MORE RAVES FOR ROBIN WELLS!

BABY, OH BABY!

"Fascinating characters, snappy dialogue and a swift pace round out this fantastic story. . . . *Baby, Oh Baby!* is a fun story that will have readers howling with delight!"

—*Romance Reviews Today*

"A dramatically touching romance. Ms. Wells adds the right mixture of wit to a serious story line and pulls off a passionate tale for readers to enjoy."

—*Romantic Times*

PRINCE CHARMING

"Ms. Wells's talent shines on every page of this terrific story. . . . An enchanting read filled with humor, passion and a cast of desirable characters. *Prince Charming* had me laughing out loud with delight. A must read for connoisseurs of laughter and romance."

—*Rendezvous*

"*Prince Charming* is an enjoyable and humorous contemporary romance that readers will fully enjoy. . . . Ms. Wells will charm readers with this offbeat novel."

—*Affaire de Coeur*

MAGNETIZED

"You know Isabelle needs you."

The words made Stevie feel all wrung out, like a wet paper towel. "But a phony marriage isn't what *I* need," she said, her voice almost a whisper.

"Well hey—there's no reason it has to be entirely phony." His eyes held a heat that made her blood rush hot and fast. He took a step toward her and put his hands on her arms. "There's chemistry between us, Stevie. That kiss last night—that was amazing."

It certainly had been from her perspective. A hot chill shivered up her spine as his hands slid up her arms.

"If we get married, there's no reason we can't make the most of it." A seductive smile played at the corner of his lips. "Marriage does have its compensations, you know."

ROBIN WELLS

THE BABE Magnet

LOVE SPELL NEW YORK CITY

LOVE SPELL®

June 2004

Published by

Dorchester Publishing Co., Inc.
200 Madison Avenue
New York, NY 10016

ISBN 0-505-52536-4

Visit us on the web at www.dorchesterpub.com.

THE
BABE
Magnet

Chapter One

Holt Landen didn't need to pull his gaze from his computer screen to know that his assistant, Lanie, was looming in the doorway of his office. The purposeful *clump-clump-clump* of her size-eleven pumps lumbering toward him served as an early warning system.

"You're not answering your intercom," the somber-faced woman chided.

"I told you I don't want to be disturbed."

"I know, but there's a call you need to take on line two."

Holt sighed. Tall, long-necked and heavy-bottomed, the gray-haired woman always reminded him of a dinosaur—the fierce kind, the kind that would eat her own young. Lanie was the T. rex of administrative assistants.

Which made her perfect for her job. She took no nonsense from the demanding CEOs who hired Holt to save their failing companies, and she put the fear of God into the accountants, attorneys and other consultants Holt in turn hired to help with the task. She was intimidatingly efficient, untiringly industrious and doggedly determined.

Unfortunately, those traits could occasionally turn and bite him on the butt. Like now.

"Unless it's the president, the pope or Catherine Zeta-Jones calling to say she can't live without me, the call can wait," Holt told her.

Plan, prioritize and focus; that was Holt's motto. Most of the floundering companies that enlisted his services had gotten into trouble in the first place because they'd lost sight of their priorities, and that was a mistake Holt didn't intend to make himself.

Especially not on this account. Allen Industries employed nearly a thousand workers, and their jobs depended on whether or not he could keep the company afloat. The responsibility weighed heavily on Holt's shoulders.

"It's a sergeant with the Dallas Police Department," Lanie persisted. "He says it's urgent police business."

"Dallas?" That was weird, considering this was New Orleans—especially since Holt hadn't set foot in Dallas in three or four years, except to change planes at DFW. "What does he want?"

"He wouldn't say. He insists on speaking directly to you."

Holt scanned his mind for any Dallas connections—any business accounts or friends or associates there—and came up blank. He turned his attention back to his computer screen. "He's probably trying to sell tickets to the policemen's ball."

"This is *not* a solicitation call." The conviction in Lanie's voice was as unwavering as her hairsprayed coif. "This is one you need to take."

Lanie usually screened Holt's calls like a Rottweiler guarding a crack house, but when she thought he needed to take one, she'd sink in her teeth and not let go. It would take longer to convince her he didn't need to talk to this officer than it would to just take the call. Holt blew out a sigh and lifted both hands in surrender. "Okay, okay. But no more interruptions the rest of the afternoon."

Satisfied, Lanie turned and thundered back down the hall.

Holt gazed out his window as he swiveled away from the computer and toward the phone. Two of the walls in his antique-filled office were glass, and the twenty-story vantage point of his Canal Street office gave him an unobstructed view of the Mississippi River's crescent curve at the foot of the French Quarter.

He watched a freighter chug around the bend as he jabbed at the blinking red button on his speaker phone and leaned back in his tall leather chair. "Holt Landen here."

"Mr. Landen, this is Sergeant Bill Jones with the Dallas Police Department," boomed a baritone Texas twang.

Holt watched a cruise ship sail downriver on its way to the Gulf of Mexico and impatiently drummed his fingers on his rosewood desk. "What can I do for you?"

"I'm afraid I'm calling with some unfortunate news, sir. I'm sorry to have to inform you of this, but . . ." The officer hesitated.

The pause caught Holt's attention. His fingers paused in mid-drum. "What?"

"Well, sir . . ." Another brief pause. "I'm afraid Ella Sinclair died in a traffic collision last night."

Ella Sinclair. The name seemed vaguely familiar, but Holt couldn't quite place it.

"Are you there, sir?" the sergeant asked.

"Yeah." Holt leaned forward, his brows beetled in a hard frown. Who the hell was Ella Sinclair? He turned the name over in his mind, trying to put a face with it. Ella Sinclair, Ella Sinclair . . .

Ella Sinclair! Now he remembered. Big blue eyes, straight blond hair and more curves than a slalom ski trail. They'd met at an Aspen ski resort a little over a year ago and had a one-night fling. It wasn't the sort of thing he usually did, but he'd been a little wasted and she'd been more than willing. Their encounter had been brief and purely physical, and they hadn't seen or spoken to each other since.

"Ella's dead?" he said.

"I'm afraid so, sir."

Holt frowned at the phone, completely bewildered. "Gee, I'm sorry to hear that. That's a real shame." He hesitated. He hated to sound callous, but the question had to be asked. "So . . . why are you calling *me*?"

"Well, you're listed as the person to contact in case of an emergency."

"*Huh?*"

Silence pulsed through the line. "You sound surprised," the sergeant finally said.

"Well, yeah. I hardly knew her." They'd had a good time on the slopes and between the sheets, but that had been the extent of it. It had been a one-night fling and nothing more.

Truth be told, Ella was too flighty for his tastes. She was the heiress of a minor oil fortune, a poor little rich girl with lots of Daddy's money and nothing to do but spend it. He usually went for women who were as serious about their careers as he was about his, and Ella didn't work at anything but having a good time.

"I don't understand why she'd list me as a contact."

The officer paused for a long moment. "Well, sir, I'd imagine it's because of the baby."

Holt froze. His spine felt like a bagful of ice dumped down the back of his shirt. "The *what?*"

"The baby."

Holt sat perfectly still. The word flapped around his brain like a sparrow looking for a place to light.

"You there, Mr. Landen?" the officer asked.

"Um, yeah. I'm here."

"I thought maybe we had a bad phone connection."

Holt grabbed up the receiver. "The connection's fine, but you've got the wrong person."

"Is this Holt Everett Landen?"

"Yes, but . . ."

"At Ten-thirty-one Canal Street in New Orleans?"

"That's my office address, but I don't have a baby."

"According to this birth certificate, you do."

The icy feeling crept back up his spine. "What birth certificate?"

"The one I'm lookin' at right here. Isabelle Elizabeth Sinclair Landen, born September twenty-first, two thousand and four, to Ella Christine Sinclair. Holt Everett Landen is listed as the father."

Was this a joke? He didn't know anyone sick enough to think this was funny, but it couldn't be real. It had to be a mistake. Or a scam.

But what kind of scam involved a dead woman and a baby?

Holt hunched over his desk. "Look, I don't know what you're talking about. I don't have a baby."

The officer's respectful tone turned harsh. "So that's how you're gonna play this, huh?"

Holt bristled. "I'm not playing anything!"

"Riiiight." The officer gave a disgusted snort. "Man, I don't know how you deadbeat dads can live with yourselves."

Deadbeat dad? The words hit like a lead pipe to the stomach—especially the "dad" part. "Hey—I haven't talked to Ella in well over a year, and I don't know anything about a baby. This is the first I've heard about it."

There was a long silence. "Holy crap," the officer finally muttered. "You're not kiddin', are you?"

"Not at all." Holt said tersely, "How about you? Did someone put you up to this?" Holt willed the man to say yes.

"Oh, wow." The sergeant let out an incredulous whistle. "Wow."

Holt heard a muffling sound that must have been the officer fitting his hand over the mouthpiece. "Hey, Charlie!" he heard the officer call in a muted tone. "This guy didn't know he'd had a baby with that DOA!"

The officer's voice once again sounded clearly through the receiver. "You really didn't know, did you?"

"There's nothing to know," Holt said irritably. "This is all some kind of mistake."

"Well, your name is right here on this birth certificate."

"Look, I don't know what kind of document you've got there, but it's got to be a fake. I never signed any birth certificate."

"Fathers don't sign 'em. Mothers fill 'em out at the hospital."

"You mean a woman can put down any man's name she wants?"

"Well . . ." The officer paused, as if he was considering it. "Hmm. I guess she could. So you think this Sinclair dame put down your name to get child support, huh?"

But that didn't make any sense. Ella wouldn't have needed child support. Holt made good money, but Ella could probably buy and sell him a dozen times over.

Come to think of it, he couldn't think of a single reason she'd put him down on the birth certificate as the child's father.

Unless he was.

That sick, whacked-in-the-gut feeling hit him all over again. He shifted the phone to his other ear. "This is crazy. If she thought I was the father, why the heck didn't she get in touch with me?"

"I dunno. But then, who knows why women do half the stuff they do? I've been married fifteen years, and I still can't figure them out."

This was insane. This was surreal. This couldn't be happening. "What's the date on that birth certificate?" Holt demanded.

"September twenty-first."

Holt did some fast calculations. He'd gone skiing right before Christmas, which meant he'd been with Ella in December. December to September was . . .

Nine months. Oh, jeez!

No. No way. He'd been with her for one lousy night. Well, actually, it hadn't been lousy—it had been quite pleasurable, but still . . .

One night. And she'd had his baby?

It couldn't be. How the heck did she even know it was his? She'd been a party girl, not a vestal virgin. And she hadn't acted as if having a one-night stand was exactly out of character.

Besides, he'd worn a condom. He always wore a condom. He knew they weren't foolproof, but it certainly reduced the odds.

Could one have broken? With a sick feeling, he vaguely recalled a rip, but he thought he'd torn it while he was pulling it off. He hadn't been all that clear-headed. They'd had a few drinks, and the high altitude had made every drink seem like three.

Holt drew a deep breath. "Let's back up a moment. Where did you get my name and number, and where did you get this birth certificate? I want to hear the whole story."

"Well, like I said, there was a car accident last night. I've got the report right here." Holt heard some papers rustle. "At approximately two A.M., a motorist called nine-one-one to report that a white Jaguar had crashed into the side of an underpass on Stemmons Freeway." The officer spoke in the stilted tone of a not-overly-proficient reader. "Two police units, two fire trucks and an EMT ambulance responded. The EMT arrived first and reported that the victim was not breathing and had no detectable pulse. Resuscitation efforts were commenced. The victim, a Caucasian female ID'd from her driver's license as Ella Sinclair, was transported to Baptist Medical, where she was declared DOA." The sergeant's voice took on an apologetic tone. "Officers responding said there was a strong scent of alcohol in the car. The coroner is doing an autopsy."

"Was anyone else involved?"

"Not directly. Let's see . . ." He resumed his reading voice. "Witnesses said the victim was, quote, going very fast and swerving, end quote. They reported that she veered toward a silver minivan in the next lane. The driver honked, she overcorrected and apparently lost control of her car."

Oh, man. "So how did you get my name?"

"An officer went to her home to notify her next of kin—we always go in person if we can." The sergeant resumed his reading voice. "The door was answered by a . . ." Holt heard more papers shuffle. "A Mrs. Greta Mitchell, who identified herself as the baby's nanny. She said she wasn't all that well acquainted with the deceased on account of the fact that she'd only been working there about a week, but she did have three names and phone numbers to call in case of an emergency. One was the baby's pediatrician, one was an attorney and one was the baby's father." The officer stopped reading. "That would be you. Your business card was attached to the paper, along with a copy of the birth certificate."

Holt forced himself to take a deep breath. *Think,* he told himself. He needed to set aside his emotions and think. Facts. He needed facts. All of them.

"Give me the name and number of the attorney and the nanny."

"Uh—sure."

Holt jotted down the names and phone numbers, his palm sweating so profusely he had a hard time holding the pen.

"You're also going to need the number of Children's Services," the officer said.

"Why's that?"

"Well, they have the baby. According to the attorney, there aren't any other living relatives, so you need to come and get her."

Get her? The air evaporated from Holt's lungs again as the implications sank in.

Ella was dead. She had no family. He was listed as the child's father, and he was expected to take her.

Dear God in heaven. He was a bachelor. He worked long hours, traveled often, ate leftover pizza for breakfast and dated long-legged brunettes. His refrigerator was completely empty except for a six-pack of beer and a carton of orange juice.

He couldn't have a baby. He couldn't even keep a houseplant alive.

Besides, he liked his life just the way it was. This had to be some kind of horrible mistake.

DNA—that would prove it. He'd call his attorney and get him to arrange a DNA test. Scientific evidence would exonerate him.

But what if it didn't? whispered a niggling little voice in the back of his head.

What the *hell* would he do with a baby?

Chapter Two

Two weeks later

A gust of cold March wind caught the glass door of the Dallas County Health Clinic as Holt pushed it open, causing it to bang heavily against the doorstop. The temperature was in the low thirties, quite a difference from the balmy seventy-three degrees he'd left behind in New Orleans that morning.

Well, it was only appropriate that the weather should be chilly. It matched the bone-chilling mission that had brought him here. He was about to become a father.

No, not *become,* he mentally amended; technically, he already was one, and had been for the last six months. But since he hadn't even known the baby existed until two weeks ago and he hadn't been sure it was his until two days ago, he figured his official foray into fatherhood would start today, when he took custody.

Custody. Fatherhood. A baby. The concepts made his stomach roil. He still couldn't really believe it, but a DNA test had confirmed it to a 99.9 percent certainty the day before yesterday: Isabelle Elizabeth Sinclair Landen was indeed his child.

It had all happened so fast—so fast his head was reel-

ing. His attorney's voice had been somber as an under-
taker's when he'd called with the news. "The test results
are in, Holt. Are you sitting down?"

Holt's world had started to topple the moment he'd
heard his attorney solemnly intone, "You're a definite
match," and "The baby is unquestionably yours." For the
last two weeks, he'd clung to the hope that this was all a
big mistake. He'd been so sure that the genetic test
would exonerate him that he hadn't seriously considered all the implications.

Amazing, how quickly one's world could change.
One minute he was an unencumbered bachelor, and
the next . . . boom! He was a single father, responsible
for raising a child he'd conceived with a woman he
scarcely knew.

Just how scarcely he'd known Ella had become clear
when Holt had phoned the former nanny, Mrs. Mitchell.

"I don't want to speak ill of the dead, but Ms. Sinclair
was *not* the motherly type," Mrs. Mitchell had said, her
voice full of nasally disapproval. "She never spent any
time with the baby. She was hardly ever home; during
the week I worked for her, she took two overnight trips
and spent the rest of her time out who-knows-where doing who-knows-what with who-knows-who. She expected me to work around the clock." She sniffed with
disdain. "I was going to resign, but she died before I
could."

"How unfortunate for you," Holt had been unable to
resist saying.

The sarcasm had been lost on the old biddy. "And
that baby!" she'd continued, her voice taking on a horrified tone. "Good heavens, that was the most difficult
child I've ever seen."

"What do you mean, 'difficult'?" Holt had asked warily.

"She cries all the time. She's very unhappy."

Well, no wonder, Holt had thought. *I'd be unhappy with a mother who ignored me and a shrew of a nanny, too.*

"I'm not the only one who found the situation impossible," Mrs. Mitchell had continued. "I was the seventh nanny my agency sent to care for that baby, and I understand that Ms. Sinclair had run through two other nannies prior to that."

The attorney, Arthur Greenwood, hadn't cast Ella's mothering skills in a much more favorable light, even though he'd tried. "I've been the family attorney for decades, and I've known Ella since she was a child," the grandfatherly-faced man had told Holt when he'd dropped by his office that morning. "I'm afraid her upbringing was somewhat . . . indulgent. Her mother died when she was just three, and her father . . ." The attorney had sighed and toyed with his gold cufflinks. "Well, Edgar was probably just a bit too generous where Ella was concerned."

Nice way of saying Ella was spoiled rotten, Holt had thought dryly.

"Ella never had a lot of focus. She'd try something for a while, then lose interest and move on to something else." Mr. Greenwood's expression had grown apologetic. "I'm afraid she treated motherhood much the same way."

According to the attorney, Ella had initially been pleased to be pregnant. Mr. Greenwood had taken advantage of Ella's early enthrallment with the idea of motherhood to convince her to prepare a will and set up a trust for the baby. The child had been named as Ella's heir, and Holt had been named as the child's guardian.

"If she knew I was the father, why didn't she tell me about the baby?" Holt had demanded.

"I tried to convince her, but Ella refused," the attorney had replied. "She said she didn't want to have to share."

Holt had known some selfish people, but Ella took the cake. "In that case, why did she even put my name on the birth certificate?"

"The Sinclair name had been quite a burden to Ella, and she wanted the child to have something different," the attorney explained. "And she said the child would eventually want to know who her father was."

"How did she plan to explain my absence from the child's life up to that point?"

Mr. Greenwood sighed. "I'm afraid Ella had a rather Scarlett O'Hara approach to problems. It would be years before the baby was old enough to ask any questions, so I imagine she just postponed thinking about it."

The memory made Holt close the clinic door harder than necessary. He stepped through another set of glass doors into a drab reception area, where a dozen or so people sat on black plastic chairs lined against the white walls.

The receptionist seated behind the low gray counter appeared to be trying to make up for the lack of color in the decor. She wore a parrot green dress and bright red lipstick, and had a nose that resembled a hooked beak. "May I help you?" she chirped.

"I'm Holt Landen, and I have an appointment with Mrs. Tucker."

The woman tilted back her head and peered through round glasses at a computer screen. "Oh, yes! You're here to pick up your daughter."

Your daughter. The words jolted him. He wondered how long it would take to get used to the idea.

She slid a sheet of paper toward him. "Sign here, please. And I'll need to see some ID."

Oh, right—as if he'd impersonate someone to get in this situation. Holt silently pulled out his slim leather wallet and extracted his driver's license.

The woman cocked her head to one side and examined it. Apparently he passed muster, because she handed it back with a smile that made her nose look even longer and more curved. "Mrs. Tucker is picking up your baby from the foster home. She should be here shortly, then the doctor will give her a check-out physical." She picked up a clipboard and handed it to Holt. "In the meantime, I need you to fill out this form, please."

Holt took the form and sat between a round-shouldered, middle-aged woman and a young Hispanic mother holding a sleeping toddler. He scribbled in his name, address and other vital information, then hesitated at the line marked RELATIONSHIP TO CHILD. It was the first time he'd acknowledged, in writing, that he was the child's father. He scribbled the word hurriedly and moved on.

CHILD'S NAME. Isabelle Elizabeth Sinclair Landen, Holt wrote. The next line gave him pause: BIRTH WEIGHT. He had no idea. And no idea what to put for TERM OF PREGNANCY or TYPE OF DELIVERY, either. He left them blank, a strange mix of guilt and anger gathering in his chest. He hadn't been there for any of that. He'd been completely left out of his child's birth, and the disturbing thing was that he didn't know if he was more relieved or upset.

It was easy to be angry at Ella, and he was. She'd had no right to have his child without letting him know. The least she could have done was to pick up the phone or drop him a line, instead of treating him like an anonymous sperm donor. He was angry at the way she'd treated the child, as well. From the sound of things, she'd been inexcusably self-centered, shallow and negligent.

The problem was, he was equally angry at himself. He'd had a one-night stand with a woman he didn't know and wouldn't have liked if he had, based on nothing more than her looks. That was pretty darn shallow on his part. So was the fact that he'd treated the whole encounter as if it were no more significant than a game of tennis.

It never entered his mind that they might have made a baby.

What would he have done if he'd known that they had? He had no idea. The only thing he knew for sure was that he wouldn't have married Ella—not permanently, at least. He might have considered some sort of short-term marriage of convenience just to make the child legitimate, but he would have insisted on a tight prenup and a definite divorce date.

He came from a broken home, and he knew how tough divorce was on kids. No kid of his was ever going to go through that. A child was better off having unmarried parents from the get-go.

Besides, he wasn't the marrying kind. He'd watched his parents divorce, marry other people, then divorce again, and from what he'd seen, marriage caused nothing but misery.

Holt scrawled his signature on the bottom of the form, rose from his chair and carried it back to the bird lady. He'd just taken his seat again when the door at the front of the reception area opened. "Mr. Landen?" said a dark-haired woman in flower-patterned scrubs.

Holt jumped to his feet.

"You can come on back."

Holt followed her down an antiseptic-scented corridor, his heart pounding. The wail of a baby echoed from the far end of the hall. Was that his daughter? If it was, she sure had some lung power.

The woman led him to a small office where he was greeted by a plump, pleasant-faced woman in a navy pantsuit. "I'm Virginia Tucker," she said, holding out her hand.

Holt shook it. "Holt Landen."

She gestured to one of the two black vinyl chairs in front of the large, government issue desk. A nameplate on the desk read, DR. J. E. SMITHERS. Three diplomas on the wall testified to the fact that he'd completed college and medical school and was a board-certified pediatrician. "Please—have a seat. I have a few things to go over with you, then I'll get the baby."

"That crying—is that Isabelle?"

"Yes." Mrs. Tucker drew two forms out of a brown folder and attached them to a clipboard. "First of all, I need you to sign these release forms." Mrs. Tucker handed him the clipboard. Holt scrawled his signature across the bottom line.

"Why is she crying?"

"Babies do that," she said. "There are lots of possible reasons."

Holt drew his brow together. "Well, shouldn't someone be doing something to calm her?"

Mrs. Tucker smiled. "Don't worry, Mr. Landen. She's with another social worker who's wonderful with children. I'm sure she's doing everything she can."

Holt pulled his brows together. *If a professional can't stop the baby from crying, what the hell am I going to do?* "Is something the matter with her?"

"Some babies cry more than others. The doctor will be in shortly, and he'll explain everything," Mrs. Tucker said soothingly.

But Holt refused to be soothed. Alarm bells jangled in his mind. "What do you mean, *everything?* What needs to be explained?"

Mrs. Tucker hesitated. "Well, I need to discuss a matter with you, Mr. Landen." She tapped the stack of papers on her lap, straightening them into a neat pile. "The first foster mother who watched Isabelle reported that she was rather . . . difficult."

It was the same word that disagreeable nanny had used on the phone. Holt hadn't even met his daughter, yet he took offense at anyone sticking such a negative label on her. "Difficult how?"

"Well, she cries a lot, and she isn't easily calmed. And she resists human contact. We were concerned enough about her behavior that we took her to Children's Hospital for a thorough evaluation."

The door opened abruptly, and a tall, middle-aged man in a white coat walked in.

Mrs. Tucker's face registered relief. "Here's Dr. Smithers. He can explain it all much better than I can. Dr. Smithers, this is Holt Landen. I was just starting to explain Isabelle's condition."

Condition? Holt shook the doctor's hand, impatient to get to the bottom of this. "What condition?" he demanded as the doctor seated himself behind the desk. "Is something wrong with her?"

"There doesn't appear to be anything physically wrong," the doctor said, his blue eyes somber. "We ran a complete battery of tests and I just checked her over again, and everything seems fine. But she's not gaining weight the way she should, and she's developmentally behind for her age. She's nearly six months old, but she looks and acts like a baby two months younger."

Oh, sheeze! "So what's the problem?"

"She's got a nonspecific condition called Failure to Thrive. Given her history and the fact that she seems to dislike human contact, I'm afraid she's developing Attachment Disorder."

Holt tensed. "What's that?"

The doctor tapped his long fingers together. "Well, all infants need to form a strong attachment to one main caregiver. If that attachment isn't formed, the child can develop all kinds of mental and behavorial problems."

Oh, man. This sounded serious.

"AD isn't usually diagnosed until a child nears adolescence, but by then the damage is done. The best course of action is to identify at-risk children and do what we can to prevent it from causing permanent problems."

The doctor flipped through the pages of the medical chart. "From what we can ascertain, the baby has had nine different caregivers—eleven, if you count the two foster mothers—during her first six months of life. She hasn't had adequate time to develop an emotional bond with any of them."

Holt leaned forward. "You said we could head off future problems. How do we do that?"

"You need to give Isabelle stability." The doctor pushed his glasses up on his forehead and rubbed his nose. "She needs one person who'll be with her for the long haul. Someone extremely patient and empathetic, who'll hang in there despite all of her fussing and fuming and pushing away."

"She's got me."

"The doctor smiled. "Well, then, she's a lucky little girl."

"So what do I need to do?"

"For starters, you need to arrange your schedule to be with her around the clock."

Holt froze. "Around the clock—as in twenty-four/seven?"

"Exactly."

"For how long?"

"At least six months. A couple of years would be better."

Holt's stomach sank. "I can't do that. My business would collapse if I took off for six months! And my current clients would sue my pants off."

"Well, it doesn't have to be you. It just needs to be someone who'll commit to being with the child for the foreseeable future." The doctor lowered his glasses and fixed Holt with a solemn gaze. "The worst thing that could happen would be for her to get attached to someone and then abandoned again. That would make her withdraw even further."

"I've hired a nanny." Actually, Lanie had handled the hiring; Holt hadn't even met her yet. She'd also handled having all of the baby's belongings moved from Ella's home to Holt's, where a spare bedroom had been converted into a nursery. "Can the baby form attachments to both a nanny and to me?" Holt asked.

"Oh, sure. Most children attach to two or more people. But they attach first to one specific person—normally their mothers. Their security in that primary, one-on-one relationship is what allows them to trust other people. That's what Isabelle has been missing." He steepled his hands together. "You need to make sure this nanny is willing to make a long-term commitment."

Holt nodded. "Six months to two years."

"Oh, no. That's just the amount of time needed for the intense, bond-forming stage. Ideally, this primary caregiver would remain in Isabelle's life indefinitely. At least until she's school age."

"Holy schmoly," Holt muttered. Where was he going to find someone who'd agree to that?

Mrs. Tucker leaned forward. "Do you have any family members who might be able to help? Maybe your mother?"

Holt shook his head. "She's in California."

"Your father?"

Oh, that was a good one. "No."

"An aunt? Or a sister? Or maybe a cousin?"

Holt shook his head. "I don't have any close family."

"Well, you need to find someone who intends to stay with the job, because the last thing little Isabelle needs is any more people coming into her life only to disappear after a week or two." The doctor placed his hands palm down on the desk, as if he was about to stand up. "Do you have any questions?"

Too many to ask. Holt didn't know the first thing about regular babies, much less babies with issues. "Any special instructions?"

"Try to get her to take a bottle as often as possible. She needs to gain weight. And she should be under the care of a local pediatrician. If she doesn't put on weight pretty soon, she'll need to be hospitalized and put on a feeding tube."

Holy diaper pails. Holt swallowed back a rising sense of alarm. "What do I feed her?"

"Formula mixed with a supplement."

"We have all of that written down," Mrs. Tucker added, handing him a typed sheet. "Here you go."

The doctor pulled a sheaf of papers out of the folder and handed them to Holt as well. "And here are Isabelle's medical records. You'll need to get her next immunization in two weeks, but she should see a local pediatrician before then—preferably in a day or two. Her weight needs to be closely monitored."

"O-kay." Holt folded the papers and shoved them in his jacket pocket.

The doctor rose and circled the desk. "It was nice meeting you. Good luck." He shook Holt's hand and left the room.

Mrs. Tucker smiled, as if the need to find a nanny who'd make a five-year commitment and the potential of feeding tubes were cheery things to contemplate. "Well, why don't I go get little Isabelle? I'm sure you're anxious to meet your daughter."

An unaccustomed wave of nervousness washed over Holt as she bustled out the door. The crying grew louder and louder, and then Mrs. Tucker walked back in the room, carrying what looked like a screaming pink dress.

There was a baby hidden among the layers of frills and ruffles, but it took Holt a moment to spot her because her face was the same shade as her clothing. Holt stared at the child. She had a tuft of white-blond hair, red cheeks and a pair of the pinkest tonsils he'd ever seen, which she was showing to full advantage.

"Isabelle, here's your daddy," said Mrs. Tucker.

Holt hesitantly reached out his arms, and Mrs. Tucker placed the baby in them. Isabelle stiffened, kicked her toothpick-thin legs against his chest, then cranked up the volume of her yowls.

She was so tiny—and so thin! The only fat on her body was in her cheeks. With that shock of hair, she looked like a troll doll. "Hey there, sweetheart," Holt said. The baby drew back and screamed even louder.

What the heck was he supposed to do now? He looked questioningly at Mrs. Tucker, but she was smiling like a sunbeam, as if everything was perfectly fine. She held out a pink ruffled diaper bag. "She's just been fed and changed, so she's all set to go. Do you have a baby seat in your car?"

Holt nodded. Equipment was a topic he could understand; you couldn't play a sport or tackle a job without the right equipment. He was fully outfitted with baby gear. Unfortunately, he didn't know how to use any of it. A man at the car rental agency had helped him fasten the baby seat into the back of the car.

Man, it was hard to think over the baby's screams.

"Well, good. Sounds like you're all set."

All set? Surely they weren't going to just turn the child over to him, with no training or further instructions. Holt looked questioningly at Mrs. Tucker. "You mean . . . we're done?"

Mrs. Tucker nodded. "She's all yours. We don't need to do anything further since you're the natural father."

He was the *biological* father, which was quite a different thing from being a natural. It seemed completely irresponsible of these people to just hand a baby over to him—especially one who was screaming like Isabelle.

He raised the child higher on his shoulder and awkwardly patted her bony back. She stiffened and pulled her head away, as if she wanted as little of her body touching him as possible, and yelled all the louder.

"Good luck," Mrs. Tucker called.

Man, am I ever going to need it, Holt thought as he headed down the hall, gingerly carrying the screeching baby, the pink diaper bag dangling from his arm. From the way this fatherhood gig was starting off, he was going to need boatloads, truckfuls and cargo carriers full of luck just to get her home to New Orleans.

Chapter Three

A week later

Stevie pressed the blinking telephone light on the sound booth console. "This is 'Parent Talk' with Stevie Stedquest. You're on the air."

"Um, yeah—I'm callin' 'bout that kid who bit his friend," rasped a male voice with the thick, Bronxlike accent of New Orleans's Ninth Ward.

Stevie leaned closer to the mike, brushing aside a strand of dark blond hair that escaped her ponytail. "Yes?"

"Yeah. Your advice stunk. You shoulda told that mom to bite him back, good and hard."

Stevie shot an alarmed glance at her producer, Hank Norton, through the window that divided the sound booth from the control room. The pudgy, gray-haired man gave an apologetic grin and lifted his shoulders in a he-didn't-sound-like-a-kook-when-I-screened-his-call shrug.

Stevie didn't buy it for a minute. She was certain Hank deliberately selected the weirdos to make her Sunday-night radio call-in show more lively.

She forced her voice into a calm, nonjudgmental tone. "Well, sir, biting is a form of violence, and violence should never be used against children."

"Hey, if a kid's gonna act like an animal, he oughta be treated like one. An eye for an eye, I always say. When my oldest son started biting other kids, I gave him a taste of his own medicine, and believe you me, that shaped him up but quick."

Stevie choked back an outraged retort. She was here to educate, not berate, she reminded herself. It would do no good to tell this creep that idiots like him had no business raising children. She knew all that, but it was still a struggle not to tell the man to do the world a favor and book an immediate vasectomy. Castration would be even better; she'd even offer to do it for him.

Instead, she forced her voice into a deliberately respectful tone. "There are much better methods of correcting a child's behavior, sir. For example, giving him a time-out would have . . ."

"Time-outs are for sissies," the man interrupted. "What my kid needed was his old man's teeth marks on his arm, and that's what he got."

"You bit him hard enough to leave *teeth marks?*"

"Sure. Gotta show 'em you mean business. But don't you worry—I didn't leave no scars."

"I would hope not!"

"Hey, I got a few from my folks, and I'm none the worse for it."

"I'm afraid you probably are."

His voice grew suspicious. "Are you insultin' my parents?"

No, Lunk Head, I'm insulting you. "I'm simply saying that family violence tends to get passed down from generation to generation."

"It wasn't violence. It was discipline."

"If it leaves a mark on a child, it's abuse. And even if it doesn't leave a mark, all the experts agree that physical discipline is not only harmful but ineffective."

The man gave a derisive snort. "Experts, schmexperts. Those jerks don't know what they're talking 'bout. Hell, most of 'em don't even have any kids. I bet you don't, either."

The words hit a nerve, but Stevie chose to ignore them. She was worried that this caller's children were victims of ongoing abuse. "Tell me about your children. How old are they?"

"You're changin' the subject."

"That's because this isn't about me."

"Sure it is. You're on the air tellin' everyone in New Orleans how to raise their kids, so we got a right to know how many *you're* raising."

Stevie shifted uneasily. "All of my parenting suggestions are documented by studies and research."

"Studyin' something ain't the same as doin' it. Unless you're doing it, you ain't qualified to give advice."

"If you're concerned about my qualifications, I have an undergraduate degree in education, a double masters in early childhood development and social work and I've managed the Parents Resource Center of New Orleans for the last six years."

"Well, la-di-da and whoop-de-do. You still haven't answered my question, which makes me think I'm right on the money. You don't have any kids, do ya?"

She was cornered. If she didn't answer the question, she'd look like she was trying to hide something. "No," she reluctantly admitted. "No, I don't."

"That's what I thought." Smugness clung to his voice like dog poop to a shoe. "You got no business tellin' people how to raise kids if you're not willin' to practice what you preach."

"It's not a matter of being willing. It just so happens I'm not married."

"Well, can't say as I'm surprised. With a name like Stevie, you probably got some kinda alternative lifestyle goin' on."

"No!" Too late, she realized her startled reply might

sound as if she condemned people who did. "I-I mean, I, uh, just haven't met the right man yet," she sputtered, then immediately wanted to kick herself. It was none of this jerk's business, and she shouldn't have allowed him to put her on the defensive.

"So you like men, huh?" The information had the unlikely effect of immediately mellowing the caller's mood. "Well, what do you look like? My sister had trouble finding a guy, too, until she lost a hundred and fifty pounds and started using Nair on her chin."

Through the soundproof glass, Stevie saw Hank double over as if he were having a spasm.

"I got a buddy I could fix you up with if you're not too bad lookin'," the caller added.

"Thank you, but I'm afraid I'll have to pass." She looked away from Hank, who was practically rolling on the floor. "Let's get back to talking about your children. How old are they?"

"Seventeen and eighteen."

Stevie breathed a sigh of relief. "I suppose that means you're no longer using corporal punishment."

"Corporal?" The man sounded mystified. "I don't know what you're talkin' about. I'm not in the military."

Through the glass, Hank was slapping his thigh.

"I meant physical punishment," Stevie patiently explained.

"Oh. No, I can't hit 'em no more." Regret tinged his voice. "They're both bigger than me now, and they can whip my ass."

Which I hope they do on a regular basis. "Well, thank you for calling, sir." Stevie punched the red button and the phone disconnected with a satisfying click.

"Disciplining children is one of a parent's most challenging tasks," Stevie said into the mike. "And it's one of the many topics you can get help with at the Parents

Resource Center. For a free brochure about positive parenting and a list of the parenting classes we're offering, give us a call or stop by the center at twelve hundred and ninety-two Prytania Street." Through the window, she saw Hank making a circle in the air, indicating she needed to wrap it up. "We have to take a break right now, then we'll be back with more 'Parent Talk.' If you have a question about your children, call me at five-five-five-fourteen-sixty-five."

Stevie clicked the off-air button as Hank started a sixty-second spot for Chuck E. Cheese. Rising from her chair, she crossed the tiny sound booth and opened the door. "Thanks a lot for that last caller," she said dryly.

Hank chortled. "Hey, he was one of the tamer ones. A lady wanted to know if you could tell her how to potty train her cat, and another one thought that because the show's called Parent Talk, you could contact her dead mother."

Stevie arched a brow. "And you resisted the urge to put those calls through?"

Hank's beard twitched as he grinned. "Believe me, it was tough."

"I bet. Thanks for exercising such incredible restraint."

"Don't mention it." Grinning, he rubbed his grizzled chin. "Must be a full moon, the way the oddballs are calling."

The direct line into Stevie's sound booth rang.

Hank's grin widened. "Speaking of which, tell your mom I said 'Hi.' "

Stevie rolled her eyes, then pulled the door shut and headed back to the phone. Her mother was the only person who called on her private line, and did so with unswerving regularity during the five-minute midshow break.

Stevie sat back down in the swivel chair and picked up the phone. "Hi, Mom."

"You should have taken that man up on his offer to fix you up," Marie Stedquest scolded.

Stevie rubbed her forehead, where she felt the beginnings of a tension headache forming. "Please tell me you're kidding."

"You need to get out there and socialize, Stevie."

"Mom, you can't really want me dating a jerk like that."

"You wouldn't be dating *him*, dear. He was going to fix you up with a friend."

"And he's likely to have a friend you'd want fathering your grandchildren?"

"Well, I'm sure he has a doctor and a dentist—maybe he was going to fix you up with one of them. He might even have a lawyer."

"Court-appointed, no doubt," Stevie said.

"Honestly, Stevie—you don't know who you might have met. They say every person has two hundred and fifty people in their sphere of influence, and one person leads to another. He might have introduced you to someone perfectly wonderful."

"The man bit his own child, Mom—hard enough to leave teeth marks! The odds of him socializing with anyone wonderful are about the same as of me winning the lottery."

"To win the lottery, you have to buy a ticket," Marie chided. "It's the same thing with dating, Stevie. To be in the game, you have to get out there and mingle."

"I'm not going to mingle with child-biters," she stated flatly.

"All right, all right, but you can't afford to be too picky. You're not getting any younger, honey."

As if she needed reminding. She'd just turned thirty-one, and her biological clock was ticking like a time bomb. She loved children, and had always longed to have one or more of her own. The only problem was, having a child involved having a relationship with a man, and Stevie's skills in that department stunk.

"I just read an article about how fertility drops off after thirty a lot faster than scientists once thought," her mom continued. "A lot of women who put off settling down end up regretting it."

"I'm not putting it off, Mom." You couldn't postpone something you couldn't control.

"You never should have let that wonderful Peter Marston get away."

"I didn't let him get away, Mom. He left me for someone else." Three someone elses, Stevie thought darkly, but who was counting?

"Well, you could have at least put up a fight for him."

"Oh, and how should I have gone about that? Asked the other girl to put up her dukes?"

"Of course not. But maybe you could have complimented him more, made him feel more special. Sometimes all a man needs to change his ways is the love of a good woman."

"And sometimes a man is just a two-timing jerk and that's all there is to it."

A long sigh hissed through the phone. "If you want a family, honey, you're going to have to be less picky. Just last month you refused to go out with Mrs. Anderson's nephew a second time, which I don't understand at all. He was so charming—and so handsome! Why, most women would be thrilled to date a man like that."

That had been the whole problem. The cocktail waitress, the restaurant hostess, the woman in the slinky red dress at the next table—they'd all made goo-goo eyes at him, and he'd made goo-goo eyes right back. He'd been

just like Peter—and just like every other single man who
was too good-looking for his own good. Why should he
settle for just one dish when he could have the whole
smorgasbord?

"He wasn't interested in settling down, Mom. Babe
magnets like him never are."

"They're not all that way. Your brother's not."

Her brother was hardly a babe magnet either, but
Stevie knew there would be no point in trying to convince her mother of that fact. "Mike's the exception,"
she said diplomatically.

"Well, I still think if you'd done more to let Peter know
how special he was . . ."

"It wouldn't have done any good."

"I don't know how you can say that for certain."

*Because he was sleeping with three other women at
the same time he was sleeping with me!* The thought
still sent a sharp pang through her heart. Not a pang of
pain anymore, or even anger—those had faded in the
past two years. The thing that hadn't faded was the humiliation.

And the ozone-sized hole it had left in her self-
confidence, which hadn't been all that solid to start
with. She might have dropped sixty pounds six years
ago, but in her mind's eye, she was still the overweight
girl all the other kids made fun of. "Let's drop it, Mom.
It's over."

"Well, look, dear . . . I'm catering a wedding Saturday
evening—a lovely affair at the Westman estate. You
should come."

Her mother had started a catering business last win-
ter, and to the surprise of the entire family, it had taken
off like a rocket. One secret to her success, Stevie was
sure, was the fact that Marie treated each event as if it
were her own personal party. Unfortunately, she some-

times took her ownership of the events she catered a little too far.

"You're forgetting one little detail," she told her mom. "I'm not invited."

"Oh, that's no problem. You can come as my assistant."

"Is something wrong with Betsy?"

"No, no—she's just fine. You're missing the point, dear. You wouldn't actually be *working*. That would just be your cover."

"My cover—as if I was a narcotics agent or a jewel thief?"

Mrs. Stedquest huffed out an I-can't-believe-I-raised-such-an-ungrateful-daughter sigh. "I mean you'd be free to circulate and dance."

"You know I don't like dancing, Mom." *Don't like* was a gross understatement; *hate, abhor, detest* were more accurate terms. Just the thought of dancing stirred up a snakepit of painful memories that made her palms damp and her stomach queasy. "Besides, I've got plans for Saturday."

"Some plans." Mrs. Stedquest sniffed. "Baby-sitting your brother's kids."

"I happen to enjoy the twins, and I don't mind the drive to Baton Rouge. It's good for Mike and Kirsten to have an evening alone together."

"I know, and I agree. But Mike and Kirsten could find another baby-sitter. Why, your father could do it." Her mother's voice took on a note of disgruntled exasperation. "Lord knows he needs something to do since he retired."

Stevie's brow knit in a worried frown. Her parents had always had what Stevie considered an ideal marriage, but since his retirement from the D.A.'s office six months ago, things had changed. Her mother had grown increasingly critical, and her father, who had always been the quiet type, had become positively taciturn. "How *is* Dad?"

"Cantankerous and always underfoot. I swear, that man is going to drive me crazy."

"Well, retirement's a big adjustment."

"Yes, and I'm the one doing all the adjusting."

Her mother's voice held a bitter note Stevie had never heard before. "Be patient," she advised. "Give it some time." She glanced up and saw Hank pointing at his wristwatch through the soundproof glass. "Speaking of time, I need to go, Mom."

"So you'll come on Saturday?"

"No. I told you—I'm baby-sitting."

"You'll never meet Mr. Right if you don't make an effort!"

"Gotta go. Talk to you later."

Stevie hung up the phone before her mother had the chance to protest. She knew her mother only wanted the best for her, but it was depressing the way the woman constantly harped about her single status. Her mother acted as if she needed to go out and track down a husband like a big game hunter.

Maybe she was a hopeless romantic, but Stevie had always thought that love would find her, not the other way around. She'd always believed that love was part of a divine plan, that there was someone meant for everyone and that when the timing was right, her soul mate would somehow just appear.

At least, that's what she used to believe. She was no longer so sure. Instead of winding up with Mr. Right, she kept winding up with Mr.-What-on-earth-was-I-thinking.

Well, she was tired of it. She'd rather be alone than with a man she couldn't trust. After her last failed romance, she'd decided that she needed to establish some guidelines to keep her from repeating her mistakes. She now had three strict rules:

Rule Number One: Avoid babe magnets. From here on out, she refused to date a man who was prettier than she was.

Rule Number Two: Avoid men with a history of hit-and-run romances. A man with a track record of one-night stands and brief affairs was not a good prospect for lifelong love.

Rule Number Three: If a man's actions and words don't match, believe the walk and not the talk.

Through the window, Stevie saw Hank hold up his hand and start the countdown by folding down each of his fingers, one at a time. When the last pinkie disappeared, Stevie leaned toward the microphone and punched the on-air button. "Welcome back to 'Parent Talk.' This is Stevie Stedquest, and I'm taking your questions about parenting." She punched the first blinking red button, glad to turn her thoughts to someone else's problems.

"This is Jan," said a young woman with a high-pitched voice. "I called last week about whether or not I should quit working after my baby's born."

"Oh, yes. Jan. Nice to hear from you. Have you made a decision?"

"I'm still thinking about it, but I just wanted to say, I feel kinda misled. I thought you were giving me advice about something you'd been through yourself."

Stevie's stomach sank like a box of rocks. "I-I never claimed to be talking from personal experience. I'm sharing things I've learned from study and research, and from my work at the parenting center."

"Yeah, well, it's not the same thing. And you gave me a bunch of statistics, not a real answer. If you'd ever been through it yourself, maybe you'd be able to give some advice that people could actually use."

Alarm shot through Stevie. "There aren't any one-size-fits-all answers. What's right for me might not be right for you and your family."

"You're darn right, because you don't have any children. I don't think they should give a parenting show to someone who's not a parent."

Apparently the rest of the population of New Orleans didn't think so either. When Stevie punched the off-air button thirty minutes later, she'd never been so glad to end a show in her life.

"You really took some heat," Hank observed when Stevie emerged from the soundbooth.

"No kidding. I feel like the pig at a luau."

"Well, controversy's good for ratings."

"Not when it's my credentials in question. I never should have admitted I don't have any children."

"You were cornered. The guy left you no choice."

Stevie pulled the strap of her black leather purse up on the shoulder of her bulky white sweater. "I don't see why it's such a big deal. Nobody feels like a doctor has to have cancer to treat it."

Hank grinned. "Kids and cancer—hey, that's a pretty good analogy. They're both expensive, painful and hard to get rid of."

Stevie pretended she was going to swat him with her purse. "That's not what I meant and you know it. The callers acted like I'd somehow betrayed them."

Hank scooted out of range. "They're just jealous that you're footloose and fancy free, while they're poor, suffering parents."

"You have two kids and you're not suffering."

"That's because they've moved out of the house."

Stevie shook her head and gave him a knowing grin. His two grown kids were his pride and joy, and she got weekly updates on their activities. "Seriously—do you think this could cause problems? Is the station likely to cancel my show?"

"Nah. They have to carry a certain number of public service programs, and yours gets great ratings." He waved his hand in a shooing motion. "Now go on and get outta here. And have a great week."

Nothing about her week promised greatness, Stevie thought dismally as she stepped out of the bright, modern studio and into the deserted hallway of the old building. Nothing about her month or year or the rest of her life promised it either, when it came right down to it. In fact, the chances of anything great happening to her were about as dim as the lighting in the empty reception area.

It wasn't as if she was longing for fame or fortune. All she wanted was love, marriage and a family with a nice, steady, good-hearted man. Unfortunately, all the men who fit that description were already married to nice, steady, good-hearted women. Nice, steady, good-hearted women who just happened to be thin, she thought with a sigh. Stevie strongly suspected that while she was trapped in an oversize body, some skinny girl had snagged her Mr. Right.

Stevie stepped into the creaky old elevator of the empty building. Maybe it was time to move on to Plan B. Maybe instead of looking for a romantic relationship, she should forget about men and focus on becoming a single parent. She'd promised herself that if she wasn't married or engaged by the time she was thirty-two, she'd check into artificial insemination.

Her family would have a fit, but by the time they found out about it, it would be too late. She was certain they'd love any child of hers, regardless of how it was conceived.

She was still pondering the matter as she let herself out the self-locking station door onto St. Peter Street and paused to search her purse for her keys under the light by the building entrance.

The night air was cool and ripe with the scent of river water and old buildings, a smell that Stevie privately thought of as Eau de French Quarter. A whiff of horse mingled with it as a tourist-laden carriage clopped loudly by.

"Excuse me," called a deep, masculine voice when the carriage had rattled past.

Stevie looked up, startled, to see a man emerging from a black BMW in the no-parking zone across the street. The squawl of a baby radiated out the car door.

He strode across the street toward her, his face in shadow. "Are you by any chance Stevie Stedquest?"

A shiver of alarm chased through her. There were some real kooks out there. What if this were a crazed listener upset by her childfree status? She backed toward the station door, her pulse pounding, but it had already swung shut and locked behind her.

Oh, dear—as usual, the building's security guard was nowhere to be seen. She groped behind her, trying to act casual, and felt the brick wall for the buzzer. Not that it would do any good, she thought belatedly; it only sounded in the reception area, which was deserted on Sunday nights.

The man drew closer. She still couldn't see his face, but his size was intimidating. He was at least six-foot-two and had a lean, muscular build. She drew a deep breath and tried to formulate a response that would neither affirm nor deny her identity. "Is she expecting you?"

"No, but I was hoping to catch her before she left the station. I'm having some trouble with my daughter and I hoped she could help me." The muffled wail of the baby in his car echoed through the night.

He didn't sound like a kook, but she decided to proceed with caution anyway. "You should have called during the show."

"I tried, but the lines were busy and I couldn't get through." He stepped into the gleam of the streetlamp. He was in his early thirties, and handsome. Head-turningly handsome—the kind of handsome that made women drool, the kind of handsome that Stevie had vowed to avoid like the plague.

He didn't have pretty-boy good looks; he had heavy-on-the-testosterone, full-throttle, manly-man good looks, complete with a five o'clock shadow, thick black eyebrows and a deeply cleft chin. His face was all angles and planes, except for piercing dark eyes and a pair of lips that looked shockingly sensual in such a hard-chiseled face.

Stevie realized his lips were moving.

"You're her, aren't you? You're Stevie. I can tell because my baby stopped crying."

"I beg your pardon?"

"Your voice seems to have a calming influence on my daughter."

Sure enough, the crying had stopped. Stevie opted to continue sidestepping the identity question. "You shouldn't leave your baby unattended in the car."

"Oh—right. I'm still trying to get the hang of this fatherhood thing."

He rapidly strode across the street to the car, opened

the back door and unbuckled the baby from the infant carrier. The baby yowled as he lifted her out and carried her back to Stevie. "I can't get her to calm down."

The howling child was the most pathetic sight Stevie had ever seen. She had a red, blotchy face, skinny arms that flailed like windmills and legs as thin as spaghetti strands. White-blond curls stuck to the side of her round, wet face as she struggled to hold her head away from the man's shoulder.

Stevie's heart turned over. The poor baby was the very picture of distress.

So was the man, now that she got a good look at him. A large stain sprawled across the shoulder of his starched white shirt, the wet collar stood up on one side by his ear and his expensive-looking pants were wrinkled and covered with splotches of what appeared to be dried baby formula. From the dark circles under his bloodshot eyes, he was seriously sleep deprived.

He awkwardly patted the baby's back, doing his best to quiet the child, but she was having none of it. "Look, I'm sorry to waylay you on the street like this, but I'm kinda desperate." He had to speak loudly to be heard over the baby's screams.

He shifted the baby to his left arm and held out his right hand. "I'm Holt Landen, and this is Isabelle."

His fingers folded around hers, strong and warm. That warmth traveled up her arm and down her spine in a hot shiver. *Down, girl. Any man with a baby that age has got to be married.*

He shifted the baby to his other arm. "Look—I can't get Isabelle to stop crying, but when she heard your voice on the radio, she got quiet, so I thought maybe you could help."

"Is she ill?" Stevie reached out and laid her palm on the baby's forehead. It was cool to the touch, but the baby jerked back and let out a screech, as if the touch hurt.

"No. Not physically. But she has something called Attachment Disorder."

"She has trouble forming connections with people?"

"Yeah. Are you familiar with it?"

"I've heard of it." Stevie searched her mind, trying to recall what she knew. AD usually occurred in children who'd been neglected as babies—deprived of a consistent caretaker, infrequently held, seldom touched. If memory served, it was most commonly found in children who'd been raised in foreign orphanages, where the staff didn't understand the importance of human interaction.

Stevie looked at him quizzically. "Where's her mother?"

"She was killed in a car crash."

"Oh, how awful!" A rush of sympathy flooded her heart. Stevie was a soft touch for any baby, but a distressed, motherless baby melted her heart like microwaved fudge sauce.

Holt stepped closer, close enough that the lamplight revealed the golden brown of his eyes.

"Look—I'm at my wits' end. My nanny quit during the middle of a business trip to Atlanta, and I had to cancel all my meetings to care for Isabelle, and she's been crying nonstop. I've tried everything I can think of to calm her down, but nothing works. I was driving home from the airport, flipping through the stations on the radio in hopes of finding some music to soothe her, when I landed on your show. Your voice had this amazing effect on her, and you seem to know what you're talking about, so I thought—well, I was hoping you could help me."

The man's eyes were dark and intense and persuasive. Even without the baby, he was the kind of guy women would have trouble refusing. Some self-protective instinct warned her to do just that.

"I'm sorry, but I don't see clients outside of the parenting center. You can call in the morning and make an appointment, and . . ."

"Please. I need help now."

The baby turned a pathetic little face toward Stevie, mouth open in a pitiful wail.

"What kind of help are you looking for?"

Holt shifted the baby so she was screaming in his other ear. "Well, for starters, she hasn't eaten since this morning. I can't get her to take a bottle. She's underweight, and the doctor says she needs to eat every three or four hours. Since your voice calmed her, I thought maybe you could get some food into her."

She shouldn't even be considering it. It set a bad precedent, meeting radio listeners outside of the parenting center. But the tear-streaked face of the obviously miserable baby was impossible to resist.

So were the father's pleading brown eyes, but that was another story.

"Please," he begged. "We could go to the Café du Monde. It's just a couple of blocks away."

Bad precedent or not, there was no way Stevie could refuse to feed a hungry baby. "Okay," she agreed. "I'll try to give her a bottle. But if you need more help than that, you'll have to come to the parenting center."

Chapter Four

A wave of relief swept through Holt. For a moment there, he'd thought she was going to refuse, and he didn't know if he could handle another hour of Isabelle's unrelenting howls.

"Where's her bottle?" Stevie asked.

"It's in the car."

"I'll hold her while you get it."

Isabelle let loose another round of yells. Holt practically had to shout to be heard over her. "I have to warn you—the only thing she hates more than being held is being passed off to someone else. She's likely to cry even louder the minute I hand her to you."

"That's okay."

Stevie held out her arms, and Holt gave her the bawling infant. Sure enough, the child stiffened as Stevie touched her, then burst into a lung-ripping screech.

"I'll get her baby carriage out of the trunk," Holt said. "She hates to be carried."

Stevie walked beside him as he crossed the street. If he was a less responsible person, he'd be tempted to dash ahead, climb into the car and speed away. Unfortunately, he was the most responsible person he knew.

Responsible, and he dealt with stressful situations every day, but he'd never experienced stress like trying to care for this baby. It wasn't just that he was sleep-deprived, or that Isabelle's demands were constant and unrelenting; the worst part was how powerless and incompetent the baby made him feel. He was used to

solving problems, not standing by like a helpless oaf as
they escalated. He was frazzled to the point of snapping.

Maybe he already had. The fact that he was here certainly pointed to the possibility. He didn't normally
hatch wild schemes involving women he'd never met,
then waylay them in dark parking lots. But then, nothing had been normal since he'd taken custody of Isabelle. In less than a week, he'd gone from being the
man with all the answers to being so confused and
overwhelmed that he wasn't even sure of the questions.

When Isabelle quieted at the sound of Stevie's voice,
he'd had a brainstorm. He'd always been a creative
problem solver, but this idea was nothing short of genius. It was a perfect solution, so perfect it was almost
eerie. Now, all that remained was convincing Stevie.

He popped the trunk, hauled out the pink baby
stroller that had been shipped with Isabelle's belongings and unfolded it on the sidewalk.

Stevie lifted a pink baby blanket inside the stroller
and gently settled the crying baby inside. "Hey there,
sweetie. It's okay. I'll bet you're hungry and don't even
know it."

The baby stopped in mid-yowl and put her fist in her
mouth.

"Sounds like you've had a rough day," Stevie
crooned. She tucked the blanket around the baby.
"You'll feel much better once you get some food in your
tummy."

Holt pulled out the pink diaper bag, slung it over his
shoulder and slammed the trunk shut. He fell into step
beside Stevie as she pushed the carriage down the sidewalk, talking softly to Isabelle.

"I can't get over how much she likes your voice," he
said.

"Do I sound like her mother?"

Holt hesitated. "Maybe. I'm not really sure."

Stevie shot him an odd look. "You don't know?"

"I can't remember, exactly." Holt admitted, "It's been a while."

Stevie's brows pulled together. A group of men in business suits and convention badges passed between them on the sidewalk, and when Holt stepped back beside her, she was still frowning. "How old is Isabelle?" she asked.

"Six months."

"So your wife can't have been dead that long."

"It's been three weeks." They stopped at the curb of Decatur and waited for the light to change. He cut her a sideways glance. "And she wasn't my wife."

A chastened expression crossed Stevie's face. "I'm sorry. I just assumed . . . but I should know better than to make assumptions. We get lots of single parents at the parenting center."

"It's okay. My situation is kind of unusual."

"I'm sure it's nothing I haven't heard before."

"I wouldn't be so sure of that," Holt said.

Judging by Stevie's incredulous stare across the table at Café du Monde ten minutes later, she'd never heard anything like his brief explanation of how fatherhood had dropped in his lap so abruptly.

"So, until the police called, you had no idea you had a baby?" she repeated.

"None at all."

He gazed down at Isabelle, who was greedily sucking on a bottle in her lap. It had only taken a few minutes for Stevie to coax the child into taking it—a feat Holt had struggled to perform all day.

Stevie shot him a puzzled look. "Isabelle's mother never mentioned it when you spoke with her?"

Holt squirmed on the green outdoor chair as the green-and-white awning flapped overhead. He'd told her he'd met Ella during a ski vacation, but he hadn't given her any details. "I, um, never talked to her after Colorado."

Stevie's gaze made him feel like a bug under a microscope. "Why not?"

Oh, jeez. There was no way to explain it without sounding sleazy. "We, um, just didn't stay in touch." He looked down at his coffee cup, but he could feel the heat of her stare. "It wasn't that kind of a relationship."

"So what kind was it?"

Her cool tone told him she knew exactly what kind it was, and she didn't approve. Well, that figured. To Holt's way of thinking, there were two kinds of women: women who loved sex, and women who didn't. Women in the first category wore makeup, attractive hairstyles and flattering clothes to make themselves attractive to the opposite sex. Women who didn't care, didn't bother. With her fresh-scrubbed face, pulled-back hair and shapeless clothes, Stevie apparently fell into the didn't care category.

Which was a shame. She was actually quite attractive in a low-key, understated kind of way—a lot more attractive than he'd expected. Radio personalities weren't known for their great looks, and the fact that she wanted to be married but wasn't hadn't boded well, either.

She was about five-foot-four and curvy, although it was hard to tell much about her figure under that long, baggy sweater. Her eyes were large and wide-set, her nose small and freckle-sprinkled, her mouth wide and generous. She wore her honey-colored hair pulled back in a ponytail that hung just below her shoulders. She wasn't his type—he usually went for smoldering Catherine Zeta-Jones brunettes, and she was more like Reese

Witherspoon playing a librarian—but she was attractive all the same. Her blue-gray eyes were intelligent and bright, and when she looked at him, as she was doing now, he felt a pull that made him wonder if he'd pegged her wrong.

Her eyes were fixed on him expectantly now, waiting for him to explain his relationship with Ella.

He took a swallow of café au lait, wishing it was something stronger. "It wasn't much of a relationship at all. It was pretty much just physical."

"In other words, a one-night stand."

Oh, man. Her voice was so frosty it nearly iced his coffee. "Look, it's not something I routinely do. But I was on vacation and I'd had a few drinks and the altitude amplified the effect of them, and . . ." He hated people who tried to excuse their behavior, and here he was, doing just that. "Hell, it just happened," he finished gruffly.

"And afterward, you just said 'Good-bye, nice knowing you,' and went on your merry way?" Little Miss Parenting Authority was looking at him as if he were a primitive life form several evolutionary rungs below pond scum.

"No," he said defensively. "I gave her my business card and told her to call me if she was ever in New Orleans."

"Well, gee, that was sure nice of you." Her sarcasm was sharp enough to poke out an eye.

"She knew how to reach me if she wanted to."

"So why didn't she? It seems like she would have at least contacted you for child support."

"She didn't need support. Ella's father left her a very generous trust fund. In fact, her attorney said one of the reasons she didn't contact me was that *she* was afraid *I'd* want child support."

Stevie looked down at the baby and mulled that over. "How did the police know to call you?"

"She left my name and number on a list of people to

call in case of an emergency. And she put my name on the baby's birth certificate. I didn't believe I was really the father, but DNA confirmed it."

Stevie gazed down at the baby, whose eyes were growing heavy. "So, how long have you had the baby?"

"Six days." He rubbed his jaw ruefully. "Six of the longest days of my life."

"Who had her until you got her?"

"Dallas Child Services."

"And how long was she there?"

"Two weeks."

Stevie's brows hunched in a frown. "That isn't nearly enough time for her to develop Attachment Disorder."

"She already had it. Her mother . . ." Holt's voice trailed off. He hated to speak ill of the dead, but there was no way of explaining the situation without casting Ella in a bad light.

"What?" Stevie prodded.

Holt hesitated. "Well, let's just say she didn't have very strong maternal instincts."

"She neglected Isabelle?"

Holt watched a mime stroll down the sidewalk away from Jackson Square. "I don't think it was technically neglect. Isabelle was always looked after. Ella just didn't do it personally."

Stevie lifted an eyebrow. "So who did?"

"A string of nannies. Unfortunately, none of them stayed longer than a couple of weeks."

"Why not?"

"Ella apparently expected them to work around the clock. She would go off on trips and leave them alone with Isabelle for days with no time off. If a nanny complained about the hours or suggested that Ella spend more time with the baby, Ella fired her."

Stevie's eyes grew somber. "Did she ever try to care for Isabelle herself?"

"For a few days, but apparently the novelty wore off fast. A week after giving birth, Ella left the baby with a nanny and went for a week-long stay at a spa in Arizona."

"You're kidding."

"Nope. Her top concern was getting her figure back."

"How could a mother just abandon her baby?"

Holt fingered his coffee cup. "I don't think she saw it as abandonment. She financially provided for the child, and the way she saw it, that fulfilled her obligation. I think she was just raising Isabelle the way she'd been raised herself."

Stevie looked down at the baby in her arms. The exhausted infant had fallen asleep, her cupid's bow lips still curled around the plastic nipple. Stevie eased the bottle out of the child's mouth, her heart aching with sympathy. Poor little sweetheart—from the sound of things, she'd been motherless long before her mother died.

"When I picked Isabelle up at Child Services, they said she'd been at two different foster homes in the two weeks they had her," Holt was saying. "The foster parents said she was too difficult to handle, and they couldn't get her to eat."

"Did they take her to a doctor?"

Holt nodded. "They ran a bunch of tests and couldn't find anything wrong with her. That's when she was diagnosed with Failure to Thrive and Attachment Disorder. Apparently Isabelle's had such a turnover in caregivers that she didn't form a solid connection with any of them."

"Poor little thing," Stevie murmured.

"The doctor I took her to here in New Orleans said it's

rare to see such pronounced symptoms in a baby this young. Apparently children usually aren't diagnosed until it's too late to do anything."

That fit with what Stevie knew about the disorder. "Did he tell you what to do to correct it?"

"He said Isabelle needs one person who'll be with her during most of her waking hours—someone extremely patient and empathetic, someone who'll hang in there despite all of her fussing and fuming and pushing away."

"In other words, someone who loves her."

Holt nodded. "And that someone needs to stick around for at least a couple of years. Otherwise, she's likely to feel abandoned again and withdraw even further." He paused. "But it leaves me with a big dilemma. Isabelle needs someone around the clock, and I can't just stop working and stay home to care for her."

"Can you take a leave of absence from your work? The Family Leave Act assures that—"

He shook his head. "It doesn't apply. I run my own business."

"What do you do?"

"I'm a crisis management consultant. I step in and tell troubled companies what to do to turn around their businesses. Right now I'm finishing up a contract with a computer manufacturer in Atlanta and starting a new one with Allen Industries here in New Orleans. They'd both sue the pants off me if I just stopped work. Besides, if the companies fold, hundreds of workers will lose their jobs." The corner of his mouth twisted in irony. "Great situation, huh? I'm in the business of solving problems for other people, but I can't solve this one for myself."

"Maybe you could adjust your schedule so you can care for Isabelle while you work." Holt blew out a sigh.

"I tried it after my first nanny quit. It was a fiasco."

"What happened?"

"Isabelle cried so much I couldn't even talk on the phone, much less attend a meeting. I hired a baby-sitter through one of those licensed and bonded sitter services in the Yellow Pages to temporarily help out. I came home to hear her shrieking threats at Isabelle."

"Oh, dear!"

"It really scared me. She said Isabelle's crying made her snap. I hate to think what she might have done if I hadn't gotten home when I did."

Stevie had seen enough abused children to know it was a real concern. "Thank goodness you didn't have to find out."

"Yeah. Anyway, it's got me wary of hiring just any baby-sitter. And Isabelle is really hard to feed. She's dropped weight lately instead of gaining like she should. The doctor warned me that if she loses another pound, he's going to put her in the hospital on a feeding tube."

Stevie stroked the baby's white-blond hair, her throat tight.

"I've got to find someone I can trust, and that's not easy."

"Finding caregivers for special needs children can be hard. And if you can find them, it's hard to keep them, because there's a high burn-out rate."

"A pretty fast one, too, apparently," Holt said glumly. "I've already gone through two nannies. My assistant hired the first one before I took custody of Isabelle, and she didn't even make it through the first day before she gave notice. I thought the second nanny was perfect. She was a private pediatrics nurse looking for a long-term position. She said she loved babies, and she had references as long as my arm."

"Sounds great."

"Yeah. She was." He blew out a big sigh. "Until she quit three days later."

"Why did she quit?"

"She said she couldn't deal with a baby she couldn't console. She couldn't handle it emotionally."

Stevie gazed down at the child. Isabelle looked like a sleeping cherub, lips slightly parted and breath blowing in and out in tiny little puffs that tickled Stevie's forearm. It was hard to believe that such a tiny thing could be such a big problem.

"It's a real dilemma," Holt said. "I can't be sure that anyone I hire is going to stay, and Isabelle can't afford to form attachment only to have the person abandon her."

He had a problem, all right. Stevie puckered her brow, thinking hard.

"I need to do something soon, because Isabelle sure doesn't seem to be bonding with me. If anything, she's getting more and more agitated. The flight back from Atlanta this evening was a nightmare. Isabelle bawled the whole way, and by the time we landed. everyone on the plane was ready to kill me. Hell, I was ready to kill myself."

He picked up his coffee cup and took another swill. "Once we got in the car, I started scanning the radio dial, thinking that if music soothes the savage beast, maybe it would soothe Isabelle. Nothing worked until I landed on your program, and then it was like magic. Your voice just mesmerized her. So I stayed tuned to your program and started listening myself."

His gaze fastened on hers, and Stevie's heart began to pound irrationally. Good heavens, but he was sexy. When he looked straight at her like that, it was easy to understand why Ella had agreed to a fling.

"I really liked the things you had to say. You seemed to really care about kids."

"That's because I do."

"Well, it came across. Your advice made a lot of sense. And when I heard those callers giving you grief about not having any kids of your own . . . well, I thought you handled it really well. So it made me think that you might be my answer."

It was hard to hold a thought when those piercing brown eyes were aimed at her. Stevie averted her gaze to watch a white-aproned waiter bring a plate of powdered-sugar–glazed beignets to the couple at the next table. "I'm sorry, but I'm afraid I don't have any advice to offer beyond what the doctor told you."

"Oh, I didn't want to ask you for advice." Holt set down his coffee cup and leaned forward, his dark eyes earnest. She made the mistake of looking into them, and a jolt of attraction made her stomach do a funny little jump. *Trouble,* her mind warned her. *Trouble with a capital* T. LADIES' MAN was written all over him. He was exactly the kind of man she'd vowed to stay away from. All the same, an unbidden shiver shimmied up her spine.

"I wanted to ask you . . ." He paused and cleared his throat.

"Yes?"

"Well, I wanted to ask you to marry me."

Chapter Five

She stared at him as if he'd lost his mind—and maybe he had. But Holt plunged ahead anyway.

"Look—I know it sounds absurd, but please, hear me out."

Her eyes were large and wary, as if she expected him to start foaming at the mouth.

He spoke quickly, wanting to overcome her objections before she could voice them. "Think about it. It's a way all three of us can get what we need. You said you want children, and you took a lot of grief tonight because you don't have any. I need someone to take care of Isabelle. And Isabelle needs a mother."

"But . . ."

He raised both his hands. "Please—hear me out. First of all, let me just say up front that it wouldn't have to be a real marriage. I mean, there wouldn't have to be anything physical."

Although it wasn't an entirely unappealing idea, if she weren't such a little Goody Two-shoes.

A red stain started creeping up her neck. "I—I don't . . ."

"Just hear me out," he repeated, leaning forward. "We'd stay married long enough for Isabelle to bond with both of us and for you to adopt her. Stepparent adoptions are very easy in Louisiana—I have a friend who just got one, so I'm familiar with this. After you became her legal mother, we'd get divorced and share custody."

Stevie stared at him, her lips parted. "I couldn't . . ."

"After the divorce, she could live with you until she was old enough and secure enough to handle splitting her time between us."

Stevie sat there, her expression stunned. He hoped her silence meant she was considering the proposition.

"Look, I know it sounds crazy. It *is* crazy. But it's also a great solution for all of us. Just think about it. I need someone to take care of Isabelle, but Isabelle doesn't just need a nanny; she needs a mother. And you're a parenting expert who needs a child."

It was an insane proposition. She didn't even know the man, and he'd just asked her to marry him!

Her first proposal, and it had to be from a crazyman.

Although he wasn't entirely crazy. Stevie looked down at the sleeping child in her arms and felt a rush of tender warmth. The poor baby *did* need a mother. Not just a paid caretaker, but a mother who would love her and care for her and be there for her.

"Don't answer right now," Holt said. "Take some time and think about it."

"I don't need to think about it. I couldn't possibly . . ."

The loud bleat of a towboat foghorn on the Mississippi over the levee made the baby jump in Stevie's arm and open startled blue eyes. She gazed into Stevie's face, then opened her pink bud of a mouth and let out a loud wail.

Stevie rocked her, trying to soothe her back to sleep, but Isabelle refused to be soothed. The infant's body stiffened, and she pulled her head away from Stevie's arm.

What a sad little sweetheart. She was so small, so helpless and needy, pushing away from the very thing she needed most—love and connection and closeness.

"It's okay, Isabelle," Stevie crooned, gently rubbing the bawling baby's back. "It's okay." The infant turned inconsolable blue eyes at her. Something in that gaze reached out and curled around her heart like a tight fist, squeezing hard.

"You'd be generously compensated," Holt continued. "Isabelle has a large trust fund, and as Isabelle's co-guardian, you'd receive . . ."

"Money has nothing to do with it. I would never marry for money."

"Well, what would you marry for?"

The bluntness of the question startled her, although she didn't know why. After all, the man had just proposed marriage after knowing her all of twenty minutes. "Marriage is a lifelong commitment," Stevie replied. "I would only marry for love."

Holt raked both hands through his hair. "Well, that's the one thing I can't offer. I don't believe in lifelong commitments."

"That's why you can treat marriage so casually." Stevie put the plastic nipple to Isabelle's mouth, and the baby settled into eating again.

"I'm not treating it casually. It's a serious legal commitment. I don't think it's possible for two people to say how they're going to be feeling about each other twenty or thirty years from now, but I *do* think it's a great way for all of us to get what we need."

"I'm sorry, but—"

"Look, when I mentioned the financial benefits, I wasn't trying to buy you. I simply wanted to point out that you'd have the financial resources to be a full-time mom to Isabelle, if that's what you chose to do."

A full-time mom. It wasn't a well-paid or prestigious career choice, and the hours were a killer, but it had always been Stevie's dream. And it was just what poor Isabelle needed.

Still, she couldn't even consider it. If and when she married, it would be for keeps. She shook her head. "No. There's absolutely no . . ."

He held up his hands. "Look—I understand this sounds bizarre and outrageous. It is. But I'm in the business of coming up with creative solutions, and often the ideas that work the best are the very ones that seem the most ridiculous at first blush."

Stevie curved her lips into a smile. "Well, this certainly passes *that* test."

"People get married for a lot less valid reasons. And fifty percent of all marriages end in divorce, anyway."

"I can't believe you're serious about this."

"I'm completely serious. Just take some time and think about it," he asked earnestly.

"There's nothing to think about. Marriage is a sacred commitment."

"So is raising a child." He leaned forward. "This is a win-win situation for everybody."

Stevie shook her head. "I'm sorry, but it's out of the question."

Nothing was ever really out of the question. Everything was negotiable. It was the basic tenet of Holt's business philosophy.

But another basic tenet was that timing was everything. Sometimes the best way to win an argument was to give the other party time to get used to the idea, then take a different approach. For the time being, he'd back off.

He blew out a long sigh. "Well, I knew it was a long shot, but I figured it was worth a try."

The wariness in her eyes melted to sympathy. "You must really feel desperate, asking a stranger to marry you."

"Desperate is a pretty good description. But just so you know . . ." He looked into her blue-gray eyes. "I wouldn't have asked just any stranger to be Isabelle's mother. Something about you really connected with her." He paused briefly. "And with me."

Their eyes locked and held, and the remark suddenly seemed colored with sexual overtones. He hadn't meant it that way, but that was how it had come out.

Apparently Stevie took it that way as well, because her cheeks blazed as she gazed down at Isabelle. He watched her tongue dart out and moisten her lips.

Well, well, well. There were definitely sparks in the air. Probably because they were discussing marriage, he reasoned; after all, marriage implied sex, and asking her to marry him was sort of like asking her to have sex with him—even though he'd stated up front that sex wouldn't be part of the deal.

Still, the idea of sex—even the idea of not having it—seemed to have lit something.

He cleared his throat. "You're probably involved with someone, anyway."

"No. I-I'm not."

"Me neither."

Another lick of heat flared between them. Stevie adjusted the blanket over the baby in her lap. "Too bad. Then you could propose to someone you actually know."

He shook his head. "The women I date aren't exactly the motherly type."

Her mouth curved. "Apparently not, if Isabelle's mother is an example."

"I've never been interested in settling down, so I deliberately date women who aren't, either," he snapped. What was it about her that made him so defensive? He didn't usually feel the need to explain himself. "Look—I'm trying to be up front about this," he rationalized. "I'm not the family-man type. But now I have this baby, and I want to do right by her, and she needs a mother."

"She needs a father, too."

"She's got that."

"So you wouldn't consider putting her up for general adoption?"

He shook his head. "No. I'm her father, and I won't abandon her. But stepparent adoption is fast and easy, and it would give everyone what they need."

Stevie gently stroked Isabelle's hair. "There's got to be a better solution. Do you have any family?"

Holt shook his head. "Not nearby. My mother's in California, and my dad lives in Ohio."

"Any brothers or sisters?"

"I'm an only child."

"Well, how about friends or neighbors?"

He shook his head. "They're all like me—they have full-time jobs."

Stevie's brow furrowed. "Well, if you keep looking, I'm sure you'll find the right person."

I've already found her. She just doesn't know it yet.

"There are some local services that locate nannies. I can get you their names and numbers, if you like."

"I've already contacted two agencies, and they're searching." He leaned back and decided to try another tack. "What about you? If you won't consider marrying me, would you consider becoming Isabelle's nanny? I'd pay you twice whatever you're currently making."

She shook her head. "I couldn't do that."

"Why not?"

"I get too attached." She gently removed the bottle from the baby's mouth. "I tried being a foster mother, but it tore me up when it was time for the child to leave. I knew it was in her best interests—she was being adopted by a wonderful couple, and I knew she'd be loved and cared for—but still, it broke my heart."

"Sounds to me like you'd be perfect for Isabelle."

Stevie shook her head. "I'm sorry. I can't let myself get that attached to any child that's not my own."

"So make her your own."

"We've already covered that."

Time to try a fresh play.

"Well, hopefully one of those nanny services will come through, but for the next few days, I'm in a real bind." He blew out a long sigh. "I suppose I'll just have to put Isabelle into day-care until I can find her a full-time caregiver."

Stevie's brow creased. "The last thing Isabelle needs is day-care."

"I know, but after coming home to a screaming sitter,
I don't like the idea of leaving her alone with someone I
don't know."

Stevie looked down at the dozing child. Poor little
thing—she'd gotten off to a hard start in life, being shuffled around from person to person, never feeling as if
she belonged to any of them. A group environment like
a drop-in day-care service was the last thing she
needed.

"I can watch her," she found herself saying against
her will.

"Really?" Holt's face lit with a smile that took him from
handsome to devastating. He had a dimple in his right
cheek that matched the cleft in his chin. "Oh, man, that
would be great. Better than great. It would be terrific!"

"It's just temporary," she warned. "Just until you find a
nanny."

"I understand. Thanks a million."

Was he playing her? His eyes met hers with an almost
physical force, making it hard for her to gather her
thoughts. She swallowed hard. "The center opens at
nine, but my assistant and I get there at eight-thirty."

"Well, then, if it's all right, I'll drop her off around
eight-forty-five."

Stevie nodded. He smiled again, and her stomach
gave a funny little flutter.

Get a grip, she told herself. He broke Rule One and
Rule Two. He was a definite babe magnet and a wom-
anizer of the first order.

Still, she couldn't help but feel a buzz when her eyes
met his.

"This is just temporary," she repeated. "Only for a few
days."

"I understand. I really, really appreciate your help."

She was doing it for the baby, Stevie told herself. The fact that Holt made hot chills race up and down her spine had nothing, absolutely nothing, to do with her decision.

Chapter Six

The high-pitched wail of a baby pulled Stevie's attention away from the April class schedule she was creating on her office computer the next morning. The cry had a forlorn tone that Stevie immediately recognized, a tone so plaintive and sad that it tugged at Stevie's heart. It could only mean one thing: Isabelle had arrived.

Which meant Holt was here, too. To Stevie's dismay, her pulse began to skitter.

Her assistant, Michelle, burst through Stevie's office door, her dark eyes bright with excitement, her straight brown chin-length hair swinging. "He's here!"

Michelle wasn't just Stevie's co-worker; she was her dearest friend. Stevie had met the married mother of two at a Weight Watchers meeting nearly seven years ago, and she'd immediately been drawn to the stylish brunette's warmth and humor. The two women had supported each other as they'd worked toward their weight-loss goals and formed a close bond in the process. Michelle had begun volunteering at the parenting center, then started working there full-time when her two children started school.

Stevie had told her all about the previous evening's encounter with Holt and Isabelle.

"Why didn't you tell me he was such a hunk?" Michelle demanded.

Stevie lifted her shoulders. "I was focused on the baby."

Michelle raised her eyebrows at a mocking angle. "Too focused to notice that the man looks like a cross between George Clooney and Tom Cruise?"

Stevie gave an embarrassed grin. She was either way too transparent or Michelle was way too perceptive. "Well, maybe I noticed, but it didn't really seem relevant."

"Uh-huh." Michelle put her hands on her hips and shot her one of those who-do-you-think-you're-kidding smiles. "Apparently it was relevant enough to make you put on some mascara and lipstick for a change." She gave a teasing grin. "And don't even try to tell me that you wore it for the kid."

Stevie gave a sheepish grin. "Don't get all worked up. There's no potential for romance there."

"Why not? He *proposed* to you, for heaven's sake!"

"The proposal was practically sight unseen," Stevie reminded her. "He would have proposed if I looked like Quasimodo."

"But you don't. You're beautiful."

"Yeah, right." Stevie knew she had some good points—good skin, decent hair and she'd finally lost the extra pounds that had made her so miserable for so many years—but she didn't kid herself. She was no bombshell, which was no doubt the kind of woman Holt dated.

Michelle blew out a sigh. "I wish you'd see yourself as other people see you."

"You're great for my morale, Michelle, but you're out of touch with reality."

"No, I'm not. The reality is, there's a gorgeous hunk of a man out there who's used the M word."

"Yes. And it stands for motherhood." Stevie clicked

the SAVE icon on her computer screen. "He's looking for a permanent nanny, not a wife."

"Maybe you can change his mind."

Stevie shook her head. "He flat-out told me he's not interested in *love* and marriage."

"No man ever is, until he meets the right woman."

"So what are you saying? I should enter into a love-less marriage with a guy who goes around having one-night stands?"

"No. But don't be so quick to write him off, either."

Stevie's chair creaked as she rose. "Do me a favor and don't tell anyone about any of this proposal nonsense, okay? As far as the staff and our clients are concerned, let's just say I'm watching Isabelle to help out a friend."

"Okay." Michelle grinned mischievously. "I promise not to tell anyone but your mother."

Michelle was well acquainted with Stevie's mother's matchmaking efforts. Stevie narrowed her eyes. "You wouldn't dare."

"You're right. I wouldn't."

"That's more like it." Tugging down her loose blue sweater, Stevie smoothed her black slacks, drew a deep breath and headed out of her tiny office. Her stomach did a funny flip when she saw Holt across the large, brightly colored room. He looked even better this morning than he had last night. His thick, dark hair was combed, his face was freshly shaved and he wore an expensive dark suit that accentuated his broad shoulders. He oozed masculinity, and the fact that he was pushing a ridiculously frilly pink stroller around the room in a fruitless attempt to quiet the sobbing baby only made it more pronounced.

Holt's face broke into a relieved smile as he spotted Stevie. "Hi."

"Hi, yourself." She found it distinctly unsettling to be the focus of his smile. She turned her attention to Isabelle, who was caterwauling like an angry Banshee inside the carriage. The baby's skinny legs kicked at the embroidered hem of her delicate white linen dress, flailing against the silk padding of the carriage. Her face was red and angry above the high-buttoned collar. "Hello, there, Isabelle."

The baby stopped in mid-squawl and stared up through teary eyes. Stevie smiled. "I like your dress, Isabelle."

The baby stuck her fist in her mouth.

"One thing Ella did well was shop," Holt said. "Isabelle has more designer clothes than most stores."

"It's very pretty. But it might be more comfortable if it were turned around."

"What?"

"She's wearing it backward. It buttons up the back."

"Oh, man." He blew out a frustrated sigh. "No telling what else I'm doing wrong. I've got a stack of books about baby care, but they assume a level of basic knowledge that I don't have."

Stevie gave him a reassuring smile. "There's a learning curve for every new parent."

"Yeah, well, my curve is about the size of the earth's circumference. Everything about this baby business is a mystery."

"You're doing fine."

"No, I'm not. Isabelle is miserable, and I have no clue how to make her happy."

Poor guy; he looked completely frustrated. "I'll see if I can find some literature that might help you. And we have a basic baby care class starting in a couple of weeks. You might want to consider signing up for it."

"Isabelle needs more than I'm going to get out of a

book or a class. She needs a mother." He looked at Stevie, his brown eyes pleading his case more eloquently than words ever could. "Any chance you've changed your mind?"

"Afraid not." She forced her eyes away from his compelling gaze and looked at the baby, who was sucking on her knuckles. "Looks like Isabelle's hungry."

"I tried to feed her this morning, but she wouldn't take more than a couple of swallows."

"You've got to eat, sweetie," Stevie crooned to Isabelle. She lifted the baby out of the carriage. Isabelle stiffened and howled as Stevie carried her to a rocking chair against the wall in the toddler play area, where Michelle was straightening picture books.

Holt dug a bottle out of the diaper bag draped on the handle of the carriage and handed Stevie the bottle. She deftly squeezed a couple of drops of baby formula onto Isabelle's lips, talking to her the whole time. The baby stopped crying long enough to stick out her tongue and taste her lips. Stevie slipped the nipple into Isabelle's mouth, and she began sucking hungrily.

"Wow," Holt marveled. "You have a magic touch with her."

Stevie shrugged. "No magic to it. Just a little experience."

"Well, the two nannies I've run through had a lot of experience, too, but neither of them had the knack of calming Isabelle like you do."

"Stevie's a miracle worker with cranky babies," Michelle spoke up, rising to her feet from her crouch before the toddler-height book shelf.

"I can tell. She's pretty good with cranky dads, too."

Stevie felt her face heat. "Have you two met? Michelle, this is Holt Landen. Michelle is the assistant director of this place."

"We met when he came in the door," Michelle said.

Holt looked around. "So, what happens at a parenting center, exactly?"

"We provide educational support for parents," Michelle said. "We hold classes, distribute information and provide counseling. We're also an educational play place where members can bring their kids."

"It looks like Disneyland for toddlers."

"Stevie set it all up. The room is divided into different centers. The classes are held here, where parents can keep an eye on their children as they play." She gestured to three rows of chairs in the center of the room. "And we've got the infant play area over there." Michelle pointed to a section covered with padded mats and padded benches, filled with baby toys. Drawings of faces, simple activity boards and a mirror were fastened to the wall at infant height, just above the floor.

She turned toward the far wall. "The toddler home center is in the corner." Michelle pointed to a plastic play house, set beside a colorful play kitchen filled with plastic stacking cups, dolls and stuffed animals. "And the action center is against the wall." Holt turned to an area filled with bigger toys, such as a plastic toddler car, a short plastic slide, a plastic hammer and work bench.

"The art center is next to it." Michelle pointed to an area surrounded by a plastic gate, with a small table and toddler-sized chairs, as well as two plastic child-sized easels. "And our book nook is in the far corner." It was a carpeted area covered with large, animal-shaped pillows next to low shelves of picture books.

"Wow." Holt looked at Stevie, who was feeding an amazingly quiet Isabelle. "I might hire you as a spatial organization consultant."

He was only half kidding. The place was clean and bright and incredibly well organized. A train mural ran along the walls, with the themes of the different centers painted behind them. "Who painted the mural?"

"Stevie did," Michelle volunteered.

"Man." Holt looked at her, more than a little impressed. "She's a woman of many talents."

Michelle nodded. "In addition to all this, she does a weekly radio show, started a single-mothers outreach program and is putting together a cookbook of nutritious kids' snacks."

To Holt's amusement, Stevie's face turned scarlet. "She sounds like a veritable renaissance woman," he said.

"She left out that I can stand on my head and pat my tummy at the same time," Stevie joked.

Holt laughed. She had a sense of humor, as well. More than ever, he was determined to convince her to become Isabelle's mother.

He glanced at his watch. "I've got to run, but I really appreciate your watching Isabelle, and I want to take you to dinner tonight as a thank-you."

The invitation apparently startled her. "Oh, gee—I . . . I . . ."

Holt headed for the door, not wanting to give her the chance to turn him down. "Gotta run. Thanks a million for watching Isabelle."

Before she could form a response, he was already out the door.

The day flew by for Stevie. She taught a new mothers class, followed by a Tame Your Toddler session for the parents of two-year-olds. While Stevie worked, Isabelle napped in her stroller, played on a large, multicolored blanket covered with textured cut-out animals in the infant play center, and stared at her reflection in the mirror. The baby fussed every time Stevie touched her, but once Stevie set her down and talked to her softly, she quieted.

In the afternoon, while Isabelle took a long nap, Stevie counseled the parents of a three-year-old who refused to sleep in his own bed, then met with the parents of a four-year-old boy who'd abandoned his potty training upon the arrival of a new baby sister. After her late-afternoon feeding, Isabelle played with a portable mobile on a blanket in Stevie's office as she returned a dozen phone calls left on the Parent Help answering machine.

Stevie had just put Isabelle in a battery-powered baby swing when Michelle's husband, Brian, walked through the door.

Michelle's face lit in a warm smile as she hurried to greet the ruddy-faced, auburn-haired man. Brian drew her into a bear hug, gave her a big kiss and whispered something that made her laugh.

"You two act like newlyweds," Stevie teased. "You've been married twelve years, for heaven's sake. When are you going to tone down the mushy stuff?"

"Never." Brian smiled down at Michelle. "We'll still be acting like newlyweds when we're in our eighties."

A knot formed in Stevie's throat. She was happy for her friend, she really was, but seeing the couple together made her painfully aware of what was lacking in her own life. It wasn't like her to dwell on negatives, but last night's radio show had left her in a funk about her future. Her Prince Charming had better hurry up and put in an appearance or else she'd end up attending the ball alone.

Maybe not completely alone, a little voice deep inside prompted. *You could marry Holt.*

She abruptly brushed the thought aside. She wanted a marriage like Brian and Michelle's, not one of convenience. If she was going to embark on single parenthood, she'd be better off doing it single from the start.

The door opened abruptly and Holt strode in. The sight of him set her nerves to jangling.

Brian looked up. "Hey . . . you're Holt Landen, aren't you?"

"Yes."

Brian crossed the room and stuck out his hand. "I'm Brian Guidry. I don't know if you remember, but we met a couple of years ago. I work with Stafford Accounting."

Holt shook the shorter man's hand. "I remember. Your firm handled the Midmain Manufacturing account."

"You two know each other?" Michelle looked from her husband to Holt, then back again.

"Sure. This is the guy who saved our biggest account from bankruptcy," Brian said. "He's probably the reason I still have a job."

"Does he always exaggerate like this?" Holt asked Michelle with a diffident smile.

"I'm not exaggerating," Brian said. "He completely turned that company around."

"I can walk on water, too," Holt added helpfully.

Brian shook his head and grinned. "More than a few people think you can." He hooked a thumb in Holt's direction. "*BusinessWeek* magazine listed this guy as one of the top crisis management experts in the country."

Stevie realized she was just standing there, staring. She abruptly turned and walked to the closet where she'd stored Isabelle's baby carriage, her mind swimming. Brian was a C.P.A. with a large downtown accounting firm, and one of the most level-headed people she knew. The fact that he thought Holt was some kind of wunderkind was disconcerting.

It was impressive, and she didn't want to be impressed by Holt.

"So what are you doing here?" Brian asked him.

"I'm picking up my baby. Stevie was kind enough to watch her for me today."

"You have a baby?"

"Yeah."

Brian cocked his head, his eyes puzzled. "Last I heard, you were listed as one of the top-ten eligible bachelors in New Orleans. When did you get married?"

"I, um, didn't." From the corner of her eye, Stevie saw Holt uneasily shift his stance. "The baby . . . well, it's kind of a long story."

"I'll fill you in later," Michelle told her husband.

Stevie unfolded the carriage, then stopped the baby swing. She felt, rather than saw, Holt cross the room and stand beside her. Like a space heater, he seemed to raise the temperature of the air. She focused her attention on unstrapping Isabelle from the seat.

Right on cue, the baby began to howl. Holt winced. "I hope she hasn't been doing that all day."

"Actually, she's been pretty quiet." Stevie lifted the protesting child from the swing. "She cried when she was handled, but she settled back down pretty easily."

Stevie passed the baby to Holt. The child stiffened and flailed her arms as he gingerly took her. There was a moment of silence as the baby drew a deep breath, then she let out a bloodcurdling yowl.

Holt patted her awkwardly. "Hey, there, sweetheart. It's okay. I'm not going to hurt you."

His words did nothing to reassure Isabelle. The child struggled against him as if fighting for her life.

Holt cast a pleading glance at Stevie. "How should I handle this?"

"Keep talking to her," Stevie said. "Hold her firmly but gently. You're doing all the right things."

"She sure doesn't act like it."

"She just needs to get used to you."

She unfolded Isabelle's stroller, and Holt placed the baby in it.

"There you go, Izzy. See?" He held up his hands. "I'm not touching you at all."

The baby's screaming lessened.

Stevie leaned down. "Don't give your daddy such a hard time, okay?"

Isabelle stopped crying at the sound of Stevie's voice and made a sound between a hiccup and a burp. Stevie smiled and handed the baby a set of large plastic keys she'd found in the diaper bag. "Look here, Isabelle. Aren't these pretty?"

The baby cooed and stuck a giant blue key in her mouth.

Holt shook his head. "Man, you really have a way with her."

"Better watch out," Brian warned. "If Stevie can charm a baby like that, there's no telling what she'll do to you."

Holt gave a crooked grin. "She's already doing it."

Stevie's heart gave a traitorous jump. She straightened and backed away from the baby carriage. "I'll get her diaper bag, then she'll be ready to go."

"Great. Are you ready, too?"

Stevie's pulse accelerated. "Me?"

"Yeah. I'm taking you to dinner, remember?"

Stevie opened her mouth to protest.

"To thank you for watching Isabelle," he quickly added.

A flush of alarm pulsed through Stevie. "That's not necessary. I enjoyed having her around. Besides, I have to close up here."

"Brian and I will handle that," Michelle chimed in. "Brian's parents are taking our kids to the mall, so we're free tonight."

Stevie searched her brain for an excuse to turn him down. "But I still have some things to do. There's paperwork—"

"Nothing that can't wait until tomorrow," Michelle said.

Stevie shot her a dark look.

Michelle blatantly ignored it. "Go on. You don't want to pass up an evening with one of New Orleans's most eligible bachelors," she joked.

Yes, I do. All of her instincts warned that this was a stupid move. Holt was exactly the kind of man she'd vowed to never date again, and she was undeniably attracted to him. If she were wise, she'd keep her distance.

"I was hoping you'd be able to give me some more pointers on how to calm Isabelle," Holt added.

"Stevie's the person to ask, all right," Brian agreed.

What could it hurt? It wasn't really a date. It was just a thank-you dinner. And it wasn't as if she had any plans for the evening beyond zapping a Lean Cuisine in the microwave.

"All right," she said before the little voice in her head could convince her otherwise. "Let me grab my purse."

Chapter Seven

Holt glanced in his rearview mirror to make sure that Stevie's yellow Volkswagen Beetle was still behind him as he waited for the pea-green streetcar to ramble past the intersection of Napoleon and St. Charles Avenue. Stevie had insisted on taking her own car, as if she didn't trust him to take her back to her vehicle after dinner.

Which probably was a wise move, considering that

the baby had screeched nonstop ever since he fastened her into her car seat. At this point, kidnapping Stevie was starting to sound like a good idea.

"It's okay, Izzy," Holt said over his shoulder. "Stevie's still with us."

And he intended to find a way to keep her with them. He'd conducted phone interviews with two nanny candidates that afternoon, and the experience had been less than encouraging. Both women had asked all sorts of questions about wages and working conditions and very few questions about the baby. One of them had flatly stated that she'd refuse to sign a long-term contract, and the other one wanted a ninety-day trial period before she made a commitment. Isabelle couldn't afford a trial period. She needed someone permanent, and she needed her as soon as possible, because he sure as hell wasn't any good at taking care of her.

He glanced in the rearview mirror, and his chest tightened at the sight of her miserable little face. He wanted to be a good father, but he didn't know the first thing about babies.

He didn't know much about fatherhood, either. After his parents had divorced, Holt had only seen his father twice a year, and during most of those visits, one stepmother or another had taken begrudging care of him while his dad had put in a sixteen-hour day at work.

Unbidden, a memory rose in his mind like the moon in the night sky: He'd been seven years old, and his father had taken him to the Cleveland airport after a weeklong summer visit. It was the first time he'd seen his dad since his parents had split up and moved more than a thousand miles away from each other. Holt had managed to choke back his tears as his father walked him to the gate, but when a stewardess put the UNACCOMPANIED MINOR airline badge around his neck, he'd broken down.

He'd grabbed his father around the waist. "I want to stay, Daddy."

"You can't, champ. Your mother's expecting you in L.A." Holt had clung tightly, hoping his father would pat his back or ruffle his hair, wanting his father's touch so badly he ached for it. Instead, his father pulled back, distancing himself.

He always distanced himself.

Holt had tried hard not to cry. His father had told him that boys didn't. Maybe if he didn't cry, his father would want to be with him.

"You could come with me," Holt had pleaded. "You could come to California, too, and we could be a real family again."

His father had looked away, but not before Holt had seen something in his eyes that looked as sad and lonely as Holt felt. "Sorry, son. That's just not gonna happen."

"Why not?"

"That's just not the way things are."

His father had smiled, but that sad look had stayed in his eyes. "See you at Christmas, champ."

Holt's jaw ached as he pulled the car into the parking lot behind Masoletto's Restaurant, just off Carrolton, and he realized he'd been clenching his teeth. He wanted to be a better father to Isabelle than his old man had been to him. He wanted to be a lot more involved in her life, and to let her know he cared about her. But he didn't know how to give her the kind of warmth and affection she apparently needed. She needed someone a lot more touchy-feely than he was, someone who knew what the hell she was doing.

She needed Stevie. He had to find a way to convince Stevie to need Isabelle, too. Stevie's car slid into the spot beside his. As he struggled to unfasten his seatbelt, she hopped out and walked toward him.

"Hey there, sweetie," Stevie said to the baby. "What's all the fuss about?"

Holt finally managed to unlatch the carseat. "The fact that her dad's an incompetent moron," he muttered as he lifted out the baby carrier, baby and all.

Stevie grinned. "Actually, I think she's unhappy about losing her pacifier." She leaned into the back seat. Her baggy black slacks stretched against her backside, revealing a surprisingly enticing shape. From what Holt could tell, she had a great figure. He wondered why she hid it under such loose-fitting clothes.

"Here it is." She drew back, holding a pink pacifier, then popped it into the baby's mouth. Just like magic, the baby's crying ceased. Holt wondered how one person could have such a soothing effect on the baby and such a stimulating effect on him.

"Why didn't I think of that?" he asked.

"Because you're still undergoing on-the-job training."

"Well, I'm glad I've got you as my personal trainer." He looked down at Isabelle. "We need to convince her to stay on permanently, don't we, Isabelle?"

Stevie's eyes took on a wary light. "I've told you, this is just temporary."

We'll see about that, Holt thought as he carried the baby carrier into the restaurant. *We'll just have see to about that.*

A short, stout man with a thick Italian accent and a bulbous nose greeted Holt as he held the heavy door open for Stevie and followed her into the dimly lit restaurant. "Good evening, Mr. Landen. Welcome."

Holt introduced Stevie to Antonio Masoletto, the

restaurant owner, then grinned as the man bowed low over her hand, the gold chain around his neck swinging forward. The restauranteur was a native New Orleanian, yet he acted as if he was just visiting from Sicily.

The restaurant looked as if it could have been air-lifted in, as well. Washed in warm shades of golden yellow and amber, its three small dining rooms had rough walls, hewn timber beams and a slate floor. The rustic decor formed a striking contrast with the fine linen, candlelight and elegant service.

The man's gaze caught on the pink baby carrier in Holt's hand. "Ah—I see you've brought not just one but two lovely ladies." He peered down at Isabelle, who was busily sucking on her pacifier. "And the little one is just as bellissima as her mother."

"Oh, I'm not her mother," Stevie said quickly.

"No?"

"No. This is Holt's baby."

Masoletto's black eyebrows flew up like a pair of crow's wings, then pulled together in consternation. Too late, it occurred to Holt that maybe this wasn't the best restaurant choice. He frequently brought dates here, and while Masoletto had always given him a wink and a surreptitious thumbs-up to indicate his approval, his vicarious enjoyment of Holt's bachelorhood apparently stopped short of illegitimate fatherhood.

"I didn't know you had a baby," Masoletto said, all trace of a smile gone.

Holt adjusted the collar of his shirt. "I've just recently gotten custody."

He could see the questioning look in the man's eyes, but he had no inclination to explain further.

"How's your brother's business?" Holt asked.

Mr. Masoletto's face lit up. "Wonderful! Fantastico, thanks to you. He is very, very grateful." He turned to Stevie. "This is a very good man. Very kind, and very, very smart. He saved my brother's bakery from bankruptcy."

"Is that right?" Stevie looked at him questioningly.

"Yes, and he wouldn't take a dime."

"Hey, I couldn't let my favorite bakery shut down. I'm addicted to his biscotti." Holt shifted his stance. "Is our table ready?"

"Of course. Right this way."

Mr. Masoletto led them to a corner table on the far side of the front dining room and pulled out Stevie's chair with a flourish. "Alberto will be with you shortly. Enjoy."

Holt set down the carrier between his chair and Stevie's. She reached down and gently rocked it by the handle. Isabelle's mouth worked vigorously around the pacifier.

"Mr. Masoletto thinks very highly of you," Stevie said.

Holt lifted his shoulder. "His brother's a talented baker. He just needed to learn a few business skills."

"How did you meet him?"

Holt unfolded the linen napkin and placed it in his lap. "I put on a few seminars to help small businesses."

"Free ones?"

"Yeah. Small businesses have a tough go. I like helping them."

"That's really nice of you."

Holt lifted his shoulders. "My father's construction company went belly up when I was a kid, so I know what it can do to a family."

Stevie's gaze grew soft. "That must have been rough."

He was glad when the waiter came and took their order. Why on earth was he telling her this? He needed to be finding out about her, not spilling his own life story.

He looked down at the baby, who had been surprisingly quiet ever since they arrived at the restaurant. "She's asleep! How did you get her to do that?"

"I rocked her carrier."

She smiled across the table. The candlelight played over her face, bathing her eyes in warmth. She had beautiful eyes, he realized—blue and long-lashed and wide set. As a matter of fact, she had beautiful lips, as well—perfectly shaped and plump, the kind of lips that looked as if they were begging to be kissed.

He was watching her lips as she lifted her water glass and took a sip. "What kind of reaction to your instant fatherhood did you get from your friends and family?" she asked.

Holt reached for his water glass. "Not too many of my friends know about Isabelle yet."

"Why not?"

"I've been busy. Between work and trying to take care of her, I haven't had much time to socialize."

"What about your parents?"

Guilt pinched his conscience. "They don't know yet, either. I want to have a permanent solution to the child-care situation before I break the news."

Stevie's brow puckered. "Are you worried they'll be upset?"

"No. I just want to lessen the shock."

"How do you think they'll react?"

"I'm sure my mom will be thrilled. She's been after me for years to settle down and make her a grandmother."

Stevie smiled. "Sounds like my mother."

Now here was a piece of information he could use. Before he could pursue it, though, the waiter came by with a wine bottle and poured them some. Stevie asked, "What about your dad?"

Holt's chest tightened the way it always did at the thought of his father. "I don't think it'll have much of an impact on him."

"Why not?"

Holt lifted his shoulders. "After my folks divorced, he was never all that involved in my life."

Stevie's eyes took on that warm, sympathetic look again. "That must have hurt."

Holt took a gulp of wine, wondering why he'd told her that. Women were always after him to talk about his childhood and his parents and his feelings, and normally he avoided it like the plague. What was it about Stevie that suddenly had him spilling his guts?

It must be this crazy baby situation.

"Do you see him very often now?" Stevie asked.

"No. We talk on the phone occasionally, but that's about it."

"What about your mom?"

"We talk and e-mail all the time, and I usually see her during the holidays." He set down his glass. It was high time to turn this conversation around.

"Tell me about *your* family," he said as Alberto set down plates of Caesar salad.

"It's a big one. I have lots of aunts and uncles and cousins who live here, and an older brother who lives in Baton Rouge. He's married and has four-year-old twins. My father retired a few months ago. He was a prosecutor with the district attorney's office." Stevie lifted her fork. "And my mother just opened a catering business. She'd been a homemaker her whole life, and everyone thought this catering thing was just a goofy idea that would never get off the ground, but it's taken off like gangbusters."

"So, you're a native New Orleanian?"

Stevie nodded as she stabbed a piece of Romaine lettuce. "My parents still live in the same house I grew up in."

"So they're still married?"

"Yep. Thirty-seven years last month."

"Wow. It's hard to imagine being that settled."

"My family takes marriage very seriously," she said with a meaningful glance.

He didn't take the bait. "You said your mother wanted you to settle down."

Stevie nodded ruefully. "She's always after me to get out and meet people, and she keeps trying to fix me up." Stevie paused as the waiter refilled her water glass. "She even thought I should have let that caller who bit his child fix me up."

Holt's eyebrows rose in amusement. "You're kidding!"

"I wish I were."

"So, why *haven't* you married yet? A woman as attractive as you must have had opportunities."

The waiter passed, carrying a fragrant dish that made their mouths water. He set it down before Stevie. "I just haven't met the right man."

"Ever come close?"

"I thought I had a couple of times." She fixed her gaze on her plate and speared a shrimp.

"So what happened?"

"Turns out I was wrong."

It wasn't much of an answer," but apparently it was all the answer he was going to get.

She picked up her wineglass. "What about you? Ever come close to surrendering your bachelor status?"

His mouth twisted into a wry grin. "Not until yesterday."

Stevie rolled her eyes. The conversation drifted to books and movies. Holt was surprised at how much they had in common, and found himself thoroughly enjoying the evening. By the time the waiter served dessert and coffee, he'd almost forgotten the reason he'd asked her out.

He was laughing at something she said when her face froze and she stared across the room.

Stevie felt her chest tighten at the horrible image before her. "Oh, no."

"What's the matter?" Holt asked.

"My parents just walked in." Of all the restaurants in New Orleans, why did they have to show up here?

Holt turned toward the door.

"Don't look at them," Stevie hissed.

"Why not?"

"If they see me, they'll come over."

"So?"

"So you don't know what you'd be in for." Stevie propped her elbow on the table and put her head in her hand, trying to hide the side of her face.

His eyebrow quirked in amusement. "And what would that be?"

"Well, my mom would give you the third degree."

He lifted his shoulders. "So? I've got nothing to hide."

"You don't understand. My mom is the sweetest person in the world, but when it comes to matchmaking, she can make the Spanish Inquisition look like a walk in the park. She'd want to know where we met, why you have a baby, what we're doing out together. . . ."

"I can handle that."

"You don't understand. She'd try to make something out of this."

"Out of what?"

"Out of you and me having dinner together. She'd think this is a date."

"Would that be so terrible?"

"Yes! If I tell her it's not, she'll want to know *why* not. Then she'd hound me for months about where you are and what you're doing and what happened between us and why I'm not seeing you."

"Hey, I like the sound of this. This could work in my favor."

"I'm glad you're amused." Stevie pulled her napkin from her lap and rose from the table. "I'm going to make a dash for the ladies room. With any luck, they'll be seated in the next room and we can get out of here without getting caught."

Holt rose as well. "Hold on a minute."

"What for?"

"For this."

Before she knew what was happening, Holt had pulled her into his arms and covered her lips with a possessive kiss.

Chapter Eight

"Why, look, Robert—there's Stevie!" Marie Stedquest said. "And she's with a man."

Robert Stedquest peered over his wife's blond curls. Sure enough, there was his daughter, rising from a table in the corner. He couldn't see her face, but he immediately recognized her all the same. His chest filled with a fond warmth.

"I wonder who he is," Marie said.

"I don't know." Whoever he was, he was tall and well dressed. Even across the room, he could tell that his suit was custom tailored. Robert watched him rise from his seat as well.

"May I help you?" asked the dark-haired man at the desk.

"Yes," Robert said, turning his attention away from his daughter. "We have a reservation. The name is Stedquest."

Beside him, Marie gave a sharp gasp and elbowed his side. Robert jerked his gaze toward his wife.

"They're kissing!" she whispered.

Robert looked back in the corner. Sure enough, Stevie and the tall man were now locked in an embrace.

Marie tugged on his arm. "Let's go see who it is."

Robert had always felt a special connection to Stevie, had always felt that her personality was more in sync with his own than Marie's, and he was more than a little certain that the last thing she'd want at the moment was an interruption by her parents. "Not now, Marie. I think we should leave them. . . ."

But Marie bustled across the room, leaving Robert no choice but to follow. It seemed to be the thing he was doing more and more, he thought darkly—following Marie to places he'd rather not go.

They arrived at the table just as the kiss ended. "Stevie, darling!" Marie exclaimed.

Stevie turned dazed eyes toward them. Her cheeks flushed with color. "H-hi, Mom—Dad."

Robert felt as embarrassed as Stevie looked.

"What a surprise!" Marie smiled brightly. "I had no idea you had plans for the evening."

The red stain on Stevie's cheeks crept down her neck. She cleared her throat. "Mom, Dad, this is Holt Landen. Holt, these are my parents, Marie and Robert Stedquest."

"Nice to meet you," Robert said, extending his hand. Holt gripped it firmly. Good, Robert thought; you could tell a lot about a man by his handshake. That Peter guy Stevie had been involved with a couple of years ago— Robert had known he was bad news from the moment he'd felt his weak, clammy grip. And sure enough, the creep had broken Stevie's heart. Robert knew the jerk had left Stevie for another woman, but he suspected there was more to the story than Stevie let on.

Robert had run Peter's name through the system, checking for any outstanding warrants or traffic violations or parking tickets, hoping to find a way to cause him grief. Unfortunately, he'd come up empty.

It didn't matter how old Stevie was; she was still his little girl, and he had a strong paternal urge to protect her.

Holt turned and shook Marie's hand, flashing her a movie star–like smile. Marie smiled back, her eyes shining in a way that said she was clearly charmed.

"Nice to meet you, Mrs. Stedquest," Holt said. "Stevie's been telling me all about you."

Marie's hand fluttered to her chest. "She has?"

He nodded. "I understand you operate a very successful catering business."

"It's taken off a lot faster than I dared hope," Marie said modestly.

Taken off? More like taken over, Robert thought grimly. That damned catering business was running their lives. It was all Marie talked about, all she cared about, all she had time for. She was so damned busy arranging other people's weddings and anniversaries that she didn't have any time for him. Hell, she wouldn't be out with him this evening if she hadn't needed to do some research for her business.

"What are you two doing here?" Stevie asked.

"I have a request for an antipasto platter for a rehearsal dinner next month, and I'd heard that Masoletto's served a beautiful one," Marie said. "I thought I'd come order one and see what all the fuss is about."

A kittenlike mewl sounded from under the table near Marie's feet.

Robert leaned to the side and peered down.

Marie gazed down as well. "Oh, my—it's a baby!"

Sure enough, a little bundle of pink lay in one of those baby carryall things, right by Stevie's chair. Stevie reached down, picked up a pacifier from the blanket and gently reinserted it in the baby's mouth.

Marie clasped her hands together over her chest. "Oh, isn't she adorable?"

She wasn't adorable; she was pathetic. Adorable babies were chubby-cheeked cherubs. This baby looked like a toothless old man. She was all red-faced and scrawny, with skinny arms and bony legs.

Apparently, women saw babies differently than men, though, because Stevie was gazing at the infant with adoration. "She's beautiful, isn't she? Her name is Isabelle."

"She's precious," Marie agreed.

Stevie's eyes got all soft and misty as she gazed at the baby. If ever there was a woman cut out for motherhood, Robert thought, it was his daughter. He'd never seen anyone who loved children as much as his daughter.

"Are you watching her for a client?" Marie asked.

"Well . . ." Stevie hesitated.

"Actually, Isabelle's mine," Holt volunteered.

"You're married?" Marie's voice held the horrified tone usually reserved for natural disasters.

Holt cleared his throat. "Um, no."

"Divorced?"

"No."

Marie's chin moved slightly forward, the way it always did when she was on a quest for information. "Where's the child's mother?"

"I'm afraid she's dead."

"Oh, how awful!" Marie's hand fluttered to her throat, her blue eyes wide with sympathy. "How absolutely awful. That poor baby. And you poor man! A widower, and a new father to boot."

"Oh, I'm not a widower. The mother and I . . . well, we never married."

Robert narrowed his eyes. He had a low opinion of men who didn't live up to their obligations. To his way of thinking, if a man got a woman pregnant, there was only one honorable course of action.

He glanced at Marie, knowing she felt the same way. Her eyes were wide and shocked, and for a moment, she seemed to be speechless. It was a sure bet she wouldn't stay that way for long. "Well, I'm sure you're grieving, all the same," she said warmly when she recovered.

That was one of the things he'd always loved about Marie: the way she was willing to let people off the hook, to assume that their intentions were better than their actions. Another woman with her convictions would have registered disapproval, but Marie wasn't one to sit in judgment. In fact, for all her faults, Marie was one of the most nonjudgmental, forgiving women he'd ever met. It was one of the reasons he'd fallen in love with her.

Which had always struck him as ironic. As a prosecutor, he spent much of his day trying to eliminate people like his wife from the jury pool.

Used to spend his day, he mentally corrected. Past tense. Back before he was forced out to pasture. The thought brought a bitter taste to his mouth.

"Actually, it's an unusual situation," Holt was saying. "The baby's mother lived in Dallas, and she and I . . ." Holt shifted his weight, looking clearly uncomfortable. "We, um—well, we hadn't been in each other's lives in some time."

"Some time?" Marie echoed, her forehead furrowed.

Holt nodded. "We hadn't talked in over a year. I had no idea she'd had a baby until I got a call from the police a few weeks ago, telling me she'd died in an accident."

"Oh, my goodness!" Marie breathed. "Oh, what a shock that must have been!"

Holt's mouth turned up in a grim smile. "It was a shock, all right."

Robert could only imagine. A call like that was every young man's nightmare. There'd been a time in his life before Marie when Robert could well have found himself in the same position.

At least Holt had stepped up to the plate when he'd found out about the child.

Robert could see the wheels turning in Marie's mind, and he knew what she was thinking. He could almost predict what her next words would be. Sure enough, here they came.

"So . . . you're unattached?"

"Yes, ma'am."

Her face brightened. She looked from Holt to Stevie, then back again. "How do you two know each other?"

Holt glanced at Stevie. She opened her mouth as if she was about to speak, but Holt beat her to it. "We met online about six months ago."

Stevie's eyes flew wide. "*What?*"

"Now, sweetheart—it's okay to tell them." Holt patted Stevie's back. Instead of soothing her, the gesture seemed to startle her.

Holt's mouth twisted in an apologetic smile. "She's embarrassed about how we met. I keep telling her that there's nothing wrong with meeting through the Internet, that it's actually the intelligent way for single people to meet each other these days, but she's a little old-fashioned."

Marie's face lit with delight. "Oh, yes," she agreed rapidly. "Sometimes Stevie can be a real fuddy-duddy. But old-fashioned girls have a lot to offer."

Holt put his arm around Stevie's shoulder. She stared up at him, her eyes as big as pasta bowls.

"That's for sure. Stevie's been giving me lots of advice about Isabelle, and she's watching her for me until I can find a permanent nanny."

Marie's eyebrows flew up. "Is that right?" She turned to her daughter, her eyes full of reproach. "Why on earth haven't you told me? I talk to you nearly every day, and you never said a word!"

Stevie's lips moved, but no words came out. "I— we . . . We didn't . . ." she finally croaked.

"We didn't actually meet in person until a couple of days ago," Holt said smoothly. "She probably wanted to see if I looked like a troll before she told you about me." He smiled down at Stevie. "I already knew from our correspondence that she was a beautiful person on the inside, but I had no idea she'd be so beautiful on the outside, too."

Marie beamed as Stevie's mouth opened, then abruptly closed.

The dark-haired restaurant owner appeared at the table and dipped his head at Robert. "Your table is ready in the next room."

"Would you like to join us here?" Holt gestured toward the table, which held two cups of coffee, a half-eaten slice of chocolate cake and a bowl of melting gelato. "I'm sure Alberto can find some extra chairs."

Marie looked ready to accept.

"No, thanks," Robert said quickly. "You two are finishing up and we've just arrived."

"But . . ." Marie sputtered.

Robert shot her a warning glance and shook Holt's hand again. "It was nice meeting you."

"The pleasure was all mine. I hope to see you again soon."

"Stevie will have to bring you to dinner at our home," Marie piped up.

"That sounds great," Holt replied.

"Wonderful! Maybe later this week?"

"I just found out today that I have to go out of town for a business meeting Wednesday."

"Well, then, how about next Saturday?"

Holt nodded. "I'd love it."

"Terrific! I'll set it up with Stevie, and she can give you the details."

"I'll look forward to it."

"Me, too. I'm so glad to meet you." Marie bent and kissed Stevie on the cheek. "Good night," she said, then added in a loud whisper, "And good going!"

"Can you believe that?" she asked after she and Robert had been seated in the next room. "She never said a word! I wonder why not."

Robert peered at a large leather-covered menu. "Most young people don't routinely consult their parents about their romantic lives."

"It's not like her to keep things from me."

Guilt twisted Robert's stomach. He was keeping something from her, too.

Marie picked up the white linen napkin and placed it on her lap. "It hurts my feelings a little that she's been so secretive."

If Stevie's little secret had hurt Marie's feelings, no telling how she'd react to his. "Maybe she didn't want you to interfere."

"I wouldn't have done that."

Oh, right. Robert suppressed a smile and kept perusing the menu.

"Do you think I interfere?" she pressed.

"Sometimes."

"I mean well. I just want to see the people I love happy."

"I know."

"Sometimes I just don't know how to make them happy." Her blue eyes held a sad, haunted look. "Especially you." Her voice fell to a cracked whisper. "Especially not in bed."

Robert's stomach curled into a ball. "Oh hell, Marie— let's not get into that here."

"Is it my weight? I know I've gained a few pounds in the last couple of years. . . ."

He felt like a complete and utter jerk. "There's nothing wrong with your weight, Marie. You look fine."

"You're just saying that."

"I'm just saying it because it's true."

After thirty-seven years of marriage, it still amazed him that she had no idea how beautiful she was. He didn't understand how she could look in the mirror day after day and not see it. He loved her body—loved her soft breasts and generous behind, loved the way she smelled and felt and looked and tasted.

"I know I'm showing my age. And I've been thinking . . . maybe I should try some Botox."

"For Pete's sake, Marie—you don't need that."

"I've heard it can really improve a woman's appearance."

"Yeah, if you want a face like a frozen snowball."

Her eyes filled with tears. "I just want you to find me attractive," she whispered.

"I do, Marie. I always have."

"Then why. . . ."

Why can't I get it up? The question hung in the air like a bad odor.

Hell, he didn't know, but it was sure humiliating.

It had started a month ago, on their anniversary. He'd bought her a pair of diamond earrings and a dozen roses and taken her to Commander's Palace for dinner. He'd done all the right things to make the evening romantic.

And it had been, until Stan Olford, a former co-worker, had stopped by their table. He'd asked how Robert was enjoying retirement, and Robert had been forced to lie.

Marie thought his retirement had been his decision. She had no idea that he'd been shoved out the door. He'd meant to tell her months ago. He'd even started to a few times, but the timing just hadn't seemed right.

Now six months had gone by, and what had seemed difficult then seemed impossible now. How the hell was he supposed to explain that he'd misled her for half a year?

At this point, the best thing he could do was just keep his mouth shut.

The evening had soured after that. Marie had prattled on and on about her business, while Robert had been hard-pressed to come up with a single topic of conversation. Talking with Stan had pointed out how insignificant his life had become. He did nothing of any consequence, talked to no one about anything that mattered and knew no news that didn't come from the newspaper or TV. He spent his days looking for something useful to do and waiting for Marie to come home. He'd felt washed up and empty, inadequate and small.

Which was exactly how his penis had behaved when they'd gotten home. Marie had put on a pretty negligee, lit some candles and crawled into bed. He'd followed her, and then . . . nothing. Nada. Zero. Zip.

He'd tried. Dear Lord, had he tried. Marie had tried, too. Hell, they'd tried everything short of rigging him up to the vacuum cleaner hose. And the harder they tried, the less hard he became.

They'd both tried to laugh it off, but to Robert, it was no laughing matter. Especially when the same thing happened the next two nights in a row. He'd thought nothing could humiliate him as much as being put out to pasture at work, but he'd been wrong. This personal failure cut deeper.

After that, hell—he'd just started avoiding sexual situations. He stayed up until Marie was asleep or, if she was out catering a late function, he went to bed before she came in and pretended to be asleep when she crawled into bed.

"You're not interested in me anymore." A tear crept down her cheek.

A stab of pain shot through him. It hurt to hurt Marie. "That's not it. I've just had a lot on my mind lately."

"Like what?"

Damn it—she *would* ask. By all rights, he should be completely stress-free. He had no job, no responsibilities, no demands on his time.

He was as useless as his limp dick.

Frustration flared into anger. "Like how much you're gone," he grumbled. "It's hard to get romantic with someone who's never there."

"I'm sorry." She reached out for his hand. "I know I've been busy, but it takes a lot of work to build a new business."

"I don't understand why you're doing it in the first place," he bit out. "It's not like we need the money."

What in the world was going on with Robert? Marie stared at her husband, trying to figure it out. He'd been her biggest supporter when she'd first started her business. He'd become a different man since he'd retired. "I'm not doing it for the money, although it's thrilling to be able to make some on my own."

"I thought I provided well enough for you."

"You did, honey."

Robert's mouth twisted in a scowl. "I still do. Thanks to our investments and my pension, our income's practically the same as it was before I retired."

Marie looked at him quizzically. What was he so defensive about? "It's not the money. You've always been a wonderful provider. But that's just it. It was *you* doing the providing. I want to test my mettle and see what I can do on my own." She leaned forward, willing him to understand.

"All these years—my whole identity was wrapped up in you and the kids. Well, the kids are grown and gone, and I finally have a chance to try my wings a little." She smiled at him, hoping to soften the tight lines around his mouth. "It's exciting, Robert. I love putting on parties. I love helping people celebrate their special occasions. And I love getting paid for it."

Robert's mouth grew even tighter. "I didn't realize you were so unhappy," he said stiffly.

"I wasn't unhappy, honey." She put her hand on top of his. "We talked about all this before I started. I thought you understood. You were the one who encouraged me. You said it would be good for me."

Yeah, but I didn't think your business would really take off. Besides, that had been when he was still employed, before he'd been shoved out to early retirement.

Robert was relieved to see the waiter approach. Good. With any luck, she'd start talking with him about food, and this whole miserable subject would be dropped.

He just needed some time, that was all. A little more time to let the humiliation lessen, to forget how weak and powerless he'd felt, to work his courage back up. A little more time and he'd start to feel like a real man again. A little more time and everything would be all right.

Chapter Nine

After Stevie's parents headed into the other room, a busboy cleared away the remains of Stevie and Holt's desserts. Alberto bustled over with the check, then Mr. Masoletto stopped by the table to ask if everything had been satisfactory.

Stevie was glad of the distractions, because she needed a few minutes to clear her head. It was spinning like a pinwheel in a hurricane. Dear heavens, what a kiss! It had done all the things she'd ever heard about a kiss doing, all the things that she'd thought were merely hype and fiction. It had left her breathless and limp-limbed and thought-impaired. It had contained enough heat to melt away her awareness of her surroundings. She probably ought to pull out her compact and see if she had scorch marks on her mouth.

The element of surprise must have made it pack an extra punch. There had been no build-up, no sense of anticipation, no warning. One minute she'd been ready to flee the room, and the next, she'd found herself in Holt's arms. She had been in shock—too shocked to protest. But when his lips had started moving softly over hers, everything else had dimmed.

It hadn't been a long kiss—probably no more than a

few seconds—yet it had an amazing long-lasting effect. Tendrils of attraction were still curling in her stomach, even as outrage was building in her chest.

When Alberto had scooped up the leather folder holding Holt's titanium MasterCard and darted away, Stevie leaned across the table and glared at Holt. "Just what do you think you're doing?"

"Paying the check," he responded with infuriating innocence.

"That's not what I meant, and you know it."

His dark eyebrows rose. She thought she saw a hint of amusement in his eyes, which only increased her fury. "You mean, why did I kiss you?"

"Exactly."

His mouth curved in a slow, sexy smile. "Well, I've been sitting here all evening staring at your mouth, and I just couldn't help myself."

Against her will, a shiver chased up Stevie's spine.

He reached out and covered her hand with his, his gaze locked on hers. "It was even better than I thought it would be."

Stevie's hand burned. She snatched it away, wishing she could snatch back her composure. "I suddenly became irresistible the moment my parents walked in the room?" She glared at him. "What the hell were you trying to do?"

"It was an impulsive, romantic gesture."

Stevie rolled her eyes. "Give me a break."

"I'm telling the truth."

She shot him a derisive look.

"I am." His gaze was disarmingly sincere. "But I'll admit there was an additional reason." He placed his napkin on the table and leaned forward. "I was trying to lay some groundwork."

"For what?"

"For marrying you." He flashed her a winsome smile. "I figured it would be easier for you to say yes if your family thought we'd known each other a while."

Of all the unmitigated gall. "I am *not* going to marry you. And I don't appreciate your telling my parents a big, bald-faced lie!"

"I don't think it was big and bald. I'd say it was more along the lines of small and fuzzy."

"You might find this amusing, but I certainly don't." She reached for her purse.

His fingers curved around her arm. "Stevie—wait. I'm sorry." His tone was remorseful, all traces of teasing gone. "I just wanted to leave the door open, that's all. I hoped to make it easier for you to say yes."

"I keep telling you, I'm not going to marry you."

"And I keep hoping you'll change your mind." His gaze was so intense it heated Stevie's skin.

"If there's one thing I can't stand, it's someone trying to manipulate me."

"That wasn't my intention."

Alberto chose that moment to return with the receipt.

Holt added a large tip, scrawled his signature across the bottom and closed the folder. "I didn't mean to upset you," he said.

"Of course not. You just meant to put me on the spot in front of my parents, lie to them about our relationship and leave me in a very awkward position."

"It was wrong of me," he agreed in a suspiciously amiable tone. "Maybe we should go tell them the truth." He tucked the credit card in his wallet, then slanted her a wicked half-smile. "Although it might be a little difficult to explain why you were kissing me back."

He was the most infuriating man she'd ever met. He was insufferably arrogant, maddeningly manipulative and . . .

Right. He was right—she *had* been kissing him back. She didn't know which upset her more—the fact he'd known she would, or the fact that she had.

No. The most disturbing fact was that she'd responded to a deliberate ploy with an embarrassing amount of passion. He'd exposed her attraction to him, and it made her feel vulnerable and foolish.

Which gave him the upper hand. This was exactly the reason she'd vowed to never get involved with a babe magnet again. Stevie plopped her napkin on the table and rose from the chair.

Holt rose, too. "Ready?"

"More than ready." Stevie pulled her purse up on her shoulder, planning to march out of the restaurant without a backward glance.

But as she started for the door, she heard Isabelle let loose a pitiful squawl. She stopped and turned. Holt had picked up the baby carrier, and Isabelle was staring up at him, her tiny face scrunched in a red ball of distress.

Stevie sighed. She couldn't walk out on a baby in misery, no matter how insufferable she found the baby's father. She took a step back and leaned over the carrier. "Come on, now, Isabelle," she murmured softly. "Don't cry, sweetheart. Everything's fine."

The baby gazed up at Stevie with round, wet eyes, her expression woeful. Stevie's heart turned over.

The baby was getting under her skin.

Unfortunately, so was the father.

Under my skin like an infected splinter, Stevie thought as she walked stiffly beside Holt out of the restaurant and through the parking lot, deliberately addressing all of her remarks to the child.

"Thank you for dinner," she finally said to Holt in a stilted tone when they reached his car.

"Stevie—I'm sorry." This time he looked it, but Stevie blatantly ignored him.

"Good night, Isabelle." She headed for her car, climbed in and slammed the door, needing to get away before the baby started crying and broke down her defenses again.

Michelle looked up from a stack of class registration forms when Stevie walked through the door of the parenting center the next morning. "I understand you had quite an evening," she said with a knowing smile.

"Where did you hear that?"

"Your mother's already called twice. She said she ran into you and Holt last night." Michelle's face creased in a Cheshire cat grin. "She said you two were kissing!"

Stevie groaned.

"So it's true?"

"It wasn't what it looked like."

"So what was it? Mouth-to-mouth resuscitation?"

Stevie blew out a sigh and crossed the room to her office. Michelle followed. Flipping on the light, Stevie plopped down in her gray fabric chair and put her purse in the bottom drawer of her desk. "What else did Mom say?"

"Well, she was full of questions. She wanted to know how long you'd been communicating with Holt on the Internet and why you'd been so secretive."

Stevie tilted her face to the ceiling and closed her eyes. "Oh, great. What did you tell her?"

"Nothing. How could I? I didn't even know you'd met on the Internet."

"We didn't. Holt made that up. He thought it would make it easier for me to agree to marry him if my family thought we'd known each other a while."

"My, oh my, oh my." Michelle's grin widened. "Well, well, well." She sat on the edge of Stevie's desk. "So . . . you two were kissing?"

Stevie blew out a hard breath. "It was a deliberate ploy on his part. He wanted my folks to think we're having a hot and heavy romance."

"Judging from your mother's reaction, it was pretty effective."

"He told them we'd been exchanging e-mails for months, but that we'd just recently met in person."

"What did you do while he was telling them this?"

"I sat there like an idiot. I was in shock."

Michelle arched an eyebrow. "Must have been some kiss."

"It was," Stevie said ruefully.

The front door whooshed open. Both women turned to see a delivery man holding an enormous bouquet of violets and red roses.

Stevie raised her eyebrows. "You must have had some evening yourself."

Michelle shot her a knowing smile and headed out to greet the man. "I don't think these are from Brian."

Sure enough, she returned a moment later, carrying the elaborate bouquet. The heady scent of roses filled the small office as she set the vase on Stevie's desk. "I was right. These are for you."

Stevie's heart pounded irrationally.

"Open the card," Michelle urged.

Stevie's fingers fumbled as she pulled the card out of the tiny envelope.

"What does it say?"

" 'Roses are red, violets are blue,' " Stevie read aloud. " 'Please forgive Dad, 'Cause I really need you.' It's signed, 'Love, Isabelle.' "

"Oh, isn't that sweet!"

It was. And against her will, Stevie's stomach knotted with emotion. "He's just trying to manipulate me again."

"Give the guy a break, Stevie. He's trying to apologize."

The door opened, and the familiar wail of a baby filled the center. "Here he is. Now play nice."

Michelle headed out to the main room to greet Holt and Isabelle. Stevie nervously rose from her chair, straightened the collar on her pink shirt and crossed the room to the file cabinet, wanting to appear busy. A moment later, Holt stuck his head in her office.

Good morning," he called over Isabelle's wails.

"Morning."

Holt set the baby carrier on Stevie's desk. She turned and leaned over it, wanting to focus on the baby rather than the disconcerting man. "Good morning, Isabelle. Thank you for the lovely flowers."

"You're welcome," Holt said in a high falsetto.

Stevie couldn't help but grin. "Why, Isabelle! When did you learn to talk?"

The baby stopped crying and stuffed her fist in her mouth.

"When my dad screwed up," Holt continued in the funny voice. "I hope you won't hold it against me."

Stevie smiled. "You can't help how your father behaves, Isabelle. Have you had breakfast yet?"

"Just some coffee and a bagel," Holt squeaked in that high voice. "No, wait—that wasn't me."

Laughing, Stevie held up her hand. "Okay, okay—enough already!"

"Good. I think I was about to strain something." He grinned at her, and despite all her intentions to the contrary, Stevie found herself smiling back. A hot flood of attraction filled the room.

"I'm really sorry about last night," he said.

Stevie shifted uneasily. She didn't want to tell him it was all right, because it wasn't.

His eyes were hard to resist. "I'm sorry I upset you, and I'm sorry I put you in an awkward position with your parents." His voice lowered. "But I've gotta say . . . I'm not sorry I kissed you."

Stevie's heart pattered hard. "Well, it better not happen again."

"It would be a shame if it didn't." His gaze was frankly sensual, his voice low and sexy. "You're one hell of a kisser, Stevie."

She fought off the wave of attraction. "And you're one hell of a smooth operator," she said briskly. "That was a low stunt."

"I'm really sorry." But he didn't look it. He looked like he was about to kiss her again.

She turned her attention back to the baby. "Did Isabelle take a bottle this morning?"

"I could only get her to drink a few sips."

"Well, then, come on, sweetie. You've got to eat your Wheaties if you want to grow up big and strong." Stevie lifted the baby out of the carrier. The child pulled back and protested, but not as vigorously as she had yesterday.

Stevie sat down in her office chair and settled the baby in her arms. Holt pulled the bottle out of the diaper bag and handed it to Stevie, and in a few seconds, Isabelle had stopped fussing and started sucking greedily.

"It's amazing how you can get her to eat," Holt said. "You're her best hope of avoiding that feeding tube."

It wasn't fair, the way Holt managed to make her feel so indispensable to Isabelle's well-being.

He rubbed his chin. "Look, I hate to do this, but I need to ask you a favor."

"I'm already doing you one."

"I know. I really appreciate it, and I wouldn't ask if I

wasn't desperate. But I have to go to Atlanta tomorrow, and I was wondering if you could come with me."

"What?"

"To take care of Isabelle. I hate to leave her alone in a hotel room with a sitter after what happened before. . . ."

A feeling of panic rose in Stevie's chest. "No. No way. I can't just up and leave. I have appointments and classes to teach. It's impossible."

"Nothing is impossible."

"This is. It's not going to happen."

He blew out a defeated sigh and cast a mournful glance down at his child. "I tried, sweetie."

It was dirty pool, the way he acted as if she was letting the baby down. Especially since it was working. "Look—I'll call the director of the parenting center in Atlanta and get the name of a visiting nurse service there," Stevie said. "I'm sure they can provide you with someone reliable."

Holt leveled a gaze at her that scored a direct hit. "Isabelle needs *you.*"

He really knew how to hit where it hurt, Stevie thought ruefully. She smoothed a strand of the baby's hair and steeled herself against the tug of tenderness. "She needs a full-time caretaker. How is your search for a nanny going?"

He blew out a sigh. "Not well. I interviewed two women over the phone yesterday, but neither of them sounded very promising."

"Have you contacted any other nanny services?"

An idea hit Holt, an idea so devious and ingenious that it surprised even him. He couldn't, could he? Yes, he could. Desperate times called for desperate measures.

"Yes. In fact, one of them is sending some candidates for me to interview this evening. Maybe you could help me."

Stevie shook her head. "I can give you a list of agencies and organizations, but I can't recommend specific caretakers. It's a liability issue for the parenting center."

"I'm not asking you to do it as an employee of the center. I'm asking you to do it as a friend."

She hesitated.

"A friend of Isabelle's."

"Now you're not playing fair."

If only she knew how unfair he was playing. But he'd bet money she wouldn't be able to leave Isabelle in the care of someone she didn't think was competent. "Please," he pleaded. "It won't take long. A half hour at most."

"I really don't think—"

"You know how important it is to hire the right person," he pressed. "And you know what to look for. Apparently I don't, because I haven't done so well the last couple of times." He could see her hesitating. "Please," he pressed. "For Isabelle's sake. She really can't afford for me to make another mistake."

She looked down at the infant in her arms, and her eyes softened. Satisfaction flooded his veins. He had her.

"We can't do it here, and I won't come to your home," she warned.

"How about my office? Around six-thirty?"

She blew out a sigh. "Okay. But this is it. I don't think it's wise for me to get any more deeply involved in Isabelle's life."

"What about in mine?" Holt asked.

A red stain crept up her neck, but she looked him directly in the eye. "That would not only be unwise but foolhardy."

Holt laughed. She was no doubt right. She was look-ing for happy ever after, and he didn't believe it existed. But if last night's kiss was any indication, they could have one heck of a good time in the interim.

Chapter Ten

"Isabelle cries a great deal, Mrs. Schultz," Stevie said that evening. She sat in Holt's office, across from his desk as Isabelle dozed in the stroller beside her. "How would you comfort her?"

The stern-faced woman folded her arms across her chest. She reminded Holt of an armored tank—squat and wide, with arms the circumference of cannons and a roll-right-over-you personality. "Vell, I vould use da binkie."

"You mean a pacifier?"

"Ya." Mrs. Schultz gave a brisk nod of her thick neck. "I vould tape it in her mouth."

"Tape it?" Stevie gasped.

"Ya. Vith zee duct tape."

Stevie's eyes narrowed with outrage.

Holt jumped to his feet. He needed to get the older woman out of here, and fast. "Thank you, Mrs. Schultz. I think that answers all our questions."

The heavyset, middle-aged woman blinked at him through thick horn-rimmed glasses. "Zat is all?"

"Yes. That'll do for now. Thank you for coming."

"Don't you vant to know my techniques on disci-pline?"

"Not at the moment. Isabelle is still awfully small."

"I am very good at disciplining small children. Zee

smaller zey are when you start, zee better. Zey need someone vith a *very stern hand*." To emphasize the last three words, she slapped the back of her left hand in her right palm as she said each one.

Stevie stared at the woman like a pit bull about to attack. "I can't *believe*—"

Holt cleared his throat and moved toward the door. "Well, I think that wraps it up. Thanks for taking the time to talk with us."

The woman rose to her feet, marched to the door, then paused. "Ven vill you make your decision?"

"Very soon. We'll let your agency know. Thanks again."

He closed the door behind the woman and walked back into the office, dropping into the armchair next to Stevie.

"Well, that was the last candidate. What did you think?"

"That was the sorriest bunch of prospective nannies I've ever seen." Stevie's face was stiff with outrage. "I wouldn't trust any of them to properly care for a goldfish, much less a baby."

Holt found it hard to suppress his elation. "They all had good references," he pointed out.

"So did Ted Bundy. Those women were *not* nanny material."

Which was not surprising, considering that they were actually actresses Holt had hired through a friend's advertising agency. They'd been told it was an audition for a commercial, and that they were to stay in character the whole time.

"That Mrs. Schultz needs to be reported to the authorities," Stevie huffed. "She was positively salivating when she talked about disciplining children. Could you *believe* that duct tape answer?"

Mrs. Schultz *had* gone a little over the top. She'd been told to play the role of a cold, unfeeling disciplinarian, but she'd overshot the mark. "Yeah, that was quite a surprise," Holt said.

"A woman like that shouldn't be allowed to get within fifty yards of a child."

"She didn't make my short list, either," Holt agreed. "What did you think about the first one?"

"The brunette with the big hair and the bubble gum? Oh, please." Stevie rolled her eyes.

Holt struggled to keep his expression neutral. "You didn't like her?"

"She took four phone calls during a fifteen-minute interview! And she didn't just answer the phone—she carried on long, involved conversations. She was more interested in booking her next manicure than in Isabelle."

"Well, what about the second one? She was the grandmotherly type you thought Isabelle needed."

"Grandmotherly?" Stevie's eyes flashed with indignation. "Whose grandmother are we talking about—Lincoln's?"

Holt didn't quite manage to suppress a snicker.

"How on earth is a woman who needs a walker and portable oxygen going to chase after a toddler in a few months? Besides, you need someone who'll stay with Isabelle for at least the next two years. That woman's life expectancy isn't that long."

Oh, this was going well. Very well, indeed. "Well, Ms. Crenshaw seemed very healthy," Holt remarked.

"Are you out of your *mind?*"

"She was very health-conscious."

"She's a health *freak*. She got fired from her last job for putting pureed garlic and strained alfalfa juice in the baby's formula behind the parents' backs, for heaven's sake!"

"Well, yes, but she admitted it when the parents got worried about the baby's bad breath."

"You can't possibly consider her."

"Well then, what about Miss Smith? She seemed very nice."

Stevie shook her head. "I couldn't get past the tattoo on her neck."

"Lots of people have tattoos," Holt said mildly.

"Yes, but not many of them say 'Satan Rules.'"

The struggle to suppress his amusement made it hard to feign the appropriate shock. "Is that what it said?"

"I'm afraid it is."

"Gee." Holt shook his head and did his best to look morose. "It's beginning to look like it's impossible to find someone who'll give Isabelle the love and care she needs."

"Surely there are better prospects out there than those women."

"Not much better. That's the third agency I've contacted."

"What was the name of it? They should be shut down."

He should have known Stevie would want to do something about it. "I don't remember offhand," he hedged. "I know it's located out of state, though."

Stevie's forehead knit. "But those women were all local."

Holt scrambled for an answer. "It's a national agency, but they specialize in locating nannies who live near their clients." He needed to change the subject before she asked any questions. "Speaking of where people live, what part of town do you live in?"

"Not far from the parenting center, but I'm looking for a new place. My landlord just sold the building. How about you?" she asked.

"I have a house uptown."

She looked at him curiously. "One of the historic ones?"

He nodded. "Built in eighteen-seventy."

"That surprises me. I would have figured you for the modern riverside condo type."

He lifted his shoulders. "I'm actually something of a history buff."

"I can see that." She looked around his office, which was carpeted with an antique Persian rug and furnished with sturdy English antiques. She rose and walked over to a side table, where a collection of old compasses sat. She ran her finger over one. "Are you originally from New Orleans?"

Holt nodded. "I was born here, and lived here until my parents split up."

"How old were you?"

"Seven."

Her eyes warmed with sympathy. "That had to be rough."

"It was no picnic."

"What happened?"

"Depends on who you ask. Mom said Dad was having an affair with his secretary. Dad said Mom left because his business went bankrupt and he was broke. All I know is that my whole world exploded." He crossed the room and stood beside her, gazing out the window at the twilight. "I remember thinking that it was all my fault, and that it was up to me to keep them from breaking up."

"Kids often think that."

"Well, I won't ever put Isabelle in that position. I figure she can't miss what she's never known."

"But she might want what she's never had," Stevie said softly.

Holt lifted his shoulders. "At least she won't go through a big trauma."

He could feel Stevie studying him. "Maybe you'll change your mind when you meet the right person."

"There's no such thing as a right person. There's only a right-now person."

Holt's words struck Stevie as infinitely sad. "You think that now, but what if you meet someone, fall in love and decide you want to be a family with Isabelle?"

"That won't happen."

"It could. People change."

"No, they don't. Not in significant ways. People are what they are."

"Wow. Not too cynical, are you?"

"I'm not cynical—just honest." He met her gaze head-on. "If you married me and adopted Isabelle, you would be Isabelle's mother—legally and emotionally. We'd have an ironclad contract. But even more ironclad would be my word. I've been through a rough divorce, and I would never do that to Isabelle. I would never disrupt her life or try to alienate you from her affections."

It was impossible to look in his eyes and not believe him.

"What if, in a year or two, I fell in love and wanted to marry someone else?" Stevie asked. Too late, she realized she'd just introduced the possibility of agreeing to his plan.

Holt's smile told her it didn't go unnoticed. "As long as you didn't move away, it would be fine. My parents' marriages to other people didn't affect me too much. Their relationships with each other and with me were what mattered." He searched her face. "So, you're considering it?"

"N-no. I—I just . . ." What *was* she doing? "I'm just thinking about the reasons it wouldn't work."

"Let's talk about the reasons it would." He angled toward her, his eyes dark and persuasive in the fading light. "Reason number one: You're perfect for Isabelle. You know what she needs and how to provide it. Reason number two: She responds to you in a way she responds to no one else. Reason number three: You want a child. You said yourself that you want to be a mother, and Isabelle could fulfill that dream for you." He hesitated. "Unless . . ."

"Unless what?"

"Unless the reason you don't want to adopt Isabelle is because she's too difficult to love."

Stevie's heart felt as if it had just slammed against her ribs. She stared at him. "How could you even think that?"

He lifted his shoulders. "I'm just being objective. She's not easy to take; she screams nonstop, she's difficult to feed and she hates human contact. Every nanny she's ever had has quit because she's so unpleasant." A shadow seemed to cross his face. "Plus there's the possibility she's so messed up she'll have problems for the rest of her life."

"Don't you ever doubt, not for even a single second, that Isabelle's lovable," Stevie said fiercely. She wrinkled her brow in a worried frown. "*You* don't feel she's too difficult to love, do you?"

"Hell—I don't know what I feel." He shoved his hands in his pockets and stared out the window. The sky was the dusky blue-black of late twilight. "Aside from sleep deprived and exhausted."

He looked very lonely, silhouetted against the dark sky.

"I want to give her everything she needs." He turned toward Stevie. "And you're what she needs the most."

Stevie's heart did another roll. How the heck had she ended up in this situation? A couple of days ago she hadn't even known that Isabelle or Holt existed. "Holt ... ."

"You know Isabelle needs you."

The words made her feel all wrung out, like a wet paper towel. "But a phony marriage isn't what *I* need," she said, her voice almost a whisper.

"Well, hey—there's no reason it has to be entirely phony." His eyes held a heat that made her blood rush hot and fast. He took a step toward her and put his hands on her arms. "There's chemistry between us, Stevie. That kiss last night—that was amazing."

It certainly had been from her perspective. A hot shiver twisted her spine as his hands slid up her arms.

"If we get married, there's no reason we can't make the most of it." A knowing smile played at the corner of his lips. "Marriage does have its compensations, you know."

Another hot shiver shot through her. "It wouldn't be a real marriage. Marriage is permanent."

"Half of all marriages don't last until one party gets the flu, much less until death does someone part."

"Maybe so, but people who are truly married don't plan their divorces before they plan their weddings. When they make those vows, they intend to keep them."

"They're just deluding themselves."

It was hard to think when he was touching her. Stevie pulled away. "And you're deluding yourself if you think I'm going to agree to any of this. I can't believe we're even having this conversation."

"Stevie, if you'll just quit being so stubborn, you'll see

that this is in your best interests, too. You said you want a child, and for all you know, this might be your best shot at it."

Stevie stiffened. "Why do you say that?"

"Well, because you want a child and you don't have one. And you're not dating anyone, so . . ."

"So I obviously don't have what it takes to attract a man?"

"What?" He stared at her, completely baffled. "I didn't say that."

"You didn't need to."

"Look. I didn't mean that the way you obviously took it. I find you extremely attractive. Hell, didn't that kiss last night tell you anything?"

"It told me you're a manipulative conniver." Stevie pulled her purse onto her shoulder and marched to the door.

"Stevie, if you'd just be reasonable—"

"Don't talk to me about being reasonable. Do you think anything you're proposing is reasonable?"

"Stevie . . ."

"I've kept my word to you, Holt. I told you I'd help watch Isabelle temporarily, and I did that. I told you I'd help you interview nannies, and I did that. I told you I'd get you the number of a visiting nurse service in Atlanta, and I've done that. So why don't you believe me when I tell you I'm not going to marry you?"

Stevie opened the door. Isabelle drew a lungful of air and released it in a loud cry. Stevie froze in her tracks, her hand on the doorknob, and looked back at the baby.

"That's why," Holt said softly.

He wasn't sure, but he thought he saw tears pooling in her eyes just before she straightened her spine, walked out the door, and pulled it closed behind her.

Chapter Eleven

The insistent clamor of the telephone jolted Stevie out of a deep sleep. Jerking her eyes open, she glanced at the glowing green numbers on the digital alarm clock at her bedside. Three thirty-seven. Anxiety crawled across her skin as she sat up and reached for the receiver. Phone calls at this hour were never good news.

"Hello?"

The plaintive wail of a baby echoed through the earpiece. "Stevie, I hate to bother you, but I think Isabelle's sick." Holt's voice sounded strained and worried. "I've got a call in to the pediatrician, but it's been an hour and he hasn't called me back yet, and . . ."

Stevie swung her legs off the edge of her bed and clicked on the lamp switch. "What's wrong?"

"Well, she woke up crying about two hours ago, which isn't all that unusual, but she feels hot and she just looks kinda weird."

"Weird, how?"

"Kind of limp and listless."

Have you taken her temperature?"

"I don't have a thermometer."

That figured. She was pretty sure she knew the answer to her next question, too, but she asked it anyway. "Do you have any Infant Tylenol?"

"No."

She should probably tell him to just wait and talk to the pediatrician. That would be the sensible thing to do. After all, this wasn't her problem, and she had no busi-

ness getting more involved with Isabelle. When she'd
left Holt's office that evening, she'd made up her mind
to have no further contact with either him or his child.
She was getting way too attached to Isabelle, and she
was way too attracted to Holt.

But the baby's wails reached through the phone like
tiny, needy fingers, grabbing her by the heart and yank-
ing hard.

Stevie had an ear thermometer and liquid Tylenol in
her medicine cabinet, left over from a baby-sitting stint
with her brother's children. She blew out a sigh. "Give
me your address and I'll be right over."

Holt must have been waiting by the door when she
pulled up in front of an imposing white house in the
lower garden district twenty minutes later, because he
immediately appeared on the wide gaslit porch, Isabelle
in his arms. He headed down the steps toward her as
she climbed out of her VW, the baby crying plaintively.

"Man, am I ever glad to see you."

A jolt of heat went through her at the sight of him.
She'd never seen him in anything but a coat and tie, but
now he was wearing jeans and a T-shirt that clung to his
body. His forearms were tan and lightly sprinkled with
hair, and she could see the curve of his biceps as he
held Isabelle against his muscled chest.

Stevie reached for the baby, who looked like a pathetic rag doll. Isabelle barely protested being handed
off at all. Her skin felt hot and dry. "She's definitely got a
fever. Did the pediatrician ever call back?"

Holt nodded. "He said to take her temperature, give
her half a teaspoon of Tylenol and bring her to his office first thing in the morning. If the fever's over a hundred and four, he said we should give her a tepid bath."

"What time does his office open?"

Holt looked at his watch. "In exactly three hours, fifty-two minutes and thirty-two seconds. Not that I'm keeping track."

Stevie grinned. "Come on, sweetheart," she said to Isabelle. "Let's go take your temperature."

Holt held the door open, and Stevie carried the baby into an elegant foyer with an enormous chandelier. "Her room is upstairs and to the left," he said.

She followed him up the wide stairs, down the hall and into the nursery. Stevie stopped in the doorway, stunned. "Oh, my goodness!"

"It's all Ella's stuff. Her attorney shipped it here." The room looked like a fairyland. It was swathed in white silk—yards and yards of sheer, floaty fabric draped gracefully across the large window and over the canopy of the most elaborate crib Stevie had ever seen. White with gold trim, the crib had four massive posters shaped like the towers of a castle.

The white-and-gold changing table sported a long silk skirt in the same fabric. An enormous matching doll house—make that a doll *castle*—sat in the corner of the room.

"It's way over the top, if you ask me," Holt was saying, "but I don't know anything about baby stuff, and it didn't make sense to go buy more baby furniture. . . ."

Stevie fingered a length of the flowing fabric. "It's gorgeous. Not baby-safe, but absolutely gorgeous."

"I didn't even think about that. I just asked the movers to set it up like it had been at Ella's place. It figures she would be more concerned with looks than safety."

"It'll be fine if you pull all the fabric out of Isabelle's reach. It shouldn't be that big a deal." She turned to Holt. "Ready to take Isabelle's temperature?"

A look of alarm crossed his face. "Me? Oh, no. You should do it. I'll just wait in the hall."

Stevie wrinkled her forehead. "In the hall?"

"Yeah."

"Well, you should at least watch and learn how."

"No. No, thanks."

Stevie eyed him sternly. "You're Isabelle's parent, and you need to know how to provide basic care. Taking your child's temperature is about as basic as it gets."

Holt shifted from one foot to the other, avoiding her gaze. "The whole idea makes me really uncomfortable."

What was his problem? Stevie was about to ask when it suddenly hit her. Holt might be a business genius, but apparently he was clueless about the advancements in thermometer technology.

She suppressed a grin. Poor guy—no wonder he was so reluctant. But she wasn't going to let him off the hook so easily. "You can do it," she said briskly. "I'll help—it's really a two-person job, anyway. Here—take Isabelle and go sit in the rocker."

He reluctantly took the crying baby and sank into the chair. "I, um, really don't . . ."

Stevie pulled her bag off her shoulder, opened it and drew out a plastic case.

His eyes widened with alarm. "Now, come on, Stevie. I . . ."

She opened the case. "Th-that's awfully big, isn't it?"

Her lip wobbled as she fought back a laugh. "No bigger than normal."

"She's an awfully little baby."

Struggling to keep a straight face, Stevie pulled out a small box of plastic tips and slid one on the end of the instrument. "Hold her still and I'll insert it."

"I—I don't think . . ."

Stevie fixed him with her sternest frown. "Are you going to help, or aren't you?"

His Adam's apple bobbed as he swallowed. He gave a

reluctant nod, his eyes full of trepidation. "Okay." He swallowed again. "Do I—do I need to remove her diaper?"

That did it. Stevie erupted in a snort of laughter.

"What's so funny?" he growled.

"You are."

"There's nothing the least bit amusing about this situation."

"Yes, there is—considering that the thermometer goes in her *ear.*"

"Her *ear?*"

The dumbfounded relief on Holt's face sent Stevie into a fresh fit.

"Really?"

She managed to nod between snickers.

"Thank God. I thought . . ."

"I know what you thought," Stevie said with a smile. "Now hold her still."

She bent over Holt and put the tip of the thermometer in his child's ear. Isabelle screamed bloody murder.

"Poor sweetie," Stevie murmured soothingly as she clicked the button and quickly withdrew the thermometer. "From the way she just hollered, I bet she has an earache."

"Did you get her temperature?"

Stevie looked at the digital readout. "A hundred and two and seven-tenths. We need to get some Tylenol in her."

Setting down the thermometer, Stevie picked up the bottle of medicine, unscrewed the lid and carefully filled the dropper to the correct line, then slipped it in the baby's mouth. Isabelle was so startled that she stopped in mid-howl and swallowed.

"Man, you're good," Holt said. "If I'd tried that, she would have choked."

"You would have managed. It's not that hard."

"Everything about taking care of her is hard for me. I can't even get her to eat."

"When was the last time she had a bottle?"

"Around eight. But she barely ate any at all."

"Let's see if we can coax her to take a little more."

Holt handed the baby to Stevie, then headed toward the kitchen to fix the baby's bottle. Stevie followed him downstairs to the living room, where she settled with the child on the leather sofa and looked around. Carpeted with an enormous Kilim rug and filled with antiques, the room reeked of money and class. Stevie studied the tasteful arrangement of brass lanterns on one side table and a dried flower arrangement on the other. The place had definitely been done by a professional.

Holt sank heavily on the couch beside her and handed over the bottle. His forehead wrinkled. "Isabelle looks so pathetic—so small and frail and sick."

"I suspect it's just an earache. She'll be fine once she sees the doctor. But she won't be up to flying tomorrow." Stevie slipped the tip of the bottle into the baby's mouth, and Isabelle's lips closed around it. "Can you postpone your meeting?"

Holt shook his head. "I've already done that once. Besides, it's too late. Thirty shareholders are flying in for it, and most of them are already there."

"What will happen if you don't go?"

A muscle twitched in his jaw. "Well, I could be sued for breach of contract, since the board of directors hired me to prepare the plan I'm going to present. My reputation would be shot, which would mean no one else would want to hire me, and I'd lose my means of supporting Isabelle and myself."

"You said Ella left a trust fund."

He shot her a scathing look. "Do I look like the kind of guy who could just lounge around and live off his daughter's inheritance?"

No. No, he didn't.

"Is there someone else who could present it for you?"

"No." He pulled in a deep breath and blew it out. "That's the weakness of not having a partner. There's no backup."

That was the weakness of being a single parent, too. He was in trouble on both fronts. "How long would you be gone?"

Holt rose and paced in front of the fireplace. "I'd be back Friday night."

The question she always advised parents to ask themselves when they were faced with a difficult choice formed in her mind: What was in the child's long-term best interests?

There was no question what was in Isabelle's. Stevie drew in a deep breath. "It's in Isabelle's best interests for you to go. I'll keep her while you're gone."

Holt turned around, his expression so relieved she couldn't help but grin. "That would be terrific. Thanks, Stevie. Thanks a million. I really owe you."

She basked in his smile, enjoying the fact that she'd put it on his face, her heart feeling all light and fluttery. Catching herself, she looked away. She had no business having any feelings for him, she told herself sternly.

"There's one condition," she warned. "I won't be able to watch Isabelle after this. I don't want to make her attachment problem worse, and if she spends all that time with me . . ."

Holt nodded. "I understand."

But did he?

Chapter Twelve

Marie Stedquest glanced at the clock above her double oven two days later, then looked at the kitchen table, where her bathrobe-clad husband was chewing a mouthful of Cheerios with maddening slowness as he leisurely perused the newspaper. Impatience rose in her chest. She needed to use that table to assemble 200 bite-sized crawfish pies for a reception tonight, but Robert would get grumpy if she asked him to hurry up or move.

He got grumpy about all kinds of things these days. More and more, she felt like she was tiptoeing around him, doing her best not to set him off.

She watched him turn the page and carefully fold back the newspaper, aligning the tops of the pages with precision, making sure that the crease was exactly straight. She fought down a growing sense of aggravation. He was such a perfectionist, always insisting on doing things just so. The sash of his white terry-cloth bathrobe was tied in a precise knot, and every silver-streaked strand of hair was in place. She'd always admired his sense of order, always liked the effortless way he kept everything about him smooth and neat and organized. Since he'd retired, though, it only seemed like a royal pain in the neck.

He didn't have deadlines and appointments and time schedules. With limited staff and oven space, she had to carefully plan her day so that all the food was ready at the same time. If she wasted a moment, her whole schedule would fall apart. But Robert seemed oblivious.

He took another bite of Cheerios and began the excruciatingly lengthy chewing process. Annoyance bubbled inside her. Turning away, she reached for the cordless phone and pressed the redial button.

To her relief, Stevie answered.

"Thank heavens you finally picked up," Marie said. "I was getting worried about you." She moved out of the kitchen and away from Robert, into the formal dining room. "What in the world is going on? I see you with a man you've told me nothing about, then you don't return any of my calls to your cell phone. When I called the center, Michelle said you aren't coming in for the rest of the week because you're watching a sick baby, but when I tried your home number, you didn't answer."

"It's a long story, Mom."

"Well, I'm anxious to hear it."

"I really don't have time right now. I'm awfully busy."

Stevie sounded as if she was about to hang up. Marie knew that tone all too well. Lately, Robert used it on her when they weren't even on the phone.

She spoke quickly, wanting to get as much information as possible in the shortest period of time. "Is this the same baby I saw at the restaurant?"

"Yes."

"She's precious—but so thin!"

"She had a rough life before Holt knew about her."

"Poor thing." Like Stevie, Marie had a soft spot for children. Especially her own. More than anything, she wanted to see Stevie settled and happy. "Are things serious between you and Holt?"

"No. I'm just helping with his baby."

"Judging from the way you two were kissing, you're more than just a baby-sitter."

Stevie huffed out an exasperated sigh. "I'm watching his baby while he's out of town," she repeated. "She has an ear infection, so he couldn't take her with him."

Marie searched her mind for a way she could help. "If you're going to be cooped up with a sick baby all day, you'll be ready for some company this evening. Why don't I come by after my reception?"

"That's not necessary, Mom. Besides, I'm not at my place."

"Where are you?"

"I'm staying at Holt's house while he's gone. All the baby's things are here—her swing, her crib, her changing table. Plus, it's the best way to keep her life as normal as possible. She's got some problems from having too many changes in her life."

"Poor dear." Marie's brow knit with worry. "What kind of problems does she have?"

"As you noticed, she's way underweight, and she doesn't like to be held or cuddled. Listen—she's crying, Mom. I've got to go."

This time the hang-up voice had a firm finality. "Okay, sweetheart. I'll talk to you"—the receiver clicked in her ear—"later."

Marie hung up the phone and walked back into the kitchen. Robert was pouring a second bowl of cereal and picking up the sports section. "She finally answered her phone, I gather," he said.

Marie nodded. "She's staying at that man's place and watching the baby while he's on a business trip."

"That's nice of her."

"Awfully nice. She's taking off work to do it, too." Marie pulled an enormous covered container of crawfish out of the refrigerator. "She said they're not serious, but she wouldn't know serious if it jumped up and hit her in the face. She has next to no experience with men."

"Oh, and you're an expert?"

His voice had the old teasing tone, the one he used when they playfully bantered back and forth. The problem was, she didn't feel playful. She felt pressured. She had a lot to do before tonight's reception, and he acted as if she had all the time in the world.

"No, I'm no expert. Especially not lately."

"Oh, for God's sake, Marie." Robert's face disappeared behind the sports section. "Don't start the day off with that."

"For your information, this isn't the start of my day. I've been up since five-thirty and I've been working for three hours."

The paper lowered. He looked at her with steely eyes. "That's your choice, Marie. You know you don't have to work."

"I *want* to work."

"Well then, don't gripe to me about the hours."

"I'm not griping. I'm just worried I won't get everything done."

He jabbed his finger in the air, pointing at an invisible spot. "That's the problem right there. This business has you worried all the time. You're tense and wound up and you snap at me like you're a box-headed turtle."

"*I* snap at *you?* Boy, you're one to talk. You ought to hear yourself. And you think *I'm* a turtle? I'm not the one who takes all morning to eat a bowl of cereal when someone else needs to clear off that table and get to work."

Robert slammed down the paper and rose to his feet, standing so abruptly that his oak chair toppled off its legs and clattered onto the tile floor. Marie jumped.

"You want the table? All you had to do was say so." He spoke in a low, precise manner far more chilling than a shout. He made a grand, sweeping gesture with his hand. "It's all yours."

Marie found herself fighting back tears as her husband stormed out of the room, leaving the chair on the floor, mute testimony to his anger. A moment later, the bedroom door slammed shut.

How appropriate, she thought bitterly—albeit a little redundant. He'd already closed the door on their love life.

Hot tears scalded her cheeks. They hadn't made love in nearly six weeks—thirty-eight days, to be exact. And the last three times they'd tried, he hadn't been able to maintain an erection.

He'd acted as if it didn't bother him, but Marie knew better. He was a perfectionist, a man who drew out the best in others by demanding the best of himself. Failure of any kind was unacceptable.

She'd made several overtures. She'd put on his favorite slinky nightgown, she'd invited him to join her in a candlelight bubble bath and she'd offered to give him a massage. She'd even flat out said, "Let's make love." He always had some excuse: he'd pulled a muscle playing golf, he was too tired, it was too hot.

She'd tried to talk to him about it, but he refused. Even worse, he refused to even acknowledge there was a problem. Nothing was wrong. Everything was fine. He was fine. She was fine.

Well, if everything was so blasted *fine*, why did she feel as if she was married to a stranger?

She didn't understand. This was supposed to be the happiest time of their lives. Robert was free to do as he pleased, and she was finally getting to fulfill her dream of running her own catering business. She loved nothing more than hosting parties; she loved all the planning and coordinating, she loved cooking and she loved—above all—being in the midst of people who were having a good time, knowing that she'd played a key role in bringing them together.

When she'd first broached the topic of opening her

own business with Robert, he'd been completely supportive. He'd encouraged her to go back to college and he'd provided a generous amount of start-up money. But once her business had taken off, all that had changed.

Why wasn't he pleased at her success? She'd put her personal ambition on hold to be a good wife to him and a good mother to his children. She hadn't resented a minute of it; she'd loved her life, loved knowing that she was the family's anchor, loved being Robert's sounding board and personal cheering section. But now it was her turn, and he wasn't willing to do the same for her. Their marriage was beginning to feel like an uncomfortably one-sided arrangement.

She'd been there for him. Why couldn't he be there for her?

Robert stalked into the master bathroom, peeled off his bathrobe and jammed it on the hook behind the bathroom door like a butcher hanging up a slab of beef. Damn it. Damn it all to hell! He couldn't even eat his breakfast in peace.

Scowling, he turned toward the sink, then caught a glimpse of himself in the mirror under the blazing row of round light bulbs. His hands froze on the faucet handles. Dear God, how had he ended up like this? He barely recognized who he saw looking back—a scowling old man, gray-headed and stubble-jawed.

A sense of disgust filled his chest. Hell, he was pathetic. He was nothing but a washed-up has-been, of no use to anyone. He had nowhere to go, nothing to do. He couldn't even stay home without being in the way.

He turned the taps and splashed water on his face. Damn it—this wasn't what he'd worked for all his life. This wasn't the retirement he'd envisioned.

But then, it wasn't a retirement he'd been ready for, either. Memories washed over him, as dark and bitter as day-old coffee.

He'd been in the middle of a huge insurance fraud case when the D.A. called and asked to see him. Robert had assumed they were meeting to review upcoming cases. As chief prosecutor for Orleans Parish, it was a regular occurrence.

Boy, had he been wrong.

The meeting was burned into his mind like a brand. The minute he'd walked into Larry's office, he'd known something was different. For starters, Larry had asked him to close the door, then had circled his desk and sat beside Robert in one of the two wing-backed chairs.

"We've got a problem," he had said.

That was nothing new. Their job was made up of problems. But Larry's tone was different this time. "Robert . . . the defense is claiming you planted evidence in that insurance case."

"That's ridiculous."

"I know, but they're claiming they've got proof."

"What kind of proof?"

"They're claiming the papers on those fraudulent claims were forged."

"What?"

"The papers in evidence are copies, not originals. They've produced other copies, and the dates and numbers don't match."

"That's ridiculous. The papers we tagged as evidence were the originals."

"Well, now they're not."

"*What?*"

"It gets worse."

Robert had felt his blood start to chill, the way it did when he had to view particularly gruesome crime scene photos. "How?"

Larry squirmed uncomfortably. "We got an anonymous tip that the real originals were in your office. So last night, after you went for home . . ."

Outrage built in Robert's chest. "You went in and looked?"

"We had to."

Robert had nodded tightly, choking back the sense of betrayal. "Of course." A cold fist of fear gripped his gut. "Good God, Larry—don't tell me you found something?"

"I'm afraid we did."

"Holy mother." A wave of nausea hit him so hard he thought he was going to lose his lunch. "I didn't—I wouldn't—" Robert had swallowed hard. "What the hell did you find?"

"Just what they wanted us to find—the altered originals."

"Where?"

"In the back of your desk files."

"Good Lord." Robert slumped in the chair. "They were planted."

"I know."

"They got to someone in the evidence room."

"I know. I have the utmost confidence in you. And I know the players in this case have long arms and lots of cash." Larry's eyes had looked sad and troubled. "Unfortunately, it looks bad."

"Did you dust for prints?"

He nodded somberly. "Nothing. It was a pro job."

Robert felt like a boa constrictor was squeezing his chest.

Larry squirmed uncomfortably. "I've already talked to Judge Briar."

He'd talked to the judge in Robert's case without Robert's knowledge? The breach of protocol hurt almost as much as the frame job. "And?" he had asked tersely.

"And he said that if they present this evidence—which you know they will—he'll have to throw out the whole case."

"They'll just walk?"

Larry nodded. "I'm afraid so. And that's not the worst of it."

Robert didn't think that was possible, but his spirits sank still lower. "How?"

"If they present the evidence, Judge Briar will have to report the findings and launch a full-scale investigation into the department."

"Oh, hell."

"We'll be crucified in the media. And every criminal you've ever convicted is going to come back and claim you fabricated evidence on them, too. And Robert—you could be indicted on criminal charges."

This was a nightmare. An absolute nightmare. And it was an election year for Larry.

"We have one way out of this." Larry's mouth had thinned until his lips disappeared.

"What?"

"We dismiss charges against them now. And you retire, effective immediately."

The memory left a bad taste in Robert's mouth. He reached for his toothbrush and squeezed out a dollop of Crest, hoping to brush it away.

He'd had no choice. There had been no way of fighting it. It would have ruined the department, ruined his good name. He would have lost his retirement benefits, racked up a fortune in legal bills, and most likely been disbarred anyway. Hell, there was a good chance he'd have wound up behind bars with the very criminals he'd put away.

He'd spent his whole career fighting crime and it had ended with him being accused of committing one. It was more than galling; It was devastating. It was as if they'd taken a knife, cut out his heart and served it to him for dinner.

He'd done nothing wrong, yet he felt such a sense of shame—shame and embarrassment and humiliation.

And he'd felt so alone. He'd wanted to tell Marie, but when he came home that evening, he just couldn't. She'd been happily preparing for her first big reception and he hadn't wanted to bring her down.

So he'd put it off, figuring he'd just wait for a good time to tell her. But her career was taking off like gangbusters just as his was collapsing and there never was a right time. He'd simply told her that he was burned out—that he was tired of prosecuting criminals, tired of office politics, tired of work days that sometimes lasted until midnight. He'd announced that he wanted to retire, and he wanted to do it as soon as possible.

His family and friends had all been surprised, but his decision had been accepted without question. Larry had thrown him a swank retirement party at Ruth's Chris Steakhouse and given him the proverbial gold watch. His co-workers had made elaborate toasts, lauded his accomplishments and wished him a happy retirement. Then everyone had gone on with their lives, everyone except for Robert, who felt like his life was over.

Time had marched on, one empty day piling on top of another, until six months had gone by. How the hell was he going to explain to Marie that he'd kept a secret of this magnitude all this time?

He scrubbed his teeth so hard his gums hurt, then spat a mouthful of toothpaste into the sink. At first he'd tried to cheer himself up with thoughts of spending time with Marie. Finally, he'd thought, they'd be able to just hang out together—to travel, to take long walks, to make love in the afternoon like they used to when they were newly married.

Yeah, right.

Robert rinsed his mouth and spat again. Marie was never around to hang out with. She was too busy with her precious catering business, which ate up all her time and attention. And as for making love . . . hell, he didn't even want to think about his failures in that department.

He picked up a can of shaving cream and squirted some into his palm. He didn't know why he even bothered to shave. He didn't have anywhere to go. He used to enjoy playing golf, but that had been when it was weekend recreation. Now that he could do it every day, it had lost its appeal.

Hell. *Life* had lost its appeal. Instead of using his razor to shave, he might as well use it to cut his damned throat. The thought of ending it all had crossed his mind more than once.

But that was the coward's way out, and Robert wasn't a coward. Besides, that would hurt the very people he'd retired to protect.

He drew the razor neatly down his lathered jaw, shaving a wide swath in the foam. He didn't need a way out; he needed a way through—a way to make it through another long, meaningless, lonely day. "Happy retirement," he muttered to his reflection. "Happy friggin' retirement."

Chapter Thirteen

Stevie looked through the peephole of Holt's front door a little after eight that evening to see her mother standing on the front porch. She blew out a sigh and opened the door. "Mom—what are you doing here?"

Marie held up a couple of foil-wrapped plates. A delicious aroma wafted from them. "I brought you some food from the reception. I was afraid you'd be so busy taking care of the baby that you'd forget to take care of yourself." She peered through the doorway. "Oh, my—what a beautiful place!"

"How did you know where I was?" Stevie asked.

"It wasn't hard. Holt is listed in the phone directory." Marie stepped into the foyer and looked around. "Oh, Stevie—this place is incredible!"

Stevie agreed. After Isabelle had finally fallen asleep the night Holt called, he'd taken her on a tour of the place, and her eyes had no doubt been as wide as her mother's were now.

Marie peered into the deep red dining room, taking in the enormous mahogany table, the antique upholstered chairs, the enormous chandelier and all the exquisite accessories. "Oh, my! Not exactly the typical bachelor pad, is it?"

"No."

"Did he inherit the place or something?"

"No. At least, he didn't say so."

Stevie's mother looked at her oddly.

"I'm sure he would have mentioned it if he had," she said quickly. It was irritating, having to pretend that she'd known Holt for six months. She hated keeping up the pretense, but it would be difficult to explain why Holt had lied and why she'd gone along with it—especially since she didn't really understand it herself.

It was easier to just play along. "He's had a a lot of work done on the place. He said he didn't change the exterior, but the inside was pretty much gutted and reconfigured."

"He must have had a team of interior designers falling over each other," Marie remarked.

Just one—falling all over him.

The doorbell had rung around eight the night before, and Stevie had answered to find a tall, gorgeous brunette standing on the other side. She'd worn a low-cut tank top and tight jeans, and held a tall arrangement of dried flowers in her hands.

"Hello," the brunette had said with a condescending smile. "Are you Holt's housekeeper?"

Stevie suddenly had become painfully aware of the fact that she was wearing a baggy T-shirt and sweat-pants. All of her feelings of inferiority—her fat feelings as she privately called them—washed through her in a rush. She'd lifted her head. "No. I'm a friend watching his baby."

The woman's brow had furrowed. "Baby? Holt doesn't have a baby."

"Oh, yes, he does."

"Since when?"

"Well, the child is six months old." *Do the math, glamour girl,* she'd wanted to say.

"Who's the mother?"

"I think Holt should be the one to pass along that kind of information."

The woman had forced a phony smile. "Of course. Is he here?"

"No. He's out of town. May I help you?"

"I'm a friend of Holt's—I did the interior design on this house—and I was bringing over a spring arrangement for his coffee table."

"I'll make sure he gets it," Stevie said, reaching for the dried flowers.

The woman reluctantly handed them over. "Ask him to give me a call."

Stevie had arched a brow. "And you are?"

"Charlotte." She'd smiled brightly. "He has the number."

And I have yours, Stevie thought. A rush of unexpected jealousy had shot through her.

Stevie's mother jerked her out of her thoughts. "Did he say who the designer was?"

"Charlotte something."

"Well, she has wonderful taste. Maybe I should hire her to help up some of our venues." Marie pulled her gaze from the room back to Stevie. "So, how's the baby?"

"She's better. She's asleep right now."

"That's good." Marie grinned. "And the father?"

"Busy. He'll be back from Atlanta on Friday evening."

"You two seem to have gotten awfully tight awfully quick."

Stevie looked down at the floor, weighed her options and decided that the safest course of action was silence. It didn't take long for her mother to fill it.

"Of course, when the chemistry is right, you can meet someone and feel you've known them all your life. That's how it was with your father and I."

Stevie seized the opportunity to change the subject. "How's Dad doing?"

A cloud passed over Marie's face. "Fine, I guess."

A twinge of concern filled Stevie. "You guess?"

"I've barely seen him all day. He was a terrible grouch this morning, then he left the house and I've been busy. . . ." Marie gave a smile that struck Stevie as overly bright. "I'd better get this food to the kitchen. Is it through there?" Without waiting for an answer, Marie headed toward the swinging door in the dining room. She paused just past the doorway. "Oh, Stevie—this is fabulous!" she repeated.

Stevie nodded in agreement. The room was large and open, with brick floors, granite-topped counters and tall oak cabinets. A rustic iron chandelier hung over a large oak table in the breakfast room.

"Oh, look! A Sub-Zero fridge, a stainless-steel cooktop— and oh, my! He's even got a double convection oven!"

In Marie's eyes, that no doubt made him a candidate for sainthood.

"Does Holt cook?"

"No." Stevie almost laughed at the irony.

"Well, you could make him some wonderful meals in this kitchen." Marie set the plates down on the granite counter and gave her a sly smile. "You know what they say about the way to a man's heart."

"Who says I care?"

Marie looked startled. "Why on earth wouldn't you?"

"Oh, gee, I don't know." Stevie's voice was full of a sarcasm. "Maybe I'm a little bothered by the fact that he had a baby with a woman he'd known less than twenty-four hours."

"Well, that's certainly not an ideal situation, but anyone can have a lapse in judgment."

"A lapse in judgment?" Stevie couldn't believe her mother was going to let Holt off the hook that easily.

"It takes two. Apparently the woman was more than willing." Marie crossed the room, opened the stainless-steel oven and peered inside. "And he's taking responsibility for his actions. It can't be easy, raising a baby alone."

He had no intention of raising it alone; he was trying to coerce her into helping him, Stevie thought indignantly.

"Anyone can make a mistake. I hope you don't hold it against him, because I really liked him." Marie shot her a sidelong smile. "And I could tell you did, too, from the way you two were canoodling at that restaurant."

"*Canoodling?* For heaven's sake, Mom . . ."

"I'm looking forward to getting to know him better when he comes to dinner."

"Mom, he's not coming to dinner."

"Of course he is. He accepted my invitation."

"Yeah, well, I'm unaccepting it."

"You can't do that. That would be rude."

Stevie blew out a sigh. There was no point in arguing with her mother now. She'd deal with it when Holt got home.

The squall of the baby echoed through the monitor clipped to Stevie's waistband. She gratefully grabbed at the interruption. "I need to go see to Isabelle. Thanks for the food, Mom."

"I don't have to leave just yet. I'll come with you." To Stevie's dismay, Marie followed her down the hallway and up the stairs to the nursery, exclaiming over the house at every turn.

Marie stopped short as she walked into the nursery. Her hands flew to her face. "Oh, my goodness! This looks like a fairyland! Oh, it's like a dream!"

"For a fabric salesman, maybe," Stevie said dryly. "You should have seen it before I pulled the canopy back out of the way. It was a real safety hazard."

"Holt's decorator did all this?"

Stevie bent and lifted the baby from her crib. "No. Everything in here belonged to Isabelle's mother."

Marie's brow furrowed. "But I thought she neglected Isabelle."

"Emotionally, not materially. She bought practically everything money can buy. But she never spent any time with her, and the poor thing never bonded with anyone. That's why she hates to be held."

Marie watched Stevie carry the child across the room. "Looks to me like she likes it just fine."

Surprised, Stevie looked down at the child. Sure enough, Isabelle was staring quietly up at her. Stevie froze in her tracks and stared back, her heart standing still. She was afraid to move, afraid to breathe, afraid of breaking the magical silence.

Isabelle wasn't crying. She was gazing up at Stevie, her eyes clear and trusting, making direct eye contact, like a normal, healthy child. Stevie's heart felt too full for her chest. It pressed against her rib cage, tender and swollen with emotion.

The soft ring of a cell phone broke the silence. As Marie pulled it from her purse and answered it, Stevie carried the baby to the changing table. To her amazement, Isabelle lay quietly as Stevie unfastened her yellow velour sleeper and changed the child's diaper.

Marie clicked her phone closed as Stevie resnapped the inseam of Isabelle's pantleg. "I've got to go," she announced. "That was Betsy, and she just remembered she promised the rental agency we'd return the china tonight. I'm going back to help her load it up."

"Okay," Stevie said absently, her eyes fixed on the baby.

" 'Night, dear. I'll just let myself out."

"Okay. Goodnight."

The click of Marie's heels faded on the stairs. Stevie smiled down at the still-quiet baby, whose blue eyes were wide and clear. "You must be feeling better, sweetheart."

To her complete astonishment, Isabelle drew up her legs, grabbed her own toes and gave a gummy grin.

Stevie gasped. "You're smiling!"

The baby's smile was as bright and warm as sunshine. Tears of joy welled in Stevie's eyes, and her heart melted like a popsicle in the sun.

And then it hit her. Oh, dear God—the baby was bonding with her!

Isabelle didn't need another broken attachment. Stevie had accompanied Holt to the pediatrician's office before he'd left on his trip, and the doctor had stressed the need to find a permanent caregiver.

"The worst thing you could do is let Isabelle get attached to another person who's going to leave," the doctor had warned.

Stevie had worried that this very thing might happen. She'd asked the doctor how long she could take care of the baby before the child became attached to her.

"I don't really know," he replied. "But if you keep it under two weeks, you should be fine."

Stevie had thought she was safe. She'd only been in Isabelle's life for five days. But apparently Isabelle had a schedule of her own.

A knot formed in Stevie's throat as Isabelle beamed up at her. That goofy little grin was the most beautiful sight she'd ever seen—more magnificent than the Grand Canyon, more amazing than a starlit sky. Nothing had ever touched her as deeply as this needy baby's smile.

Until the child lifted her skinny arms.

Stevie's heart constricted. "You—you want me to pick you up?"

It was pretty clear that the baby wanted just that. She was six months old, more than old enough to communicate a desire to be held, but it was such a radical departure from any behavior she'd ever exhibited before that Stevie could hardly believe it. This baby who always screamed and stiffened and cried at human contact was begging Stevie to hold her?

Apparently so. The baby whimpered and stretched out her arms, her eyes pleading.

A ripple of fear washed through Stevie. The last thing she wanted was to harm this child. She probably shouldn't do anything to encourage the baby to bond with her any further.

But Stevie could no more refuse the child's silent plea than she could stop her own heart from beating.

"Come here, sweetie." Stevie scooped up the baby and held her close, the way she'd held her dozens of times before. But this time was different.

This time, Isabelle was silent, and Stevie was the one who cried.

What was she going to do? Stevie stayed up most of the night pondering the question.

After feeding Isabelle and putting her back to bed, she sank into the rocker in the corner of the nursery, listening to the child's rhythmic breathing in the darkened room.

The child not only had stopped resisting, she'd actually reached out to her. It was a major breakthrough—and it posed a heart-wrenching dilemma. If Stevie walked out of the child's life now that Isabelle had begun to trust her, it might do irreparable harm. But if she stayed . . .

She gazed out the window at the almost-full moon, her heart twisting like a pretzel. She couldn't just be Isabelle's nanny. She'd cared for a foster child for four weeks, and even though she'd known she was going to a loving home with parents who'd been eagerly waiting to adopt a child for four years, it had devastated Stevie to give her up. She couldn't live with the possibility that a child she loved could be taken from her. She wasn't cut out to be a nanny; she was cut out to be a mother.

Isabelle's mother. She felt it like a calling. She knew it, deep in her soul. The baby wasn't the only one who had formed an attachment; in the matter of just a few days, the child had wrapped herself around Stevie's heart.

But becoming Isabelle's mother meant becoming

Holt's temporary wife, which presented a whole other set of problems. Stevie had always promised herself that she'd only marry for love. Marriage was supposed to be a lifelong commitment.

And yet, there was a good possibility that a lifelong marriage just wasn't in Stevie's future. There were no guarantees that Mr. Right was out there, or that she'd ever find him if he were. Before Isabelle and Holt even entered the picture, she'd been contemplating single motherhood via artificial insemination—not because she felt a biological urge to give birth, but because she felt an emotional need to love and nurture a child.

No child would ever need love and nurturing more than Isabelle. And no one could give her more than Stevie, if Stevie were given the chance.

But Isabelle came as a package deal, and the other half of that package was Holt.

The thought of him made Stevie's stomach tighten. Holt was everything she'd vowed to avoid in a man, and then some. Could she really marry him, all the while planning to divorce him as soon as the adoption went through?

She rose from the rocker and crossed the room to the crib. The baby lay on her back, her matchstick arms flung out, her tiny legs sprawled, her fine hair sticking out like fluff on a dandelion. Tenderness flooded Stevie's veins.

She'd told Holt that she'd only marry for love. Well, if she married him to become Isabelle's mother, she'd be doing just that, because she loved this child with an intensity that was almost frightening.

Tears filled Stevie's eyes as she reached down and caressed the sleeping child's soft cheek. She'd always known that when the time was right, the love of her life would appear. She just hadn't known that the love of her life would be a six-month-old baby.

Chapter Fourteen

It was nearly eleven o'clock on Friday night when Holt climbed the red brick steps to his house. He usually had to fumble in the dark to unlock the front door, but not tonight. Tonight, the gaslights on his porch flickered a welcome, and the glow of a lamp in the living room crept through the drawn drapes.

"Stevie?" he called as he closed the door behind him. "I'm home."

It was weird, knowing that someone was there waiting for him. Weird, but not exactly unpleasant.

Stevie rounded the corner of the hallway, tugging at the neckline of a bulky blue sweater that had slipped low on one shoulder. She wore blue jeans and bare feet, and her hair swirled around her shoulders in loose curls.

"Wow. You look a lot different."

Stevie self-consciously ran a hand through her hair. "I-I was reading, and I fell asleep on the couch. I must look like a mess."

"No. You look great."

Attraction sizzled in the air like a steak in a hot skillet. So this was how she'd look in bed, Holt thought. The thought caused a pang of hunger.

It was odd, the way she affected him. With most women he was initially bowled over by their looks, but as he got to know them, their beauty seemed to fade. Stevie was just the opposite. Every time he saw her, she seemed to grow more attractive.

But then, everything about Stevie was different. For

starters, he was pursuing her for the sake of his child, not for himself. Somehow he kept forgetting that. With most women it was out of sight, out of mind; but Stevie stayed in his thoughts with surprising tenacity. And most women loved to talk about themselves. He'd called Stevie every day while he was away and she'd given him detailed updates on Isabelle, but virtually no information about herself or what she was thinking.

"How's Isabelle?" he asked.

"Great. No fever, and she seems to be out of pain. She's asleep. Want to go up and take a peek at her?"

"Sure." Holt dropped his computer case and clothes bag on the sofa and followed Stevie up the stairs.

Her backside was at eye level, and Holt couldn't help but admire it. She had a J. Lo bottom—full and round and well-shaped. He liked to look at it.

He liked to look at Stevie, period. He enjoyed seeing a woman with genuine curves. Why did she hide them under baggy clothes?

But her looks weren't the reason he wanted her around, he reminded himself. He wanted her around for Isabelle. The baby desperately needed a mother, and Stevie was perfect for the job.

He followed her down the hall into the darkened nursery. It was lit by only a nightlight, and it took a moment for his eyes to adjust to the dimness. He stopped beside Stevie and peered into the crib. Isabelle was dressed in pink flowered pajamas, and she was hunched up, bottom in the air, her thumb stuck firmly in her mouth.

Jeez, she was tiny—and so skinny! It was almost frightening, how fragile she looked. She was so helpless, so needy, so defenseless. A funny warmth shot through his chest, along with a fierce sense of protectiveness.

"Is it okay for her to sleep on her stomach like that?"

he whispered to Stevie. "I read that babies were supposed to sleep on their backs."

"That's true for young babies. But Isabelle's old
enough to turn over by herself, so it's okay."

They stood there a moment longer, staring down at
the slumbering child, then headed for the hall. Stevie
shot Holt a curious glance as they went down the stairs.
"So you've been reading up on baby care, huh?"

He lifted his shoulders. "I want to be a good father."

Stevie gazed at him somberly for a moment. "Well
then, I'm sure you will be."

That funny warmth spread through him again. He
fought it down, irritated that such a gratuitous remark
could affect him so. "So, that's all there is to it?" he chal-
lenged. "Just want to be one, and I will?"

"You wouldn't want to be a good dad if you didn't
care about her," Stevie said.

"There's only one problem: I don't know what a good
dad does. My own was never around."

"Just be the kind of father you wished you'd had."

A cold knot formed in his belly. He'd wanted a lot.
What if Isabelle did, too? What if he couldn't meet her
expectations?

Stevie followed him into the kitchen. "How often did
you see your dad?"

"A couple of times a year—once in the summer, then
at either Thanksgiving or Christmas." He opened the refrigerator and pulled out a bottle of Chardonnay. "My
folks took turns."

He'd hated the holidays—hated leaving one parent
alone, hated trying to convince the other he was having
fun, hated feeling like it was somehow his fault that his
parents were so unhappy.

"What did you do when you were together?"

Holt rummaged in a drawer for a corkscrew. "We'd go

to a game or two together—baseball, football or hockey—but that was about the extent of the father-son activities. He'd go to work and leave me with whichever wife he happened to have at the time, and I'd just feel like I was in the way."

"So your dad remarried?"

"Twice. Divorced two more times, too."

Holt peeled the wrapper off the cork. "He didn't know what to do with a kid."

"But you liked being around him."

"Oh, yeah. Even though I didn't like his wives, I'd get real upset when I had to leave. He always hated that. He hated emotional displays."

"He probably didn't know how to handle it."

How the hell had he gotten off on this topic? Something about Stevie made him end up telling her more than he intended. Holt twisted the corkscrew into the cork. "Tell me about Isabelle. Has she been eating?"

Stevie smiled. "Like a little horse. Her appetite seems to have really revved up."

"That's great." The cork came out with a pop. "You're awfully good for her, Stevie." And he meant it in a non-self-serving way. She really was just a wonderful mother.

Stevie looked away, then changed the subject. "How did your meetings go?"

"Good. They're going to adopt my long-term plan." He splashed some wine into their glasses. "They were originally going to slash about four hundred jobs, and this way they don't have to. I feel pretty good about it."

"You should. That's a lot of jobs."

Holt nodded somberly. "And most of them are breadwinners. Do you have any idea what it does to a family if the primary breadwinner loses his job?"

"No." But something in her eyes, something warm

and intense, said she knew that *he* did. "I imagine it's pretty traumatic."

Holt nodded. "It can tear a family apart. And in today's economy, it wouldn't be easy for a lot of those people to find work elsewhere."

She looked at him searchingly, and once again he wondered why he'd said so much.

"Well, congratulations."

"Thanks." He poured more wine into the glasses, then held one out to her.

She lifted it. "Here's to your success—in your work, and as a father."

Holt clinked his glass against hers and took a long sip. He watched her drink, too. Picking up the bottle, he refilled both their glasses, then lifted his again.

"And here's to you. The best thing that's ever happened to Isabelle and me."

She gave a small grin. "I don't know if I should drink to such a blatant exaggeration."

"It's the truth. Drink up."

They both took a long draught.

"So what went on in my absence?" he asked.

Stevie walked over to a notepad by the phone. "Well, you've had some phone calls."

Uh-oh. He did his best to act casual. "From whom?"

"Someone named Tiffany called yesterday. She thought I was the maid. She wanted to know what time you were getting home and if I'd let her in so she could be waiting here to surprise you."

Oh, hell. "I only went out with her twice. I hope she didn't give you the impression that there was something between us."

"Oh, she definitely gave that impression." Stevie's mouth twisted wryly. "Here's a piece of advice, Holt;

most women tend to think that if you sleep with them, you're in a relationship."

"I haven't slept with her."

Stevie's look said she didn't believe him.

He lifted his hand. "I swear. Things were headed in that direction, but I got the drift that she was looking for the whole commitment thing, so I decided to cool it."

"You might want to tip her off, then, because she seems to think things are pretty hot and getting hotter." Stevie looked down at the notepad. "You also had a call from Mandy."

"Who?"

"Mandy. Apparently you met her in New York last month and told her to give you a call if she ever came to New Orleans. She has a vacation coming up and was thinking about spending it here if you were going to be around."

This was not making him look good. He took a sip of wine.

"And then you had a visit from Charlotte."

Holt cleared his throat. "She's my interior designer."

Stevie smiled. "Well, she provides wonderful service, showing up all dressed to kill at eight in the evening. She brought you a spring flower arrangement."

Oh, damn.

"And then you had a call from Buffy." Stevie's eyebrow rode high. Holt wished he could slide under the counter. "I figured you for a lady-killer, Holt, but I didn't know you were also slaying vampires."

"I haven't seen her in months. That's all over. I swear."

"Yeah, well, I guess you failed to drive a stake through the heart of that relationship."

"What did she want?"

"You, apparently. She grilled me over the phone, then

showed up on your front porch. She left you a letter."
Stevie held out a sealed envelope with his name
scrawled in big, spidery letters.

Oh, *hell.* Holt took another long swallow.

"Let's see . . . you also had calls from Amber and
Sarah—and Bob." She looked up. "I must say, I was
shocked to hear that you have time for male compan-
ions. Oh—and your mother called."

Alarm shot through Holt. "My mother? What did you
tell her?"

"Relax, hotshot. I didn't tell her about the baby." Stevie took a sip of wine. "I figured you'd want to do it
yourself."

"So . . . what *did* you say?" he asked cautiously.

"That I was house-sitting while you were in Atlanta."
Stevie put down the notepad. "She seems very nice."

"Was everything okay with her?"

Stevie nodded. "She said she was just calling to touch
base—that she hadn't talked to you in a while and was
wondering how you were doing." Stevie picked up her
glass of wine. "You really ought to keep in better touch
with her."

He blew out a sigh. "I know."

"In fact, from the calls I took, I'd say you need to do a
better job communicating with all the women in your
life."

"Stevie, I swear—I'm not currently involved with any
of those women." It was true. In fact, the truth was, he
hadn't dated at all in some time. Lately it had all
seemed as if the hassles outweighed the temporary
pleasures. "The only females in my life right now are Isabelle and you." He looked at her intently. "And I'd like
to keep it that way."

She took a long swig of wine, then set down her glass.
"Holt, we need to talk."

Those words always boded ill. "About what?"

She seemed to be deliberately avoiding eye contact. "I'm concerned about Isabelle's well-being."

"Me, too." Something in her voice was so somber it alarmed him. "Is everything okay? Did something happen?"

Stevie nodded, her eyes dark and serious.

Worry flooded his chest. "What?"

"She doesn't cry when I pick her up anymore. She smiles at me and holds out her arms."

Holt's heart jumped, but he wasn't sure if it was from joy or fear. Stevie sure didn't look as if she was relaying good news. "Really?"

"Really." Stevie's face was somber, worried. "Holt, she's starting to bond with me."

A knot of worry tightened in his stomach. He'd taken a gamble, but he might have been wrong. "She started bonding with you when she first heard your voice on the radio," he pointed out.

"I mean *really* bond. In a way that could hurt her if I disappear from her life."

Oh, dear God—he couldn't stand the thought that his scheming had backfired, that Isabelle might end up hurt as the result of his actions. "Well, then, you've got to stay," he said hopefully.

Stevie twisted her fingers together and avoided his gaze. "I've done a lot of thinking about it."

"And?" The knot in his gut cinched tighter.

She drew a deep breath. Holt held his. *Please, please, please,* he prayed.

"I've bonded with Isabelle, too," she said. "I'm crazy about her, and I can't stand the thought of leaving her." She paused. "If your offer is still on the table, I'd like to take you up on it."

Joy flooded Holt's veins. "Oh, it's on the table, all

right." He set down his glass and crossed the kitchen. "This is great!" He grabbed her in a bear hug and lifted her off her feet.

Stevie gasped and reflexively grabbed his shoulders as he twirled her around. The feel of her invaded his senses. He could smell her soft, sweet perfume, feel the silk of her hair against his neck, see her lips part in laughter as he set her down. Heat flooded him at all the points of contact—his arms around her waist, his belly against hers, her breasts against his chest. From the way she was looking at him, she felt it, too. Electricity zinged between them, hot, melting, magnetizing.

And then she dropped her arms and drew back. It took a great effort, but Holt did the same.

She folded her arms across her chest and cleared her throat. "There are, um, a few conditions."

Holt nodded, trying to ignore the way the blood pounded through his brain and the imprint of her body burned into his skin. "Just name them."

She stepped back still farther and leaned against the black granite counter. "Well, first of all, my family takes marriage very seriously, and it would devastate them to know I was marrying with the intent of divorcing. I'd rather let them think we had real feelings and tried but just couldn't make the marriage work. So that's Condition Number One: As far as everyone else is concerned, the marriage has to seem like the real deal."

That was easy enough. Holt nodded. "No problem. I don't want to do a lot of explaining, either."

"That brings us to Condition Number Two." She cleared her throat nervously. "While we're married, you have to *act* married. I don't want to be humiliated by you running around with other women."

"By 'act married,' you mean sleep only with you?"

She shot him a look that said this was not the time for

jokes or wisecracks. "That's Condition Number Three. You and I will *not* be sleeping together," she said firmly.

"At all?"

"At all."

"So I'm not going to sleep with anyone for the duration of our marriage?"

"Right."

"Gee, this sounds like a real marriage, all right."

"I'm serious!"

"I am, too."

"You expect me to be celibate the whole time?"

"That's the deal. Take it or leave it."

He wasn't about to do either. "How about this—I promise to be faithful to you while we're married. And I agree not to exercise my husbandly rights until you invite me to."

"Until?" She rolled her eyes. "You'd better not hold your breath."

"That'll be my plan of last resort—to make you give me CPR."

"Can you be serious for a moment?"

"I *am* serious. Anything else?"

"Yes. Condition Number Four is that you have to behave like a loving husband in front of my parents and friends."

He pulled her close. "You mean put my arm around you and nuzzle your neck and . . ."

She wriggled out from under his arm.

He grinned. "Yeah, I think I can handle that. Anything else?"

"Yes. Condition Number Five: You will be a loving, involved father to Isabelle. A child needs two parents, so don't think you're going to just hand over all your parenting responsibilities. You have to agree to bond with her and be a big part of her life, for *all* of her life."

"That's my intention."

"Good."

"Is that all?"

Stevie nodded. "That's it."

"So this means we're engaged?"

She looked away, as if the concept flustered her. "I guess it does."

"Well, this calls for another toast." He refilled their glasses and stepped toward her. "To Isabelle's new mother."

"Isabelle's mother," she murmured wonderingly. Her eyes grew misty and soft as she clinked her glass against his and took a drink.

He lifted his glass again. "And here's to Isabelle, the luckiest little girl in the world."

"Well, I don't know about that."

"I do. Drink up."

Stevie drained her glass. He refilled it.

"And last but not least, here's to us."

"Us?"

"Sure. We're about to get married."

"Yes, but it's not a real marriage."

"No, but it's a real partnership—a partnership in parenting. Surely that deserves a toast."

Stevie clinked her glass against his, then took a long drink. Holt started to refill it, but she stopped him by putting her hand over the top. "All of these toasts are making me dizzy, and we have a lot of details to work out."

"Right. Like when and where we're going to get married."

"Before we get to that, we need to get our story straight."

Holt's eyebrow rose. "Our story?"

She nodded. "Of how we got engaged. My family and friends will want to know how you proposed."

"Oh, right." He hadn't even considered. "Proposals are big deals to women, huh?"

"*Very* big deals. And I'm afraid I'm not a very convincing liar."

"Well, in that case, I'd better do it for real."

The least he could do was give her a good proposal. After all, she was agreeing to spend the next eighteen years raising his child. He hadn't really thought about all that marrying him would involve—deceiving her family, lying to her friends, foregoing the big first wedding that most women dreamed about.

She was giving up a lot. If she wanted a romantic proposal, then by golly he'd see to it she got one. His family had a proposal tradition that would more than fit the bill. He might as well use it; it wasn't as if he was going to need it later.

Holt put down his glass and raised his hand, his index finger up. "Wait right there. I'll be right back."

Chapter Fifteen

Stevie climbed on an upholstered bar stool as Holt left the kitchen, grabbing the counter as the room seemed to tilt. She really wasn't much of a drinker. She shouldn't have had all that wine.

But maybe it wasn't just the wine, she thought as she carefully adjusted herself in the center of the iron-backed chair. Maybe her head was still spinning from the way he'd picked her up and swung her around as if she weighed no more than a sack of flour. The feel of his hard chest against hers, his arms firm as granite around her, had definitely contributed to her light-headedness.

She heard his footsteps descending the stairs. A moment later, he poked his head out. "Stay right there. I'm setting the scene."

Stevie's heart pounded. This wasn't real, of course, but it was still pretty thrilling.

Soft music floated in the air. Holt reappeared a moment later. "Okay. We're all set."

"For what?"

"Come see." Stevie rose to her feet, feeling none too steady.

He took her hand and led her into the living room. It glowed with candlelight. Five fat crimson candles of varying heights gleamed on the coffee table, while three more burned in the fireplace.

Holt led her to the sofa and sat down beside her. "I have something for you."

Stevie's pulse raced as he pulled a small black box about the size of a deck of cards from his shirt pocket.

"Go ahead. Open it."

Stevie's hands trembled as she lifted the lid.

She gingerly lifted a battered gold object from its velvet nest. "A pocket watch?"

"No. It's a compass."

Stevie turned it in her hand, fingering the dented case, then looked up at him questioningly.

"It originally belonged to my great-great-great-great-great grandfather Ben on my father's side. This compass has been passed down to the oldest male heir of each generation ever since."

"Wow. What a treasure."

Holt nodded. "Ben fought in the battle of 1812. He and a soldier named Frank were on a reconnaissance mission when they had a skirmish with six Redcoats. Frank was shot and badly wounded. Ben was hit as well, but his compass stopped the bullet. The impact broke a rib and cracked the glass, but the compass saved Ben's life."

Stevie fingered the dent.

"Once they got away from the soldiers, they were deep in the swamps, and Frank was bleeding badly. Just when it looked like there was no hope, they stumbled onto the cabin of a French trapper and his beautiful daughter, Elise, who gave them food and water and tended their wounds. Ben was smitten by the daughter; it was love at first sight. He wanted to stay and marry her, but he needed to go back to warn the Americans that the British were closer than they'd thought.

"Frank was too ill to travel, so Ben left him in their care. Before he left, he gave Elise his compass as a sign of his love. At first she refused to take it, saying he would need it to find his way back.

" 'No,' he told her. The compass had protected his heart so he could give it to her, and the heart was a much surer guide than any compass. He would return to marry her when his duty to his country was over."

"Oh, that's so romantic!" Stevie breathed. "Did he?"

Holt nodded. "He was as good as his word—but it took him nearly a year to get back. In the meantime, Frank's wounds had healed, and he, too, had fallen in love with Elise.

"Her father thought she was wasting her life waiting for a man who would never return. He tried to convince her to marry Frank, but she repeatedly refused. After an argument, the father took the compass and hurled it into the swamp."

"Oh, no!" Stevie murmured.

"The loss of the compass seemed to break her spirit, and Elise reluctantly agreed to marry Frank. Her father arranged to trade an alligator skin for a wedding dress. As he gutted the alligator, the compass fell out of the creature's belly. The girl fainted dead away. The father said it was a sign and called off the wedding."

Stevie held her breath.

"Three days later, on the very day she was supposed to marry Frank, Ben returned to claim his bride." Holt paused. "My great-great-great-great-great grandmother."

"Good heavens," Stevie whispered. "Did that really happen?"

Holt lifted his shoulders. "I'm skeptical, but my father said his great-grandfather swore it was true. And every firstborn male descendant of Ben and Elise has given the compass to his intended bride ever since, with the words I'm about to say to you."

He pulled a yellowed piece of paper from his pocket, then dropped to one knee in front of her and reached for her hand, pressing the compass against her palm. Stevie's pulse roared in her head.

" 'You are my true north, the one I have been seeking, and I am lost without you,' " he read. " 'You give my life meaning and direction. My heart rests in the palm of your hand. You have the power to crush it or fill it with everlasting joy by the answer you give to my earnest plea.' " His dark eyes searched her face. "Stevie, will you marry me?"

Stevie's eyes clouded with tears. She felt as if her heart were in her throat.

"This is where you're supposed to say yes," Holt prompted.

Stevie's mind felt all fuzzy and misted over, like a soft-focus photograph. "Yes," she whispered. "Yes, I will."

"There's one other part of this tradition we need to fulfill," Holt said. His eyes glittered in the candlelight as he pulled her to her feet.

He was going to kiss her. The thought mesmerized her. She wasn't sure if it was the wine or the circumstances that made her wobble as she stood, but it didn't matter, because he steadied her as he drew her into his arms.

The first brush of his mouth was gentle, more of a hovering than an actual touch. Restrained and soft and almost reverent, it was a mere whisper of a kiss.

And then his lips pressed more fully against hers, moving in a slow, sensual slide. He tasted of wine, dark and delicious and intoxicating. Desire, swift and hot, kickboxed her low in the belly, heating her blood, making it pool there. He tugged at her lower lip, provoking her, teasing her. She breathed in the starch of his white cotton business shirt, the musk of his skin, the earthy scent of his hair, and grew more aroused with every breath.

His tongue slid along the seam of her lips, urging her to open and let him in. Her lips parted and he deepened the kiss, plundering. She wrapped her arms around him, clutching the compass in one hand and pressing the hard muscles of his back with the other. His chest was warm and firm. She pressed her breasts against it, yearning to get closer, yearning for more. Her blood seemed like liquid fire, pumping hard and fast through her veins. Even the metal of the compass in her hand was growing warm.

She moaned and moved against him, feeling the hard proof of his arousal against her belly. His hands moved low on her back, then even lower to cup her buttocks. She rose on her tiptoes, trying to align herself more intimately against him, and curled a leg around his thighs.

She heard him gasp. He tightened his grip on her buttocks, picked her up and carried her the remaining two steps to the sofa. She pulled him down with her, longing to feel the heat and hardness and weight of him on top of her.

A baby's cry cut through the air, plaintive and loud.

Stevie's mind was so fogged with passion that it took a moment for the who, what, when and where of the situation to register. *Isabelle was crying. She was at Holt's house. She was in his arms, on his sofa, locked in a very intimate embrace.*

She abruptly wriggled out from under him. "I-I need to go see to Isabelle."

As her mind returned to earth, alarm shot through her. What was she thinking? He was a womanizing babe magnet, a heartache waiting to happen. She'd agreed to marry him? She'd believed all he said? The wine must have gone to her head—the wine and the romantic setting.

But the proposal . . . Her fingers tightened around the compass. Oh, dear Lord—that was the most romantic thing she'd ever heard.

Yet it hadn't been real. He hadn't been really asking her to marry him. Somewhere along the line, she'd lost sight of that.

The baby's cries grew louder. Stevie struggled to her feet.

Holt's brow knit. "Do you think something's wrong?"

Oh, something was wrong, all right. It was completely wrong that she'd been lip-locked with Holt in a horizontal position.

She smoothed her rumpled sweater, wishing she could smooth this awkward situation as easily. "She's probably just hungry. The doctor said she needed to eat every three or four hours since she's so underweight, and she's starting to do that. It's a good sign that she's getting back her appetite." Stevie was babbling, but that was what she tended to do when she was flustered. And she definitely felt flustered.

"I'll fix her a bottle," Holt said.

"Okay. I-I'll go and see to her." Steve fled up the stairs, wishing she could flee from the confusing maelstrom of emotions churning inside herself as well.

"She ate like a real little chow hound," Holt said twenty minutes later, after Stevie had set a full and sated Isabelle gently back in her crib.

"I told you her appetite's picked up," Stevie replied.

"You weren't kidding. I couldn't believe how she stopped crying when you picked her up." Holt looked at Steve as they headed downstairs. "She's crazy about you."

"Well, it's mutual." Steve carried the empty bottle to the kitchen. "I'm crazy about her."

"And I'm crazy about you." Holt reached out for her, but Stevie ducked out of his way. She placed the bottle in the sink and faced him.

"Holt—I can't do this. If we're going to make this arrangement work, we can't have this stuff going on."

Holt grinned. "What stuff?"

"You know exactly what stuff I mean." Her expression said this was not the time to joke around. "What we were doing earlier."

Holt took a step toward her. "Stevie, we're going to be living together. There's chemistry between us. I don't see a problem."

"Well, I do. I don't get physically involved unless my heart is involved, and if my heart in involved, I want a permanent commitment. We both know that's not what this is about. There's no point in muddying the waters."

"Stevie . . ."

"It's one of the conditions you agreed to," she warned.

He blew out a frustrated sigh. He didn't want to sour the deal now that he'd finally gotten her to agree. She was amazing with Isabelle, and the child clearly adored her. But he was going to find it damn near impossible to live in the same house with her and keep it platonic—especially after that kiss.

But he had no choice. He ran a hand over his face. "Okay," he reluctantly conceded. "I won't make another move on you unless you initiate things."

"Dream on, Landen."

"Oh, I'll be dreaming about it, all right."

She walked back to the living room and he followed her. Avoiding the sofa, she sat in a wing-backed chair by the fireplace. "We need to make a few practical arrangements."

He sprawled on the sofa. "Like what?"

"Well, since Isabelle is going to be waking in the night and needing to be fed until she puts on some more weight, I probably should stay with her from here on out. So I think we need to get married as soon as possible."

"Terrific." He was anxious to close this deal before she had a chance to change her mind. "How do you want to handle the wedding? If her earache's cleared up, we could go to Vegas or Reno tomorrow."

She shook her head. "I can't get married without my parents. It would break their hearts."

This parent thing was turning into a real grind. "Well then, how about City Hall? I can get my attorney to draw up the papers and we can get the license on Monday."

She shook her head. "We can't get the license until we tell my folks. They'd be hurt. Besides, you have to ask my dad for my hand."

Oh, man. Holt stared at her in dismay. "You're kidding."

"He's very old-fashioned. He expects it."

"He's told you that?"

"Not exactly, but he's joked about it. All my life, whenever I did something goofy, he'd threaten to tell my fiancé about it when he asked for my hand in marriage."

It was hard to imagine Stevie being goofy. "Oh, yeah? What kind of things?"

"I don't know—stupid stuff."

"I need specifics. I don't want to appear too shocked if he makes good on his threats."

She grinned. "Well, he's threatened to show a picture of me with my hair rolled around orange juice cans."

"You roll your hair on orange juice cans?"

"I did when I was fifteen, because I read it was supposed to give me smooth hair. He thought it was the funniest thing he'd ever seen."

"And he took pictures?"

"I never let anyone take pictures of me." He wondered why, but before he could ask, she hurried on. "You're losing sight of the point here. The point is, he expects the man I marry to ask for my hand."

"Okay." If he had to walk over hot coals, he'd do it to seal this deal. "When should I do it?"

"Well, we're supposed to have dinner with them tomorrow night. I guess you should take him aside before dinner; then we can break the news afterward."

This was all getting a lot more complicated than he'd thought. But what the hey—it was a small price to pay for insuring that his baby had a mother. A great mother. He nodded. "Okay."

She nodded back, then nervously moistened her lips with her tongue. His gaze locked on her mouth. Damn, but she was some kisser. He couldn't recall ever feeling that degree of passion that fast. He never would have expected someone who looked so buttoned down to be such a wildcat. He was getting aroused all over again just thinking about it.

She rose from the chair. "Well, I guess we'd better try

to get some sleep." She folded her arms across her chest. "I'm staying in the room next to Isabelle's."

She started for the stairs.

"Let me know if you want some company," he called.

"Don't hold your breath."

"Maybe I should, so I can get some of that CPR we talked about."

"You won't get it from me. I'll call nine-one-one and get a big, burly paramedic named Fred to do it."

"Scratch that idea, then."

Her lips curled in a dry smile. "Scratch anything you like. You'll be sleeping in total privacy."

Holt grinned as she marched up the stairs.

She had a mouth on her, that Stevie. He liked that about her. He liked it a lot.

He especially liked the way she used it on his.

Chapter Sixteen

"This looks like the parking lot of the Superdome during a Saints game," Holt said the next night as he drove past a line of vehicles parked in front of a rambling white brick house in the Lakeview section of New Orleans. "I thought it was just going to be us and your parents."

"Me, too." Stevie's brow knit. "It looks like Mom's invited half the family."

Great, Holt thought grimly. Not only was he going to have to face her parents and ask for Stevie's hand in marriage, now he'd also have to make nice with a whole slew of her relatives. "Who's here?"

"Well, that's my brother's van . . . and Great-Aunt Sophie's Cadillac, Uncle Chuck's Toyota, Uncle Joe's pickup, and my cousin Mona's Taurus. . . . I'm not sure about the others." She blew out a chagrinned sigh. "I had no idea Mom was going to do this. Isabelle's going to hate this crowd."

She won't be the only one, Holt thought glumly. "Anything I need to know about anyone?"

"Well, my brother's very protective of me. He's a police detective in Baton Rouge, so he's likely to ask a lot of questions."

Oh, boy—this promised to be a real fun evening.

"Uncle Joe is hard of hearing, but he likes to act as if he knows what's being said, so he repeats words he catches and says, 'Hear, hear!' a lot. And Uncle Chuck will talk your ear off. If he corners you, you'll be there all evening, so be sure you're with my mother or another family member who can rescue you when you meet him."

Oh, yeah. Big fun was in store, all right. "Anyone else?"

"Well, my great-aunt Sophie . . ." Stevie hesitated.

"What about her."

"Well, she's a bit of a flirt. She's eighty-five, but she doesn't seem to realize it."

"Doesn't realize it, how?"

"Well . . ."

"Well, what? Is she senile?"

Stevie held her thumb and forefinger about half an inch apart. "Maybe just a wee bit. But only where men are concerned."

Yes, indeed, the evening promised to be a barrel of laughs. Holt finally found a parking spot two houses down. He circled the car and opened the door for Stevie. "Do you want me to bring Isabelle in her car seat?"

She shook her head. "I'll carry her in my arms. Mom still has a crib set up from when my brother's twins were babies, so hopefully she'll fall sleep before we eat dinner."

Stevie opened the back door and leaned in. "Hey, sugar," she said to the baby.

"Oh, wow—look at that smile!" Holt exclaimed.

"I told you we were bonding."

Holt watched as Stevie stretched forward to unfasten the baby's car seat. The neckline of her long black-and-white print dress gaped open, revealing a peek of generous cleavage and a lacy black bra. Fire raced through him.

This might not be a love match, but lust was certainly a component. He couldn't get Stevie's kiss out of his mind. It had plagued him all of last night.

He walked beside her to her parents' front door, which swung open before the doorbell even quit ringing. Stevie's mother appeared, wearing a bright pink dress, matching lipstick and a wide smile.

"Hello, Holt—Stevie!" Marie kissed Holt on the cheek, then turned and did the same to Stevie. "And Isabelle—it's so wonderful to see you!" As Marie leaned forward and smiled at the baby, Isabelle turned her face and cried.

Marie's face fell. "Oh, dear. I didn't mean to upset you, sweetheart!"

"Don't take it personally," Holt said. "She's very shy."

"We didn't know you were planning on having the whole family over," Stevie remarked.

"It's not everyone," Marie answered defensively. "I just thought it would be fun to have a little get-together." She stepped back from the door and smiled at Holt. "Come in and meet everyone." Holt followed Stevie and Isabelle inside, through a white-tiled foyer into a crowded living room.

Isabelle's face grew red, and her cries turned into screams. "She's not accustomed to crowds," Stevie said.

"Why don't you take her into the kids' bedroom while I introduce Holt around," Marie suggested.

Holt longed to go with Stevie—or better yet, to bolt out the door. Instead, he forced a smile as Stevie shot him an apologetic look and headed down the hall with his child.

"Come on in and let Robert get you a drink," Marie said, leading him through the spacious living room.

The walls, the carpet and the furniture were all in shades of taupe and beige, and family photos were everywhere. Holt scanned them for a picture of Stevie, but before he found one, Marie stopped in front of an old-fashioned built-in bar. Stevie's father stood behind it.

"Glad you could come." Robert greeted Holt with a smile, but there was a guarded look in his eyes. A current of uneasiness ran through Holt. Robert was not a man who would be easily deceived. When Holt spoke to him, he'd better keep to the truth as much as possible. Stevie hadn't said what would happen if her father didn't approve of their marriage, but it might just be a deal breaker. Holt shook the man's hand, dreading the thought of asking him for Stevie's hand in marriage.

"What'll you have?" Robert asked.

"A beer, please." Holt looked around. "Quite a crowd you've got here."

"We've got a large family."

"That's what Stevie said."

Robert unscrewed the top of a beer bottle. "What about you?"

"I don't have much of one." Holt accepted the beer. "I always thought it would be fun to be part of a big family."

Marie smiled. "You can always do what Robert did and marry into one." She took his arm. "Come on, Holt. Let's get you some food—and I want to introduce you around." Marie took him over to the far side of the room, where an elaborate array of spinach tarts, tiny popovers, cut vegetables, and other appetizers were laid out.

"Wow—I can see why your catering business is doing so well."

Marie beamed. "Most of this food is from a party I catered last night. I just made a little extra." She turned toward a tall man with light hair like Stevie's. "Holt, this is my son, Dan. And the lovely brunette by the back door with the twins is his wife, Casey—I'm sure she'll be over in a minute. Dan, this is Stevie's friend, Holt."

"I saw your baby when you came in," Dan said as he selected a phyllo-crusted slice of brie from the buffet table. "Cute kid. Were you married to her mother?"

Holt was pretty sure Dan already knew otherwise.

"No," he replied calmly. "I didn't even know I had a baby until about a month ago, when I got a call that the child's mother died."

"Wow. How'd she manage to keep a secret like that?"

"She lived in Dallas, and we hadn't spoken in a long time."

Dan studied him. "So you parted on bad terms?"

Holt had the uneasy sensation this was an interrogation. "No. We just parted."

Dan took a bite of brie. "Lucky for you that she didn't want child support, huh?"

No question about it; he was definitely being grilled. "Ella was independently wealthy. Her father left her a fortune."

"Oh, really?" Dan's eyebrows rose. "How'd she die?"

"Good heavens, Dan, don't treat him like a suspect," Dan's wife said, stepping up beside him. A petite brunette with short hair, she introduced herself with a friendly smile.

Holt smiled back. "It's okay. I'm used to answering

questions." He turned back to Dan. "She died in a car crash in Dallas. And in case you're wondering, I was in New Orleans at the time."

Casey laughed. "You'll have to excuse Dan. He's never entirely off the job."

"If I had a sister involved with a guy with a baby, I'd want to know the particulars, too," Holt said, putting a spinach tart on his plate.

"So you and Stevie—you're involved?" Dan asked.

Man, this guy was persistent! Holt nodded.

"Does that mean you're serious about her?"

Dan's wife elbowed him in the side. "Dan!" she chided.

"Well, she's my sister. I don't want to see her hurt again."

Again? Apparently there was some history he ought to know about.

To Holt's relief, Marie Stedquest appeared at his elbow. "Aunt Sophie wants to meet you."

"Uh-oh. Watch out," Casey warned. "She's a man-eater."

"Holt's safe," Marie said with a smile. "I explained that he's with Stevie, and you know how crazy Sophie is about Stevie."

"We know how crazy Sophie is, period," Dan muttered.

"Besides, she brought a date."

"That's not a date. That's a gigolo," Dan said.

Holt followed Dan's gaze to an elderly man wearing a bright blue jacket, an ascot and a black toupee, standing beside a shriveled redhead in a lavender dress.

Casey elbowed her husband. "Be nice."

He let Marie drag him over to the elderly couple, who apparently had met on a recent cruise. He found himself jostled from the great-aunt to a cousin, then to Marie's sister and her husband, followed by two more sets of Stevie's aunts and uncles.

Across the room, he felt Stevie's father's eyes on him. Might as well get this over with, he thought grimly. Swallowing hard, Holt excused himself and headed across the room to the bar. "Mr. Stedquest—could I talk to you privately for a moment?"

The older man froze for a second, then recovered so quickly Holt thought he must have imagined it. "Yes, of course. Let's go into my study."

"Have a seat." Robert gestured to a flame-stitched chair in front of his desk and seated himself in the one beside it. The dark green room with the wall of bookshelves was his favorite in the house, the one he thought of as his private lair.

He knew what was coming. A sixth sense he'd developed as a prosecutor told him Holt was about to ask for Stevie's hand in marriage, even though it struck him as way too soon for the relationship to be so serious.

"Mr. Stedquest, you have a wonderful daughter."

"Yes, I do." Robert sat back, his hands folded. He wasn't going to make this easy. If this man wanted Stevie, he was going to have to work for her.

"I've grown very fond of her."

Robert's eyebrow quirked up. "Fond?"

He could see Holt's Adam's apple bob. "More than fond. I—I think she's the most wonderful woman in the world. I'm crazy about her."

He hadn't said he loved her, but then, love wasn't a word that Robert said easily, either.

"And . . . I want to ask you for her hand in marriage."

Robert stared at him for a long, disconcerting moment. "Have you discussed this with Stevie?"

"Yes."

"And what was her answer?"

"Yes."

"Well, then, it doesn't really matter what I say, does it?" The words came out caustic and harsh—far harsher than he had intended. Damn it, everything he said these days seemed to come out that way.

Holt earned points for the way he kept his cool. "No, but I'd like to have your approval," he said calmly. "It means a lot to Stevie."

"Stevie means a lot to me."

"I know that, sir."

Robert leaned back in his chair, drummed his fingers on the oak desktop and fixed Holt with the long, measuring stare that used to make defense attorneys quake in their wingtips.

Holt didn't bat an eye.

"How long have you known her?" Robert asked.

"Long enough to know I can't live without her."

Robert was used to interrogating people, and he knew all the little signs that gave away lies—the micro-expressions that crossed a person's face, the quick glance away, the tightening of the fingers, the slight dilation of the pupils. Holt had none of those. "Does she feel the same way about you?"

"I hope so, sir."

Again, there was no sign of deception. He would throw the man a curve and see how he reacted.

"Are you grieving the death of your baby's mother?"

"Actually, I'm not. I was sorry to hear about it, of course, but that relationship was never very intense, and it had been over for more than a year."

"Are you looking to marry Stevie because you need a mother for your child?"

A hint of discomfort flashed across Holt's face. He unfolded his legs and adjusted his weight in the chair, but when he replied, his gaze was direct. "Well, that's a bonus, there's no doubt about it," he admitted. "For Stevie as well as Isabelle and me. And there's no doubt the baby moved things along faster than they might have gone otherwise. But Stevie and I . . ." He hesitated, and Robert saw him swallow. "Well, there's definitely more between us than just the baby."

That much was true. Robert had seen them kissing in the restaurant. There was undeniably chemistry, on both their parts.

"I've looked you up on the Internet," Robert told him. "You seem to be doing extremely well professionally. And your social life has been pretty lively, too." Robert paused. "I saw that you were named one of New Orleans's most eligible bachelors. And you've been in the society columns with some awfully glamorous women— models and actresses and the like."

To his credit, Holt didn't rush in with explanations. He sat calmly, his hands folded.

"Stevie's lovely, and as her father I think she's the greatest girl in the world, but I can't help but note that she's not the flashy sort you've gone for in the past."

Holt nodded. "That's one of the reasons I want to marry her."

Robert picked up a paperweight shaped like a golf ball off his desk. "I've got to say, I find it highly unusual that one of the most eligible bachelors in the state would resort to an Internet dating service."

Holt glanced away and shifted in the chair again. "It's not unusual if you're looking for a different type of woman than the kind you usually attract."

This line of questioning was clearly making Holt uncomfortable, so Robert pressed it. "What made you decide to look for a different type?"

"Well, to tell you the truth, I'd gotten tired of superficial conversations and game playing. After a while, dating arm candy is about as satisfying as eating noth-ing but marshmallows."

"Are you ready to devote yourself to just one woman?"

"I'm marrying Stevie with the full intention of remain-ing faithful throughout our marriage," Holt replied.

Years of questioning criminals had given Robert good instincts, and his said that Holt's answer was a lit-tle too pat, as if it had been prepared in advance. But then, it was a question a reasonable man would have anticipated from his future father-in-law. Marie's father had asked him the same thing thirty-seven years before.

The memory of sitting where Holt was now hit him like an attack of angina. He'd been scared to death, but so in love he would have faced the devil himself. He would have swum the Mississippi upriver to Des Moines, crawled through a den of rattlesnakes, wrestled a swampful of alligators if that's what it would take to win Marie's hand.

A feeling of nostalgia and sadness washed over him. Where had the years gone? They'd flown by like shoot-ing stars, burned up by work and things that really didn't seem to matter much now.

He forced his thoughts back to Holt.

Nothing in the younger man's responses indicated that he was telling an outright lie, yet something just wasn't right. Still—what the hell was he going to do about it? This whole exercise was nothing more than a meaningless tradition. Stevie was a thirty-one-year-old woman, and she was going to do exactly what she wanted, regardless of what he thought or said. His au-thority over her life had ended years ago.

The thought brought another bout of sad wistfulness. It seemed like just yesterday that she'd been a little girl with bows in her hair, begging him to push her in the backyard swing, to take her to the zoo, to teach her how to fish.

And most of the time he'd been too damn busy. His work had consumed all his time, all his energy, all his thoughts. A pang of regret pierced his chest. "Later," he'd told her. "When things slow down at the office."

Well, they'd slowed down, all right. Slowed all the way down, when he'd been shown the door. Work had been his claim to success, the definition of who he was. Now that it was gone, what did he have?

Nothing. Nothing but regret. Like a dying smoker, he'd realized too late that he'd traded his life for a meaningless addiction.

He blew out a hard sigh. Well, Stevie was beyond needing his permission, but maybe she still wanted his approval. It was the least he could give her, even though he had a gut feeling about this man who'd asked to marry her. "Do I have your word that you'll do everything in your power to make Stevie happy?"

"You do."

Robert's chair creaked as he rose and stuck out his hand. "Well then, congratulations."

"Thank you." The younger man's face broke into a relieved smile as he stood and shook his hand.

"When do you want to announce this?" Robert asked.

"How about at dinner?"

Robert nodded. "Good idea. Let's do it right before dessert."

Marie Stedquest stuck her head in the room. "There you are! I wondered where you two had gone. We're nearly ready to sit down for dinner."

Holt headed toward the door, apparently eager to escape. "I'd better go see if Stevie needs any help quieting the baby."

"Oh, the baby's asleep," Marie said. "Stevie's with Uncle Chuck on the patio."

"Well then, I'd better see if she needs help quieting Uncle Chuck."

"The baby would be a lot easier," Marie said with a laugh.

She had a lovely laugh, Robert thought—soft and musical and light as air. The sound of it used to dance through the house all the time. Where had all her laughter gone?

He'd squelched it. He used to love to make her laugh. Now all he seemed to do was make her cry.

She turned to follow Holt out of the room. "Marie, do you have a moment?" Robert called.

"Not right now, dear. I need to get the rolls out of the oven or they're going to burn."

Robert turned and stared out the window as she left the room, his gaze lighting on a sprawling red oak on the side lawn. When he'd planted it thirty-something years ago, he'd been a strong young man, and the tree had been nothing but a pathetic twig. Now the tree was going strong, and he was the pathetic one.

Right now the tree was sprouting burgundy buds that would unfurl into new green leaves. Red oaks lived up to their name twice a year: now, when the leaves budded, and again in the fall, before they fell. If the temperature didn't dip low enough, however, the leaves simply turned brown and died.

He'd hoped to face the autumn of his life like that tree after a cold snap—to blaze with color and vibrancy until the very end. Instead he was simply withering away, growing more colorless and sapless by the day.

He didn't like the man he had become, but in looking back, he wasn't sure he liked the man he used to be, either. He'd always thought retirement would be a new beginning, a time for him and Marie to finally enjoy all that he'd worked for.

It wasn't turning out that way. Nothing was turning out the way he'd planned.

Chapter Seventeen

As soon as Stevie sat back down at the table after helping serve dessert and chicory-laced coffee, Robert clinked his spoon against his water glass and rose to his feet. Stevie's heart pounded as the hubbub of conversation hushed around the long, lace-covered table that her mother had custom-ordered years ago to accommodate her large family.

"I've saved this announcement until dessert, because just like Marie's bread pudding, I wanted to save the best for last." Titters of excitement and speculation rippled around the table.

"Holt has some news he'd like to share," Robert said.

"Actually, Stevie and I have some news." Holt tugged at her hand as he stood, urging her to her feet beside him. She rose, her insides quaking.

Holt paused and smiled down at her like a man in love. She knew it was all an act, but her heart somersaulted in her chest all the same. "Stevie has agreed to marry me."

"Oh, my goodness!" Marie exclaimed, clasping her cheeks. "Oh, how wonderful!"

Murmurs rose into the air like steam from the just-poured coffee. Snippets reached Stevie's ears:

"What a surprise!"

". . . out of the blue."

". . . hear he's very successful."

". . . good catch."

"I didn't even know she was dating anyone."

Holt cleared his throat, and the table quieted. "I asked Mr. Stedquest for Stevie's hand in marriage, and he gave me his blessing."

Applause broke out among the guests. When it died down, Holt turned to Stevie. "So I have something to give you to make our engagement official." He reached into his jacket pocket and pulled out a small black box. As Stevie stood still as a stone, he opened it and pulled out a shiny ring, then lifted her left hand and slid it onto her fourth finger.

Her hand trembled as she stared down at a diamond solitaire, huge and brilliant and gleaming. She could feel it on her finger, but it seemed as if she was looking at someone else's hand.

She must have stood there for a long time, because Aunt Lou prompted, "Well, aren't you going to say something?"

"I-I don't know what to say," Stevie choked out. "I'm in shock."

"You already said the only thing that matters when you agreed to marry me," Holt said with a smile. "Hopefully this will keep you from backing out."

"Th-thank you," Stevie murmured.

"So kiss him already!" Great-aunt Sophie called.

"Already! Hear, hear!" called Uncle Joe.

Stevie turned toward Holt and awkwardly put her arms around his neck, and Holt did the rest. She was keenly aware of the dozen-plus pairs of eyes on her, but that didn't prevent her from feeling the kiss all the way to the soles of her feet.

The table erupted in applause. And then Stevie's mother was beside her, hugging her, then hugging Holt.

Stevie's father rose and embraced her, and the rest of her family congratulated her, oohing and ahhing over her ring.

It was several minutes before the pandemonium died down and everyone was reseated at the table.

"This calls for a toast!" said Uncle Chuck.

"To Stevie and Holt," Stevie's father proclaimed, his glass raised in the air. "May they have a long and happy marriage."

"Marriage. Hear, hear!" called Uncle Joe.

A long and happy marriage. The immensity of the fraud she was committing hit her hard. She was deceiving the people who loved her the most, leading them to believe that she and Holt were making a lifelong commitment. Guilt weighed on her, heavy as a barbell.

Glasses clinked around the table. Stevie forced herself to touch her glass to Holt's and to as many of her relatives as she could reach, then to take a small sip of wine. Congratulations continued to shower down on them.

"Marie, looks like you have a wedding to plan," Stevie's Aunt Lou said.

"Yes, indeed." Marie's eyes shone with excitement. "Let's see—this is late March. If we get right to work, maybe you can be a fall bride."

Holt shot Stevie a look.

"Oh, we don't want to wait," Stevie said quickly. "We want to get married right away."

"Right away? But it takes time to plan a wedding!" Marie protested.

"We thought we'd keep it simple," Stevie said.

"Even a simple wedding requires lots of planning."

"Actually, we thought we'd just get married at the courthouse next week," Holt said.

"Oh, you can't do that!" Marie exclaimed. "You'll look back on your wedding day with joy all your lives. You'll want memories to relive every anniversary, and photos to show your children and grandchildren."

Everyone at the table murmured their agreement.

"Why the big rush?" Dan asked. "You two haven't even known each other that long."

"Maybe she's got a bun in the oven," Uncle Chuck said.

Aunt Lou elbowed him hard.

"Ow!" Uncle Chuck exclaimed.

"Ow—hear, hear!" called Uncle Joe.

The table grew silent as all eyes turned in Stevie's direction. Oh, dear heaven—they thought she was pregnant! Stevie felt her face flush. "No! I'm not—I mean, there's no reason . . . I'm not . . ." She looked at Holt for assistance.

"We're not expecting, if that's what you're wondering," he said. "But we are in a hurry because of a baby."

Stevie nodded. "Holt's baby needs a mother—and I can't wait to start filling that role. We want to become a family as soon as possible."

"Still, a wedding is the event of a lifetime. You'll regret it if you don't make it special. And you're my only daughter, Stevie. Your father and I have dreamed about giving you a beautiful wedding all your life."

Oh, dear—how the heck was she supposed to respond to that? A few more pounds of guilt pressed down on her chest.

"But we really don't want to wait," she protested weakly.

"If you could wait just two weeks, we could pull something together. Maybe we could even hold it right here," Marie said. "We could set up a couple of tents in the backyard."

"Oh, that would be lovely!" Aunt Lou murmured.

"Lovely," echoed Aunt Sophie.

"Lovely. Hear, hear," said Uncle Joe.

"I don't want you to go to a lot of trouble and expense," Stevie said. *Especially for a marriage that's only going to last a short time.*

Stevie's father bristled. "Money is not an issue," he said firmly. "I've been saving for your wedding since you were a little girl."

Oh, great, Stevie thought—now she was not only breaking her mother's heart, but offending her father as well. He'd always taken pride in his ability to provide for his family, and now he probably thought she was insinuating that he couldn't afford to give her a wedding.

What a situation. She didn't want to let her parents down, but on the other hand, she didn't want them investing a lot of time and money in a phony marriage.

But they'd never know it was phony. She didn't intend to ever tell them the truth about the arrangement.

She looked from one end of the table to the other, from her mother's pleading face to her father's loving eyes. She'd known her wedding would be important to them, but she hadn't realized just how important. A few more pounds of guilt slipped onto the barbell.

Stevie looked over at Holt.

He leaned closer. "As long as it happens in the next two weeks, I don't care if it's in the lion's cage at the zoo," he murmured in her ear.

She shot him a relieved smile. Since her parents obviously wanted to give her a wedding, she might as well make them happy. "Okay," she said. "If you think we can pull it together in two weeks, then we'd love to get married here."

Stevie's mother beamed, her father smiled and the rest of the relatives cheered.

"Let's toast the bride and groom!" Uncle Joe said.

"Drink up," Holt murmured to Stevie with a sexy smile. "I love your reaction to toasts."

As Stevie raised her glass again, she wondered what on earth she'd just done.

"So, Holt—what do your parents think about all this?" Marie asked after the table was cleared and everyone had migrated to the living room.

"I haven't told them yet." He glanced at Stevie, who was seated beside him on the sofa. "We wanted to get things squared away with you first."

"Well, you've got to call them right away. Then you've got to give me their number so I can get in touch to co-ordinate things."

Cold fear rippled down his spine. "Coordinate what things?"

"Well, the rehearsal dinner, and what we plan to wear . . ."

Marie expected his parents to come to the wedding? He needed to nip that right in the bud. "My parents are divorced, and they live out of state. I don't think they'll be able to make it."

Marie's eyes grew wide. "Not make their own son's wedding?"

"Well, this is pretty short notice, and I'm sure they already have things scheduled. . . ."

"All the more reason you should call them right away. I'm sure they'll be more than happy to alter their plans."

This was spinning way out of control. He'd had no intention of inviting his parents—or anyone, for that matter—to his wedding. Hell, he hadn't planned on having a wedding at all. He'd thought he and Stevie would just make it legal without a big fuss.

"I'm afraid my parents don't get along," he said. "They can't stand to be in the same room with each other."

"I'm sure they can put their differences aside for one day," Marie said.

If they were going to put aside their differences, seems like they would have done it for Christmas or my birthday or my college graduation. "I wouldn't bet on it."

"Besides," Marie continued, "a wedding is an excellent occasion for people to mend fences."

With his parents, a wedding was more likely to be the occasion of a double homicide.

"Give them a call. I'll bet they'll surprise you," Marie said. She was nothing if not persistent.

"I'll call them, but don't count on anything," Holt warned.

"Good." Marie smiled. "Can you do it tonight or tomorrow morning? That way I can call them tomorrow afternoon and we can get the ball rolling."

Holt glanced at Stevie. She gave a small shrug, as if to say "I can't stop her."

Man, this was turning into a real pain. He hated the thought of a big production of a wedding, and he dreaded the thought of having his parents together. The last time they'd been together was twelve years ago, at his graduation from Tulane.

Just thinking about it made his stomach knot. The three of them had gone to dinner together at Antoine's, and throughout the lengthy meal, his mother had refused to acknowledge his father's presence. She'd acted as if he were invisible, as if she couldn't hear his comments. The tension stretched so tight that Holt had felt as if he were going to snap.

At first his father had just looked chagrined, but as the meal wore on he'd become angry. In the middle of the entrée, he'd thrown down his napkin and pushed back from the table.

"I won't take any more of this," he'd stated in a low, cold voice. "Holt, congratulations. I'm very proud of you. I'll be in touch."

And with that, he'd walked out. As soon as he'd gone, his mother had burst into tears.

Holt felt a nerve jump in his jaw. He'd rather face a pack of rabid wolves than find himself in that situation again. He fervently hoped that one or both of them would refuse to come.

"Good night—drive safely!" Marie called from the front door. Robert waved as Aunt Sophie backed her black barge of a Cadillac out of the driveway later that night.

"Is that everyone?" he asked.

Marie nodded and closed the door. "As usual, Aunt Sophie was the last to leave."

With a sigh of relief, Robert ambled to the living room, picked a law journal out of a basket of magazines and settled in his leather recliner.

Marie sank into the chair beside his. "I'm so thrilled for Stevie!"

"Don't you think this engagement is awfully sudden?"

"Not really. Holt said they'd been e-mailing each other constantly for months. A couple can really get to know each other through letters. Remember?"

Robert remembered, all right. He'd originally met Marie as a young soldier stationed in Germany. Her church had sponsored a support-our-troops Christmas letter-writing campaign, and he'd received a note from her addressed to "Dear Soldier."

"If some other soldier had gotten my letter, we wouldn't be sitting here now, talking about our daughter's wedding," Marie said.

How many times over the years had he thanked his lucky stars for just that? But this whole conversation made him uncomfortable. If things started getting mushy, that would lead to the bedroom, and . . . Hell, the memory of his last few attempts at lovemaking filled him with shame. He nodded, then pulled on his reading glasses and opened the journal.

"Remember how things were between us when we finally met in person?"

"Sure." He didn't want to remember. If he opened the door just a little, the memories would started crashing down on him, like junk from an over-filled closet. Remembering how sweet things used to be made the present seem more bitter.

Silence fell between them. Robert flipped to an article about the latest legislative session, but he couldn't concentrate.

"Do you ever wish some other soldier had gotten my letter?" Marie asked softly.

"What?"

"If someone else had gotten it, chances are we'd never have met." Marie's voice cracked. "Do you ever wish that had happened?"

Robert lowered the magazine. "Holy mother, Marie, what kind of question is that?"

"A direct one."

He slammed the journal shut. "No it's not. It's some kind of damned trick disguised as a question. Whatever I say, it's not going to be the right thing."

"That's not true!"

"It is, too. You're trying to force me to say a bunch of stuff you want to hear."

Tears filled her eyes. She spoke in a small voice, barely above a whisper. "Would it kill you to say something I want to hear?"

No. But it might kill him. Because if he let go of his anger, if he showed some tenderness, she'd expect him to make love to her, and he couldn't—he *wouldn't*—put either one of them through another humiliation. "Why do I have to say it?" he growled. "You know I love you."

"No, I don't. Not anymore."

Oh, hell. Her eyes swam with tears—big fat ones just waiting to fall. He hated it when she got all emotional, hated that he made her so unhappy.

"Marie—I'm sorry. I just . . ." He halted, unable to continue.

"You just what?"

He blew out a sigh and stared down at his lap. "I don't know." It was a lie, but he couldn't bring himself to tell her the truth: *I'm a has-been, a failure, a washed-up old man. I was forced out of my job and I serve no useful purpose to anyone.*

"This whole thing with Stevie's wedding." Marie's lower lip trembled. "It has me thinking about us— about how we used to be. Remember?"

Of course he remembered. Try as he might, he couldn't forget. "Look, no offense, Marie, but I don't want to stroll down memory lane. I'm uncomfortable with all that sentimental garbage."

"Memories and feelings aren't garbage." Tears streaked down her face. "They're the tenderest part of a person. You're taking the tenderest part of me and stomping on it."

The words slashed like a razor. It didn't help to know that his pain was self-inflicted. "Marie—I'm sorry. I don't mean to."

She wiped her face with the back of her hand, her eyes soft. She always forgave him so readily—too readily. "We used to talk, to share things. You didn't even tell me Holt asked you for Stevie's hand."

"I tried to, but you had some damned rolls to see to."

"You could have followed me into the kitchen."

Was that how things were now? He was supposed to just follow her around like some kind of pathetic puppy? More and more, that was what he felt like he was doing.

Her lips curved in a soft smile. "We've had some good times in that kitchen. Remember?"

That was a low blow. How could he ever forget? Before they'd had the kids, they used to raid the refrigerator in the middle of the night, ravenous after a rowdy round of lovemaking. Halfway through feeding each other grapes or crackers or whatever they managed to find, though, they'd always ended up back in each other's arms.

The memories crashed down, flashing through his mind in vivid color, leaving holes in his heart as they landed. Oh, yeah, he remembered, all right—remembered the way Marie looked spread-eagled on the dining table, remembered taking her from behind by the stove. He remembered the time they'd tried it standing up against the refrigerator, and the time they'd made love with her perched on the counter, her legs so tight around him he could barely breathe.

He could barely breathe now, just thinking about it.

She somehow knew it. She rose from her chair and moved toward him, unfastening the top button of her dress, seducing him with her eyes. "We could go in the kitchen now and see what we can cook up," she said in a sultry purr.

He wanted to. Good God, he wanted to! But the thought of failure—another failure—was more than he could face. When had he become such a coward? He didn't know, but he couldn't risk Marie finding out.

"Hell, no, I don't want to go in the kitchen," he growled. "The kitchen's the whole problem. You spend so much time in there because of your damned business that you don't have time for anything else. You want to know why I don't tell you things? It's because you're never around. And on the rare occasions when you are, you're so preoccupied with rolls and party plans and baking schedules that you're as good as gone."

Hurt slapped across her face like a palm print. Her hand froze on the second button of her dress. Her fingers fanned out to cover her chest.

He felt like a runaway train racing down a steep embankment. He knew he was headed for disaster, but his brakes were gone, and the momentum of his emotions were about to propel him over the edge. He rose from the chair, flung down the law journal and headed to the door.

"Where are you going?" she asked.

"Out."

"When will you be back?"

"I don't know. But don't wait up." He grabbed his windbreaker from the coat rack and stormed out the door, hating the way he was hurting her, hating the man he had become, hating his inability to do anything about it.

Chapter Eighteen

Holt caught Stevie gazing down at the ring on her hand as he braked at a stoplight on the way home from her parents' house.

"Do you like it?" he asked.

"I love it!" Her face shone with such unabashed delight that it delighted him as well.

"But you shouldn't have," she said. "It must have cost you a fortune, and since we'll only be married for a little while. . . ."

"You wanted your folks to think this is the real deal. What kind of potential son-in-law would I look like if I didn't spring for a ring?"

"So you spent thousands of dollars to impress my folks?"

He lifted his shoulders. "Hey—you're taking a major step here. You're going to be my daughter's mother. And by marrying me, you're taking yourself off the market, so to speak, until the divorce is final, so . . . Hell—the least I could do was get you a ring."

He turned his attention back to the road, but he could feel the warmth of her gaze on his face. "That's very sweet of you," she said. "I'll give it back to you when we divorce."

"I won't take it. It's yours to keep."

"But—"

"I want you to have it," he said firmly. Hell, he was stealing all of her romantic dreams with this sham of a marriage. He couldn't give her a forever marriage, but he could darn sure give her a ring to keep.

"That's really nice of you." She smiled again. "My family thought you were nice, too."

He moved his foot off the brake and onto the accelerator as the light changed. "I'm not so sure about your father. For a moment there, I thought he wasn't only going to turn me down but charge me with some kind of crime."

"Why? What did he say?"

"It wasn't anything he said, exactly. It was more how he looked at me, as if he thought I might steal the family china. And your brother interrogated me like a murder suspect."

"You can't say I didn't warn you."

"I think they both suspect something." He turned the corner. "If you expect them to believe that we've known each other for a long time, I'm going to need to know a little more about you."

"Such as?"

"Well, your brother brought something up about not wanting to see you hurt again."

"Oh, boy." She turned her face to the window.

"So, who hurt you?"

"Which time?"

"You've been hurt more than once?"

She kept her face averted, but a sigh escaped her lips. "I don't have very good taste in men."

"Want to tell me about it?"

"No. But I guess I better, because it's likely my family will bring it up again."

This promised to be interesting. From the corner of his eye, he saw her twist the strap of her purse on her lap.

She drew a deep breath. "I didn't date while I was in high school or college, so I was pretty naïve about men when I met Joe."

Holt's eyebrows rose. "Why didn't you date?"

"No one asked me out."

"You're kidding." He slanted her a curious glance. "I would have thought guys would have been fighting to take you out."

She looked oddly embarrassed. "Not hardly."

"Why not?"

She kept her face turned away. "I had a weight problem," she finally said. "I used to weigh sixty pounds more than I do now. Until I lost weight, no guy would look at me twice."

Holt didn't know what to say. He tried to imagine her heavy and failed.

"When you're fat, people treat you like you're either invisible or an object of ridicule. I dealt with the pain by eating, which just made things worse."

Holt glanced over at her as he changed lanes.

"You might have noticed there are no pictures of me at my parents' house," she said.

"Now that you mention it—yeah."

"That's because I wouldn't let anyone take pictures of me. But when my brother got married seven years ago, a videographer and photographer took pictures of the whole thing. I was a bridesmaid, so of course I was in the photos, and, well . . . there I was, larger than life."

She gazed out the window. "I don't know what it is about photos. I guess it's because the evidence is so solid, so irrefutable. When I saw the pictures, I looked at myself and cried. I hated myself. And I realized that if I was ever going to have a life, I had to do something about my weight."

"So what did you do?"

"What I should have done years earlier. I joined a support group and started exercising and got on a diet—the kind where you just lose a pound or two a week, not the fast-fix type I'd always tried before. It took nearly nine months, but I finally lost the weight."

"Wow—that's a big accomplishment. You must have felt really good about it."

"It was weird. I was still the same person inside, but all of a sudden, people treated me differently. Especially men."

Holt looked at her as he braked for another light. Her mouth was tight, and her eyes looked sad and faraway.

"I fell hard for the first man I dated. His name was Joseph, and he really swept me off my feet. He was a real charmer—personable, handsome and successful." Stevie's purse strap was twisted into a coil. "He lived in Houston, so I only got to see him every other week or so when his job brought him to town. One weekend, I decided to surprise him by showing up in Houston." She bit her bottom lip. "I surprised him, all right. I also surprised the heck out of his wife."

"Oh, man!"

"Talk about feeling terrible . . . I would never, ever, not in a million years have dated a married man—especially not a married man with young children. So you can imagine how I felt as a woman came to the door holding a baby, with a two-year-old peeking out from around her legs."

Stevie's mouth curled into something too sad to be called a smile. "I didn't even get it at first. Like an idiot, I said, 'I must have the wrong house—I was looking for Joe Thornton's residence.' And she said I was at the right place, that she was Mrs. Thornton."

Holt gave a soft whistle. "What did you say?"

"I was dumbfounded. I mumbled something about having made a mistake, and I turned to leave. But the woman wanted to know who I was and why I was looking for Joe and how I knew him. Then Joe came out to see what was going on, and I started crying, and . . ." She blew out a sigh. "It was a mess. He was the one who lied, but I was the one who ended up feeling like the guilty party."

"Wow. You poor kid." Knowing how she felt about marriage, he imagined she took it hard.

"It was awful. His wife blamed me, and she went a little nuts. She started calling me in New Orleans in the middle of the night. At first she'd just hang up, but then she started saying things—calling me all kinds of names, saying I'd ruined her life, threatening to ruin my life, too." Stevie looked down at her fingers, which were now wrapped in purse strap. "I didn't know what to do, so I went to my brother. He had a friend with the Houston police department go by and tell her I was going to press charges for stalking and harassment, and that if she didn't want to be arrested, she'd better stop."

"Did she?"

"Yes." She gave a small smile. "Dan has been pretty protective of me ever since."

That explained why he'd gotten the third degree, Holt thought.

Stevie stared out the window for a moment. "I didn't feel much like dating for quite a while after that."

"I can imagine."

"And then a couple of years later, I met Pete. We dated for about six months, and I thought it was getting serious. He met my family, and my mother thought he was wonderful."

"What did he do?"

"He was the marketing director for a family-owned retail chain."

"So, what happened?"

"Well, he took me to a company Christmas party. And while I was in the ladies room, the wife of one of his coworkers came in with another woman. They didn't know I was in there, and they started talking about Pete—about what a hound dog he was and how he was sleeping with three other women while he was seeing me, and how sorry they felt because I didn't have a clue."

Holt glanced over at Stevie. She was staring straight ahead, her expression pained. Anger pulsed through him. Only cowards and low-lifes misled women into thinking they were the one-and-only when they weren't.

Stevie's mouth curved in a rueful grin. "They were right—I didn't have Clue One. Apparently I was the respectable girlfriend—the one he brought to business functions to impress his conservative boss, or took out when he needed a date who wouldn't alienate his friends' wives."

"Oh, man."

"When I confronted him, he didn't even try to deny it. He said he needed some excitement in his life and that I was nice, but . . ." Her voice trailed off.

"But what?"

She gazed out the window. When she spoke, her voice sounded flat and hurt. "He said nice wasn't very exciting."

Another flash of anger shot through Holt. "He was a fool. I think you're exciting as hell."

She looked at him, surprised. Their eyes met, and a current of heat raced between them.

She abruptly looked away.

"I was the one who was foolish. I was part of a freakin' *harem* and didn't have a clue."

"Give yourself a break. Everyone's made some bad choices."

"Everyone?" She lifted an eyebrow.

"Sure. Having a one-night stand with Ella obviously wasn't a stellar choice on my part."

He could feel her studying him. "Have you ever had your heart broken?" she asked.

He shook his head. "Not really."

"How do you manage?"

He shrugged. "Unlike your pal Pete, I tell women up front that I'm not looking for commitment. And I don't hang around that long."

"How long do you hang around?"

"I don't know. A few months."

"And that works?"

"Pretty much."

"So your basic philosophy is to just not let anyone close enough to hurt you?"

"That's about it."

"Wow. Sounds lonely."

"No lonelier than your approach. And not nearly as painful."

He had a point. She blew out a sigh. "Well, at least I've got hope."

"Of what?"

"Of eventually finding my soul mate."

He gave a derisive snort.

"You don't believe in soul mates?"

"I don't even know if I believe in souls."

"So, what *do* you believe in?"

He shrugged. "That what you see is what you get. That all we've got is the here and now."

"That's really sad."

"Life is really sad, when you get right down to it." He steered the car into the driveway and killed the engine. "That's why you should enjoy what you can, when you can." He twisted toward her, lifted a strand of her wheat-colored hair and twirled it around his finger. "I can think of one thing I really enjoy."

"What?"

"Kissing you." His eyes flashed in the dark. "And I think you enjoy it, too."

"You flatter yourself." The husky tone of her voice denied the flip reply.

His eyes glittered with a dangerous heat. "You didn't like it?"

"I—I was tipsy."

"You weren't tipsy when you kissed me tonight at dinner."

Her eyes slid to his lips. She moistened her own with the tip of her tongue, then realized that was exactly the wrong thing to do. "That was an act," she defended.

"Actors need practice. Maybe we should rehearse for our next performance."

He was going to kiss her—and she wanted him to. He'd just reiterated that he didn't believe in commitment, yet here she was, tilting her face up toward him, her pulse pounding hard, drifting toward him as if he exerted a gravitational pull. It was completely irrational. It went against all her rules. And yet in another second, she'd be beyond the stopping point.

It took every ounce of willpower, but she forced herself to pull back and open the car door. The overhead light flashed on. "We need to put Isabelle to bed."

She scurried out of the passenger seat, opened the back door of the car and unfastened Isabelle.

Good heavens—what on earth was she thinking? She hadn't been thinking; that was the problem. When she got close to Holt, her brain just seemed to short-circuit. She needed to keep her distance, both physically and emotionally.

But how was she going to keep her distance from a man she was about to marry?

Chapter Nineteen

"This is Parent Talk with Stevie Stedquest. You're on the air."

"Yes. I have a suggestion for that mother with the colicky baby," warbled an elderly female voice.

"Great," Stevie said into the microphone. "We always welcome input from experienced parents. What do you suggest?"

"That mother should hang the left foot of a frog over the baby crib."

"I beg your pardon?"

"Babies cry because they see stuff we can't see—evil fairies and gnomes with little wrinkled-up faces and such. That frog's foot will keep them away."

Just when she thought she'd heard everything, another caller proved her wrong. Stevie turned and shot the producer in the control room an accusing look. Hank lifted his arms in his classic I-didn't-know-she-was-a-nutcase gesture.

"That's a very interesting theory," Stevie said. "Thank you for calling."

She rapidly punched the disconnect button, then glanced at the clock. Eight minutes until her show was over. She wondered if Holt had managed to get Isabelle to take a bottle. She was eager to get home and see to the child.

And to see Holt.

Irritated at the direction of her thoughts, she punched the next red blinking light on her phone. "This is Parent Talk. You're on the air."

"Yeah—I called last week 'cause I thought you weren't tough enough in the discipline department."

It was the biter. Stevie's stomach tensed. Man, Hank was really having fun tonight. Sure enough, he was stroking his gray beard, trying to hide his amusement. "Yes, I remember," Stevie told the caller. "Do you have a question about parenting?"

"Not exactly. I was callin' because I talked to that friend I mentioned—his name is Gus—and he said he wants to meet you, never mind how bad you might look, if you're willin' to go dutch."

Through the glass, Stevie saw Hank double over in laughter. She looked away, trying hard not to laugh herself. "Gee, I'm flattered, but . . ." She drew in a deep breath. She might as well throw this out there. "The truth is, I'm engaged."

Hank's eyebrows rose on the other side of the window. "For real?" he mouthed.

Stevie lifted her hand and pointed to her engagement ring. The producer's eyes grew huge behind his round glasses.

"Why didn't you say so?" the caller asked.

"I don't like to talk about my personal life on the air."

"When ya gettin' hitched?"

"In a couple of weeks."

"Ya gonna try to have a baby right away?"

"Actually, I'll become a mother when I marry. My fiancé has a young child."

"Oh. Well, if don't work out, just say so. I'm sure Gus'll still be lookin', 'cause it ain't like the ladies are beatin' down his door."

By the time she wrapped the show and signed off the air, more than a dozen listeners had called to offer congratulations. Stevie was touched and surprised at how many people wished her well.

Hank opened the sound booth door as she pushed back from the console.

"I thought you're supposed to be screening the callers, not holding auditions for Comedy Central," Stevie said as she rose from her chair.

He lifted his shoulders and grinned. "Sometimes it's hard to weed 'em out."

"Oh, right."

"Just trying to keep things lively." He pushed his glasses up on his nose. "Are you really getting married?"

"Yes."

He gave a teasing smile. "You don't have to go and do that to keep your job, you know."

Stevie rolled her eyes. "I didn't think I did."

"So who's the lucky guy?"

"Holt Landen."

Hank's eyes widened. "*The* Holt Landen?"

"You know him?"

"Yeah. He was a guest on our midday show a couple of months ago, answering questions from people with small businesses. He's a real nice guy."

It seemed like everybody in New Orleans knew more about Holt that she did. "I'll tell him you said so."

"He's a business whiz—has all kinds of credentials. Must have oodles of money."

Stevie gave a wry grin. "Well, he's probably more solvent than Gus."

"He's generous with it, too. He's given seed money to several small business owners, and he runs a free seminar every year to help small businesses stay afloat. I was real impressed that a big shot like him takes time to help the little guy."

Stevie said her goodbyes and headed down the narrow hall, not sure if she were more pleased or disturbed to learn about Holt's altruism. The more she learned about Holt, the more he sounded like a man she could love. Under the circumstances, that made him a dangerous man to marry.

Chapter Twenty

"Oh, how gorgeous! Oh, my goodness!" Marie fluttered a hand in front of her eyes, as if she was trying to wave away the tears pooling there.

Stevie smoothed the beaded white satin of the strapless wedding gown and stared at herself in the bridal shop mirror. She'd selected the dress a week ago, when her mother had dragged her to a bridal salon the day after the engagement announcement. Since there wasn't time to order a dress, she'd chosen a floor sample.

When she'd first tried on the dress, it had hung like a bedsheet. It hadn't been flattering, but it was better than the puff-sleeved, Little Bo Peep dresses that had comprised the rest of the selection. The saleslady had insisted that alterations would transform the gown into the dress of her dreams. Stevie hadn't believed her, but the woman hadn't been exaggerating.

The dress poured over her body like water in a shower. She stared in the mirror, taking in the way the gown dipped low enough to show a hint of cleavage at the bodice, then followed the curve of her waist and the slope of her hips on its long, sexy slide to the floor. The woman in the mirror looked nothing like Stevie's mental image of herself. In her mind's eye, she was still pudgy and shapeless.

"It's perfect." Marie sighed. "It looks like it was custom-made for you."

"Is it too tight?" Stevie asked Michelle, whom she'd asked to be her matron of honor.

"No. It's stunning." Her friend slowly walked around Stevie, admiring her from all angles. "You look absolutely breathtaking."

From her seat in the stroller by the mirror, Isabelle cooed.

"See? Even Isabelle thinks you look gorgeous," Stevie's mother said.

"I believe the actual translation is 'Looky there! I'm gettin' one hot mama!' " Michelle teased.

Stevie laughed, then turned to her mother, who was pulling a tissue out of her purse. She frowned in concern. "Are you okay, Mom?"

"Yes. I just can't get over how beautiful you look. Holt's going to think he's the luckiest man on the planet." Her mother's eyes grew wistful. "That's what your father told me on our wedding day."

"Oh, that's so sweet," Michelle breathed.

Marie's eyes filled with tears, and for a moment she looked as if she was going to bawl. Stevie was relieved when she only drew a deep breath and glanced at her wristwatch. "Speaking of sweet, I have a dessert reception this evening for an oil company. I need to get going." She kissed Stevie on the cheek, hugged Michelle, and blew a kiss to Isabelle.

"Bye, Mom. Thanks for joining us," Stevie said as her mother headed for the door.

"Oh, I wouldn't have missed it."

"I'd hope not, considering I'm doing all this for your benefit," Stevie murmured.

Michelle gave her an affectionate smile. "It means a lot to your mom, giving you a nice wedding."

"I know, but it seems like a waste, going to all this trouble for a marriage that isn't going to last."

"You only get married for the first time once," Michelle said. "Might as well enjoy it."

"I don't want to enjoy it too much." Stevie pushed the stroller toward the changing room. "It's hard enough to separate reality from fantasy as it is."

"I imagine so. Holt is pretty much fantasy material."

"Not unless you fantasize about a no-strings-attached relationship."

"Maybe you can get him to change his mind about that."

"No chance." Stevie pushed the stroller through the narrow doorway into the spacious changing room. "We've already written up the papers for our divorce."

"When did you do that?"

"This morning, when we signed the prenup. The attorney is preparing the divorce papers and, as soon as my stepparent adoption goes through, he'll file them."

The whole thing had left Stevie depressed, despite learning that Holt was surprisingly wealthy and generous. The divorce would give her Holt's house, a large cash settlement, and an enormous amount of child support. She would be set for life, yet instead of feeling pleased, she just felt empty.

Michelle closed the door as she entered the room and regarded Stevie in the mirror, her dark eyes troubled. "Stevie, are you sure you want to do this? It's not too late to change your mind, you know."

"Why would I change my mind?"

"You're giving up an awful lot."

"But look at what I'm gaining." Her gaze fell on Isabelle, who was sucking on a pink and purple pacifier. Stevie smiled at the child, and the child smiled back, dropping her binkie in the process.

Stevie picked up the pacifier from the baby's blanket and handed it to back to the child. "Did you see that?" Stevie straightened. "Two weeks ago, this child would cry if anybody looked directly at her. She was ready to be admitted to the hospital to get a feeding tube. Now she's gaining weight and smiling and even wanting me to hold her!"

"There's no doubt this is good for Isabelle. I'm just concerned about what's good for *you*." Her friend sank down on the beige velvet bench, her eyes worried. "Are you sure you want to go through with a loveless marriage?"

"It won't be loveless. I love Isabelle, and she's starting to love me back."

Michelle unzipped the back of Stevie's gown. "You deserve to have all your dreams come true, Stevie."

"They are. I dreamed of finding true love." She smiled at Isabelle as she stepped out of the gown. "And I have."

Michelle carefully hung the gown on the white padded hanger. "I just don't want to see you hurt, that's all."

"I can't think of anything that would hurt worse than abandoning this baby." Stevie reached for her white tailored shirt. "Besides, if it weren't for Isabelle, I might have gone the artificial insemination route in a year or two, and this has lots of advantages over that. I'll have a parenting partner, and my child will have a father. Plus finances won't be an issue, so I can dedicate more time to my child."

Michelle was silent. A moment later she said, "Sounds like you know what you're doing."

"I do." At least when it came to Isabelle. She was less certain about things when it came Holt.

Michelle looked at her watch. "I've got to get back to the center."

Stevie grinned. "Yes, you should, now that you're running the place." Stevie had turned in her resignation as the center's director, and Michelle had taken over the job. Stevie still planned to teach a few classes and host the weekly radio program, but she wanted to free up her time to focus on Isabelle.

"Are you still set for your Day of Bridal Beauty on Thursday?"

Stevie grimaced. Her mother had given her a gift certificate for a pull-out-all-the-stops makeover at a local spa. A hair stylist was going to figure out the best way for her to wear her hair with her veil, and a makeup artist was going to do her makeup. As if that wasn't enough, a stylist from a local store was going to select several outfits for her to wear to the pre-wedding festivities.

Stevie's mother had ignored all her protests.

"You still dress as if you're overweight. You need to stop hiding your figure," Marie said. "Besides, every bride needs a trousseau."

"Mom, trousseaus went out with dowries."

"Well, call it what you like, but this coming week is one of the most important of your life, and you need to look your best. And you'll insult your father if you refuse."

Her mother really knew how to cinch a deal. The last thing Stevie wanted to do was hurt her father's feelings.

"Bridal beauty, here I come," Stevie glumly told Michelle. "I hope they don't make me look too bizarre, because I'm meeting Holt's mother right afterward."

"Are you nervous about meeting her?"

"Only because I'm afraid I'll say something that'll give away the fact that Holt and I haven't known each other that long." She stepped into her favorite pair of loose-fitting black slacks. "Mom talked to her on the phone and says she's great. The two of them really hit it off."

"What about Holt's father?"

"He's not coming in until Friday."

"What's he like?"

"Mom said he's very nice as well." Stevie pulled on her skirt. "Holt seems to have a different opinion."

"They don't get along?"

"They don't argue, but they're distant." Stevie slipped her feet into her shoes. "His parents apparently don't get along with each other. Holt says they can't stand to be in the same room, but they haven't seen each other in twelve years, so hopefully things will have mellowed by now."

"Ought to be interesting."

"That's for sure."

At ten minutes before four on Thursday afternoon, Holt found himself stuck in traffic on the Pontchartrain Expressway, sitting behind a gray minivan.

"Is traffic always this bad?" his mother asked.

Holt had taken off the afternoon to pick her up at the airport and introduce her to Stevie. "No. There must be a stalled car or an accident ahead."

"What time is Stevie meeting us?"

"At four-fifteen." The Windsor Court Hotel was famous for its afternoon high tea so, at Stevie's suggestion, they were meeting there.

"I can't wait to meet her. I hope I don't look too rumpled."

Holt glanced over. "You look great, as usual." Caroline Landen was the most rumple-free person he'd ever known. Her chin-length dark hair was cut in a stylish bob. Her skin was smooth and unlined, despite her fifty-six years, and her cream-colored designer pantsuit still looked spotless and fresh despite her four-hour flight from Los Angeles.

"I don't know whom I'm more anxious to meet—my grandbaby or the woman who's going to be my daughter-in-law," Caroline said.

"Well, you'll get quite different reactions from the

two of them. One will probably scream and cry when she meets you."

"I hope that won't be Stevie," Caroline said with a smile.

Holt edged his vehicle forward. "She's not the crying, screaming type."

"What type is she? I've been trying to picture what sort of woman you might eventually settle down with, and I'm coming up blank."

"You'll get to see for yourself in just a few minutes."

She cast him a fond smile. "I'm interested in your opinion, not mine. What is it you love about her?"

Love. The word jolted him. He was going to have to get used to hearing it over the course of the next few days, he thought. "Well, she has this dry, low-key sense of humor. And she has a way of putting me in my place."

Caroline's eyebrow quirked in amusement. "And you like that?"

Holt considered the question. "Oddly enough, I do."

"Hmm." She gave him a teasing smile. "I must not have disciplined you enough when you were little."

Holt grinned back. "Probably not." His mother had always been a soft touch.

"Tell me about her."

He stared out the windshield at the bumper of the minivan. "She's very down to earth and genuine. And she's generous. She focuses more on other people than herself."

"She sounds wonderful."

"Yeah. Yeah, I guess she is."

"You guess?" His mother's eyebrows lifted in a bemused expression.

Too late, he realized he should sound more definite about the woman he was about to marry. He adjusted his rearview mirror. "I mean, she is. She's terrific. And Isabelle adores her."

"I wish you'd called me when you first found out about the baby," Caroline chided. "I could have come and helped you."

"You didn't have time to do that."

"I would have made time." She fiddled with the gold and diamond bracelet on her arm. "I regret not doing that more when you were little. After the divorce, I was so busy trying to build a career, and then I met Gary, and . . ."

"Hey, no apologies needed. I turned out okay, didn't I?"

"You turned out wonderfully." His mother smiled, but her eyes were sad. "I'm afraid that's something I can't take credit for, though."

"You get a hell of a lot more credit than Dad," Holt said.

Caroline looked out the window. "I shouldn't have tried to turn you against him the way I did."

Holt looked at her in surprise. "I never thought you did that."

"I spoke badly about him to you, and I shouldn't have. I see that now. I see a lot now that I didn't when I was younger."

Holt's hands tightened on the steering wheel. He disliked this depth of conversation; he wanted to keep things light and surface level. He had no desire to dive into the murky waters of the past. "Hey—that's all over and done with, and everything turned out fine. Don't worry about it."

Caroline looked at him somberly. "I didn't give you much of an example of how to have a good marriage or be a good parent, but maybe I can help you avoid some of the mistakes I made."

Holt stared straight ahead at the unmoving brake lights of the minivan. He wasn't just trapped in traffic. He was trapped, period. "Mom, we don't need to go into all that."

"Like it or not, I'm going to give you a little motherly advice. I hope that in some small way it'll make up for some of my mistakes."

Oh man—he was in for it now.

She twisted to face him more fully. "First and foremost, you and Stevie need to put your marriage before everything else. No job, no possession, no accomplishment is worth a fraction of what your marriage is worth. Don't lose sight of that. Don't let the little daily stuff gnaw away at your love for each other. Don't forget how to laugh together, how to play together, how to talk together. And keep sex on the front burner."

Oh, jeez! Holt slunk down in his seat, willing the traffic to move. He couldn't wait to get to the hotel and out of this miserable conversation.

"I've been seeing a therapist, and she's helped me see a lot of things in a new way."

"A therapist?" Holt looked at her, alarmed. "Are you all right?"

"I'm fine. I just wasn't happy with the way my life was going—especially with my inability to form a successful relationship. She's helped me realize a lot of things. One of them is that your father wasn't entirely to blame. I felt angry and hurt and betrayed, and I drew away instead of being supportive when his business went under. He wasn't right, mind you, but . . . neither was I. I see that now." She gazed out the window as the traffic began to creep forward.

"Marriages don't fall apart overnight. Little things creep in, bit by bit. You don't make time to have any fun together. All you talk about are problems, and pretty soon you find yourself caught in a spiral of negative thinking. Little things, like how the other person squeezes the toothpaste, start to irritate you. You stop confiding in each other. You criticize each other, and it starts to feel like you're living with an enemy. And then, when something bad happens, you jump to conclusions and blame each other instead of supporting each other."

She looked at Holt. "Don't let it happen to you and Stevie."

Holt drove down the Tchoupitoulas Street exit, feeling as if a pile of concrete blocks were stacked on his chest. Here was his mother, pouring out her heart in hopes of helping him have a lasting marriage, and he'd already made plans for a divorce. The hypocrisy of it galled him, and yet he couldn't tell her the truth.

He'd promised Stevie he wouldn't. Besides, if his mother knew the truth, she'd be in the untenable position of having to pretend that the wedding was real in front of Stevie's parents.

He couldn't do that. All he could do was drive the car as fast as possible to the Windsor Court Hotel while his mother continued to spew embarrassingly intimate advice.

"Your father called me last week," she said abruptly.

Holt's stomach knotted. "He did?" Holt had talked to his father the day after the dinner with Stevie's parents. He'd sounded so surprised and delighted to hear from Holt that he'd felt guilty for not calling him more often. His father had been genuinely happy about the news.

Caroline nodded. "He phoned after he talked to you and Stevie's mom. He offered to not come to the wedding if it would make me feel more comfortable."

"You should have taken him up on the offer."

"I told him there was no need to do that, that we

should both be here." Caroline hesitated. "We talked for a long time."

"You did?"

She nodded again. "We had a lot to catch up on. I apologized for the way I behaved at your graduation." She twirled her bracelet again. "I want to apologize to you, too."

"There's no need."

"Yes, there is. I'm sorry for my whole attitude toward your father after the divorce." Her eyes clouded with tears. "And I'm sorry I didn't give you a better childhood."

Ah, hell. He didn't want to deal with all this heavy stuff. "I told you—there's nothing to apologize for."

"Well, maybe I can do a better job as a grandma than I did as a mother."

"All you have to do is be half as good, and Isabelle will be one lucky little girl."

Caroline was smiling when Holt finally steered his car behind the brick wall that shielded the exclusive hotel from the street. "Here we are," he said as he braked.

A burgundy-uniformed doorman opened his mother's door and collected her luggage from the trunk as Holt turned the keys over to the parking attendant.

"It's nearly time for Stevie to meet us," he said. "I'll wait for her down here while you get checked in and settled; then you can come join us."

"That sounds great."

A moment after his mother left the lobby for her room, a familiar figure came through the door, pushing a baby carriage. Holt did a double take. It looked like Stevie, but there were major differences. He didn't remember Stevie's hair being quite that blond, and he'd never seen it styled in such a sleek sweep to her shoulders. He'd never seen Stevie's eyes and lips accented with makeup like that before, either, and he'd darn sure never seen her wearing anything remotely as form-fitting as that black pantsuit.

Not until now.

Good heavens. He'd always thought she was pretty; now she'd kicked it up to drop-dead gorgeous.

Stevie saw Holt walking toward her in the lobby and was assaulted by the usual rush of physical attraction she felt for him, one so strong she could hardly think. His mother was probably watching, so he was no doubt going to greet her with a kiss. The thought made her knees turn to jelly.

"Wow—you look great." Holt's eyes swept over her as he drew her close.

He smelled of soap and shaving cream and cinnamon breath mints. He tasted of cinnamon as well. His mouth was hot and sweet, and his lips moved over hers in an intimate caress that made heat flood her body.

She'd been telling herself that kissing him couldn't be as earth-moving as she remembered, that surely she'd been imagining the way his touch affected her, but there was no imagining the way her heart was racing now.

He pulled back at the edge of decorum. It was a good thing, because Stevie's brain had nearly ceased to function. She took a self-protective step back.

"Your hair's different." He lifted a strand and sifted it through his fingers as her breath caught in her throat. His gaze moved down to the V-neck of the hot pink blouse under her fitted jacket. "And I love what you're wearing."

Stevie's hand fluttered to the neckline. "I'm not used to wearing clothes this tight."

"They don't look tight. They just don't look as if they're about to fall off you."

She arched an eyebrow. "As opposed to the way I usually look?"

"Oh, no—you're not going to get away with twisting a compliment into an insult. All I'm saying is, you look terrific."

To her dismay, she felt her face flush. "My mother insisted on buying me a trousseau."

Holt's eyebrow quirked. "Is that right? Well, I hope there are lots of sexy undergarments in it."

Stevie tilted up her chin. "If there are, you'll never know."

His eyes gleamed. "Won't I?"

"Most definitely not."

"Well, whatever you're wearing or not wearing under that suit, you look darn hot."

Which was how Stevie's face was feeling. "Shouldn't we go join your mother?"

"She's up in her room. She'll join us in a few minutes."

So the kiss had been for his benefit, not his mother's. She started to call him on it, but he'd turned his attention to Isabelle, who was watching from her stroller. "How are you today, baby? Did you go shopping with your mommy?"

Your mommy. The sweetness of the words brought a lump to Stevie's throat. *Isabelle's mommy.* It had to be one of the most beautiful titles in the world.

Stevie looked down to see Holt staring into the carriage.

"Hey—I'm making eye contact and she's not screaming," he whispered in a low, incredulous voice.

Sure enough, Isabelle was looking him straight in the eye.

"You're starting to grow on her," Stevie said.

He stood stock still, as if Isabelle were a bomb that

the slightest movement might set off. The baby stared straight at him and blew a bubble.

He grinned, and then it happened.

Isabelle smiled back.

Holt stood there, unable to breathe, as something fiery yet tender expanded in his chest. *His daughter was smiling at him!* The brightness of her smile shone right through him, lighting up corners of his heart he didn't even know existed.

Just as quickly as it appeared, the smile was gone. But it had happened.

"Did you see that?" he asked eagerly.

"I saw it," Stevie replied.

He'd been completely unprepared. Who would have guessed that a wet, gummy grin could make him feel like Lance Armstrong at the finish line or Arnold Schwarzenegger on election day? He'd had no idea that this perverse little creature who had so completely upended his life could so suddenly and unexpectedly bring him such gut-wrenching joy.

Hell, he hadn't even known this feeling was possible.

He wanted to shout. He wanted to pump his arm in the air and jump around. But most of all, he wanted to make her do it again. Unfortunately, Isabelle stuffed her fist in her mouth and turned away to study a bellman with a shiny brass cart.

"She'll do it again," Stevie told him softly. "You're going to get lots of smiles."

Holt looked at her, surprised. He hadn't said a word, and yet Stevie had known what he was thinking. "Are you psychic, or am I that transparent?"

"You're human," she replied, her eyes soft. "And your daughter just smiled at you for the first time."

It was disconcerting, the way Stevie could read

him—disconcerting, and alarming. He didn't let people get close enough to know him that well. At the same time, it was somehow strangely comforting. She made him feel less alone than he'd ever felt in his life.

"Amazing, isn't it?" she murmured. "It changes something inside you."

It had. He no longer felt like just a man with a baby.

He felt like a father.

His tie suddenly felt too tight. He adjusted the knot, uncomfortable with these new emotions, uneasy with the way Stevie saw right through him. It made him feel raw and exposed and vulnerable.

His throat felt swollen, and when he spoke, his voice came out low and gruff. "Come on. We'd better go get a table before they're all filled."

Chapter Twenty-one

"Here comes Mom."

Stevie had already guessed that the tall, elegant woman walking into the tea room five minutes later was Holt's mother. He had her dark hair, her patrician nose, her wide, engaging smile.

Holt rose to his feet. Stevie did the same. "Mom, this is Stevie. Stevie, this is my mother, Caroline."

"It's so nice to meet you," Stevie said.

"Likewise." Holt's mother stepped forward and gave her a hug. Her faint perfume was rich and exotic, a sophisticated scent that suited her well.

"There's someone else you need to meet," Holt said, sweeping his hand toward the stroller that was facing the table. "Mom, meet your granddaughter."

"I don't want to get too close and upset her," Caroline said worriedly, gingerly peeking inside, where Isabelle lay gumming a teething ring. Caroline drew in her breath. "Oh, she's beautiful—but so tiny!"

Holt nodded. "She's six months old, but she's only the size of a four-month-old baby. But she gained nearly a whole pound just last week." He reached out and took Stevie's hand. The warmth of his fingers spread up her arm. "Stevie is working miracles with her."

"And with you, too, apparently," Caroline said with a smile. "I never thought I'd see the day you decided to tie the knot."

A uniformed waiter wheeled over a tea cart, then set Wedgwood teacups in front of them, along with a three-tiered selection of scones, tea cakes, tiny sandwiches and cookies.

"So, Stevie," Caroline said after the tea was served. "I understand you met Holt online several months ago."

Stevie averted her eyes, searching for an answer that wasn't an outright lie. "Well, it's difficult to meet single people through my work."

Holt came to her rescue. "Stevie's a parenting expert."

"That's what you told me. How absolutely perfect!"

"That's what I think." Holt smiled at Stevie in a way that gave her goosebumps, even though she knew it was an act.

"Are you planning to continue working after the wedding?" Caroline asked.

"I won't be managing the parenting center anymore, but I'll still teach a few classes and do my radio show," Stevie answered. "I want to focus on Isabelle."

"From what Holt told me, that's exactly what she needs."

Isabelle kicked her legs and whined. Stevie pulled a

bottle from the diaper bag, then rose from her chair and picked up the child.

"This is huge progress," Holt told his mother as Stevie settled the baby on her lap and gave her the bottle. "A couple of weeks ago, she screamed bloody murder if anyone touched her."

"Oh, Holt—she's beautiful." Caroline stared at Isabelle, who greedily sucked on the bottle. "She looks so much like you did as a baby! She's thinner and has blond hair, of course, but I can see your mouth and your nose. . . ."

"And she has Holt's ears," Stevie added, softly stroking the baby's head.

Too late, she realized she'd unwittingly revealed a level of interest in Holt that she hadn't intended to reveal.

Holt cocked one eyebrow and shot her an amused grin. "I didn't know you'd been checking me out so closely."

"You'd be surprised at the details a woman notices on the man she loves," Caroline said.

Stevie felt a desperate need to change the subject. "Holt tells me you sell real estate to movie stars and millionaires," she said. "That must be fascinating."

"To tell you the truth, a lot of them are a pain in the neck," Caroline confided. "Sometimes I think I'd be happier in a different market."

Holt's cell phone rang. He pulled it off his belt and glanced at the number. "I'm sorry, but I need to take this. Excuse me." He rose and headed for the lobby, the phone to his ear.

Stevie gazed down at Isabelle, nervous at being alone with Holt's mother.

"It must have been quite a shock, having Isabelle drop into the picture out of the blue," Caroline said.

"You might say that," Stevie said cautiously.

"A lot of women would have turned and run if they learned that the man they were dating had an illegitimate baby—especially one he was responsible for raising."

"I love babies, so that wasn't an issue."

"Where will you two live?"

"At Holt's place. The lease was up at my apartment, so we've already moved my things into the attic."

Caroline nodded. "I've always loved that house, but I've got to admit, it stirs up some painful memories for me."

"It does?"

"Sure."

"Why?"

Caroline gazed at her, her delicate eyebrows high, her eyes round with surprise. "Holt didn't tell you?"

"Tell me what?"

"That's the house where he lived as a child, before his father and I divorced."

The news took Stevie aback. So did the fact that Caroline was looking at her oddly. Oh, dear—if Holt's mother figured out that she and Holt didn't know each other that well, this whole charade would crumble like a house of cards.

"I-I'm sure he mentioned it early on and it just didn't register," Stevie mumbled. "It's been so chaotic with the baby, and I've had so much on my mind. . . ."

Caroline smiled sympathetically. "I probably would have forgotten my own name if I was trying to care for a baby and plan a wedding at the same time."

She was buying the excuse—or at least pretending to. Stevie sighed with relief.

"He went to great pains to buy it," Caroline went on. "It wasn't for sale, and he offered the owners nearly twice the appraised value to convince them to sell it to him." She took a sip of tea, eyeing Stevie over the rim. Stevie busied herself adjusting the white pinafore of Isabelle's pink dress.

"He's a lot more sentimental than he likes to let on," Caroline said.

After sounding so clueless about the house, she'd better say something that proved she knew Holt. "Yes. His proposal was very sentimental."

"How did he propose?"

"He gave me a compass."

"Oh—you got the compass proposal!" Caroline put down her cup and clasped her hands. "Oh, that's so wonderful! I got the compass proposal, too. It . . ."

Her voice cracked, and her eyes unexpectedly filled with tears. "I'm sorry," she said at length, her voice choked. "I guess I'm pretty sentimental, too."

It wasn't nostalgia in her eyes, but sadness—a sadness so profound and deep that Stevie averted her eyes, because it seemed too private to witness.

"Holt always said he'd never marry," Caroline said at length. "I'm shocked that he is." She gave a tremulous smile. "Shocked and delighted."

Stevie smiled back.

"You're so different from the type of woman I've seen him with in the past."

"What type is that?"

"Women who have everything except a heart. It's almost as if he deliberately steered away from anyone he might form an emotional attachment to."

That certainly fit with Holt's method of avoiding heartache.

"The divorce between his father and me hit him hard," Caroline continued. "Has he told you about it?"

"A little. He doesn't like to talk about it."

"I'm not surprised. It was a rough time in his life."

"It must have been rough for you, too."

Caroline nodded, "Vince—Holt's father—was a build-ing contractor. We'd been happily married for years when he became distracted and quiet and withdrawn. I kept asking him if something was wrong, and he told me everything was fine, that he just had a lot of projects in the works and had a lot to do.

"Well, one day he came home in the middle of the af-ternoon and told me that his business had gone un-der—that the bank had repossessed all his heavy equipment. He also said he'd put a second mortgage on the house without my knowledge, but he hadn't been able to pay it for four months, and that we were going to lose our home. We were broke—flat-out busted. And I hadn't had a clue we were even in trouble."

"Oh, my goodness!"

"It was devastating. But the thing that upset me the most was the fact that he hadn't said a word about it to me. He'd been going through all this for months, and in-stead of reaching out for me, he shoved me away. I thought there was another woman in the picture." She rolled the edge of her napkin.

"He said he'd been protecting me." She gave a tight, mirthless smile. "I can see that now, but I couldn't see it at the time. I was angry and hurt. He'd been hiding so much of his life from me, he felt more like a stranger than my husband."

She blew out a sigh. "We argued, and I left. I took Holt and went home to my mother in Los Angeles. It was a bitter breakup. Vince thought I kicked him when he was down, that I left when the money ran out. I thought his behavior was irresponsible and untrustworthy, and I was convinced he was having an affair. And poor Holt. Holt was caught in the middle."

"Divorce is always hard on children," Stevie murmured.

Caroline sighed. "He took it hard. It didn't help that his father and I refused to speak to each other except to convey the curtest of messages. And then I remarried and divorced again, and Vince did the same. Then Vince remarried and divorced yet again. By the time Holt left for college, he'd been through four divorces."

No wonder Holt was so soured on marriage, Stevie thought—and no wonder he was so sensitive to the plight of people who lost their jobs. He equated his father's business failure with the failure of his parents' marriage.

She was still absorbing the information when Holt returned to the table.

"Sorry about the interruption," he said. He looked from Stevie to his mother, then back again. "What were you two talking about?"

"You, of course." Caroline shot Stevie a conspiratorial grin.

"All good, I hope," Holt said, shooting Stevie a quizzical look.

"How could it be anything else?" Stevie smiled at him. "I was just asking your mom what you were like as a little boy."

"And she told you I was wonderful, no doubt."

"He really was. He was always more mature than his years, always very responsible." Caroline's eyes filled with fondness as she looked at him. "Too responsible, probably. Sometimes it seemed like our roles were reversed, like he was taking care of me instead of the other way around."

"In what way?"

"He'd do household chores and have dinner waiting for me when I got home from work. And he used to listen to my problems, then try to find solutions to them."

Stevie shot him a teasing look. "It's good to know what kind of treatment I can expect. Especially that making dinner part."

"Mom forgot to tell you I only served Spaghetti-Os or frozen dinners."

"I'm sure you've added a few more dishes to your repertoire over the years."

"Yeah," Holt said dryly. "Take-out chicken and Chinese."

The conversation drifted to lighter topics, but the information about Holt's childhood weighed on Stevie's mind. No wonder he avoided commitment; every marriage he'd ever witnessed at close range had come to a painful end. No wonder he was determined not to let anyone get close; from what he'd seen, intimacy always ended with a broken heart.

And yet despite all his resistance, a part of him longed for those very things. Why else would he go to such lengths to buy his childhood home? Unable or unwilling to form a loving relationship, he'd turned to the only place where he'd ever felt fully loved.

He'd gone to great lengths to avoid letting anyone get close. But one female had sneaked under the wire—Isabelle. Whether he liked it or not, Holt had fallen in love with his daughter.

And whether she liked it or not, Stevie feared she was falling for Holt.

Chapter Twenty-two

"I'm going to drive Stevie and Isabelle home," Holt told his mother an hour later. "I'll be back at eight to take you to dinner."

"Aren't they going to join us?"

Stevie shook her head. "I want Isabelle settled in bed at her regular time tonight. Tomorrow is the rehearsal and the rehearsal dinner, so it's likely to be a late night. Then the day after is the big day."

"I understand." Caroline kissed her on the cheek. "It was wonderful meeting you. I can see why Holt fell in love with you."

A lump formed in Stevie's throat. "And I can see why he's such an exceptional man."

Five minutes later, Holt's BMW pulled into the hotel drive. Holt tipped the parking attendant as the doorman opened Stevie's door.

"Your mother is terrific," Stevie said.

"Yeah. She's a special lady."

"I'm anxious to meet your father, too."

Holt's mouth tightened as he steered the vehicle out onto the street. "I'm sure he'll charm you. He does that to everyone."

Stevie studied Holt's profile. "You sound as if that bothers you."

He lifted his shoulders. "I just hate the way he cons everyone into thinking he's such a great guy."

"Maybe he is. Maybe you should give him another chance and get to know him."

"He never showed much interest in getting to know me."

"Maybe he just didn't know how."

The stiff set of Holt's jaw told Stevie that Holt wasn't likely to change his mind on the matter. She decided to change the subject.

"You didn't tell me you grew up in your current house."

He shot her a wary look. "I didn't grow up there. I only lived there until my folks divorced."

"Still, you didn't tell me."

"It didn't come up."

"Well, it did with your mother, and I felt like an idiot."

Holt blew out a sigh. "I bought it because it's a good house in a good neighborhood, so don't go reading a bunch of psychological meaning into it. I had it completely remodeled, and it looks nothing like it did back then. And in case you've got any icky Freudian suspicions, the master bedroom is now downstairs and on the opposite side of the house from where it used it be."

"I wasn't going to psychoanalyze you."

"Good."

"But if I were, I'd start by pointing out that you sound mighty defensive."

"I do not."

"See there? That's a defensive statement."

"Oh, for Pete's sake . . ." He turned toward her, his eyes narrow.

She gave him a wide grin. "Relax. I'm teasing you."

He gave an uneasy smile, then drove in silence for a moment. "While we're on this topic, I might as well tell you that I'm buying the house across the street, too," he finally said.

Stevie's eyebrows rose in surprise. "The one with the big porch?"

Holt nodded.

"I didn't even know it was for sale."

"It wasn't. I made them an offer they couldn't refuse." He braked for a pedestrian. "We haven't really talked about living arrangements after the divorce, but I'd like to live right across the street. That way Isabelle can go back and forth whenever she wants."

"That sounds great." *Except for the fact that I'll have to watch a steady parade of women going and coming from your home.* The thought sent an unexpected zing of pain richocheting through her.

This is the deal you're signing up for, she scolded herself. *This relationship is not about you and Holt; it's about you and Isabelle, and you'd better not forget it.*

"Who lived in that house when you were a kid?"

"My friend Jimmy."

"Did you spend a lot of time there?"

"Yeah. We practically lived at each other's house, so I figured Isabelle could do the same." A wary look crossed his face, as if he didn't want her thinking he was sentimental or soft. "But the reason I selected it is because it's a good house."

Stevie pretended to believe him. "It looks it. The outside is gorgeous." She gazed at the statue of Robert E. Lee as Holt guided the car around Lee Circle. "If you want, I can move there and you can stay put."

"No. You're going to have primary custody, and I like the idea of Isabelle growing up there."

His mother was right; he was a lot more sentimental that he wanted anyone to know. "Are you going to have to do a lot of remodeling?"

Holt shook his head. "It was overhauled a couple of years ago. The owners knocked down some walls and opened up the floor plan, then put in new wiring and plumbing and central air. It's pretty much ready to go."

Stevie wondered if Holt planned to use the same decorator he'd used on his current place. After all, he'd be single again when he lived there. Maybe he'd want to rekindle an old romance.

Another little jolt of pain shot through her. *Stop that!* she silently ordered.

He pulled into the driveway and killed the engine. "I'll carry in Isabelle's stuff, then help you bathe her and tuck her in."

"Okay," Stevie said.

"Who knows? Maybe I'll even get a smile out of it."

"Well, you'll certainly get one from me."

His eyes gleamed as he gave her a wolfish grin. "In that case, maybe I ought to give *you* a bath and put *you* to bed."

Stevie's heart throbbed at the tone of his voice. "Sorry. I'm a self-bather and a solo tucker."

He stretched his hand along the back of the carseat and twirled a strand of her hair. "I'll have to work on changing your mind."

Stevie glanced back at Isabelle, whose face was scrunched in red concentration. She had to hand it to Isabelle—the kid had timing.

"Looks to me like the thing that needs changing is Isabelle's diaper," Stevie told Holt with an equally mischievous grin. "Why don't you start by working on that?"

Chapter Twenty-three

Holt squinted against the early afternoon sun as he strode along the levee behind the Aquarium of the Americas on Friday, looking for his father. When Vince Landen had called earlier in the day to say he'd arrived in town and wanted to get together, Holt had suggested they meet at the foot of Canal Street and stroll through the French Quarter. Holt figured that if they ran out of things to say, they could talk about the sights.

Holt spotted his father standing by the railing, gazing out at the Mississippi. He looked like a dapper tourist dressed in pressed khakis, a starched blue-striped sports shirt and brown loafers. His father's hair was grayer than when he'd last seen him, and he was thinner. It was odd to realize that he was taller than his dad. In his mind's eye, his father towered over him.

A maelstrom of emotions swirled in Holt's chest—resentment, anger, and a weird, deep yearning. He steeled himself against them. He no longer needed his father's approval or attention. He no longer needed him at all. He'd keep this meeting brief and light; then he'd be the one to walk away.

Vince turned and spotted him. His face was etched with deeper lines, but he still had the same bright smile. "Hello there, son!" He held out his arms.

Holt wasn't going to get suckered into any phony displays of affection. He held out his hand. "Hi, Dad."

Vince shook it, using his other extended hand to clap him on the back. "You're looking great, Holt."

"Thanks. Looks like you're staying in shape yourself."

"I do my best." He gestured toward the aquarium and the casino across the street. "This place has changed a lot since I lived here."

Holt nodded. "The riverfront has, but the Quarter's still the same. Feel like taking a walk?"

"Sure."

The two men fell into step along the red-brick walkway. "Your call came as quite a surprise," Vince said. "A double surprise. So you're a father, huh?"

"Yep."

"How's the baby doing?"

Holt had briefly explained about Isabelle's problems on the phone. "Better every day. Stevie's working wonders with her."

"Well, good. Good. So you're finally taking the plunge, huh?" Vince asked.

"Looks like it."

Vince gazed out at a tugboat pushing a fleet of barges downriver and gave a self-conscious smile. "Don't guess you'll be wanting any marital advice from me."

"You guessed right." The words were harsher than Holt intended. He modulated his tone. "Mom already gave me the talk on what not to do."

"She did?" Vince's eyebrows flew up.

"Yeah." Holt shot him a curious glance. "She says the two of you had a long talk."

"We did." Vince stepped aside to let a man and a woman with a stroller pass. "So, how does she look?"

"Mom? Great. Same as always."

"That's good. Good." Vince swallowed. Holt could feel him looking over, and sensed him screwing up his courage to say something. "Look, Holt—I know I haven't been the best father to you . . ."

That was putting it mildly.

"But I want you to know it wasn't because I didn't care. I did. I cared about you and your mother more than anything."

Yeah, right. Holt cringed inwardly. What was with all this? "We don't need to get into all that. The past is the past."

"No, it's not." Vince looked at him, his hazel eyes serious. "The past is what makes up the here and now. There are a few things in our history that I'd like to get out in the open."

Was it Wax Philosophical Week? Apparently weddings

and babies made people want to haul out their old baggage, dump the contents on the ground and sort through all their mistakes.

"First of all, I want you to know that you and your mother were my whole world," Vince said.

"Yeah? Well then, why did you run off with Susie the secretary?" The words flew out of Holt's mouth before he knew he was going to say them. He'd never directly confronted his father about this before, but it had eaten at him for years.

"I didn't."

"Oh, right." He should have known his father would deny it. His mother had said he'd denied it all these years.

"Ask your mother," Vince said. "She talked to Susie just a couple of months ago, and Susie confirmed it."

"How much did you pay her?" Holt asked.

Vince's mouth hung in a sad, resigned line. "It's time I told you my version of what happened between your mother and me. I can't make you believe or forgive me, but I wish you'd at least let me say my piece."

"Say away."

He stopped and leaned against the iron railing. Behind him, a freighter slowly chugged upriver. "When my business started failing, I kept it from your mother. I didn't want to worry her, and I thought I could turn things around. I didn't know it, but she thought I was having an affair because I was working such long hours. I wasn't. I swear I wasn't. I was too busy and too worried about losing my shirt to fool around, even if I'd been so inclined." His voice had a resigned, nothing-to-lose quality that made his story sound oddly truthful.

"When my business collapsed and your mother took you and high-tailed it to California, I had nothing to live for. I was so lonely and depressed I thought about ending it all. I literally had nothing but the clothes on my back—no car, no house, nothing in the bank. Susie took me in and let me sleep on her couch, and after a few weeks one thing led to another, and that's when it happened. After. Not before. I swear."

Holt looked at his father. For the first time, he entertained the possibility that his mother had been wrong about his father's affair. Was that what she'd been trying to tell him in the car?

"Look," Vince was saying, "I know I wasn't the world's best father, but I never stopped loving you. I just didn't know what to do. Your mom said it upset you to be shuffled around, and sure enough, you were always crying when you arrived for a visit and then again when you had to leave, and you looked so damned unhappy the whole time you were with me . . . Well, I realize now I should have tried harder. I should have fought for more time with you, but I didn't want to make your life any more difficult than I'd already made it. When your mom married Gary, she said the three of you were trying to become a family, so I decided to stay out of the picture so you could bond with your new stepdad."

His father had kept his distance so Holt could bond with that Gary wimp? "I never bonded with him. I never wanted to. You were my dad. I wanted *you,*" Holt said. "I thought you were too busy with your new wife's kids to have time for me."

Vince shook his head. "I wanted you to come live with me. But every time you came to visit, you acted so angry and resentful and withdrawn that I decided you were better off with your mom."

Was that true? He'd never thought of it from his father's perspective, never thought about how his father must have interpreted his attitude.

Oh, sheeze—he'd done the same thing to his father

that Isabelle was now doing to him. He'd pushed his dad away, even though he'd desperately needed him. He'd rejected him, because he was afraid of being rejected. He hadn't let him get close, because getting close might mean getting hurt.

"In any event," Vince continued, "I just want you to know that I love you and I'm proud of you. I'm proud of the man you've become. And I envy you the chance to marry a woman you love and raise your child with her." He looked Holt straight in the eye, his expression intent. "Don't make the mistakes I made. Be upfront with them. Let them know you love them. Be there for them."

Had Holt been wrong about his dad all these years? He had spent so much time and energy yearning for his father's attention and resenting the fact that he wasn't getting it, he didn't know what the truth was anymore.

Maybe it didn't matter. Maybe all that mattered was that his father was here now. Maybe Stevie was right; maybe he should give Vince another chance and get to know him. Maybe it was time to forgive and forget and make a fresh start.

Holt clamped a hand on his father's shoulder, touching him the way he'd longed for his father to touch him as a child. Vince looked over, surprised.

"Thanks for the advice, Dad," Holt said. "Why don't we go get a beer and catch up on each others' lives?"

Chapter Twenty-four

The sky was the deep purple blue of late twilight as the wedding rehearsal began in the Stedquest backyard Friday evening. Marie stood in the back of one of two white tents flapping on the large lawn—one for the wedding, the other for the reception that would, if the weather was good, also spill out onto the patio.

Due to the shortness of time, Marie had given in to Robert's urging and hired not only a wedding planner but another caterer. She was glad she had; if she was trying to cater the event herself, she'd be supervising the placement of the folding dance floor the workers were carrying into the reception tent instead of standing at the back of this one with the rest of the wedding party.

"When the quartet begins the wedding march, the groom and his best man should step out and wait by the altar," announced the wedding planner, a buxom redhead named Lois, whom Marie thought looked like a cross between Bette Midler and Ethel Merman.

From her vantage point at the back of the white wedding tent, Marie watched Holt and his best man step front and center. "He looks so handsome," she murmured to Caroline, who was standing beside her.

"He does, doesn't he?" Caroline agreed with a proud smile. "He looks just like his father."

"Flattery will get you everywhere." Vince grinned.

"The first person down the aisle will be the matron of honor," Lois announced. Stevie's friend Michelle walked down the aisle, holding an invisible bouquet of flowers.

"Next comes the flower girl."

Marie grinned as her four-year-old granddaughter, Madison, skipped down the aisle, gaily flinging invisible petals up into the air. The child wore a blue dress with a matching bow in her blond curls. Marie thought she looked like a mischievous angel.

"Walk, don't skip. And gently drop the petals, dear— don't throw them," Lois instructed.

"Like this?" the child asked. She dipped her hand into a make-believe basket, made a fist, then opened it.

"Yes. Very good. But walk, dear. Don't run, and don't skip."

Caroline laughed. "She's adorable. I always wished I'd had a sister for Holt."

"I never knew that," Holt's father said.

Marie looked curiously at the tall man with graying light-brown hair standing beside Caroline. She could see Holt in both his parents. He had his father's build and strong jaw, but his mother's eyes and coloring. They made a handsome couple.

Holt had said that they hadn't spoken in twelve years, but it was hard to believe. Instead of the awkward silence she'd been warned to expect, they'd arrived together and treated each other with surprising warmth. With more warmth than Robert treated her, Marie thought with a pang.

"The ring bearer is next." The wedding planner gave a nod to Madison's twin, Justin. The little boy solemnly marched down the aisle, his forehead furrowed in concentration as he balanced a plastic ring on a satin pillow.

"Very good—nice job! All right—time for the bride and father."

A knot formed in Marie's throat as Robert escorted Stevie down the aisle.

He looked so handsome in his dark suit—and Stevie

looked flat-out gorgeous in a champagne-colored dress.
Marie's chest churned with emotion. It seemed like just
yesterday when it had been her, walking down the aisle
to marry Robert, her heart so full of love and happiness
she thought it would burst.

Her eyes filled with tears.

"Here." Caroline handed her a tissue.

"Th-thanks."

"I always cry at weddings, so I came prepared," Caroline said.

Lois moved to the middle of the aisle. "When the music ends, the minister will begin the ceremony. When he says, 'Who gives this woman in marriage?' that's your cue, Mr. Stedquest."

Robert nodded.

"After you give away the bride, you'll go join your wife. Stevie will hand her bouquet to her maid of honor, then turn toward Holt. I'll let the minister explain what happens next."

Beside her, Caroline sniffed into a tissue. Vince awkwardly patted her back. Caroline looked up and smiled, and Vince's arm closed around her shoulders.

A pang shot through Marie. When this wedding was over tomorrow, she'd turn her attention to her own marriage. She missed the tenderness and warmth she and Robert used to share—missed it like a body part, like an arm or a leg. She had to get it back. She didn't know how she'd do it, but somehow, some way, she was going to rekindle her romance with her husband.

The rehearsal dinner was held in the Gold Room upstairs at Arnaud's Restaurant in the French Quarter. True to its name, the room was completely gilded—the walls, the drapes, even the mantels of the room's two fireplaces.

Both Holt's mother and father had wanted to host the dinner, but Holt had insisted on doing it himself. His instructions to the restaurant had been simple: Make it a memorable evening.

Apparently they'd succeeded, because Stevie's eyes widened when she first stepped into the room. "This is amazing," she murmured. She turned around slowly looking at the room as if she were Dorothy discovering Oz. "It's like stepping into a jewel box."

It was an apt description, Holt thought. A pianist softly played a baby grand in the corner, near a small dance floor. Four round tables were draped with gold lamé and topped with white linen and sparkling gold candles. Elegant arrangements of white roses and magnolias graced the tables and the fireplace mantels, where they were reflected in the gilt-framed mirrors. The room was dazzling.

But not as dazzling as Stevie. Holt glanced over at her now as she laughed at something his best man, Evan Hensley, was saying. She wore a champagne-colored silk dress that somehow wrapped and fastened at the side of her waist. It was cut low in front, revealing a mesmerizing glimpse of cleavage. Holt wondered what held the dress together and what she was wearing beneath it.

He longed to find out. That full-body kiss on the sofa had kicked his attraction to her into high gear. He couldn't get the taste of her lips, the smell of her skin, the feel of her body out of his mind. His attraction to her grew more intense with every passing day, and the fact that she'd started wearing clothes that showed off her curves only increased her appeal. This hands-off policy of hers was driving him crazy.

But that only applied when they were alone. In public, he was supposed to act like a doting fiancé.

He leaned over and kissed her softly on the side of her neck. She looked up, surprised, and when her eyes met his he felt a crackle of electricity.

The attraction was two-sided; there was no doubt about it. He smiled as two strawberry-colored blotches appeared on her cheeks.

"I wonder how Isabelle's doing," she said in a deliberate attempt to divert his attention.

"She's sound asleep," Holt replied. They'd brought the baby in her carriage and parked it in a quiet corner of the room. "If she weren't, we'd be hearing about it loud and clear." He nuzzled her neck again.

The blotches spread. She made another stab at distracting him.

"Your parents seem to be getting along great," she said.

Against his will, Holt's gaze shifted to the next table, where his mother was laughing at something his father said, her head thrown back, her hand on his arm. A strange tightness squeezed his stomach. "Yeah, they are."

"You don't seem very happy about it," Stevie observed.

"Why wouldn't I be?"

"Well, if a person had spent most of his childhood hoping his parents would get back together and they refused to even talk to each other, it might annoy him to see them getting along when it was too late to do him any good."

Holt picked up his steak knife and cut off a bite of Beef Wellington. "That would be pretty small-minded and selfish."

"It would be perfectly understandable."

How the heck could she see right into him like that? Holt stabbed the bite with his fork. "It's just weird, that's all. But it's a lot better than worrying that they're going to start throwing dishes at each other."

"It's hard to imagine they ever had such hard feelings."

Looking at them now, it was. "They evidently talked for a long time on the phone after your mother and I called," Holt said.

"They didn't stop talking to each other at the rehearsal, either."

It was true. But before Holt could respond, his best man clinked his spoon against his glass. A friend from college who was now a corporate attorney in Boston, Evan had a friendly, boyish face and a pretty wife who was seven months pregnant with the couple's third child. They'd both taken an immediate liking to Stevie when they'd met her at the rehearsal.

"I'd like to propose a toast," Evan said, lifting his glass.

Silence fell over the room as everyone stopped talking and lifted their glasses. "To Stevie—a remarkable lady who has succeeded at something many other women have attempted in vain. I've known Holt for years, but I didn't think he knew how to spell commitment, much less make one. After meeting Stevie, though, I can understand why he's decided to resign from confirmed bachelorhood. Holt, you've made a wise decision—and Stevie, you've won the heart of one heck of a great guy. I wish you both a lifetime of love and happiness."

Stevie smiled as crystal clinked all over the room, but inside her heart was aching. She hadn't won Holt's heart, he wasn't committed to her and he had no intention of giving up his bachelorhood. None of this was real.

The problem was, she'd begun to wish it was.

Which she couldn't allow herself to do. It was one thing to be attracted to Holt—after all, what red-blooded woman wouldn't be? It was entirely another to develop feelings for him. And she was beginning to develop a definite softness in the area of her chest whenever he was around.

The toasts went on for what seemed like forever. She was greatly relieved when they ended and the pianist resumed playing.

"Let's dance," Holt suggested.

"Oh . . . I-I don't . . ." Stevie's throat grew tight, and it was suddenly hard to breathe. "No."

He looked at her oddly. "Why not?"

"I imagine everyone's ready to leave."

"No, they're not. The musician will be here for another couple of hours, and I've ordered more champagne. Come on." He started to rise from his chair.

Tentacles of panic clutched her chest. Stevie tugged at his arm, urging him to stay seated. "No!" The word came out as a high squeak.

Holt's forehead knit in a confused frown. "Is something wrong?"

She swallowed hard. It was embarrassing, but she had to say it. "I kinda freak out when I have to dance," she finally managed.

He looked at her curiously. "Why?"

She stared at the candle, not wanting to meet his eye. "It's a long story—and I'd rather not go into it here."

He eyed her with concern. "I saw the workmen putting down a dance floor in the reception tent at your parents' place," he pointed out. "We'll be expected to dance tomorrow."

"I know. And I'm dreading it." It was a relief to get the words out. "I thought I'd be okay, but when it comes to getting up and actually dancing, I feel as if I can't breathe."

He reached for her hand. "If it upsets you, we don't ever have to dance. Not now, and not tomorrow. We'll just tell your parents, and . . ."

Stevie shook her head. "It's a big deal to my father."

She paused, her throat growing thick. "When I was a little girl, I used to dance with him by standing on top of his feet. He used to talk about how we'd dance at my wedding."

"Your folks don't know how you feel about dancing?"

She shook her head. "They know I don't much like it, but they don't know how it affects me."

He gazed at her for a long moment. "Are you ready to get out of here?"

Stevie nodded.

Holt rose from the table and spoke to the room. "Thank you all for coming and sharing this wonderful occasion with us. Stevie and I have to put Isabelle to bed, but we want to encourage the rest of you to stay and dance and enjoy some more champagne. We'll look forward to seeing all of you tomorrow at the wedding."

He looked over at Evan and his wife. "Would you two do me a big favor?"

"Sure."

"Go dance. I don't want the fun to end just because we're cutting out early, and hopefully you'll get the ball rolling."

"Sure thing."

Holt and Stevie said their good-byes and headed for the door, pushing the sleeping baby in her carriage.

Isabelle awoke as Stevie lifted her to put her in her car seat, then cried all of the way home.

"I hope she's not regressing," Holt worried.

"I think she's just tired," Stevie said. "I'll bet she falls right asleep after her bedtime bottle."

The child quieted as soon as Stevie lifted her from the car seat at the house. "Now she's crying for you to hold her, instead of crying for you not to," Holt remarked.

"Isn't that wonderful?" Stevie said.

"Yeah. Maybe one of these days she'll let someone else have a turn."

"She's warming to you, Holt. I'll bet you'll be holding her before the week is out."

It was funny, how much he wanted to. He'd never known he could care about anything so much so fast. He fixed a bottle while Stevie changed the child into a fresh diaper and pink pajamas, then carried it to the nursery. He watched Stevie settle Isabelle on her lap in the rocker. By the dim glow of the nightlight, he watched the baby gulp half the bottle as Stevie softly talked to her. The child's eyes grew heavy, then slowly closed entirely. Stevie eased the nipple from the baby's mouth, lifted her and placed her in the crib.

Holt reached down and caressed the child's blond curls. The only time he could touch his daughter without setting off a squall fest was when she was asleep. Her skin was smooth as satin, her hair like spun gold. She looked so tiny, so fragile, so delicate. His heart swelled with emotion as he tucked a white baby blanket over her.

Stevie clicked on the baby monitor on the dresser, then picked up the portable receiver and carried it with her as they left the room.

"She looks like a little doll," Holt said as they climbed down the stairs.

"Or an angel."

"Yeah. I look at her when she's asleep like that, and more than anything I want to do right by her."

"You will," Stevie said softly.

"Yeah, well, the only thing I've done right so far is convince you to become her mother."

Stevie grinned at him. "I hate to tell you this, but Isabelle is the one who did the convincing."

"So I'm still batting zero, huh?" He smiled at her. "Want to go sit on the deck? It's a beautiful night."

"Sure."

Holt opened the French doors to the backyard, and Stevie stepped through. The air smelled of olive blossoms, fragrant and sweet. He followed Stevie to the wooden bench swing that hung from the porch rafters. The chains squeaked as he sat down beside her and set the swing in motion.

"Tell me about this dance phobia of yours. Have you had it long?"

She'd known he was going to want to know more about it. She gazed out at the large live oak in his backyard and sighed. "Since high school."

"Did something happen to cause it?"

"Yes." Thinking about it made her stomach knot.

He waited for her to continue. He didn't press; he just waited.

Memories tumbled through her mind like clothes in a dryer, round and round, chasing each other. Before she knew it, the words came spilling out.

"I told you I used to be overweight," she finally said.

He nodded. "I find it hard to believe, but yeah, you told me."

"Well, believe it. I was a pudgy baby, and I just got heavier as I got older. I grew up being teased and taunted. I was shy to start with, but being overweight made me all the more timid. I didn't want people to look at me. I just wanted to be invisible." Her mouth curled in a mirthless smile. "As if a one-hundred-eighty-five-pound girl could be."

She glanced at him, half afraid the number was going to repel him, wondering why she'd told him. She'd always gone to great lengths to hide her actual weight, to keep anyone from knowing how high the scales had actually gone. Maybe she wanted to repel him. Maybe that was her only protection against the tender feelings budding in her heart.

She pushed the thought aside. "It's tough being a teenager under any circumstances, but it's really tough being a fat one. There's this unrealistic expectation that all girls are supposed to look like models and actresses. The farther away you are from that ideal, the bigger a loser you are. When you're *way* far away from it, like I was, you're a freak."

Holt's arm stretched across the swing, and his hand rested on her shoulder. "Kids can be cruel," he murmured.

No kidding. She remembered walking down the high school corridor, hunched over her books, trying not to look at anyone. She could still hear the whispered names: *Tubbo, Heifer, Rhino Butt. She could still feel the mortification of some hallway comedian calling, "Watch out—Shamu's gonna blow!"* And then there had been the humiliation of changing clothes in gym class, and trying to act like it didn't bother her that she was always picked last for teams.

She closed her eyes against the painful memories.

"My folks sent me to dance class in junior high, because they insisted that no one's education was complete without learning to dance. I told them it was a waste of time; no one ever invites fat girls to dances. And no one ever did."

Holt's hand tightened on her shoulder.

"The first time I went to a dance was a week before my high school graduation. My English teacher drafted me and some other geeky kids to help out with the refreshments at the senior dance." Her mouth twisted in an ironic smile. "She thought she was doing us a favor, giving us a way to go to the dance without dates."

Stevie glanced at Holt. His eyes warm, his expression intent. She gazed out at the night and let her memories take over.

"Toward the end of the evening, one of the most popular boys in school came up and asked me to dance. I couldn't believe he was asking me. I'd secretly had a crush on him for years." She could still remember the way she'd felt as he led her out on the dance floor—like Cinderella.

"The song that was playing was 'Stairway to Heaven.'" She gave a wry grin. "It should have been 'Express Elevator to Hell.' Instead of slow dancing, he started dancing all fast and goofy—holding me too tight, whipping around too fast. I could smell liquor on his breath."

She could smell it now, just thinking about it. "Everyone started laughing. That just egged him on. It took me a moment to realize what was happening—that he'd asked me to dance to make fun of me."

She closed her eyes for a long moment, opened them and continued. "I was mortified. Everyone else stopped dancing and watched, and the laughter just grew louder and louder. I tried to leave the dance floor, but two of his buddies got in the act, grabbing me as I tried to leave and spinning me around."

"Oh, man," Holt muttered.

"I didn't know what to do. I just kind of tensed up and froze. I was in high heels, which I wasn't used to, and then . . . I fell. My skirt flew up, and there I was, with my big old queen-sized butt exposed to the world, laying on the floor like a beached whale. Everyone just stood around, staring and laughing. The whole gym was shaking with laughter."

Holt muttered a dark oath.

"It turned out I'd sprained my ankle, but that didn't hurt nearly as much as being ridiculed did. I was completely humiliated. I refused to go back to school. I didn't even attend my graduation ceremony. I didn't want to limp across the stage on crutches and risk being laughed at again."

"And your parents didn't know?"

She shook her head. "They just knew I fell and twisted my ankle."

"Weren't there any chaperones at this dance?"

"Yes, but this happened when they were all out in the parking lot. They'd caught some kids selling booze out there."

"While the kids who'd drunk it were all unsupervised inside."

"Yeah, that's about the size of it."

He drew her close and lifted her hand. It wasn't a sexual gesture; it was comforting and touchingly human, and it warmed the cold, clammy feeling the memories left in her chest.

"Ever since then, the thought of dancing makes me feel all sick and queasy." She gazed out at the night. "It terrifies me."

"Because you're afraid you'll fall?"

"No. Yes. Heck, I don't know." She gave a small sheepish grin. "It's more about being afraid I'll look foolish, I guess—or that I'll *feel* foolish. The worst part about that whole thing was feeling like such a stupid idiot."

"Those boys were the idiots. You were the victim."

She shook her head. "I was the stupid one. How could I have believed that this guy—this popular, attractive guy who could dance with any girl he wanted—would really want to dance with me? That's what's so humiliating. The thought that I could be naïve enough to actually think that he found me . . . you know . . ."

Holt's chest was strangely tight. "Attractive?"

She nodded miserably.

An odd, defensive comment she'd made when he'd been trying to convince her to marry him popped into his mind: *Obviously you don't think I have what it takes to attract a man.*

He stopped the swing with his foot. "You don't still have those doubts, do you?"

She gave a shrug, avoiding his eyes. "I'm still the same person."

"No, you're not." He spoke with conviction. "You've grown way beyond that person. The Stevie Stedquest I know wouldn't stand for being treated that way—and you wouldn't let anyone else be treated that way, either."

She refused to meet his gaze, but she seemed to be listening.

"You said you were shy," he continued. "But look at you now. You talk on the radio in front of thousands of people, and you teach classrooms full of adults. You've conquered your shyness. And you've conquered your weight problem, too."

He tipped up her chin, forcing her to look him square in the eye. "Anyone who can do all that is not stupid. And as for desirability . . . jeez, Stevie, do you have any idea what you do to me?"

She gazed at him, her eyes a mix of yearning and wariness.

"I've wanted you from the first moment I saw you," he whispered.

The wariness won. She pulled away. "You wanted me to take care of Isabelle."

"That isn't all I want you for and you know it. We've already established that you're not stupid, Stevie." His hand feathered through her hair. "Those kisses we shared must have told you something. But if for some reason you didn't get the message, I'll be more than happy to show you again."

Stevie pulled away. "That's really not necessary."

"I think it is. Apparently, your memory needs refreshing." Holt's eyes slid to her lips. He was leaning down to claim them when she sprang off the swing, sending it into an off-kilter sway.

"My memory is just fine. Yours, however, could use some improvement. I distinctly recall you saying you wouldn't make any moves on me."

"Unless you ask me to," he added, rising from the swing.

"Which has not—and will not—happen."

"We'll see." He smiled. "Just the fact that we're having this conversation is promising."

She looked as if she was going to argue further, so he grabbed her hand. "Come on."

"Where?"

"To the living room." He opened the door and pulled her through it. "We need to practice for tomorrow."

"Practice . . . kissing?"

"A great idea. But I was talking about dancing."

"Oh."

He wasn't sure, but he thought she looked a tad disappointed. "So what are we going to dance to?" he asked as he closed the door.

"Well, when my mother asked me what was our song my mind went blank, so I just said the first thing that came to mind."

"And what was that?"

She shifted from foot to foot. "It was the song that had just played on the oldies station in the car."

Holt shot her a look that clearly said, Cut the stalling. "The name of the song, Stevie. Let's have it."

She looked at the floor. " 'Boogie Nights,' " she mumbled.

" 'Boogie Nights'?" He stared at her incredulously. "Our song is 'Boogie Nights'?"

"Well, since it's not a slow song, the band isn't going to play it first."

"So what are they going to play?"

" 'We've Only Just Begun.' "

Holt grimaced. "Great."

"I know, I know. I had the gag-me-with-a-spoon reaction, too."

"Who needs a spoon?"

"I don't guess you have that in your CD collection."

"I hate to admit it, but I'm afraid I do. Someone gave me a collection of the greatest hits of the sixties and seventies." He opened the armoire that held all his electronic equipment, rummaged through a stack of CDs and pulled one out. After reading the back case, he put it in the player and pushed some buttons. The familiar tune began to waft through the air. He held out his arms.

Stevie hesitated, her heart thumping.

"Come on," he coaxed. "It's just you and me. I'm not going to laugh, and I promise I won't let you fall."

"I know it's silly, but I'm scared."

"Nothing's going to hurt you," he said softly. His mouth quirked in a grin. "Well, there's the possibility the song might make your ears bleed, but aside from that, you're perfectly safe."

She smiled and crossed the room on legs that felt like rubber. He put one arm around her and took her hand with the other. "So far, so good," he murmured.

She smelled the starch of his shirt and the soft scent of shaving cream on his neck. He slowly began to move. The memory of that long ago dance rushed into her mind, making her stiffen.

He ran his hand gently down her back. "Focus on the here and now, okay? That's the game plan. The best way to drown out old memories and fears is to just be in the moment."

"How do I do that?"

"Focus on your sensory impressions—on the sounds and sights and feelings you're experiencing right now."

"I don't know if I'll be able to get past the sight of people standing around watching."

"Sure you will. You can close your eyes or look at me."

She hesitantly looked up into warm, dark eyes.

"Want me to show you how this works?"

"Sure."

"Okay. I'm going to describe my impressions." His hand slid slowly down her back, then back up. "I feel warm silk. It's soft and slinky sliding under my hand, and it's warmed by your body heat."

Her heart thudded hard. He nudged her thigh with his, and she stepped back as he stepped forward.

"I feel the pressure of your body against mine. I can feel your breasts against my chest, and it really turns me on."

His thighs nudged hers again. Stevie realized they were slowly moving across the floor. Stevie's heart rate ratcheted up to the speed of a sprinter nearing the finish line.

Tightening his arm around her, he dipped his head and inhaled. "I can smell your hair. It smells like a garden at night. It makes me think of those orgasmic shampoo commercials, only I'm the one who's excited."

A flush of heat spread through her body.

Holding her tight, he guided her in a turn. "There's something about the way your hair smells that shampoo can't account for, though—something faint and sexy, something I smell on your neck, too, along with your perfume." He lowered his head closer to her neck. "I love your perfume, but this other scent—man, it's driving me crazy. It's like catnip to a cat. It's human nip, I guess."

She heard him draw in a deep breath. "It's the sexiest thing I've ever smelled. I have to get real close to catch it, and then it makes me want to get even closer." He tightened his arm around her, resting his cheek against her hair.

"I can't see you very well right now because we're so close, but I know just how you look because I've been staring at you all night. You're gorgeous, and the amazing thing is that you don't seem to know it." He turned her around. "You remind me of a fruit salad."

Stevie's blood was pounding so hard that she could hardly think. Her mouth wobbled when she tried to grin. "Don't you mean fruitcake?"

"Fruit salad. You're too fresh and delicious to be fruitcake. Your hair is the color of the inside of a banana, and your skin is peaches and cream. Your lips look like you've been eating raspberries—I guess you're wearing lipstick, but it looks like a berry stain—and all night I've been wanting to kiss you, to see if you taste as sweet as you look."

Stevie swallowed.

"I'm going to kiss you tomorrow," he said. "At the end of the wedding ceremony, then again when this song ends—like it's doing now."

"The song's over?" Stevie said, even as the last notes died away.

Holt stopped moving and looked down at her, a small smile on his lips. "Yep. That was pretty painless, wasn't it?"

Painless wasn't the word Stevie would have chosen. Stimulating, hot, erotic, sensational—dozens of words came to mind, but none of them had anything to do with pain.

"It'll be just like that tomorrow," he promised. "We'll focus on sensations and you'll get through it just fine."

She might get through the dance, but how was she going to get through the rest of the marriage? She was falling for Holt.

She stepped out of his arms as a Bee Gees song started playing. "Thank you."

"Do you feel better about things?"

It depended on which things he was talking about. "I feel a lot better about the dance. You're very good at offering a distraction."

"You're mighty distracting yourself."

His voice was low and gravelly, and his eyes had a light that sent hot goose bumps chasing up her spine. For a moment, she thought he was going to kiss her, and then she remembered he'd promised not to unless she asked him to. An irrational wave of disappointment washed over her. She folded her arms protectively around herself. "Well, it's getting late."

"Yeah." He stepped forward and brushed her cheek with the backs of his fingers. "Thank you for doing this, Stevie. Isabelle is one lucky little girl, and I'm a lucky guy."

Stevie stepped back, unnerved by his nearness.

"I'd better let you get some beauty sleep. Not that you need it."

Stevie rolled her eyes. "You can stop with the phony compliments already. We're no longer dancing."

He looked at her, his gaze steamy. "They aren't phony, Stevie. I mean every word."

Chapter Twenty-five

The faint strains of a string quartet playing Beethoven wafted on the evening air as Robert waited with the wedding party behind a flower-covered lattice partition outside the white tent.

The wedding planner bustled around, arranging the coronet of flowers in Madison's hair and straightening the ribbon on the matron of honor's bouquet. Lois had a chest like a cartoon opera singer. She must wear some kind of industrial-strength, whale-bone–enforced undergarments to keep her ample assets from jiggling, Robert thought, because the only thing that moved above her waist was a lavender fabric flower flopping on her chest like a dead fish.

He'd always loved the way Marie's breasts moved when she did. He'd been gazing at them for thirty-seven years, and they hadn't lost their fascination for him.

He glanced over at her as she conferred with Lois.

Marie looked gorgeous in a deep pink dress with her hair all done up in a French twist. She still took his breath away. So many times through the years he'd wondered why such a lovely woman had consented to marry the likes of him. He still wondered.

Marie was probably beginning to wonder, too, he thought with a pang. He hadn't made love to her in weeks, and she'd always been a passionate woman. He hadn't intended to let this celibacy business go on this long; he'd thought time would allow the memory of his bedroom failures to fade and his confidence would return. But instead of time making it easier to get back in the saddle, it had made it more difficult. Now it had become this big, huge deal, and he felt more pressure than ever.

He hadn't compensated for his lack of amorous attention in other ways, either, he thought guiltily. If anything, his behavior toward her had only become more standoffish and curt than ever. He didn't understand himself. Why did he treat strangers with unfailing politeness, yet behave like a jackass with the woman he loved?

"It's ten minutes after," the wedding planner said, looking at her watch. "Do you think all the guests have arrived?"

"If Aunt Sophie is here, they probably have," Marie said. "She's always the last to show up for anything."

Robert stepped forward and peered into the tent, where two rows of people sat in white-draped folding chairs. His eyes lit on a blue hat sitting above blue-gray hair.

"I see her," Robert said to Marie as he stepped back. "She's with her gigolo."

The wedding planner blinked in shock. Robert glanced at Marie and grinned. She smiled back. For a moment it felt like old times, back when they shared lots of inside jokes.

God, he missed that sense of closeness and camaraderie and emotional intimacy. And as for physical intimacy—dear Lord, how he missed the feel of her body, the sweetness of being buried deep within her.

A surge of arousal pulsed through him at the thought. That was the confounding thing about this whole . . . disability. When he was in a situation where he couldn't do anything about it, he'd find himself completely capable.

"If you think everyone's here, then we're ready to seat the groom's parents," Lois said. "Do you know where they are?"

"In the house with Isabelle," Marie said.

"I'll go get them." The wedding planner bustled off.

Marie smiled up at him. "Caroline and Vince are completely smitten with their grandchild."

"And with each other, from the looks of things," Robert agreed.

Marie looked at him in surprise. "Do you think so?"

"Well, they're spending all their time together. More than we are."

A defensive look crossed Marie's face. "I'm sorry, but I've been really busy lately. Organizing a wedding in two weeks isn't easy."

Hell. Why did she take everything he said as a criticism? He bristled, then realized the person he was actually annoyed with was himself.

Damn it all—who could blame her? He hadn't exactly been Mr. Supportive lately. "I know, I know. And you've done a wonderful job. Everything looks really nice."

"Especially Stevie." Marie turned and gazed at the bride, who was laughing at something Michelle said. Her eyes grew warm and misty. "Doesn't she look beautiful?"

"Yes." *And so do you.* He knew he should say them, but the words stuck in his throat. Why did he choke on the tender phrase, when harsh phrases came out so easily? It was all so convoluted and wrong. He wanted to let her know how he felt, but he was afraid of where it might lead.

"Ready to go, Mom?"

Robert turned to see their son, who'd been pressed into usher duty. He looked so handsome and dashing in his black tuxedo. Marie always said Dan looked just like him. Had he ever been that good-looking? He sure wasn't now.

He looked from Dan to Stevie, who was so gorgeous in her white gown that it made his heart swell. He and Marie sure had some fine children—amazing children, bright and beautiful and successful. Marie deserved most of the credit. He knew he hadn't been around as much as he should have been. He should tell her that, let her know how he admired and appreciated her. So many things pressed on his heart. There were so many things he wanted to say to her, but the words all just balled up in his throat like paper towels in a clogged toilet.

"You're next," Lois said.

Marie looked at him.

Say something, he ordered himself. *Tell her how you feel.* He swallowed hard. "You look real nice."

You're pathetic, Stedquest, he thought, but Marie reached up and adjusted his white rose boutonniere, her touch soft, her eyes tender. "You look very handsome yourself."

"All right, Mrs. Stedquest," Lois said. "You're up."

Stevie's heart fluttered as she watched her mother disappear into the tent on the arm of her brother.

"As soon as she's seated, I'll signal the musicians," Lois said.

Stevie took her father's arm. He patted her hand. "You look gorgeous, sweetheart. Are you nervous?"

"A little."

His eyes grew somber. He leaned down close to her ear. "It's not too late to change your mind, you know."

The Babe Magnet 247

The remark took her aback. "Why would I want to do that?"

He lifted his tuxedo-clad shoulder. "You haven't known Holt all that long, and sometimes people regret making big decisions in a hurry. So if you have any doubts . . ."

"I don't." Not about Isabelle, at least. And that was what this whole thing was about. She wanted to adopt Isabelle, to become the child's legal mother. She looked her father directly in the eye, knowing he'd put more weight on that than on her words. "This is what I want to do."

"Okay. Just checking."

Stevie's heart filled with love for her father. Even after spending all this money and going to all this trouble, he was more than willing to let her back out. That's what love was, she thought—second chances. "I love you, Dad."

His eyes grew moist. "Love you too, pumpkin."

The strains of the wedding march filled the air. Lois signaled from the edge of the door. "We're ready for the matron of honor."

Michelle stepped up to the doorway, clutching a bouquet of gardenias and calla lilies against her rose-colored dress. Stevie gave her a thumbs-up. Michelle smiled and headed down the aisle.

"All right, flower girl," the planner said a moment later. "Are you all set?"

Stevie's four-year-old niece nodded, blond curls bouncing. She looked like an angel in a white gown tied with a wide rose sash. A very mischievous angel.

"Now remember—walk, don't skip," Lois reminded her. "And don't throw the petals. Drop them gently."

Beaming broadly, Madison grabbed a handful of flower petals and started down the aisle. Stevie heard a chorus of appreciative murmurs, followed by a titter of laughter.

Stevie grinned at her father. "I can't wait to see the video. I bet she's throwing them like confetti."

Her father smiled back. "I bet you're right."

"Ring bearer, are you ready?"

Justin nodded solemnly. He was dressed in a white suit with a bow tie, his blond hair carefully combed, and he approached his task with all the seriousness of a heart surgeon.

At last, it was Stevie's turn. "All right," Lois said. "Here we go."

Stevie and her father stepped into the doorway. Her first impression was of flowers and faces, all turned toward her. The heady scent of roses and gardenias filled her senses. The music swelled, and the crowd rose to their feet.

And then she saw Holt, standing at the flowered altar at the front, looking more handsome than any man had a right to. It seemed like a scene right out of one of the storybooks she read to Madison—a handsome prince, a fairy-tale setting, a beautiful gown. The whole thing seemed too wonderful to be real. She floated down the aisle and through the ceremony as if it were all a dream.

Until it was time to say the vows. And then, all of a sudden, the proceedings seemed very real.

"I, Stephanie Ann Stedquest, take you, Holt Everett Landen, to be my lawful husband, to have and to hold, to love and to cherish, for better or for worse, for richer or for poorer, until death do us part."

This wasn't just a step in an adoption process; this was the holy joining of her life with Holt's. She was making a sacred vow, and there was no way she could rationalize that fact away.

Before she could absorb it all, Holt had pledged the same to her. The minister smiled. "And now, by the power vested in me by the state of Louisiana, I pronounce you man and wife. You may kiss the bride."

She turned toward Holt. He put his hands on her upper arms and pulled her to him. *My husband*, she thought. *He's my husband.* And then his mouth was on hers, and she was back in fairyland. His lips were both soft and hard, tender and intoxicating, and she was floating again, lost in a wondrous, thrilling dream.

It ended all too soon, leaving her light-headed and dizzy. The next thing she knew, they were walking down the aisle and out of the tent, circling around to the back as the wedding planner had instructed.

Holt grinned at her as they waited for the guests to file out so they could go back inside for photos. "Well, we did it."

"Yes," she murmured.

But a question burned in her heart as his kiss still burned on her lips.

What, oh, what have we done?

The reception passed in a blur of greetings and toasts, with a sit-down dinner that Stevie barely touched. She did drink quite a bit of champagne, however—and she looked a little like she was feeling the effects when Holt took her hand and led her onto the dance floor for the first dance.

He smiled and took her in his arms as the quartet struck up the opening chords of the song they'd practiced.

"They're all staring at us," she whispered.

"Don't think about that. Look at me."

She stared up into his dark, warm eyes.

Holt gazed down into wide, frightened eyes. His heart

lurched. "Now think about the here and now, and tell me your sensory impressions. What are you feeling?"

"Terrified."

"No. I mean physically."

"I'm physically terrified."

He squeezed her fingers. "Do you feel my hand?"

"Yes."

"Describe how it feels."

She took a shaky breath. "Warm. Strong. Tight."

"Good. Very good. Can you feel any other part of me?"

"I-I feel your arm around me. And your chest against mine. It feels . . . nice."

"It feels nice from this side, too. Any other impressions?"

"Your tuxedo. It's smooth and warm."

"Warm seems to be a recurring theme," he said, moving her across the floor.

"I guess it is."

"What else do you feel?"

"Your thighs. They're kind of urging mine to move."

I can think of other things I'd love to urge your thighs to do, Holt thought. "Let's check out your other senses. What do you smell?"

"You."

"Uh-oh. Guess my twelve-hour deodorant gave out."

She grinned. "No. You smell like soap and starch. And I can smell your boutonniere."

"My boutonniere? I'm so embarrassed."

She laughed.

"You've got a great laugh."

"So do you."

"Yeah?"

"Yeah. It kind of rumbles against my ear."

"Are you sure that's not my stomach?"

"Pretty sure. And if I put my ear against your chest, I can hear your heart beat."

He wondered if she could hear it do a funny flip. He drew her closer.

She looked up at him. "I see a pair of very dark eyes. Dark and bright, with black lashes and black brows. I can see the shadow of your whiskers. And I see your mouth."

Holt swallowed. His breath seemed trapped in his lungs.

"I smell a hint of champagne on your breath," she whispered. "It's very, very sexy."

Good God almighty.

"Maybe I should check out your taste."

"Stevie—are you tipsy?"

"Maybe a bit. There were quite a few toasts." She snuggled closer, fitting her pelvis against him.

A rush of arousal pulsed through him. It was a good thing the song was ending, because he was about to make a sensory impression that would no doubt embarrass her to describe. "Stevie . . ."

"Yes?"

"The song's over."

She looked up and gave a dreamy grin. "Drat."

Chapter Twenty-six

"For a gal with a dancing phobia, you sure danced up a storm tonight," Holt said as he unlocked the door to their house late that night.

"I did, didn't I?" Stevie cradled the sleeping baby

against her chest, very pleased with herself. After the dance with Holt, she'd danced with her father, then Holt's father, then the best man, all the ushers and most of her uncles. It was only when the orchestra started packing up their instruments that she'd left the dance floor.

"I think I'm over it."

"I think you are, too." He opened the door and held it.

Stevie looked at him. "I owe you one. Thank you."

"Hey, the pleasure was all mine."

No, it wasn't, Stevie thought. Not all of it. She carried the baby inside, then paused at the bottom of the stairs. "I'm afraid I'll trip on my gown if I don't hold it up."

Holt's mouth curved in a sexy grin. "You could take it off and carry Isabelle in your skivvies."

"I have a better idea. You can carry her."

She could see trepidation on his face. The baby had not yet let him hold her without protesting.

"She's asleep," Stevie said, with more sureness than she felt. "It'll be fine."

She carefully handed the baby to Holt. He gingerly cradled Isabelle in his arms. The exhausted child lay there, eyes closed, breathing deep and rhythmic.

"Well, what do you know?" Holt said. He gazed down at Isabelle as if he were holding a little miracle.

Tenderness flooded Stevie. Lifting the skirt of her gown, she followed him as he slowly carried Isabelle up the stairs and into the nursery, moving with a degree of caution that would have been amusing if it wasn't so touching.

Stevie watched him gently lay the child on the changing table. He gazed at Stevie with an expression that said, "Can you believe it?" and "I did it!" and "Isn't she something?" all at the same time.

Emotions, tender and green, sprouted in her heart. "Want me to take over?" she whispered.

He shook his head. "I'm on a roll, so I might as well go for broke. Besides, you're still in your wedding gown. You can go change into something more comfortable while I put her in her jammies."

"This is actually very comfortable." The truth was, Stevie didn't want to leave the room. The sight of Holt with his child was too touching, too moving, too special. She held her breath, praying that Isabelle wouldn't awaken and scream and ruin the moment.

There was another reason she didn't want to change. If she took off the dress, the magical evening would end, and she wanted to prolong it as long as she could.

Isabelle barely protested as Holt changed her diaper then dressed her in a yellow sleeper. Her eyes closed again nearly as soon as he lowered her into her crib.

He stood by the edge of the crib, gazing down. Stevie stood beside him, as the baby's breathing resumed the deep, slow rhythm of sleep. "That's the first time I've held her and changed her that she hasn't screamed," he said.

"I know. That's wonderful."

"Yeah."

Stevie's heart warmed as she watched him gaze down at his child. "She's attaching to you."

"Do you think?"

"Most definitely." *And Isabelle's not the only one.* His arm brushed hers, and her blood seemed to heat and speed up. She must be still a little tipsy from the champagne, she thought. It was a dangerous combination—champagne and these tender, hothouse feelings.

She backed toward the door.

"Well, it's late. I guess I should go to bed."

"But it's our wedding night."

There it was again—that delicious hot shiver.

"Besides, there's something we forgot to do," Holt said.

"There is?"

Holt nodded and put his hand on the small of her back, guiding her down the hall.

"What is it?"

"Come outside and I'll show you."

She looked at him quizzically but followed him down the stairs and out to the porch. The air outside was cool, the quiet punctuated by the occasional chirp of a cricket. "So what is it?"

"This." He abruptly scooped her up in his arms, one arm under her knees, the other around her back.

Stevie gasped, her blood racing, and wrapped one arm around his neck for balance.

"I need to carry you across the threshold." And he did just that, closing the door behind them with his foot as soon as he'd carried her inside.

He inundated her senses. His clean-shaven beard rasped against her face. His starched shirt rubbed her bare shoulder. She inhaled his clean, masculine scent, and felt his hair brush her arm as she clung to his neck. It was an altogether intoxicating sensation, being carried by a man. It made her feel petite and feminine.

Holt made her feel petite and feminine. And attractive. And desirable.

Especially when he looked at her the way he was looking at her now. Her pulse pounded in her ears so loudly she was certain he must hear it, too. He carried her to the sofa. She thought he was going to put her down, but he didn't. Instead, he rolled her toward his chest and held her tighter. Tighter and closer, with his face mere inches from her own. It was her move to make, and she made it.

Before she knew what she was doing, she leaned forward and placed her lips on his.

It started out soft, then flared into a wildfire—hot and hungry and all-consuming. She parted her lips, and his tongue plundered her mouth. Stevie's brain fogged over like a mirror in a steamy bathroom.

He lowered her feet to the floor, but only to align their bodies more fully. His arms pulled her tight against him, flattening her breasts against his chest. His arousal pressed against her. She stood on tiptoe, angling her aching center against it.

"Good God, Stevie," he moaned.

His passion fueled her own. Liquid heat burned low in her belly, setting her on fire, eradicating everything except the blistering, demanding need. His hands roamed up the sides of her dress, stroking the sides of her breasts, running his thumbs across the tips. The dress she hadn't wanted to take off was now an encumbrance she couldn't wait to shed. She reached for the hidden side zipper under her arm. He found it for her, pulled it down, then slowly eased off the gown.

The air was cool on her belly as the dress fell to the floor, leaving her in a strapless bra, lacy white panties and thigh-high stockings. She felt his gaze roam over her, and for a split second, the fog of desire parted enough for self-consciousness to seep in. She started to pull back, but he wouldn't let her. "You're beautiful," he murmured. His hands moved up her hips, over her waist, up to her breasts. His mouth dipped to the swell of her breasts above the lace of her bra. "So beautiful."

His lips moved to her neck, then her ear. His hands moved down, and his fingers toyed with the elastic of her panties. "There's another threshold I want to carry you over," he whispered.

Her mind seemed disembodied, her ability to think clouded by the thick smoke of desire. "Where?"

"My bedroom."

"Take me there," she whispered against the side of his mouth.

He scooped her up again and carried her down the hall to his bedroom. He set her on the navy-and-tan comforter of his king-sized bed, then knelt over her, his eyes glittering in the dim light filtering through the door.

She reached up and undid the silver studs of his shirt. He yanked it off and tossed it aside, then leaned back over her. The sight of his naked chest—of his muscled pecs, his hard stomach, the feathering of masculine hair on his chest that narrowed like an erotic arrow to disappear in his waistband—made her breath hitch in her throat.

His biceps swelled with the weight of his body as leaned over her. "My turn," he whispered, reaching behind her to unfasten her bra. He eased it off, revealing her breasts' rigid pink tips. "Beautiful. Stevie, you're so beautiful."

His touch made her quiver. And then his mouth was moving—down her neck, across her chest. He took a pebbled nipple in his mouth and sucked, sending a flash of heat straight to her core, as if a hot wire connected the two erogenous zones. He treated her other breast to the same pleasures as her fingers splayed across his back and into his hair. She sucked in a sharp breath as his mouth slid down, kissing the underside of her breasts, then slowly blazed a hot trail down her belly. He tugged at the edge of her panties with his teeth while his fingers executed exquisite torture on her inner thighs, moving with excruciating slowness toward the ache that longed to be stroked and filled.

She was dying with need when he finally pulled off her panties. His hot breath on her most secret parts made her moan.

"I want you in me," she murmured.

"Not yet." And then his mouth settled on her, setting

off a round of sensation so amazing, so dazzling, so intense that the pleasure almost hurt.

Stevie's world narrowed to a laser focus—just this moment, just this man, just this feeling—and then, without warning, exploded into a million shards of pleasure.

When she drifted back to earth, he was hovering over her. She pulled him down, wanting to give him all that he'd just given her, wanting to feel his weight on top of her, his length within her.

He groaned with pleasure as he slowly filled her. "Sweet," he whispered. "You feel so sweet."

She clutched at his back, pulling him closer, urging him on. To her amazement, it was happening again—the pleasure flooding and rising and cresting again, overflowing in a hot, rushing torrent. It was deeper this time—deeper and fuller and more profound, because this time, she took him with her.

Chapter Twenty-seven

It was nearly two in the morning before Aunt Sophie and her elderly beau finally left the Stedquest home. Marie closed the front door behind her and returned to the living room, where she collapsed on the beige chenille sofa beside Robert. "They say it's the sign of a good party when the guests don't want to leave," she said.

"It was definitely a good party."

"And the ceremony was lovely, don't you think?" Marie said.

Robert nodded. "It was altogether the finest wedding I've ever seen. Excepting ours, of course."

Marie smiled, her heart full and happy. It had been a wonderful day. And one of the most wonderful aspects was that Robert had been more jovial and outgoing and affectionate than he'd been in weeks—almost like his old self. Maybe things were getting back on track.

"Wasn't Stevie gorgeous? And didn't Holt look dashing?"

Robert nodded. "They make a handsome couple."

"You looked dashing, too. There's something sexy about a man in a tuxedo."

Robert gave her the teasing grin she'd missed the last few months. "I'll have to watch you around waiters, then."

She laughed. "You're the only man who has that effect on me." She scooted closer to him and rested her hand on his chest. "I find you incredibly sexy, Robert, whatever you're wearing—or not wearing." She tugged at his bow tie and smiled suggestively. "At the moment, I'd prefer you to be wearing a whole lot less."

She felt him stiffen, felt his shoulders tense. Even his voice grew tight. "It's awfully late."

She reached around him and began rubbing his shoulders. "I've done some reading about ED, and . . ."

"Who the hell is ED?"

"It stands for erectile dysfunction. It's very common as men grow older, and . . ."

Robert jumped off the sofa as if it were electrified. "For God's sake, Marie—I don't have any kind of dysfunction."

"Something's wrong, Robert. You never want to make love anymore."

"I might, if I didn't feel so pressured."

"You feel pressured?"

"Damn right." His voice held a hard edge. "You're pressuring me right now."

Her stomach clenched. "I don't mean to."

"Well, that's what you're doing."

Her eyes filled with tears. "Robert, honey, this is *our* problem. I'm affected, too. This is something we need to solve together. I've been doing some research, and there are medicines. If you'd just go see a doctor . . ."

"I don't want to go see any damn doctors. And I damn sure don't want to have to live up to your expectation that just because it's a special event, I've got to perform like a trained monkey."

Hot tears coursed down her face. "I just want to be close to you. Lovemaking doesn't have to involve intercourse."

"Oh, right," he ground out. "Like dinner doesn't have to involve food."

"There are other things we can do, other ways to be intimate."

"I don't believe in starting a job I can't finish."

"Robert, if you'd just see a doctor, I'm sure . . ."

But he was storming out of the room, pulling off his bow tie as he went. "I don't need a doctor. I need you to back off and leave me alone." He stalked into his office and closed the door.

Marie leaned against it and closed her eyes, despair and anger raging in her chest. He was too proud to seek help. Too proud, and too stubborn. Apparently he would rather let thirty-seven years of love wither away than admit he had a problem.

Which was a problem in and of itself. Ever since his retirement, he'd been like a different man—moody, morose, short-tempered and critical.

She suspected he regretted retiring. Whenever anyone asked how he liked it, he said it was great, but his behavior said otherwise. This other Robert—this dark Robert—had emerged about the time he'd announced he was throwing in the towel.

Maybe quitting work had left him depressed. From what she'd read, ED could be caused by depression. But Robert would no more talk to a doctor about depression than he would talk to a doctor about his sex life.

And he was too proud to call his old office and say he'd changed his mind, that he didn't want to retire after all. Once he made a decision, he didn't back down from it.

But if he was invited to come back, that would be a different story.

Marie abruptly straightened. Excitement pulsed through her veins. That was it! If his old boss knew that Robert missed working, Marie was certain he'd ask Robert to come back. That would solve everything. And Robert need never know she was behind it.

This was it. She'd found the solution.

Chapter Twenty-eight

Stevie awoke the next morning with a throbbing headache. Over the sound of her blood pulsing in her ears, she heard Isabelle crying in the distance and wondered why the baby sounded so far away; she could usually hear Isabelle clearly since she slept right next to the nursery.

Blurry-headed and disoriented, she opened her eyes, only to become further confused by the glare of sunshine in her face. She closed her eyes against the painful brightness, wondering where the light was coming from. Her bedroom didn't have a window facing east.

But Holt's did.

Her eyes flew open, confirming her worst fear. Oh, dear Lord—she was in Holt's room. In Holt's bed.

Naked.

The events of the night before came flooding back. "Oh, me. Oh, my. Oh, dear. Oh, *damn*," she muttered, abruptly sitting up.

The sudden movement made her stomach queasy. What, oh what, had she done?

Well, for starters, she'd apparently drunk too much champagne. And then she'd let Holt carry her across the threshold.

Two thresholds. And several more, if she counted the metaphorical kind.

And oh, dear heavens—it had been exquisite. That was the terrible part. It had been the most amazing, moving, magnificent night of her life. Holt had aroused feelings in her that she'd never thought actually existed.

And not just physically. Emotionally. He'd stirred feelings that were deep and dangerous, feelings that were perilously close to all-consuming love.

A fresh bout of queasiness struck. *Dear Lord—she was in love with him.*

No. She couldn't be. She wouldn't be. She wasn't going to love another man who didn't love her back—especially not a man she'd have to see on a regular basis for the rest of her life. Throwing off the covers, she climbed out of bed, just as Holt appeared in the doorway.

Stevie dove back under the covers and pulled the sheet up to her chin.

Holt leaned in the doorway, wearing jeans and nothing else, looking like he belonged on a hunks of New Orleans calendar. He gave her a sexy smile. "Good morning."

From what Stevie could see, there was nothing good

about it. She gripped the sheet as if it were a life raft. "Morning."

"No need to be so bashful." Holt's mouth curved in a wolfish grin. "You sure weren't last night."

Oh, dear! She had to set things straight, but her throbbing head made it hard to think. "About last night . . ." she began. But he was looking at her with so much heat in his eyes that her limited ability to form a coherent thought vaporized entirely.

"It was terrific," he said. "*You* were terrific."

She swallowed hard, her mouth suddenly dry.

"I was just closing the door so you could get some sleep," he said. "I know you didn't get much last night."

"I heard Isabelle . . ."

"I got up with her. I couldn't get her to take a bottle, but I changed her and put her in her swing. She's happy for the time being." He grinned. "Why don't you try to get some extra shut-eye? You'll want to be rested for Isabelle's naptime." With a wink, he closed the door.

He thought they were lovers. He thought what happened last night was going to happen during Isabelle's naptime, then again tonight, then tomorrow night and the next night and the next and so on.

Until they divorced.

The thought brought a lump to her throat. Then it would all be over, and Holt would start dating other people. He'd do all the incredible, amazing, intimate things he'd done with her last night with someone new.

And Stevie would be living across the street, watching other women leave his house in the morning, all bed-rumpled and smiling.

The pounding in her head sounded like sonic booms. She threw back the covers and headed for the bathroom, tears coursing down her face.

Yesterday had been a fantasy—a wonderful fantasy, but completely unreal. She and Holt might have said wedding vows, but this wasn't a real marriage, regardless of what she'd allowed herself to believe last night. This was an arrangement, a step in the custody process and nothing more.

She opened his medicine cabinet, found a bottle of ibuprofen and swallowed two pills. Then she turned on the shower and stepped inside, letting the steaming water pour over her throbbing head. The heat felt good, and as her headache eased, her thinking cleared.

There was nothing she could do about last night. It was over and done. But there was something she could do about the future. She could prevent this from happening again.

Isabelle yowled and squirmed on Holt's lap as he tried to give her a bottle. "Come on, sweetheart. You know you're hungry." Holt tried to slide the nipple into her mouth, but the baby just averted her head and screamed.

He was relieved to see Stevie walk into the kitchen, wearing his white terry-cloth robe. Her hair was wet and her face freshly scrubbed. She looked beautiful.

"Are you giving your daddy a hard time?" Stevie asked.

"Yes, she is."

The baby stopped howling and looked at Stevie, then held out her arms.

"Man, do I ever feel rejected," Holt said.

Stevie took the child, then sat at the breakfast table. Holt handed her the bottle, and Stevie expertly guided it to the baby's mouth. Isabelle latched on and sucked as if she was starving.

That's the same bottle I was trying to give you, Izzy girl," Holt chided.

Stevie gave him a sympathetic smile. "Give it a little more time. In another week or so, she'll be begging you to pick her up."

He shot her a rakish grin. "Kind of like you?"

"Holt . . ." Stevie drew a deep breath and looked back down at Isabelle. "Last night was a mistake."

Holt's stomach tightened. "You seemed to like it just fine."

"That's the problem."

"You would prefer not to like it?"

She kept her gaze on Isabelle, her cheeks flaming. "What I'm trying to say is . . . I can't separate my heart from my body. I can't handle casual sex."

"It's hardly casual. We're married." He gave his most winsome grin.

"We went through a wedding ceremony. That's not the same as being married."

"It is in the eyes of the law."

"Not in my heart. Holt, I don't want to get hurt." Her voice was somber, and when she looked back up from Isabelle, her eyes were, too. "I can't have sex with you and not get emotionally involved."

Hell. The last thing he wanted to do was to hurt her. He had no intention of permanently settling down, and she was looking for a lifelong commitment. He'd known that going in.

What he hadn't known was how strong his attraction to her would be. Last night had been the most amazing sex of his life, bar none.

"We're going to be in each other's lives from here on out," she continued. "Let's not do anything that will make it awkward or difficult to be around each other."

"What if I find it difficult to be around you and not touch you?"

She gave a small smile. "That's one you'll have to deal with on your own."

"So from here on out, we're just going to act like buddies and pretend last night never happened?"

She nodded. "We just forget about it."

Holt shrugged. "There's no way I'm going to forget how gorgeous you look naked." *Not to mention how your legs feel wrapped around me, or how your breasts feel in my hands, or that soft sound you make, or how you arch your back when you come.*

Her face flushed furiously. "Apparently you've got me confused with someone else."

"Correct me if I'm wrong, but I believe you were the only woman in my bed last night."

"Yeah, well, I'm far from gorgeous."

"I think you are."

She gave a derisive snort.

"You don't believe me?"

"Look, I worked hard to get to a healthy weight, and I work hard to stay there, but I don't kid myself. I don't have a body like your interior designer friend or the other women you're used to. And I don't like hearing a bunch of glib stuff you're used to telling those other women."

Those cretins in high school had really worked a number on her. She had no idea what she really looked like. "That's not what I'm doing."

"Well, it doesn't matter, because you're never going to see me that way again."

"I'm never going to see you as gorgeous?"

"No. Naked."

It turned him on, just hearing her say the word. She

must have realized it, because she abruptly set about readjusting the feet on Isabelle's pajama bottoms as if it was a matter of urgent importance.

"I don't want to talk about this anymore. I want to forget about it and focus on Isabelle."

Holt rose from the table. "We'll do this your way, Stevie. But if you think I'm going to forget any part of last night, you're sadly mistaken."

Chapter Twenty-nine

"Marie, it's so nice to see you!" Larry Martin rose from his leather chair as Marie entered his office at City Hall, his ruddy face creased in a smile. The pudgy, middle-aged prosecutor circled his large glass-covered desk and kissed her on the cheek. "You look wonderful. This new catering business of yours is apparently agreeing with you."

"Yes, I'm enjoying it," she said.

"Robert said it was taking off like a rocket. He's very proud of you."

The remark took Marie by surprise. "Really?"

"Yes, indeed."

"When did you talk to him last?'

"Not since his retirement party, I'm ashamed to say. I've been meaning to call him, but things have been awfully busy around here." He gestured toward a chair across from his desk.

Marie sat down, adjusting the skirt of her gray suit. Larry sat down in the one next to her. "How's he enjoying retirement?"

"Actually, that's what I came to see you about." She

tightened her fingers around her gray leather clutch. "He misses work."

Larry's eyebrows flew up.

"He doesn't say so, but he's been out of sorts and unhappy ever since he quit."

"I'm sorry to hear that," Larry said somberly.

"I think he made the decision too rashly. He hadn't even talked about it; he just came home one day and announced that he was ready to retire. I know that last case he worked on completely frustrated him, and I think he was just temporarily burned out. So I was wondering . . ." Marie leaned forward. "Would you ask Robert to come back—at least on a part-time basis?"

"Marie . . ."

Something in Larry's face alarmed her. She leaned forward. "I know it's not my place to do this, but you know Robert. He's very stubborn, and once he makes up his mind about something, he doesn't like to back down. On his own, he'd never admit he made the wrong decision, but if he were to get a phone call . . . Well, I'm sure he would jump at the chance."

"I'm sorry, Marie, but . . ." He cleared his throat and adjusted his tie, looking very ill at ease. "I'm afraid I can't do that."

"Oh, I figured his job had been filled—I didn't mean on a permanent basis. I meant as a consulting attorney. I know you sometimes hire them to help out on the big cases, and with Robert's expertise, he'd be perfect for that."

Larry steepled his fingers. "This is very awkward, Marie."

A cold chill seized her chest. Marie sat perfectly still.

He tapped his fingertips together. "There's something about Robert's retirement that apparently you don't know."

The chill in her chest turned to ice. "What?"

Larry exhaled a long breath. "He didn't just decide to retire. He was *asked* to."

Marie furrowed her brow. "I-I don't understand."

"That last case he was on—it involved the mistress of a very high-ranking government official."

Marie nodded. "He told me." That was back when Robert used to talk to her, when she felt like a real part of his life. A twinge of longing shot through her. "That was the insurance fraud case."

Larry nodded. "The woman was just a bit player, and everyone advised Robert to go easy on her, to go after the big fish and leave her out of it, but he didn't want to cut her any slack just because of who she was sleeping with."

That was just like Robert, Marie thought fondly. She'd always been proud of how he treated everyone the same. He didn't believe that wealth or privilege or connections made anybody above the law.

"In the middle of the preliminary hearing, some papers mysteriously surfaced that made it look as if Robert had deliberately falsified evidence."

The hair rose on the back of Marie's neck. "He would never do that!"

"I know. Everyone in the office knew it, too. But the defendant's friend was very powerful and well connected, and it looked convincing. We're sure those papers were planted, but we'd never be able to prove it."

"Oh, dear Lord," Marie whispered.

"The charges were dropped, and all the defendants walked. Off the record, the judge said he believed Robert was innocent, but under the circumstances, he was going to have to report it unless we took appropriate action."

Marie's fingers clenched around her purse so tightly

that her nails left dents in the leather. "Appropriate action. Meaning what?"

"Terminating Robert."

"No!" Marie's head reeled. "You just said the judge thought Robert was innocent!"

Larry blew out a harsh breath and slowly nodded. "I know. But the judge had no choice. Technically, he's supposed to report any suspected misconduct, which would have put our whole office under investigation. It would have been a nightmare. And there's a strong possibility Robert could have been indicted."

"Oh, dear God." Marie's voice came out a whispered croak.

"Robert was given the option of retiring, and he took it. At least that way he was able to preserve his reputation and his retirement benefits."

Shock, confusion and disbelief tumbled through her mind. "I-I had no idea."

"I'm sorry, Marie. I thought you knew."

She shook her head. It seemed like a bad dream. "I don't understand why he didn't tell me. Why would he keep something like this from me?"

Larry lifted his shoulders, his expression embarrassed. "This was a very bitter pill for him to swallow. Maybe he just didn't know how to break it to you."

"But I'm his wife!"

He gazed down at his desk and picked up a glass paperweight. "I don't have the answer to that."

No wonder Robert had been depressed since he'd retired. It hadn't been his decision at all. Why had he put so much energy into making her think that it was?

Larry regarded her with empathetic eyes. "I know it's small comfort, but Robert took the fall for all of us. If he'd opted for an investigation, the press would have had a field day. It would have made the whole department look bad. Once there's a hint of corruption, the stink clings to everyone."

Marie's mind swam. How humiliating it must have been for Robert. He'd spent his whole life fighting crime, only to be forced out of his job because he was accused of it himself. What a nightmare this must have been for him!

And he hadn't said a word—not a single word. He'd borne this on his shoulders all alone. He'd shut her out.

"Does everyone here know?"

Larry's chair squeaked as he shifted. "We tried to keep it as quiet as possible, but you know how people talk. Something like this spreads pretty fast."

So everyone knew. Everyone but her. All the people at his retirement party, all the people who'd made speeches and toasts—they'd all had information Robert hadn't told his own wife. She'd thought the staff had seemed a little overly emotional, but she'd chalked it up to the fact that he was well liked and they hated to see him go.

She felt so foolish. Foolish, embarrassed and hurt.

"We're all in his corner," Larry said. "We all know he's a straight arrow—as straight as they come. He's held in very high regard here."

She had to get out before her emotions exploded. Scooting to the edge of her chair, she nodded numbly. "Thank you for telling me. I know it couldn't have been easy."

"Can I get you a cup of coffee or anything?" Larry's expression was kind—so kind she almost crumpled. She rose to her feet.

"No. I need to be going. I'm meeting a friend for lunch." It happened to be the truth; she was supposed to meet Caroline in twenty minutes. If she hadn't had plans, though, she would have made some up. Anything to get out of there.

Larry looked troubled. "I'm sorry, Marie. I hate it that things worked out this way."

She didn't trust herself to speak.

"I'll give Robert a call soon and see if he wants to get together for lunch."

"I'm sure he'd like that." She headed for the door. "Thanks again. And give my regards to Brenda."

"Will do. We'll have to see about the four of us getting together for a night out."

It would never happen, but Marie went along with a polite chuckle. "That sounds lovely."

She made it out of the office in a daze, forcing a smile and waving to people she knew, walking swiftly so she wouldn't have to stop and talk to anyone. She endured the ride in a crowded elevator by silently repeating the Lord's Prayer, then managed to make it out of the building and to the sidewalk before the tears began coursing down her cheeks.

The maître d' led Marie into the Garden Room at Commander's Palace, where Caroline was already seated and sipping an iced tea. The attractive brunette smiled and rose as Marie approached. As usual, Caroline looked elegant in a navy-trimmed pink suit that clung to her slim figure. She enveloped Marie in a perfume-scented hug. "It's so nice to see you."

"Sorry I'm late."

"I just got here myself."

Marie could feel Caroline watching her as she sat down in the chair the maître d' pulled out for her. When he left the table, the woman leaned forward, her forehead creased in concern. "Are you all right? You look a little pale."

To Marie's dismay, fresh tears pooled in her eyes.

"What's the matter?"

"It's Robert." Marie wiped at her cheek with her napkin. "He's been depressed since he retired, and I thought that if I went to his old office and told them he missed work, they'd ask him to come back part-time or as a consultant. But instead I found out . . ."

Fresh tears forced her to draw a deep breath. "I found out that he didn't retire because he wanted to—he was forced out over an incident that wasn't his fault."

"Oh, Marie; I'm so sorry."

Marie dabbed at her check with a napkin. "He didn't tell me, Caroline. He pretended he wanted to retire and acted like it was all his idea. And all the while, everyone in his office knew the truth. I went to his retirement party and everyone knew except me, and . . ." She wiped her cheeks again. "He shut me out. He's been so distant since he retired and I don't understand why."

Compassion shone in Caroline's eyes. "My guess is, he's ashamed."

"But I'm his wife!"

"That might have made you the hardest person for him to tell."

Marie's brow creased. "It should have made me the easiest. I'm the one closest to him. Or, at least, I thought I was."

"Your opinion matters more to him than anyone else's. He doesn't want you to think less of him."

Marie gazed at Caroline. Her voice had the ring of truth. "That's what happened with Vince and me."

"Really?"

Caroline nodded. "He lost his business. And not just his business, but everything we owned—our savings, our home, even the college fund we'd put aside for Holt's education. He'd sunk all of it into trying to save his company, and it went belly up. I didn't find out until everything was being repossessed."

"Oh, Caroline!"

"I felt shocked and hurt and angry, but most of all, I felt *betrayed*. If he'd only told me what was going on, we could have worked it out together. If he'd just talked to me instead of taking desperate measures to fix and hide it from me, I wouldn't have been so hurt."

"I feel the same way," Marie said.

"What I didn't understand was that Vince's whole identity—his ego, his sense of self-worth, his self-confidence—was tied up in his work. I didn't see that; I only saw that he'd gone behind my back and put up all our assets as collateral. I didn't look at what had driven him to do it."

"And what was that?"

"When his business started sliding, he felt like a failure. He needed one place where he didn't feel like a screw-up—one place where he felt admired and loved, because he darn sure didn't admire or love himself." Her voice lowered. "He was afraid that if I knew, I'd leave him."

Caroline's eyes grew moist and her voice thickened. "The awful thing is, I did. But not because of the business failure and our financial loss—I could have dealt with that. It was the breach of trust. And just like you said happened with Robert, the secret had driven a wedge between us before I even found out. I knew something was wrong, but he insisted everything was fine."

"That's exactly what Robert's doing!"

"Vince was working long, long hours, and he was never home. Sometimes he'd get phone calls at home that he didn't want me to hear—I'd walk into a room and he'd stop talking. I thought it was another woman. Then I found out about the business and that we were losing our home. We had a big blow-up. I took Holt and went to my parents' place in California." She fingered the stem of her water glass. "I thought he'd come after me and beg me to come back, but he didn't. He thought I'd kicked him when he was down, walking out on him like that. And then his former secretary stepped in to console him—she'd had a crush on him for years—and then there really *was* another woman. Of course, I was convinced that he'd been having an affair with her all along."

"Was he?"

"No. But I believed that until she called me a few months ago. She'd joined a twelve-step program, and apparently one of the steps is making amends to everyone she'd harmed. She wanted to apologize for any role she played in the end of my marriage. She said Vince had been completely faithful to me until I left him. She even admitted that she'd done her best to seduce him, that she'd been in love with him for years, but that he was completely true to me."

"Oh, Caroline! You and Vince have talked about this?"

Caroline nodded. "When Vince called me about the wedding, it was my turn to make amends." She placed her hand on Marie's. "Don't let the same thing happen to you and Robert. Don't be angry that he didn't tell you. Believe it or not, it's a sign of how deeply he cares for you."

"What do I do now? He'll be furious if I tell him I went to his office and tried to get his job back."

"Maybe you can find a way of getting him to open up to you, to tell you himself."

"How do I do that?"

"I don't know. But if you put your mind to it, I'm sure you'll think of something."

She had to, Marie thought. She had no choice. If she wanted to save her marriage, she had to find a way to make Robert tell her the truth.

Chapter Thirty

Holt walked into his kitchen the following Thursday to find Stevie testing the temperature of a spoonful of baby cereal on the inside of her wrist. He stopped in the doorway and watched.

"Guess what, sweetie," he heard her say. "I've got a special treat for you."

Man, I wish you were talking to me. Living with Stevie without sex was driving him crazy. Everything she did reminded him of that amazing night of passion.

It wasn't that she was deliberately provocative. Right now, for example, she was wearing a fuzzy blue robe that looked more like it had come from the Disney Store than Victoria's Secret. There was nothing sexy about it, except for the fact that he knew what was underneath—long, smooth legs, lush, curved hips, pink-tipped breasts and a soft thatch of hair that he'd like to disappear into like the Bermuda Triangle.

The robe covered every inch from her chin to her ankles, yet the minute he walked into a room, she'd adjust the neck and tighten the robe to make sure he didn't glimpse anything—which had the perverse effect of making him want to glimpse something all the more.

"Are you ready to try something new, sweetie?" she asked.

You bet. How about doing it on the kitchen table?

"Do you want to sit on my lap, or in your chair?" she asked.

"The lap sounds great, but it'd work a whole lot better if you sat in mine."

Her head jerked around as he stepped into the kitchen. Her face flushed. "G-good morning." Sure enough, she reached for the neck of that blasted robe and tugged it tighter. "I didn't see you standing there."

"I just walked in," he lied. He strolled toward Isabelle, who was laying under a baby gym in the breakfast room, batting at a dangling Cookie Monster. He squatted down beside her. "Good morning, sunshine."

Isabelle's lips drew back to expose an expanse of pink gum and the tips of two white teeth. His heart grew big and soft and melty like a microwaved marshmallow. It was amazing, the way that smile made him feel.

He made a goofy face, and Isabelle laughed aloud. Surprised, he looked up at Stevie. "Did you hear that?"

"I sure did."

Holt turned back to the baby. "Hey, Izzy—look at this one." He twisted his mouth, scrunched his face and crossed his eyes.

The baby laughed again. After the fourth face, though, she began to fuss.

"I think she's hungry," Stevie said. She lifted and settled the baby on her lap, then picked up a tiny spoon and dipped it into the bowl. She held it to the baby's lips. "It's rice cereal, Isabelle. What do you think?"

Isabelle cautiously tasted, her eyebrows gathered in concentration.

"She looks like a professional wine taster," Holt said.

Stevie grinned. "I wonder if it's a good vintage."

Apparently it was, because Isabelle swallowed, then opened her mouth for more. Stevie grinned and held out the spoon to Holt. "You want to feed her?"

"Do you think she'll let me?"

"You'll never know unless you try."

He crouched in front of Stevie, took the spoon and slowly aimed it for Isabelle's lips. Sure enough, the baby's mouth opened like an automatic garage door. Holt's heart bounded in his chest. "It's working!"

Stevie smiled. "Like a charm." She handed over the cereal bowl.

Holt knelt at her feet and spooned another tiny scoop into his daughter's mouth.

Stevie watched Holt's face, her heart warm. He looked like a little boy on Christmas morning—or like the tree itself, all lit up and glowing. He knelt at her feet and spooned another scoop into Isabelle's mouth. "Can you believe this?"

"Sure. I knew you'd win her over."

Just like you did me. The thought sent a rush of alarm racing through her.

Holt dipped the spoon back in the cereal. "She's only going along with this because you're holding her."

Stevie readjusted her grip on the squirming child. "So? Raising a child is a team effort."

"You and I make a pretty good team."

Almost like a real family. The thought walloped Stevie in the stomach, setting off a deep, aching hunger. *Don't think along those lines,* she ordered herself. *Don't wish for things you can't have.*

The rumble of a loud engine made her look up and out the front window. A moving van was pulling up to the house across the street.

"Looks like our neighbors are clearing out," she remarked.

"Yeah. I'm closing on the property in a couple weeks."

Stevie swallowed. She'd known he was buying the house, known he was going to move out when the adoption went through, but it had seemed so far off and distant. Now it seemed all too near. They'd only been married a week and it was already the beginning of the end.

Well, it was a good thing, she told herself sternly, because she was growing more attached to Holt with each passing day.

Just last night she'd been headed to bed after a long, fragrant bubble bath, and she'd stopped by Isabelle's room to check on her. When she'd peered into the crib, she'd been alarmed to discover it was empty.

"Over here," whispered a man's voice from the corner.

Stevie had whipped around, her heart in her throat. Holt sat in the rocker, holding the sleeping baby.

Stevie had folded her arms across her chest, acutely conscious that she was wearing only a mid-thigh–length camisole. "You gave me a scare."

"Sorry." Holt gave a sheepish grin. "The only time she lets me hold her is when she's asleep."

Mr. I-Don't-Get-Close-To-Anyone was sitting in the dark, holding his sleeping daughter. A tender lump had formed in her throat.

"I thought maybe if I held her while she slept, she'd subconsciously get accustomed to me," he said.

He couldn't just admit that he simply wanted to hold his child, she'd thought wryly; he'd had to have a practical reason for it. Stevie had nodded, more than willing to go along with his excuse.

Isabelle brought her thoughts back to the present by spitting out a mouthful of cereal.

"Does that mean she's had enough?" Holt asked.

"Looks like it." Stevie gently wiped the child's chin with a napkin. "But you got her to eat a lot more than I thought she would."

Holt beamed. "Good going, Izzy." He leaned forward and kissed the child on the cheek. As he did, his jaw grazed Stevie's breast.

Attraction, swift and strong, roared through her. Holt looked at her, and the sexual undertow nearly swept her out to sea. For a heart-stopping second she thought he was going to kiss her. Then he abruptly pulled back and straightened. A rush of disappointment swept through her, even as she told herself it was wrong.

"I've gotta go." His voice came out low and gruff.

"Don't you want some breakfast?"

"I'll grab something on the way to the office." He picked up his computer case and headed for the door.

He locked it behind him, a protective gesture Stevie found touching and sweet. She wished she could lock up her emotions as easily, but there were no deadbolts to throw, no chains to fasten, no bars or barriers that could keep Holt from creeping into her heart.

Chapter Thirty-one

"We've really missed you around here," Michelle said, four weeks later, as she helped Stevie set up chairs in the parenting center for a class called Motivating Your Teenager.

"It hardly looks like it." It was Stevie's first class after her four-week marital leave, and the center looked just the same as when she'd left it. She picked up a chrome-and-plastic chair against the wall and carried it to the center of the room. "Looks like you're doing just fine without me."

"How's motherhood?"

"Fantastic." Stevie glanced over at Isabelle, who was laying in the infant play area, banging at a plastic rabbit and laughing as it squeaked.

Michelle followed her gaze. "Well, it obviously agrees with Isabelle. I've never seen a child change so much so fast."

It was true. In the past month, Isabelle had blossomed. Her weight was now within the normal range for her age, and her motor skills had improved by leaps and bounds. But of all the changes, the one in her personality was the most pronounced. Instead of a squalling, inconsolable bundle of anxieties, Isabelle was now smiling and happy, as cheery as the bright yellow playsuit Stevie had dressed her in that morning. She'd not only bonded with Stevie but with Holt. To Holt's delight, Isabelle now smiled when he entered the room and reached out her arms toward him, wanting him to pick her up. She was even starting to respond to strangers.

"So how's married life?"

"It's great, too." Stevie picked up a chair against the wall and carried it to the center of the room. "Unfortunately."

Michelle raised a quizzical eyebrow. "Unfortunately great?"

"Well, you know the circumstances."

"I was hoping they'd changed."

Me, too, Stevie thought, then immediately tried to suppress the thought.

"So . . . what's it like?" Michelle asked.

"What do you mean?"

"Describe a typical day."

Stevie crossed the room and picked up another chair. "Well, we get up with Isabelle."

Michelle picked up a chair as well. "Both of you?"

"Pretty much."

"From the same bed?"

Stevie shot her a look. "You know better than that."

"No, I don't. You and I haven't had a chance to talk in a while."

"Well, nothing's changed in that regard." Stevie set down the chair. "We have breakfast together, then Holt gets dressed for work. When he gets home, we usually have dinner together. We bathe the baby and put her to bed."

"And then?"

"Holt usually has a lot of work. He'll work on his laptop in the living room while I read. Sometimes we watch TV or movies, or we'll listen to music and talk."

"And then?"

"We go to our separate bedrooms."

"So you haven't . . ."

Stevie tried to change the subject. "Do you think we have enough chairs, or should I get some more?"

Michelle straightened and grinned. "You have!"

It was a safe assumption that they weren't talking about chairs. Stevie blew out a sigh. "We did. Once. And just to save you from asking—not that it seems to bother you in the least—it was wonderful. More than wonderful. But . . ."

"But what?" Michelle asked softly.

"I can't let it happen again." Stevie felt a knot form in her throat as she turned to her friend. "I'm falling in love with him."

"Oh, Stevie," Michelle said. "Maybe he feels the same way."

"No."

"I've seen the way he looks at you."

"There's attraction, but it takes more than just that."

"It sounds like you two get along really well."

"We do." And they did. Holt talked to her about his work, about the problems and personalities he dealt with. They discussed movies and current events. They shared a similar sense of humor, and he liked to make her laugh.

Stevie shifted a chair to line up with the ones she'd already placed. "But he's determined not to really commit. He's seen his parents divorce and remarry, then divorce again, and he insists he's not going to put Isabelle through that."

"Maybe you can change his mind."

Stevie shook her head. "It's completely made up. He bought the house across the street and plans to move into it after we divorce. Plus, he's got his attorney working on the adoption, which looks like it's going to go through any time. Everything is going forward as planned."

"Have you talked to him about your feelings?"

"No."

"Why not?"

"What's the point? It'll only make things awkward between us, and we're going to be in each other's lives from here on out." Stevie adjusted a chair. "If he can't commit, it's better not to get involved at all. It's better for me, and it's better for Isabelle."

Michelle's brow furrowed. "Stevie, I hate to see you shortchange yourself."

"Look—I went into this to get a daughter, and I have." She gazed at Isabelle, who was smiling at her reflection in a mirror on the floor, and her heart swelled. "I can't tell you how wonderful it is, seeing her grow and thrive and flourish. That was the deal. I've gotten what I wanted. End of story."

"I just want to see you happy."

"I am happy." She looked at the clock. "Come on. Our students will be getting here any minute, and I need to copy the handouts and set up the VCR."

She picked up her folder and headed for the copy machine in the back room, but she could feel

Michelle's worried gaze following her, and she wasn't sure if her friend quite believed her. She wasn't even sure she believed herself.

After they put Isabelle to bed the following evening, Holt sat beside Stevie on the sofa, reading his e-mail on his laptop computer. Stevie suddenly cringed.

"Oh, no!" she exclaimed, covering her eyes with both hands.

Holt looked over and grinned. "Relax. It's just a TV show."

"I know, but they're walking into an ambush."

"If it upsets you, maybe I should turn it off," he teased.

"Don't you dare!"

Holt laughed. Stevie watched the police drama every week and always got so worried about the characters that she was literally biting her nails. Holt loved to tease her about it.

But mostly he loved just being with her. He liked the way she got all caught up in whatever she was doing. He liked her enthusiasm and her compassion, even when it was aimed at fictional characters on TV. He liked her sense of humor and the sound of her voice—and the way lamplight shone in her loose hair, and how her upper lip looked like the top half of a heart, and how her blue T-shirt stretched across her breasts, and . . .

Stevie straightened abruptly and pointed at the TV. "Hey—there's the Nazi nanny!"

Holt looked up to see a commercial for a local bakery. To his dismay, the stocky woman pulling a pie from the oven was the actress who'd played the overly strict Mrs. Schultz.

"She doesn't have a German accent!" Stevie said.

Sure enough, the woman's accent was as American as the apple pie she was slicing.

Oh, great. Holt turned his attention to his computer. He could feel Stevie looking at him.

"What's a professional nanny doing in an ad for a bakery?"

Holt squinted at his computer screen. "Maybe she made a career change."

"Or maybe she was never really a nanny at all." Something in Stevie's voice sent a chill down his spine.

He hunkered lower over his computer. "I don't know what you mean."

"Oh, I think you do."

Uh-oh.

"Anything you'd like to tell me?" she asked.

She was on to him. Time to come clean. "Yeah, I guess there is." He looked up and sighed. "Those nannies— well, they weren't really nannies. They were actresses."

Stevie folded her arms and looked at him, her silence more disconcerting than any words she could have spoken.

"I know it was wrong, but I figured if you thought there weren't any qualified nannies out there, you'd agree to stay with Isabelle. I knew you wouldn't leave her in the care of an unqualified person."

"In other words, you were taking advantage of my fondness for children."

Man, she had a way of making him feel like a worm. "Um, yeah. I guess you could say that."

"That was a really low-down stunt," she said flatly.

There was no denying it. He gave a miserable nod. "You're right. I'm really sorry."

For a long, wretched moment, he waited for the ax to fall.

But then her lips curved in a dry smile. "I wondered how long it would take you to tell me."

Relief rushed through him. "You knew?"

She rolled her eyes. "I saw the 'Satan Rules' tattoo lady—sans tattoo, by the way—in a newspaper ad for mattresses a couple of weeks ago. And last week the bubblegum-chewing cell-phone talker was on TV selling health insurance."

"Oh, man!" She'd known, and she hadn't said a word for all this time? "Weren't you ticked off?"

Her mouth curved in a crafty smile. "Oh, I was plenty ticked. I considered hiring them to come to your office and pretend to be IRS auditors."

He winced.

"I also considered dressing them in police uniforms and sending them to arrest you during an Allen Industries board meeting."

"Ouch!"

"But then I decided against it."

Thank God. "What made you change your mind?"

Her eyes got a tender look that made his stomach do a funny spin. "After I got over the sneakiness of it, I realized you were just trying to convince me to be Isabelle's mom. And how could I stay mad at you for that?"

Something as sweet and soft as a ripened persimmon quietly burst inside him.

"I love her," Stevie said. "She's the best thing that ever happened to me."

"And you're the best thing that ever happened to her."

And to me.

The thought alarmed him so much that when the phone rang, for a moment he thought he'd imagined it. It rang again, and he jumped to his feet, setting his laptop on the coffee table. "I'll get it." He was glad of the diversion, glad of something concrete to do, glad of a reason to pull his thoughts off the dangerously tender path they were traveling.

* * *

"That was Mom," Holt said when he re-entered the room ten minutes later. "She's coming to town this weekend."

Stevie clicked off the TV and turned toward him. Holt had changed into jeans after work, but he still wore the starched blue shirt he'd had on with his suit. The sleeves were rolled up to show his tan forearms, and the neck was unbuttoned, revealing a hint of chest hair. He looked sexy as sin.

She tucked her bare feet under her own jean-clad bottom. "Really?"

Holt nodded. "She's thinking about relocating here."

"No kidding?"

"She said she's sick of dealing with the high and mighty, that she wants to sell homes instead of monuments to ego."

Stevie laughed.

"But the real motivator is that she wants to be close to Isabelle. She's gone into serious grandmother mode."

"It would be terrific for Isabelle to have her nearby."

Holt nodded and sank back on the sofa. "Mom's thinking it would be great from her perspective as well." He leaned forward and lifted his laptop off of the coffee table.

"Great. Except . . ." Stevie's stomach sank as a thought hit her. "Except she's going to think our marriage is on the rocks if she discovers we're in separate bedrooms."

"She's going to have to think that sooner or later."

"It's too soon," Stevie said.

"Well, you can move into the master suite with me."

She must have looked as alarmed as she felt, because he smiled.

"Relax. I'll sleep on the floor." His voice lowered to a rumble. "Unless you invite me to share the bed."

The thought electrified her. She'd been longing to do

just that for weeks. But she couldn't. She was already way too fond of him as it was.

"In your dreams," she said lightly.

"As a matter of fact, I have been dreaming about it."

So have I. "Maybe you should stop eating pizza before bedtime."

"Pizza's not my problem." He reached out and twirled a strand of her hair. "You are."

Heat pulsed between them like a third heartbeat. "You're wrong," she said softly. "Your problem isn't with me. It's with commitment."

His hand stilled. His eyes grew dark and troubled. "Stevie . . ."

His expression told her all she needed to know, and all she didn't want to hear. Nothing had changed. She forced a light note she didn't feel. "Your biggest problem this weekend, though, will be whether or not you've got a comfy sleeping bag." She rose from the sofa and flashed him a smile, trying for an offhand tone. "It's late. I'm going to turn in."

She hurried from the room, not wanting him to know how she'd longed for a different response, not wanting him to see the tears pooling in her eyes.

Chapter Thirty-two

"It's so nice of you to put me up," Caroline said to Stevie as they climbed the stairs to the guest bedroom on Friday evening. Holt followed behind, carrying his mother's bags.

"We're glad to have you," Stevie said. And she was. She genuinely liked Holt's mother and was delighted to see her again. But she was more than a little nervous about the sleeping arrangements.

"I'm sorry to be arriving so late. The flight was due at eight, but it was delayed two hours. I suppose Isabelle is asleep."

"She is, but we can look in on her, if you want."

"I'd love to."

The two women headed into the nursery while Holt dropped his mother's bags in the bedroom Stevie had just vacated.

"Oh, my heavens! I can't get over how much she's grown," Caroline whispered as she gazed down at the sleeping child.

"She's turned into a regular little chow hound," Holt said. He'd quietly entered the room. "The doctor said she's within the normal range for her height, and she's catching up developmentally. And she's getting friendlier every day."

"She's become a real daddy's girl," Stevie added. "She lets Holt hold her and feed her and change her."

Caroline smiled. "That's wonderful."

Judging from the proud smile on Holt's face, he thought so, too.

The three of them stepped into the hall. "Are you hungry?" Stevie asked Caroline. "I can heat up some jambalaya."

"No, thank you, dear. I've already eaten. It's been a long day, though, so if you don't mind, I think I'll turn in early."

"We don't mind." Holt put his arm around Stevie, playing the newlywed role to the hilt. "Do we, babe?"

"N-no." It was hard to think when he was so near. "Not at all." She turned to Caroline. "Do you need anything?"

"I'm all set." Caroline headed into the guest room. "See you in the morning."

Holt kept his arm around Stevie until they got to the stairs. "I guess we need to turn in, too," he said. "It would seem odd if newlyweds weren't in a hurry to go to bed."

Stevie felt her face heat up. She lagged behind as he strode down the hall to the master suite.

Holt noticed, because he turned and smiled at the door. "I won't bite," he said.

It wasn't biting that she was worried about. She tentatively entered the room, feeling awkward and strangely shy.

"Do you want to shower first, or should I?"

"You go ahead," Stevie said.

He went into the master bath and closed the door. She rummaged through the belongings she'd moved into the room earlier in the day, looking for the novel she was reading. She heard the shower turn on, and heard its glass door open.

Holt was on the other side of that door, *naked*. She tried to expunge the thought from her head, but it refused to leave. She climbed onto the bed, propped some pillows against the headboard and turned her attention to the novel. She read out loud to focus her thoughts.

" '*He pulled her into his arms and claimed her lips in a savage kiss. Desire poured through her like molten lava.*' "

Oh, great—a steamy love scene. Not exactly what she needed tonight. Sticking the bookmark back between the pages, she put the book on the nightstand and crossed the room to the entertainment armoire. Opening the door, she picked up the TV remote and clicked it on, determined to get her thoughts on something besides Holt.

But her mind refused to cooperate, especially when she heard the shower shut off. She meant to keep her eyes fixed on the news when he stepped out of the bathroom, but her gaze swerved to him all the same.

Her breath caught in her throat. He was wearing nothing but a towel around his waist.

"I usually sleep nude," he said. "But in honor of your presence here tonight, I'll put on some sweats. I just forgot to take them into the bathroom with me."

She swallowed. Good heavens—she hoped he wasn't going to drop the towel and don them then and there.

She grabbed up her overnight bag. "I'll, um, give you some privacy to do that." She ducked into the bathroom without a backward glance, and closed the door firmly behind her.

She stayed in the shower until the hot water ran out, then dried off and pulled on her baggiest pajamas. Made of blue flannel, they were covered with sheep and numbers. She'd made up her mind beforehand that she wouldn't wear anything that looked even remotely seductive, and these more than fit the bill. Still, she felt strangely shy as she opened the door and stepped into the bedroom.

The TV was off, and so was the overhead light. A lamp beside the bed provided the only light in the room. Holt sprawled on the bed, wearing only a pair of gray sweatpants. The sight of his naked chest made her heart flutter. She realized he was reading her novel.

He lowered the book. "Hey, this is some pretty hot stuff."

"You have to read the whole story to understand the context," she said defensively.

His mouth curved in a mischievous grin. "Oh, I can understand it just fine."

She reached for the book, but he snatched it away, rolling out of reach on the king-sized bed. " 'His hand moved under her gossamer camisole, across her smooth belly, then slid up to cup her ample breasts,' " he read aloud.

She felt her face heat. "Give me that," she demanded, climbing on the bed and grabbing for the book.

He lifted it out of her reach. " 'He flicked his thumb across her dusky nipples,' " he read.

She made a lunge for the book. He rolled toward her, causing her to come down on top of him. He wound one arm around her, holding her tight, and extended the book high above him. " 'She moaned and reached for his belt buckle.' "

"Let me have it!" Stevie demanded, writhing against his steely grasp. He flung a muscled thigh over her flailing legs, pinning her in place.

" '*Let me have it*,' she pleaded," he pretended to read. " 'I beg you to hurl me to the throbbing heights of most excellent ecstasy.' "

"Hey, that's not in the book!" She attempted to reach for it again, but he'd pinned one of her arms against his side, and the other was caught in his iron grasp.

" 'Please, I beg of you,' she breathlessly panted," he continued. " 'Hurl me now or I shall expire of desire.' "

"Oh, you're going to expire, all right," Stevie muttered, digging her elbow into his side.

"Ow!" He yelped, grabbing his side and rolling away from her.

She hadn't meant to hurt him. Worried, she leaned over him. "I'm so sorry— Are you okay? I was just playing around, and—hey!"

Before she knew what was happening, he'd flipped her onto her back.

She gazed up into his laughing eyes. "Faker," she accused.

"He blazed with desire," Holt said, still pretending to be reading. "His loins burned for her."

"Oh, right." She rolled her eyes, then adopted his phony reading voice. "Hot flames shot out of his crotch where she kneed him in the family jewels."

"You wouldn't."

She arched a brow. "Willing to bet your family jewels?"

"On second thought, maybe not." He cautiously removed his hands from her arms, but still stretched over her, smiling down. She grinned back, and as their eyes caught, the playful mood shifted to something deeper. Attraction, hot and primal, unfurled in her belly.

His gaze held her more firmly than any physical grasp ever could. He was so close she could see the individual hairs of his shaved jaw, smell the toothpaste on his breath and—oh, dear heavens—feel the thick heat of his arousal against her belly.

He caressed her cheek with his knuckles. "Stevie," he breathed.

That was all he said, just her name, but it seemed as if her heart had been waiting all her life for a man to say her name just that way. She reached up, curled her arms around his neck and tugged his head down until his lips were on hers.

The kiss was like lighter fluid on an already burning fire. It surged into flame and blazed out of control. He pulled her bottom lip between both of his, sucking the soft flesh. She moaned and pulled him tighter. Her hands splayed across the muscles of his back, then moved down to his hard buttocks as she rocked against his even harder erection. The kisses lengthened and deepened, drugging her with desire.

Holt moved back enough to unbutton her pajama top. Pushing back the blue fabric, he exposed her breasts to the lamplight.

A wave of self-consciousness washed through her. "Turn off the lamp," she murmured.

"I want to see you."

"I—I don't want you to."

"Why not?"

"Because . . ." She turned her head away, embarrassed. "Because . . ."

"That does it." His voice held a time-to-end-this-nonsense note. "Come here." He rolled off the bed and pulled her to her feet.

Alarm shot through her. "Where are we going?"

"To the mirror. It's high time you took a good look at yourself."

"No. I-I . . . This is probably all a bad idea. We shouldn't—"

But he was tugging her over to the walk-in closet opening the door, exposing a full-length mirror mounted on the back. He stood behind her, his arms around her waist. "Look at yourself," he ordered.

She reluctantly lifted her eyes, then cringed at the sight, red-faced and embarrassed, standing there in baggy sheep-printed pajamas with shirt gaping open. She started to rebutton it, but he put his hands on hers, stopping her.

"I want you to *see* yourself. Now just stand there and watch while I take you on a guided tour."

She met his eyes in the mirror, and something in his gaze compelled her to obey. She stood stock still and stared in the mirror as his fingers combed through her hair. "I see a beautiful woman with beautiful, soft, silky hair." He sifted a strand through his fingers, then moved his hands to her temple. "I see smooth, creamy skin and intelligent eyes." His fingers slowly skimmed her cheek, moving down to her mouth. One index finger traced her bottom lip in a languorous caress. "And a highly kissable mouth."

The sensation made her tremble. His hands moved

down her neck to her shoulders. She caught her breath as he slipped her pajama top off her arms. The air chilled her skin. She started to fold her arms across her chest, but he covered her breasts with his hands before she could. The sight of his tan, masculine hands on her pale chest was simultaneously shocking and erotic. She felt oddly removed, as if she were watching a movie.

"Your breasts are beautiful—full and round and soft." Her knees quivered as his hands moved over her skin. "I love to touch them and look at them. . . ." He moved his hands so he could do just that, cupping them from below. "And taste them." He moved in front of her and took a pebbled nipple in his mouth. Stevie's breath caught at the sensation, even as her gaze stayed riveted on the image in the mirror, locked on the erotic sight of his dark hair contrasted against her pale skin, his naked back before her naked chest. He shifted to her other breast, then slid his hands slowly, slowly down. "I love your torso," he murmured. "I love the curve of your waist and the slope of your belly."

He sank to his knees in front of her. Kissing his way down her stomach, he untied the drawstring on her pajama bottoms. The pants fell to the floor, leaving her naked except for a pair of pink panties, which she normally didn't wear with pajamas but had put on as some kind of extra psychological barrier.

"I love the curve of your hips," he murmured.

Stevie tried to turn aside. "They're too big."

He held her in place. "They're sexy as hell. I like the way they flare out right here . . ." His hand slipped over her hips, just below the waist. "And here." His fingers warmed her flesh as they moved around to the back. "And I love the curve of your bottom." Goose bumps chased through her as he cupped her buttocks. "Especially this spot right here, where they meet your thighs."

His finger slowly traced the sensitive flesh right below the swell of her bottom.

His hands slid farther down the back of her legs, blazing a trail of pleasure that left her weak.

"I'm crazy about your thighs."

"They're too large," she murmured.

"They're perfect." His caresses changed direction, now sliding upward. "I look at them and I want to part them so bad I can hardly stand it."

The words sent a hot rush of desire pulsating through her. She could barely breathe as his fingers moved to her inner thigh.

"And when it comes to what's between them . . . well, just thinking about it makes me ache for you."

An answering ache gripped Stevie. She watched in the mirror, mesmerized by the image of his hands on her skin, as his fingers inched still higher. He ran his palm across her sex, then slowly pulled down her panties. His forefinger langorously stroked her until her legs trembled.

He stood and moved behind her again, his hands roaming over her hips and belly and breasts. "Look at yourself, Stevie. You're an erotic dream. You've got me so excited I'm likely to finish before we even get started."

She felt his erection pressing against the small of her back and saw desire, dark and smoky, reflected in his eyes. He wasn't just handing out empty compliments; he genuinely craved her.

"Look at yourself, Stevie, and see what I see in you."

She watched his face in the mirror as he looked at her naked body. He thought she was sexy. For the first time in her life, she looked at her nude reflection and thought so, too. He made her feel that way—sexy and beautiful and desirable. She even felt a little proud, because her body excited Holt.

"It turns me on to look at you naked," he murmured. "So let me, okay?"

"Okay," she whispered. "As long as I get to do the same."

He grinned. "Deal." She smiled back, then tugged off his sweatpants. He stood there, aroused and huge, letting her look all she wanted.

And then he scooped her up in his arms and carried her back to bed. And by the soft light of the bedside lamp, he did all the things to her he'd just done in front of the mirror, only longer and slower and more intimately, until she was trembling and moaning.

"Please," she begged him. "Please . . . 'hurl me now.'"

A laugh rumbled low in his chest as he leaned over her, but it changed to a sharp intake of breath as he entered her, inch by exquisite inch.

Stevie gasped as well, pulling him down, urging him in, aching for all of him, because as he filled her body, he also filled her soul. Her heart overflowed as he carried her up a dizzying slope, to a pinnacle higher than heaven. He pushed her through the clouds and she pulled him to the summit, and they arrived together, breathless and spent and shaken.

The words must have come straight from her soul, because they bypassed her brain and tumbled from her mouth before she even knew she was going to say them.

"I love you," she murmured. "I love you, Holt."

Chapter Thirty-three

Holt was drifting back to earth from the most intense orgasm of his life when he heard the fateful words, the words that were the death knell to romance. He tried to tell himself that he'd heard Stevie wrong, that she'd actually said "I loved that," or "That was lovely," but then she went and said it again. This time she even tacked his name on.

"I love you, Holt."

He gazed down at her, and her eyes held so much tenderness that it took his breath away. He put his finger to her lips. "Shh. Don't say that."

"I didn't intend to, but the words just wouldn't stay inside."

Oh, hell. He was a bastard, an absolute SOB. He knew how she felt about sex and love, and he'd gone ahead and made love to her anyway.

He rolled away and onto his back, his arm over his eyes. "Stevie, you don't really love me. You're just feeling good because we just had amazingly good sex."

"That's not true." She grinned. "Well, it's true it was amazingly good, but the other part . . ."

He rolled onto his side toward her, scared to death that she was going to say it again. "Look, Stevie—ah, hell, I'm sorry." He blew out a harsh sigh. "It was crappy of me to lure you into bed, knowing how you feel about love and sex going hand-in-hand."

"You didn't lure me. I came of my own accord."

He hauled himself to a sitting position and leaned

against the headboard. "I don't want to mislead you, Stevie. Nothing's permanent. This is not a permanent thing."

"It could be," she said softly.

He needed to burst her bubble, and quick. "No, it couldn't. I'm not cut out for commitment. The cleave-only-to-one-woman gene skipped me over."

"How do you know if you've never tried it?"

"I know how this works, Stevie. Sooner or later, things'll head south and we'll split up. And when that happens, if Isabelle has gotten used to us being together as man and wife, it'll crush her. I won't do that to her." His voice softened. "I don't want to do it to you, either."

"I don't think you will."

"Damn right I won't. Because we have an agreement." He swung his legs off the side of the bed. "This is about Isabelle, not us. You knew that. *We* knew that. Don't go thinking anything's changed, because it hasn't."

From the corner of his eye, he saw her bite her lip, as if she were trying to hold back a sob. His chest felt heavy and tight. Turning away, he pulled on his sweat-pants, crossed the room to his bureau, yanked open a drawer and pulled out a T-shirt. "You think you know me, but you don't. The truth is, I'm an SOB."

"No, you're not."

He tugged the shirt over his head. "Trust me on this."

"I trust my own instincts."

Damn it, why wouldn't she just quit? She was forcing him to be cruel. If he didn't disillusion her now, she'd be hurt worse when he inevitably disillusioned her later. "Yeah, well, you won't think I'm so great when we divorce and I start seeing other women."

Predictably, her eyes filled with tears. Unpredictably, it cut him to the quick. He tried to explain, "You don't really love me, Stevie. You love the idea of us being a family."

"Maybe I love both."

He folded his arms across his chest. "Damn it—I don't want a lot of intense emotion here. Things get ugly when you start dragging in emotions. If you get attached, you'll be angry, and that'll make sharing custody difficult. I saw what it did to my parents. I know what it's like on a kid. I'm just trying to spare all of us a lot of pain and misery."

"There's no reason to think we'd be like that."

"You're darn right we won't, because we won't stay together that long. We have an agreement, and we're going to stick to it. When the adoption goes through, I'm outta here."

She turned away from him and faced the wall. She didn't make a sound, but he knew she was crying. It made him feel sick inside.

"Come on, Stevie. Be reasonable. You don't want to go and spoil everything."

"*I'm* spoiling everything?" she asked in a small sob-soaked voice.

He blew out an exasperated breath. "I warned you I'm an SOB." His keys rattled as he snatched them from his bureau.

"Where are you going?" she asked.

"Out."

"But what about your mother?"

"I'll be back before she gets up in the morning." He grabbed his wallet and stalked out of the room, hating himself, hating what he was doing to Stevie, hating this whole complicated situation where hurting her was the kindest thing he could do.

* *. *

Stevie tossed and turned in Holt's bed for most of the night, replaying the events of the evening in her head, her emotions swaying back and forth like Isabelle's mechanical swing. As morning light crept into the room, she rose from the bed and walked to the window. Wrapping her arms around herself, she gazed out at the huge live oak in the backyard as the gray sky lightened to blue.

She was in love with Holt. She hadn't realized it until she heard herself saying it, but it was true. She loved him. The episode in front of the mirror had sealed the deal. It had touched her as she'd never been touched before; it had changed the way she saw herself. Holt had shown her her own beauty; he'd freed her to accept her body, to revel in its uniqueness. When she'd looked in the mirror before, she'd seen only flaws. Last night, she'd seen a body lovely enough to excite the man she loved.

It had changed the way she saw Holt, as well. He'd unwittingly given her insight into his soul. He cared for her, she was sure of it; he couldn't have been that tender, that concerned, that affectionate if he didn't. The problem was, he refused to acknowledge it.

He claimed he was incapable of love, but she knew otherwise. He wasn't incapable; he was simply afraid. Not so much of getting hurt, but of hurting her or Isabelle.

Which only served as further proof that he cared.

She hadn't meant to tell him she loved him; the words had just welled up inside of her and burst out, surprising her as much as they'd surprised him. She'd terrified him when she'd said it. Instead of lowering his barriers and opening his heart, he'd raised his defenses and tried to scare her off.

Holt thought love was a time bomb just waiting to explode. He thought it was a negative emotion. He thought it inevitably led to tears and arguments and re-criminations. He thought it would end up hurting everyone involved.

Well, she'd show him differently. Holt didn't need to learn about love through words. He needed to see it in action.

He probably expected her to be emotional and upset and angry, so she'd be cheery and warm and loving. She'd act as if his storming out in the middle of the night was no big deal.

Isabelle's wake-up babble sounded through the baby monitor. Grabbing her robe, Stevie headed out of the bedroom. As she pulled it on, she also pulled her mouth into a purposeful smile.

If Holt saw that she didn't fall apart when he deliberately tried to hurt her, maybe he'd lose his fear of accidentally doing so. And if he lost his fear of hurting her, maybe he would also lose his fear of loving her.

Holt walked through the kitchen door to find Stevie, Isabelle and his mother already in the kitchen.

"Good morning, dear," his mother said. "Did you have a good run?"

So that was the cover story. Holt shot a glance at Stevie, then smiled at his mother. "Yeah. It was great."

The truth was, he'd spent a restless night on his office couch. He couldn't get Stevie's words out of his mind.

I love you.

Damn it, why did women always have to make things so complicated? In the past when he'd told a woman he didn't love her, she always got hurt and angry. Now Stevie was probably going to act all strained and pained around him, and turn his life into a living hell.

He watched her warily as she moved around the kitchen, mixing Isabelle's cereal and talking to his mother. So far, he couldn't see any change in her behavior.

"Do you want to feed Isabelle?" she asked him cheerily.

"Sure," he said. He took the bowl from her cautiously, halfway expecting her to dump it on his head. Instead she smiled and fastened Isabelle into her highchair.

It was a good thing his mother was here, he thought. That was probably the reason Stevie was acting so civil. Once she got him alone, she'd no doubt rip him a new one.

"So where are you looking at property?" Stevie asked Caroline as she poured a cup of coffee.

"In the Garden District and on the lakefront."

Holt looked up, the baby spoon in his hand. "I thought you wanted a condo."

"I thought I did, too, but I've decided I need more space."

"What for?"

"So Isabelle can come and visit. And because . . ." She nervously fiddled with the sash of her red silk robe. "I've got some news."

"Yeah?"

"I'm not moving to New Orleans alone."

Holt sat bolt upright. His mother hadn't said anything about dating anyone. "Is that right?"

"Yes." She hesitated a moment, then blurted, "Your father is moving here, too."

"Dad?"

She nodded, her face lit up like the sky on the fourth of July. "We're going to remarry."

Holt froze, the baby spoon in mid air. "You're kidding."

"No, I'm not."

"But . . . why?"

"We never stopped loving each other."

"What do you mean, you never stopped?" A feeling of something close to outrage rose in Holt's chest. "What about all those years when you were so angry you wouldn't even speak to each other?"

His mother's eyes were warm and sympathetic. "We were two stubborn fools, too stubborn to get together and talk things out. I hope that you and Stevie will never be so dense and thickheaded." Her mouth curved in a sad smile. "I hope you'll be wiser than to ever put Isabelle through what you went through."

You can bank on that. Holt frowned.

"This is awfully sudden, don't you think?"

"No. We think we've wasted too many years already."

"But . . . have you really thought this out? Are you sure of what you're doing?"

"Surer than I've ever been about anything."

Stevie rose and hugged Caroline. "This is wonderful. I'm so happy for you!"

Wonderful? This was a disaster!

Caroline hugged Stevie back. "We have you and Holt to thank, dear. If it wasn't for your wedding, we might never have spoken to each other again."

Was there some kind of love potion in the water? Stevie had said she loved him, and now his parents were getting back together.

Isabelle banged on her high-chair tray, protesting the lack of service. Holt dipped the baby spoon back in the cereal and fed her another bite.

"I have another surprise." Caroline sat back down on the bar-stool. "I talked to Vince this morning, and he's flying in this afternoon. And I was wondering—well, would it be all right if he stayed here tonight?"

"Of course. Absolutely," Stevie said.

Great. Just great. His parents would be getting busy upstairs while he either spent another night in his office or slept on the floor.

"This is fabulous, isn't it, honey?" Stevie said, putting a cup of coffee on the table beside him and giving him a look that clearly indicated he should agree.

"Yeah. Right. Fabulous," he said flatly.

"I imagine it's quite a shock for Holt." His mother shot him a sympathetic look.

That was putting it mildly. He reached for the coffee cup and took a long swig. "It's going to take some getting used to."

A whole hell of a lot of getting used to, in fact. Holt was still trying to wrap his mind around it an hour later when his mother headed out to the airport to pick up his father. He watched Stevie place Isabelle in her swing.

"Man, I can't believe that."

"That your folks are getting back together?"

"Yeah." The memory of the night they'd broken up was still etched in his mind so vividly that he felt sick just thinking about it. He could still hear the sounds— the angry voices, the slamming doors, the revving car engine, his mother's sobs. He could still feel the sinking feeling in his gut, like he'd swallowed two pounds of chewing gum and it was sitting in a heavy wad at the bottom of his stomach.

"She's going to get hurt again," he said. "Commitment doesn't work for the old man any more than it does for me."

Stevie turned on the mechanical swing. "You don't know it doesn't work for you."

"Hey, I've never crawled inside a lit oven, but I know I'd get burned." He'd rather climb into a broiler right now than get into a discussion about last night, but something needed to be said. "Look, Stevie—about last night . . ."

She smiled brightly. "That was wonderful, wasn't it?"

Her cheery attitude took him aback. "Well, yeah. I'm talking about . . . afterward."

"Afterward?" She scrunched her brow together as if she couldn't quite remember what he was talking about.

"What you *said*."

"Oh, that." She gave a little laugh and turned toward the sink. "You were right. That was just post-coital happy talk. Don't worry about it."

How could he not worry about it? He didn't want to hurt her, but he didn't want to encourage her into thinking this was going to turn into anything permanent, either.

"I got carried away," she said breezily. "Sorry if I upset you."

Oh, she'd upset him, all right.

She picked up a plate and loaded it into the dishwasher. "I think it's just great about your parents."

She was upsetting him again. Holt pulled his brow in a frown. "If they were going to remarry, I wish they'd done it a long time ago. I tried my darnedest to make it happen when I was a kid."

"What did you try?"

"What *didn't* I try?"

"Give me some examples."

Holt watched Isabelle swing back and forth, and let his thoughts go back in time. "Well, I thought if I could get them in the same room, everything would work out, so I came up with all kinds of schemes. My first thought was that if I got really, really sick, Dad would have to come see me in the hospital, so I ate some cat food."

Stevie gasped. "You're kidding."

He shook his head. "It didn't work. It made me sick, all right, but not sick enough to go to the hospital." He grinned at her expression of shock. "To this day, though, I can't stand tuna."

Stevie snickered, but her eyes were warm with sympathy. She sat on the barstool beside him. "What did you try next?"

"I jumped off the roof, figuring I'd go to the hospital for sure if I broke some bones."

"Oh, Holt!"

"I sprained my ankle, but I didn't break any bones. The sprain hurt bad enough that I gave up trying to injure myself, though."

"Thank goodness!"

"My next brainstorm was to go out for sports. I figured that if I did really great, Dad would come watch me play. Unfortunately, the Little League coaches made sure everyone got equal play time, so there was no chance to become a star."

He watched Isabelle kick her feet as she swung. "Plan D was to get the role of Robin Hood or Friar Tuck or King Richard in the school play, and Dad would have to come see me." He shook his head. "Instead, I ended up playing a tree."

"Good casting," Stevie teased.

"That was followed by an attempt at playing piano. Man, did I hate those lessons! But I stuck it out because Dad agreed he'd come to my recitals."

"Did he?"

"Yeah." A bitter taste filled his mouth. "With his new wife and her two daughters."

Holt could still remember his stomach churning at the sight of the buxom blonde and her two flaxen-haired girls sitting by his father in the audience, while his mother sat alone on the other side of the room. "I felt physically ill, like I was going to blow lunch," he told Stevie. "Instead, I blew the music—blew it big time."

A cold sweat broke over him at the memory. He'd sat down at the piano, and the room had taken on an expectant hush, so deep and quiet that he could hear the rustling paper of someone's program—and then he'd gone blank. He couldn't remember a thing. He'd stared at the keys, and they'd looked like rows of monster teeth with big black cavities. The teacher had finally come on stage and put the sheet music in front of him. He'd made a weak start, then stumbled through it. It had been the most humiliating experience of his life.

"When I finally finished, I looked up, and those damned girls were laughing."

Stevie's eyes were so full of compassion, it was like she was trying to sponge up his hurt. "That had to be awful for you."

"Yeah." He drummed his fingers on the counter. "After that, it seemed like Dad just kind of pulled out of my life, and he and Mom started playing musical chairs with marriage. Mom remarried, then Dad got a divorce, then Mom divorced and Dad remarried, then Dad divorced all over again. I felt like the caboose of a runaway roller coaster."

"No wonder you have a negative impression of marriage."

"Negative impression?" He gave a derisive snort. "That's putting it mildly. It's a sinkhole for happiness."

"Not all marriages are like that."

"All of the ones I've seen have been. And believe me, I've seen quite a few."

"If your parents had worked things out, they never would have had those other marriages," Stevie said softly. "Those probably failed because your folks were still in love with each other."

"If they couldn't work things out back then, I don't think they'll be able to now."

"I think they realize they made a huge mistake, and they want to give their love a second chance."

"And I think they're lonely and sad and getting older, and this is a pathetic attempt to re-create their youth."

"Well, regardless of what you think, they're your parents and we need to do something to celebrate their engagement. I think we should invite my folks over tomorrow and have a barbecue."

"Why celebrate something that's doomed from the start?"

Stevie shot him an exasperated look. "Because they're your parents, Mr. Sunshine. And because you love them and wish them well. And because they're visitors in our home and we want to help them celebrate their good news."

"Good for whom?"

"For them."

Well, it sure wasn't good news for him. Just the thought of it made him feel like the floor had been kicked out from under him—what little floor was left after last night.

Her blasé attitude today had him completely bewildered. She acted as if using the L-word was no big deal, but he wasn't buying it. He knew how she felt about love, and if she was mentioning it, she was emotionally involved.

There was only one course of action to take: From here on out, he had to enact a strict hands-off policy. No physical contact of any kind. He couldn't risk hurting Stevie or ruining things for Isabelle.

It was the honorable thing to do, but it was going to make for some long, lonely nights, some frustrating days and an awful lot of cold showers.

Chapter Thirty-four

Isabelle kicked her feet against the red plastic play mat on the deck and whimpered.

"Sounds like she's ready for her nap." Rising from her wrought-iron chair, Stevie picked up the baby.

Marie gazed fondly at Stevie, who looked adorable in blue print Capris and a blue knit shirt. "We'll clean up the dishes, dear."

"Yes," Caroline added across the large umbrella-shaded table. "You go on and see to the baby. And thank you for a delicious lunch."

"Don't thank me. Thank the barbecue crew." She inclined her head toward Holt.

He dipped his head. "Thank you. Thank you very much," he said in a bad Elvis impersonation.

Everyone laughed.

"Well, you get credit for that scrumptious chocolate cake and all the other fixings," Caroline said.

"It was all delicious," Vince added.

"Glad you liked it." With a quick smile, Stevie disappeared into the house with the baby.

"She got your cooking genes," Caroline said as she picked up the platter of leftover barbecued chicken and followed Marie into the kitchen.

"I'm afraid she also got Robert's secretive genes." Marie put the stack of dishes in the sink. "Something's wrong, but she keeps saying everything's fine."

"She wasn't feeling well this morning," Caroline said. "She made coffee, then said the smell of it was making her ill. I wondered if it might be morning sickness."

"Oh, my goodness!" Marie clasped her hands together, delighted at the concept of another grandchild. "Oh, wouldn't that be fabulous!"

"Yes." Caroline smiled. "And Vince and I will be here to share it."

"I'm so happy for you two," Marie said. "I'm thrilled that you're going to be living here, and it's wonderful that you're getting back together."

"I only wish it had happened a couple of decades earlier—but better late than never, right?"

"Absolutely."

Caroline scraped a plate over the trash. "So, how are things with Robert?"

"Well, he still sulks every time I cater an event. And he's still sleeping in the spare bedroom." Marie had already told Caroline during one of their frequent long-distance phone conversations that Robert moved into the guest room shortly after Stevie and Holt's wedding. He'd said it was because he had insomnia and didn't want to wake her, but Marie was certain it was to avoid intimacy.

"Has he told you the truth about his retirement?"

Marie shook her head. "I keep trying to give him openings, but so far, no luck. I've mentioned newspaper articles about people losing jobs, and I've talked about how hard it must be on their egos, and how understandable it would be if they were reluctant to tell people, but he doesn't say a word." She placed the glass in the dishwasher. "But lately I've seen some signs of improvement."

"Really?"

Marie nodded. "His black mood seems to be lifting. He's become more talkative and outgoing. We went to a movie last week, then out to dinner last night, and it almost seemed like we were dating again."

"That's encouraging."

Marie leaned over. "But the really encouraging thing is, he's agreed to go to the doctor."

"Really?"

Marie nodded. "I've been after him to get a physical, and he refused. A week ago, he said if I made an appointment for him he'd go." And then he said, in a really offhand manner, that he might ask the doctor about Viagra."

"That's great!"

"Evidently one of the men he plays golf with said something about going for a physical and getting Viagra, so all of a sudden it doesn't seem like such a big deal." Marie rinsed a plate in the sink. "I'm hoping that if we get physically close again, he'll open up emotionally. I think men are the opposite of women—we want to connect emotionally before we connect physically, but men are the other way around."

"I think you're right." Caroline spooned leftover baked beans into a plastic container. "And I'll bet that's just what will happen."

"Here they come now."

Vince strolled up and put an arm around his ex-wife, trailed by Stevie and Holt. "We need to be getting to the airport. Our flights leave in less than two hours, and we have to return the rental car."

"I know. I'm all packed and ready to go." Caroline turned to Stevie. "Thank you so much for putting us up. Hopefully next time we come, it'll be to close on our new house."

"Where is it?" Robert asked.

"Two blocks off Napoleon and St. Charles. It's an old Victorian." Caroline smiled. "Kind of like this house, but not as large. We wanted to have enough of room for Isabelle and any other grandchildren Holt and Stevie might give us."

Marie shot them a teasing smile. "Any news along those lines?"

The color drained from Stevie's face. She took a moment too long to answer. "N-no. Of course not."

Marie looked at Holt. He was staring at Stevie, his face like granite. *Oh, my.* From the look of things, she'd apparently stepped onto a land mine. Either they disagreed on the timing, they were trying and having no success or Stevie was pregnant but didn't want anyone to know yet.

Across the room, Caroline caught her eye and raised an eyebrow, indicating that she thought something was up as well.

Marie tried to smooth things over. "Well, when and if there's any news along those lines, we'll all be eager to hear it."

"Yes, indeed," Caroline said. She turned to Vince. "You'd better get our bags, dear."

"I've already brought them downstairs. I'll go load them into the car." He rose from the kitchen bar stool.

Marie closed the dishwasher door and looked at Robert. "We need to be going ourselves."

Holt barely managed to wait until the door closed behind their guests before he turned to Stevie. "Anything you want to tell me?" he asked tersely.

"About what?"

"You know about what."

"I-I don't think so. I mean . . ." She looked down at her shoes. "I hadn't even thought about it until my mother brought it up."

He drew a deep breath. "Stevie, are you using some form of birth control?"

Two stains appeared on her cheeks. She refused to meet his gaze. "I-I wasn't seeing anyone when I met you.

And I didn't think you and I would . . . that we'd . . . you know."

"In other words, no."

She nodded glumly.

"We didn't use any protection the other night. And . . ." His stomach knotted like a sailor's rope. Emotions rolled through him so strong and fast he had no idea what they even were. "We didn't use any on our wedding night, either."

"No. It just happened."

It just happened. How could he have let it "just happen"? He wasn't a green high school kid. Damn it, he'd already had one baby accidentally—and that was when he *had* been careful. Stevie seemed to mess with his head. His desire made him all foggy. When she was in his arms, he didn't think about coherent things like protection or emotional involvement or repercussions. When he was with her, he didn't think at all. He swallowed. "Is everything, you know—on schedule?"

Her face grew pale.

His fingers tensed in his palm. "Talk to me, Stevie. Are you late?"

"A . . . a little."

"How little?"

"Four or five weeks."

"For the love of . . ." He slapped his hand against his forehead and turned around. He abruptly swiveled back. "And that didn't concern you?"

"I-I haven't thought about it. There's just been so much going on. . . ."

He strode into the kitchen and grabbed his keys from the counter. "I'll be right back."

"Where are you going?"

"To the drugstore to get one of those tests. And when I come back, you're going to take it."

* * *

Stevie stared at the little window on the white-and-blue plastic wand, a feeling of disbelief curling in her gut. Pregnant. She was pregnant!

"No way," she muttered. But there were clearly two lines in the window on the wand. She picked up the instructions from the counter by the sink and scanned them again. No, she hadn't misread them: two lines meant pregnant. And the test claimed to be more than 99 percent accurate.

But she couldn't be. How could she be so unlucky? Everyone she knew who'd had a baby had used ovulation predictors and thermometers and tried for months.

She stared at herself in the mirror. Such a momentous event should register somehow in her appearance. There ought to be something different about her, some change that she could see. "Pregnant," she whispered. "You're pregnant."

A confusing jumble of emotions tumbled through her—disbelief, worry, joy, fear. Holt's baby was growing inside her. Isabelle was going to have a little brother or sister. Her mouth curled into a smile as joy overrode all other thoughts, all other feelings.

But Holt wasn't likely to have the same reaction. She jumped as a knock sounded on the bathroom door.

"Stevie—are you all done?"

Oh, dear. Placing her hands protectively on her belly, she drew a deep breath and tamped down her elation. Holt wouldn't welcome this news. He wouldn't want another child. He didn't want to be married, didn't want to be emotionally involved. If they stuck with their original plan, they would already be divorced when this baby was born.

The thought sent another roller-coaster of emotions

screaming through her. She couldn't allow that to happen. She needed to buy some time.

"Stevie?"

One thing was for sure: she couldn't buy time in here. No matter how much she dreaded it, she had to face Holt.

She slowly opened the door. He stood on the other side, his hands shoved in his pocket, his hair sticking up in front as if he'd been jamming his hand through it. His expression was anxious.

"Well?" he demanded.

"Well . . ."

"So, are you?"

She started to speak, but words wouldn't come out. She settled for simply nodding.

He stared at her. She couldn't read his reaction, couldn't tell what he was thinking behind those dark, dark eyes.

"Are you sure?"

"Look for yourself. Two lines, pregnant." She held out the wand.

He gazed at it and swallowed.

"According to the box, the test is awfully accurate. But I guess I need to go to a doctor to confirm it."

"You'll make an appointment tomorrow." The words came out as a directive. "The sooner we know for sure, the sooner we can decide what to do."

Stevie straightened her spine. "There's nothing to decide. If I'm pregnant, I'm having the child."

A nerve flexed in his jaw. "I figured you'd feel that way."

Her stomach wrenched. "And you don't?"

He turned away and jammed his hands through his hair. "Hell, Stevie—I don't know what I feel. I never intended to have any kids, and all of a sudden I'm some kind of damned baby-making machine." He walked away, then turned back, his face twisted with frustration. "Damn it all, I never meant for this to happen."

Her insides curled up like the toes of the Wicked Witch of the West. "I didn't plan it either. But it did."

He propped his hands against the closet door and stood there, his head down. At length he pushed off the door and turned to face her, his eyes grim. "Well, this doesn't change anything."

As far as Stevie was concerned, it changed things considerably. "What do you mean?" she asked cautiously.

"I'll provide for you and this child just like I'm providing for Isabelle, but, Stevie—we're not staying married."

She tipped up her chin. "Who says I'd want to?"

"Well, from what you said the night before last . . ."

"Oh, that." Regardless of how sincerely she'd meant it, it had been a mistake to tell him she loved him. It had scared him to death. It had made him back off. And the last thing she wanted to do—especially now that she was pregnant with his baby—was push him away.

"I got carried away and said the first thing that popped into my head. I didn't mean it."

He regarded her suspiciously.

"The truth is, you're not the kind of guy I really want as a husband, anyway."

His suspicious look turned into a scowl.

"No offense meant." She gave him a smile. "But we'll have to postpone the divorce awhile. My parents would never forgive you for divorcing me while I'm pregnant with your child. And you're going to need to be around for the first few months to bond with this baby, too."

Holt's Adam's apple bobbed as he swallowed. "I hadn't thought about that."

"If we divorce in, say, a year, you'd be around for the first few months of the new baby's life, but Isabelle will still be under two years old. That's plenty young enough that she won't remember us ever living together."

"I suppose that makes sense."

"So you agree?"

He blew out a sigh and shoved his hand through his hair, then reluctantly nodded.

Good—she'd bought some time. She had a year to change his mind—a year during which she would love him so passionately and thoroughly that he would have no choice but to love her back.

She prayed that he would. Because she couldn't bear to think about the alternative.

"Hold still, Isabelle."

The baby wriggled and yowled on the changing table like a coyote in a bear trap as Holt struggled to change her diaper later that evening.

"Come on, girl. Work with me here."

The baby kicked her scrawny legs and squalled. She had been unhappy ever since Stevie left for the radio station thirty minutes ago. The baby seemed to have picked up on Holt's mood, which had been dark and stormy ever since he'd learned that Stevie was pregnant.

Another baby. What the hell was he going to do with another baby? He couldn't even handle this one.

And that wasn't even the worst of it. Stevie's pregnancy meant he was going to have to stay married to her for a full year. A full year! How was he going to live with her for a full year and not touch her?

She'd said she loved him, for Pete's sake. He couldn't sleep with a woman who loved him! That was just courting disaster.

Stevie had retracted the L-word, but Holt was wary. The safe thing to do—the honorable thing—was to keep his distance.

But that was going to be damn near impossible, now that he knew how she tasted, how she responded, how she sounded when they were making love. Just the thought of it turned him on. Was he supposed to live in a state of unrequited arousal for a whole friggin' year?

He must some kind of sick bastard, because the thought of his baby growing inside of Stevie struck him as oddly erotic.

He finally managed to fasten tape around the top of Isabelle's diaper. "There!" He picked up the baby, who didn't seem any happier to be carried than she was to be changed. "Let's go turn on a radio and see if Mommy's voice can calm you down."

He carried the baby to the living room, set her on her play mat, then opened the entertainment armoire and flipped on the radio.

"This is Stevie Stedquest with Parent Talk. You're on the air."

Sure enough, Isabelle abruptly quieted at the sound of Stevie's voice. To Holt's annoyance, her voice had the opposite effect on him.

"I'm pregnant," said a woman caller, "and lately I've been lying awake at night, worrying that I won't be able to handle another child."

"How many children do you have now?"

"Just one. He's a two-year-old boy."

"And what, specifically, is your concern?"

"I'm worried I won't be able to love another child as much as I love the one I already have."

"It sounds like you love your child a lot."

"I do. He's the light of my life."

"Well, it may be hard to believe now, but you're going to love your new baby just as much."

"I don't know if that's possible."

"Sure it is. Love isn't a limited resource. It's an ever-expanding, infinite power."

"I don't understand."

"Well, I'm sure you already had people in your life that you loved before you had your son. And you still love them, even though you love your son, now, too, right?"

"Yeah."

"So you were able to make room in your heart for him. And you'll be able to make room for this new baby, too. The amazing thing about love is, the more you give, the more you have to give."

"I hadn't thought about it like that."

"Well, that's how it works."

"Thanks. I feel better about things."

Stevie had a knack for making people feel better, Holt thought. He felt better, and he didn't even know if he believed any of the stuff she'd just said.

Isabelle felt better, that was for sure. Instead of crying, she was lying quietly under her baby gym, listening to Stevie's voice and batting at the Sesame Street characters dangling there.

Maybe a second baby wouldn't be so bad after all. Stevie was a terrific mother, and Isabelle would have a little brother or sister. As an only child, Holt had always longed for a sibling.

He wondered what the baby would look like. If it was a girl, he hoped it had Stevie's hair and Stevie's eyes.

Thinking about Stevie's eyes made his stomach do a funny flip.

He scowled. He was *not* going to get all mushy about

Stevie just because she was pregnant. Emotions caused problems when couples separated, and he and Stevie were going to separate before Isabelle was old enough to remember them ever being together.

But *he* would remember. And he wasn't quite sure how he was supposed to deal with that.

Chapter Thirty-five

"Look at you—you're positively glowing!" Michelle exclaimed later that week when Stevie pushed Isabelle's stroller into the parenting center. "Pregnancy really agrees with you."

Stevie parked the stroller against the wall and unbuckled the safety strap. "I'm pretty thrilled about it."

"I bet your parents are, too."

Stevie smiled. She'd dropped by her parents' house on her way home from the doctor's office four days earlier, after having the pregnancy confirmed. "Mom literally jumped up and down, and Dad got all choked up."

"Oh, that's so sweet!"

Stevie lifted Isabelle from the stroller. "It was so good to see Dad happy, Michelle. He seems to be coming out of that funk he's been in ever since he retired."

"That's terrific." Michelle followed her to the infant play area. "How did Holt's parents take the news?"

"They're over the moon. They're nuts about Isabelle, and the thought of having another grandchild to dote on is their idea of heaven."

"I can imagine."

"They signed the contract on that house they

wanted," Stevie added. "Vince sold his share of his business to his partner, and he's moving into a temporary apartment here so he can supervise the renovations while Caroline wraps up her business in California."

Michelle smiled at Isabelle, and the baby grinned back. "With two sets of grandparents in town, you're going to be such a spoiled little pumpkin!"

Isabelle laughed.

"So how's Holt dealing with things, now that he's had a chance to get used to the idea of another baby?"

"He's adjusting. I think he's more excited about it than he lets on. He asked this morning if I'd want to know if it was a boy or a girl before the baby was born."

"That's a good sign. What did you say?"

"I told him I don't want the doctor to have any information about our baby that we don't have. If Dr. Arnold can tell, I'll want to know, too." Stevie adjusted the elastic cuff on the bottom of Isabelle's flowered overalls as she set the baby on the play mat. "Holt agreed."

"Another good sign." Michelle watched Stevie select a plastic toy from the shelf and place it in front of the baby. "How are other things?"

Stevie straightened and pushed her hair out of her face with a sigh. "Well, I scared him but good when I told him I loved him. So we're back to separate bedrooms."

She'd come home after her radio show the night his parents left to discover that he'd moved her things back into the guest room. Under the circumstances, they needed to keep some distance, he'd claimed.

"You need to change that," Michelle said. "Because regardless of what you may have heard . . ." She leaned close as two young mothers and their toddlers walked through the door. "The way to a man's heart is *not* through his stomach."

"I've already figured that out," Stevie agreed with a smile. Now all she had to do was figure out what to do about it.

Chapter Thirty-six

"Oh, Stee-vie! I'm ho-ome."

Her heart skipped at the sound of his voice. She rose from the living room sofa, grinning at Holt's lousy Ricky Ricardo impersonation. Over the course of the last few weeks, she'd discovered that Holt had quite a repertoire of bad impersonations.

But then, she was doing one herself, trying to impersonate a woman who wasn't in love. She smoothed her blue tank top over her jeans as he walked through the door, lugging his overnight bag and computer case.

"How was your trip?" she asked. He'd been in Atlanta for the last three nights, and Stevie had missed him more than she thought possible.

"Good. When this final audit is over, I'll be finished with that account." He set down his bags and looked through the mail on the side table. "How were things here?"

"Isabelle's asleep. She's doing great, but I think she missed you."

Holt grinned. "And I missed her."

Silence hung between them, along with the unsaid words: *I missed you, too.*

He shoved his hands in his pockets. "How are you feeling?"

Stevie drew a deep breath and screwed up her courage. It was time to put her plan into action. "Well, I've been having a little trouble sleeping."

"Insomnia, huh?"

"Yes." She cast him a sidelong look, trying not to show her quaking nerves. "I keep having these . . . urges."

"Like for ice cream or pickles?"

"No. For . . ." She swallowed. *Nothing ventured, nothing gained*, she reminded herself. "For sex."

Holt froze, mail in his hand.

"One of my pregnancy books mentions that expectant women often have especially strong sexual appetites."

Holt put down the unopened envelopes and stared at her. "Oh, really?"

Stevie nodded. "That seems to be what's going on with me." She clutched her hands together to keep them from shaking. "So I, um, would like to propose a solution."

He appeared to be all ears. "What is it?"

"Well, I know you don't want us to get emotionally involved, but I need a way to deal with this . . . tension. It's not good for the baby."

She saw him swallow.

"So I was thinking . . . maybe we could make love, but pretend we're each somebody else. That way we could keep our emotional distance."

He ran a finger around his collar, even though it was unbuttoned. "How would it work, exactly ?"

"Well, if you were to pretend that I was, say, a stripper . . . and if I were to pretend that you were, say, a cop . . . that would keep us from getting emotionally involved, don't you think? Especially if we keep things light and playful."

* * *

The image of Stevie in stripper garb raised the temperature of the room considerably. Holt pulled off his jacket and tried to sound thoughtful, as if he was mulling it over. "Well, I suppose that might work."

"If I was able to relax and get enough sleep, it would be good for the baby."

"We definitely want what's best for the baby." It wouldn't be too bad for him, either. Just thinking about it had him harder than first-year trigonometry. Living with Stevie and not being able to touch her was driving him crazy. If she thought putting on costumes would keep her from getting attached, yet allow them to make love, he'd dress up as anything she wanted.

"I suppose there could be no harm in trying it," he said.

"I hoped you'd see it that way." She smiled. "Stay right there a moment." She darted down the hall. He heard a closet door open, then a moment later, she returned with two small shopping bags. She handed him one.

"What's this?" he asked, opening it.

"Your costume."

He cautiously pulled out a policeman's cap, a pair of handcuffs and a skimpy pair of silky briefs printed with badges and pistols. Writing ran across the front. Holt's eyebrows rose as he read it. " 'Fully cocked and ready for action'?"

Stevie's face grew red. "It was the only policeman's costume they had in stock."

"Not exactly a regulation uniform. Where the heck did you get this?"

"A little shop in the French Quarter."

She'd certainly been busy in his absence. "Where's yours?"

"Right here."

"When do I get to see it?"

"When I put it on."

Oh, man—he could hardly wait. "And when will that be?"

"How about now?"

He grinned. "I think I can clear my schedule."

She grinned back. "Give me five minutes, then come into the bedroom. Pretend it's after hours at a strip club and you're a big, bad, mean cop. A playful one. If I don't do everything you say, you're going to haul me off to jail."

"You want me to play a big, tough cop?"

She nodded. He lifted the handcuffs. "Do you want me to actually use these?"

"Sure." Her smile was pure tease. "I want you to use everything you've got."

Stevie drew a deep breath, then zipped up the red-fringed miniskirt that went with the skimpy red-fringed top.

Pretend you're someone else, she told herself as she slipped into a pair of ludicrously high-heeled mules—*someone daring and bold and sexy.*

Her nerves quivered as she teetered across the room to dim the light. She'd just put on a CD entitled *Songs of Seduction* when a knock sounded on the door.

"Come in, officer," she called. She struck a pose, one arm braced on the armoire, the other on her thrust-out hip, and tried for a sultry expression.

The door opened slowly. Holt stepped inside, wearing the policeman's hat and a pair of jeans with the handcuffs dangling from the pocket. He was shirtless, and the sight of his muscled chest made her heart pound.

"Hey, there, little lady." He sounded like John Wayne. Sort of. "You got a license to carry all that equipment?"

"What equipment?"

"The equipment you've got under all those clothes."

Stevie widened her eyes with feigned innocence and spoke in a breathy Marilyn Monroe voice. "Why, no, officer. I didn't know I needed one."

"Oh, but you do. On my beat, all of your equipment has to be licensed and inspected." He gave a wicked grin. "*Closely* inspected."

"Really?"

He nodded. "In fact, I require a strip search."

She batted her eyes. "You do?"

"Yessirree. So I want to see your best striptease." He pulled the handcuffs out of his pocket and, toying with them, sat down on the edge of the bed. "And it better be good, or I'll have to haul you in and throw you in the pokey."

"The pokey?"

"Yep. It might sound hokey, but I'll throw you in the pokey."

Stevie snickered.

"Hey! I didn't give you permission to laugh, missy. Now start takin' off those clothes and give me plenty of bump and grind while you're at it."

"First I'll need to see some proof that you're a real police officer."

"What kind of proof do you want to see?"

"Well, maybe a badge or a gun. Or maybe you could show me your official police-issue underwear."

He grinned. "I'll show you my gun just as soon as you get down to your skivvies. And if you're very, very naughty, I might even show you my nightstick."

"Oh, my. I'd better do as you say."

"If you know what's good for you."

Stevie swiveled her hips and unbuttoned the skimpy

shirt, playing it for laughs and getting a grin. She pulled off the fringed shirt to reveal a lacy red bra, then turned around and wriggled her backside as she unzipped her short red skirt. It dropped to the floor and she stepped out of it, revealing a red thong. She danced toward him, grabbed his hand and pulled him to his feet. "Let's see if you're a real policeman," she said, reaching for the button at the top of his jeans. "If you are, you should be packing heat."

He grinned as she unzipped the fly. "Oh, I'm packing heat, all right."

Was he ever. A rush shot through her as he pulled off his jeans. "My, oh my," she murmured. "You're certainly living up to that motto on your briefs."

"Your clothes aren't coming off nearly fast enough, lady," he murmured.

"Sorry, officer." Stevie turned around to unfasten her bra. Before she got it unhooked, he stepped toward her.

"That does it. I'm afraid I'm going to have to take you into custody."

"What for, officer?"

"For concealing evidence." He took her hand and tugged her to the bed. "Get over here so I can frisk you."

"Oh, good. I'm definitely feeling frisky."

"In that case, I better handcuff you," he told her. She stretched out on the bed, and he leaned over her. "This is for your own protection."

"Whatever you say, officer."

"Put your hands over your head," he ordered. She did as he requested. He handcuffed her wrists together.

He leaned over her. "First I need to frisk your mouth."

His lips came down on hers, hard. She kissed him back until they were both breathless and panting.

He kissed his way down her neck to her shoulders,

then pulled away and unfastened her bra. He tugged, only to realize he couldn't completely remove it with her hands cuffed together.

"I seem to have made a tactical error."

Her nipples hardened under his gaze.

"Well, you're way too dangerous to unhandcuff now. We'll just work with it." He moved the bra up her arms to her hands, then lowered his head to her breasts. Hot darts of pleasure shot through her as he teased her nipples with his tongue.

"No signs of illegal activity so far," he breathed against her skin, "but I need to search the rest of the premises." He moved lower on the bed and tugged down her panties. Desire filled her belly as he slid them off her legs.

"Officer, is this an undercover operation?"

"Most definitely."

"Well then, aren't you supposed to be dressed like the suspect, so you'll blend in?"

"Oh. Right." He peeled off his briefs, then slid his hands up her thighs. "Okay—spread 'em."

"Do you have a search warrant?"

"If you have nothing to hide, I shouldn't need one."

Stevie was too far gone with need to thwart him. She spread her legs.

He watched, his eyes dark. "Very good." He slipped his hands up her inner thighs, moving so slowly that she thought she'd die before they reached her aching center. When they did, she gasped at the contact. He stroked her with his fingers and blazed a hot trail of kisses up her leg until she was moaning and panting.

"Please," she begged at length. "Please. I can't stand any more."

He obviously couldn't either. "Well, I don't want you

complaining about police brutality." He leaned over her and slowly drove into her tight, slick body.

"Oh, Holt," she moaned, wrapping her legs around him. Together they escaped to a place with no laws, no rules, no restraints—a place where they each held the key to the other's sweet release.

Chapter Thirty-seven

Holt walked into the kitchen two weeks later to find Stevie feeding Isabelle in her highchair. Stevie's dark blond hair shone like burnished gold in the late afternoon sun. Holt stopped in the doorway and watched her, overcome by a surge of emotion.

She was so damned beautiful it hurt. After this amount of time around a woman, Holt usually discovered that his infatuation faded into boredom, but that wasn't the case with Stevie. Just the opposite. The more he was around, the crazier he grew about her. Just the sight of her gave him a loopy feeling in his stomach.

Stevie looked up and smiled. "Hi!"

"Hi, yourself." He crossed the room, grabbed her around the waist and gave her a hard kiss. Isabelle loudly banged her fist on her highchair tray.

"Hello to you, too, sweetheart," Holt said to the baby, bending down to kiss her cheek.

"You'll never believe what she learned to do today," Stevie said.

"Ah dah." Isabelle banged her hand on the plastic tray. "Ah dah dah."

Holt's pulse pounded. "She learned to say 'Daddy!' "

He squatted down, his face level with Isabelle's. "Say it again, sweetie," he urged. "Say Da Da. Daaa—daaa."

Instead of calling his name, Isabelle blew a loud, wet raspberry.

Holt jerked out of the line of fire.

Stevie laughed and handed him a paper towel. "You guessed wrong. I was about to tell you she learned how to give a Bronx Cheer."

Holt wiped his face, his mouth twisted in a wry grin. "So I see."

"You're lucky she swallowed most of that last mouthful of peaches." Stevie leaned a jeans-clad hip against the counter. "She got me good with applesauce at lunch."

"Did you blow applesauce on Mommy, Izzy?" Holt asked. Isabelle gave a toothless grin and razzed again.

"Guess what else she did today."

"I'm almost scared to find out."

"She sat up all by herself—no pillows, no propping, no back support of any kind."

"No kidding." Holt beamed, as pleased as if she'd won a Nobel Prize. "Wow, Izzy. You're coming up with new tricks so fast I can hardly keep up with them." He straightened and shot Stevie a sexy grin. "Kinda like your mom."

Stevie grinned back. Ever since their little costume party, she'd been sharing his bed, and he'd discovered she was full of surprises. Bedtime had become his favorite part of the day.

But then, this part wasn't bad, either. He loved coming home to Stevie and Isabelle.

"I've got a little good news of my own," he said, climbing onto a barstool.

"Oh, yeah?" Stevie spooned more pureed peaches into Isabelle's mouth.

"I started to call and tell you, but I decided it would be more fun to tell you in person." He paused dramatically.

Stevie looked up. "What is it?"

"The adoption went through. The judge signed the papers this morning. You are now legally, officially, Isabelle's mother."

Her face lit with joy. "Really?"

Holt nodded. "Really."

Stevie let out a whoop, then jumped up and down. "Did you hear that, sweetie? Mommy's really your mommy!"

Isabelle responded with a laugh and another raspberry. Stevie unfastened the tray, unlatched the safety strap and lifted the child in her arms. "You're mine! I'm yours! We're a family!" She danced around the room, the baby in her arms, singing a couple of verses of "We Are Family" in a sweet, off-key voice. Isabelle giggled. "Can you believe it, Isabelle? I'm really, truly your mommy!"

Holt watched, his heart warm and full. "You've been that child's mother since the first time she heard your voice," he said. "She picked you, you know."

"And I'm so glad she did." Stevie beamed at the baby in her arms.

"I'm glad, too," Holt said.

"Oh, yeah?" Her tone was playful, but there was something hopeful in her eyes. "And why would that be?"

Because I love you. The thought sent a bolt of alarm ripping through him.

Did he? Heck, he didn't know. His feelings for Stevie were all jumbled up and confused. He craved her physically. He loved her laugh and her smile and her wit and her warmth. He even took an inexplicably intense pleasure in the fact that his baby was growing in her belly.

And there was something more—a sense of rightness, a clicking into place like the last piece of jigsaw puzzle, a feeling of being at home when he was with her. When he was with Stevie, he was somehow a better version of himself.

Was this what love was like?

If it was, then maybe it wasn't so bad. Maybe, just maybe, this whole marriage thing could work. After all, lots of couples made their marriage stick. Stevie's parents had been together for thirty-seven years, and her brother seemed happily married.

Even his own parents were saying they never should have split.

"Let me guess," Stevie teased. "You're glad Isabelle picked me because I make such great jambalaya."

"Is that what I smell?" Holt asked, moving to the stove and lifting the lid on a pot.

"Yep."

He breathed in the spicy scent. "Mmm. That must be it. Plus your skill at teaching Izzy how to blow raspberries." He dropped another kiss on her lips, then reached for the stack of mail.

He sorted through a stack of envelopes and advertising flyers.

"Looks like you got a card from your interior decorator," Stevie remarked.

Holt pulled out a card-sized envelope with a return address sticker for Charlotte's Interior Design. He opened the envelope and pulled out a flowery card with the words Thank You emblazoned on the front. He opened it.

Holt—
Thank you so much for recommending me to your mother. I'm looking forward to meeting with her during her visit next week. And I can't *wait* to

work with you again on your new project. I've
missed seeing you!!

Love, Charlotte.

Stevie looked up from wiping Izzy's mouth. "What's
that all about?"

Holt put the card down. "I ran into Charlotte downtown a couple of days ago and mentioned that my
mother was looking for an interior designer. They're going to hook up when Mom comes to town."

Stevie's face got a funny look. "Oh." She untied the
Big Bird bib from around Izzy's neck, then unfastened
the highchair tray and set the baby on the red play mat
in the corner. "So what's in the note?"

Holt handed it to her. Stevie quickly read it, then
looked up, her mouth tight. "What's your new project?"

"The house across the street."

Stevie visibly tensed. "You're hiring her to work on
that?"

Holt felt oddly defensive. "She asked if I had any new
projects, and it came to mind. I liked the job she did on
this one, so why not? She's coming by in a day or two to
get the key."

"I see." Stevie stiffly turned away to stir the jambalaya
on the stove.

"Do you have a problem with that?"

"As a matter of fact, I do."

"Why?"

Gee, I don't know." Stevie's tone was sardonic. "It
might have something to do with the fact that she's an
old girlfriend."

Holt prickled. "That doesn't have anything to do with
it. That's over."

"Not in her mind, it's not. She showed up for a bootie
call a few weeks ago."

A creepy sense of déjà vu hit Holt. This was just the sort of thing his mother used to say to his father about his secretary. It was all eerily familiar—the hurt tone, the suspicious expression. A clammy tension stretched through him.

No. He refused to go through this again.

"It really isn't any of your business who I hire," he said curtly.

For a moment, Stevie looked like she'd been slapped. Then her chin shot up. "Yes, it is. You agreed not to embarrass me by running around with other women while we're married."

"I'm not running around. I'm hiring an interior designer."

"Who happens to be pursuing you."

This was just the sort of thing that had broken up his parents. He'd been kidding himself, thinking that he and Stevie would be any different.

He couldn't get sucked into the marriage vortex. When it ended, it pulled everyone involved into a suffocating downward spiral. He wouldn't do that to Isabelle, and he wouldn't do it to his unborn child.

"Stevie, you're starting to sound annoyingly like a wife."

Two pink spots blazed on her cheeks.

Holt pushed off the counter and headed for the door.

"Where are you going?"

"To the gym."

"But dinner's almost ready."

"Go ahead and eat without me. I'll grab a bite while I'm out."

He strode from the room, his gut wound tight. He'd been kidding himself, thinking this marriage might last. He knew better. Nothing lasted forever. It was in the best interests of everyone concerned if he stuck with the original plan.

He needed to cool things off before they got any more overheated. He needed to back off and create some distance. If he wanted to be able to break up in a year with no hard feelings, he was going to have to put the brakes on things now.

Chapter Thirty-eight

Marie glanced at her watch, then fastened her left earring in the mirror of her bedroom vanity. Robert should be home any time now, and she was anxious to find out how his doctor's appointment had gone.

It had taken two weeks to get after she'd called for the appointment, but today was finally the day. Robert had gone to see the doctor at eleven. Marie had wanted to go with him, but she'd had a dessert reception to prepare for tonight. She'd made plans for her assistant to handle the event by herself. If she could give Betsy more responsibility, she would have more free time for Robert.

She had high hopes for the evening. Robert had even kissed her on the cheek as he left the house, and told her to plan on going someplace special for dinner. She'd stopped at Victoria's Secret in the New Orleans Centre shopping mall and bought a sexy red bustier and thigh high stockings. She'd hurried home to shower and change, hoping that before the night was over, Robert would discover the sexy lingerie she was wearing under his favorite red dress.

She was dabbing perfume on her neck when she heard Robert's key in the front door. Her pulse quickened under her finger.

"I'm in here honey," she called, replacing the cap on the perfume bottle. She heard his footsteps draw closer. "How did things go at the doctor's?" She looked up and caught sight of him in the mirror, and her smile froze on her lips.

Robert's face was a mask of anger. His lips were a hard straight line, so tightly pressed together that they were practically colorless. A vein bulged in his temple, and his eyes spit fire.

Fear gripped her gut as she turned to face him. "W-what's wrong?" she asked.

"How dare you!" His voice was low and cold, far more fearsome than a yell. He advanced into the room. "How *dare* you go to my office and demean me like that?"

Oh, no. He'd found out. "I-I didn't go to demean you."

"What did you think you'd do, going in and asking for my job back?"

"I thought I'd help you."

"*Help* me? You thought it would *help* for my wife to go into my former workplace and grovel on my behalf?"

"I wasn't groveling. I-I just thought that you weren't enjoying retirement, and that you were too proud to tell them you'd made a mistake, but that if they called you and offered you some consulting work, you'd accept and be happier."

"Happier? You want me to be happier?" He took another step toward her.

"I—I didn't know the circumstances. If I'd known, I never would have gone."

"You never should have gone, period. That was not your place."

Marie rose from the gold damask vanity stool on wobbly legs. "Why didn't you tell me about your job?"

"Why didn't *you* tell *me* that you were contemplating such an underhanded stunt?"

"Don't go pulling that lawyer act on me, answering a question with a question. You're the one who was deceitful."

"*I* was? You set me up to look like a total ass."

"What happened?"

"What *happened* was I went for a beer with Larry."

His face was red, redder than she'd ever seen it, even redder than when he'd gotten that awful sunburn at Destin Beach three years ago.

"Larry starts talking about you coming into the office, and how he hoped he hadn't put me in an awkward position. For crissake, Marie, I'm sitting there trying to figure out what the hell he's talking about, and when I do, I want to crawl under the friggin' table."

"Oh, no. I'm sorry, Robert." Her voice was a raw, tormented whisper. "It's just that you were so unhappy, and our relationship was so mixed up and sour—I just wanted to fix it for you."

"Damn it, Marie, you're my wife, not my mother. You're not supposed to fix things for me."

"And you're not supposed to hide things from me! You've been going through one of the worst times of your life and you shut me out of it."

"With damn good reason, apparently." He stormed across the room, yanked open the closet door and pulled down his suitcase—the big black leather one he'd bought for their twenty-fifth wedding anniversary trip to Europe. Flopping it open on the floor, he began emptying the drawers of his bureau into it—socks, underwear, T-shirts, sweats. He stormed back to the closet, pulled a half-dozen pants and starched shirts off the rack, then snatched up a handful of ties.

A wave of fear washed over her. "W-where are you going?"

"Somewhere else."

"Where?"

"I don't know."

She started to ask "For how long?" but the words froze on her lips. She didn't want to know. She was afraid of what his answer might be.

She stood and watched as he stormed out of the house. Through the window, she watched him throw his suitcase in his trunk, then pile clothes hangers full of suits and shirts on top of it. She watched him slam the trunk, circle around and climb in the car.

His tires shrieked on the pavement as he drove away. Marie buried her face in her hands, but she didn't cry. She'd cried enough. If Robert was going to be like this, she didn't want him around anyway. She wasn't his doormat or his whipping boy. She wasn't his enemy. She wasn't his mother.

She was his wife. She was supposed to be his confidante, his friend and his lover. If he wouldn't let her be those things, then there was nothing of their marriage left to save.

Robert drove aimlessly around town, seething and fuming, so angry and upset he couldn't even think of a place to go. As night settled in, he headed across the causeway to the north shore of Lake Pontchartrain, simply because it was twenty-four miles of bridge—twenty-four miles when he didn't have to make a decision about which way to turn.

Because he didn't have a clue. This thing with Marie—boy, had he ever been blindsided.

The day had started well. He'd been pleased when Larry had called and asked him to lunch. He had declined because of his doctor's appointment but had agreed to meet his old friend for a beer that afternoon. Robert had looked forward to it.

They'd grabbed a table near the front of a familiar watering hole by the courthouse. They'd swapped the usual pleasantries and each ordered a beer. And then Larry had leaned forward, his forearms on the table. "Hey, buddy—sorry I spilled the beans to Marie a couple of months ago."

"What?"

"You know—when she came by the office to see me."

"What are you talking about?"

Larry's face blanched, and then reddened. "Oh, man—not again."

An unpleasant feeling had slithered up Robert's spine. "Not again what?"

Larry took a long gulp of beer. "Look, I'm sorry. Forget I said anything."

"What the hell is going on?"

Larry shook his head. "Ask Marie."

Robert could only think of one reason Larry would look this uneasy when discussing Marie. Jealousy, terrifying in its width and depth, roared through him. "I'm asking *you*," he'd said tersely.

Larry had caught his drift. He'd sat back, his eyes wide, and put up his hands. "Oh, hell—it's nothing like that."

"So what is it?"

Larry heaved a reluctant sigh. "She came to the office a couple of months ago. She said you'd been depressed since your retirement, and that you were too proud to say you'd made a mistake retiring so early. She wanted to know if I'd offer you a part-time position or some consulting work."

Robert's gut had wadded up. "*What?*"

"You heard me. I didn't know you hadn't told her about the, um, circumstances of your retirement. I ended up telling her the whole story."

Humiliation had flooded Robert like hot water on a cotton T-shirt, shrinking to the size of a pin point the minute amount of self-esteem he had left.

"I can't believe she'd go behind my back like that," Robert had said. "I'm sorry."

"Hey, she was trying to do you a favor. She had your best interests at heart." Larry had pulled his heavy gray eyebrows together over concerned eyes. "You and Marie—you two need to talk more."

The last thing he'd wanted to get at that point was marital advice. "Look—I gotta go. Sorry you got pulled into the middle of things."

Bright lights came up fast behind him, pulling his thoughts back to the present. He was nearly in the center of the bridge, and some a-hole was riding his bumper, the headlights on high.

Robert's jaw clenched. He was tempted to slam on his brakes and let the idiot plow into him. With any luck the impact would push him off the bridge and put an end to his problems.

The thought alarmed him, because it had distinct appeal. He'd always thought suicide was the coward's way out. During his years as a prosecutor, he'd worked closely with police detectives, and he'd come across all kinds of cowards—jumpers and shooters and rope swingers, pill swallowers, slashers and gas breathers. The only ones who had any class were the ones who managed to make it look like an accident, and from what he'd seen, only two types ever succeeded in doing that: drowners and car crashers. With his luck, though, he'd float instead of sink—and if he crashed the car, he'd probably just end up a vegetable.

Not that it would be that big a change from what he was now. After all, he was such a big loser that Marie had to fight his battles—and then she'd been afraid to tell him because he was such a wuss that she thought he couldn't take it.

And hell—she was right. A wave of self-loathing crashed over him.

He was nothing. A big zero, a washed-up old man. He was a loser at everything, and he was making the only woman he'd ever loved miserable.

The image of her face flashed in his mind. It was funny, how he always thought of her smiling and happy. She sure didn't smile much anymore.

His anger at her evaporated, replaced by anger at himself.

God, what a jerk. He should have realized that she'd known. Hadn't she told him all kinds of stories about men who lost their jobs and how it affected their self-esteem? Hadn't she harped on how Vince had lost his business, and because he hadn't told Caroline about the trouble he was in, their marriage had collapsed?

She'd been trying to get him to tell her.

Why was it so frigging hard?

The car on his bumper finally roared around him, accelerating as it went. It was a beat-up white Chevy, and Robert could see the glow of the man's cigarette embers as he flicked them out his open window. Robert watched the white car weave from the left lane to the right, then back again. A drunk. If there was one crime he hated worse than any other, it was drunk driving.

Noting the car's tag number, he reached into his pocket for his cell phone and dialed 9-1-1. "I'm northbound on the causeway and there's a drunk driver ahead of me, weaving all over the road."

"Where are you?" the dispatcher asked.

"I just passed the mile twelve marker."

And then it happened—so fast that Robert wouldn't have seen it if the vehicle hadn't been less than a hundred yards in front of him and under a bridge light. It hit the guard rail, tilted up, then flew off the bridge in a freakishly graceful arc, like a giant white pelican diving into the water. "Good God—the drunk's car just went in the water!" Robert shouted into his cell phone.

Screeching to a stop, he climbed out and dashed for the concrete railing. He paused to shuck off his brown tassel loafers, then jumped into what looked like a black hole.

The water was cold—cold and slightly salty. He looked down. The lake was only about twelve feet deep at this point, and the roof of the white car was visible through the dark water. Holding his breath, he swam down to the driver's door. The man was buckled in his seat belt, alive and panic-stricken. One arm flailed wildly through the open window.

Robert shot to the surface to breathe. Drawing in a deep gulp of air, he dove back down and tried to open the car door, but it wouldn't budge. It was a good thing the man was a smoker, he thought grimly, because his window was open. It was probably the only time in history that smoking might actually save someone's life.

Reaching through the open window, he unbuckled the man's seat belt. The man clawed at him, frantic. Robert's lungs burned. He tried to pull the man through the window, but instead, the man was pulling him into the car.

And then the man went limp. In that instant, Robert realized he had a decision to make, and only a split second to make it. The man might be dead already. If he wasn't, he deserved to be. If Robert stayed with him, it would all be over in a minute or two. It would look like an accident. Robert would even die a hero.

But Marie would think he died angry at her. She would think it was all her fault, that she'd caused his death.

He could not, would not do that to her. He loved her.

He loved her. The immensity of it filled him, like water in the sunken car. *He loved her, and she loved him.* Love was what mattered. Love was the reason for life. Love was the reason to live.

It was also the reason this other guy could not die tonight, the reason Robert had jumped in the lake in the first place: Someone, somewhere might love this stupid, pitiful drunk. Even if no one did, he still deserved a second chance.

Robert desperately needed air. He gave a mighty yank and hauled the unconscious man out through the window. It might be too late, he thought as he lugged the guy upward. He had only a second or two before he passed out from lack of oxygen. He was headed toward a brilliant glow, and he'd always heard that souls traveled toward a bright white light. Was this what it was like to die? He'd never dreamed that it required such excruciating physical effort. His lungs burned and his muscles slackened. The light dimmed, then began to fade away.

And then his face reached heaven—a breathable heaven of air. He gulped in a lungful and opened his eyes. He'd made it to the surface—and the light was back, shining in his eyes, bouncing off the brackish white caps slapping his face.

"There they are!" called a voice from above.

Robert looked up at the source of light and saw something being lowered from the bridge. A life preserver—two life preservers. He trod water, trying to keep the man's head up with one arm, and grabbed a life preserver with the other.

A rope ladder unfurled down the side of the bridge. Robert slowly made his way toward it as a man descended. "Are you all right?" the man called.

Robert grabbed the rope and nodded, still gasping, not able to spare the energy to speak a single unnecessary syllable. He inclined his head toward the man under his arm. "Unconscious."

The rescuer rapidly fitted a harnesslike apparatus around the unconscious driver, then looked up and signaled to someone above. The rope to the harness tightened. The rescuer grabbed a lead line connected to the harness. "I'll take him up, then come back for you," he told Robert.

Robert watched as the unconscious drunk was lugged out of the water and into the air. The rescuer climbed up the ladder, steadying the man with the lead line, until he disappeared over the edge of the bridge.

In a matter of seconds, the rescuer climbed back down. "Are you injured? We can lift you out if you can't climb."

"I'm fine," Robert said. And he was. For the first time in a long time, he was.

For the first time in a long time he was glad to be alive. And he couldn't wait to get to Marie, to hold her in his arms, to tell her that he loved her, and to plead for a second chance.

She didn't answer the phone. He tried her cell number as he sped across the causeway a little while later, heading back toward New Orleans. It took a couple of rings before she answered, and when she did, her voice was wary.

"Marie, I need to see you," he said.

She hesitated for a second. Robert's heart faltered. She was always so ready to forgive, so eager to make peace.

"Maybe we should wait a day or two, Robert. Maybe we need a little space."

An arrow pierced his soul. Space was the one thing they'd had way too much of. Had he used up all her forgiveness, all his second chances? Robert's damp hand tightened on the cell phone. "Where are you?"

"I have a dessert reception at Gallier Hall." There was a detached tone to her voice that he hadn't heard before. "Betsy was going to handle it, but after you left, I decided to come help."

"I'm on my way."

"I don't think that's a good idea. I think . . ."

"I'm on my way," he repeated.

Marie was replacing a mirrored tray of chocolate petit fours on the satin-draped buffet table when she heard a hush fall over the room. She looked up as a sea of sequined gowns and tuxedos turned toward the entrance. She watched the sea part, and a dripping wet man with a fiercely determined look on his face stalked through their midst and straight toward her.

Robert.

Marie's heart stuttered. She rushed toward him. "Good heavens—you're drenched!"

"I know."

"What happened?"

"It's a long story."

She was keenly aware that people were staring. The first law of catering was that the staff should never disrupt the event. Marie took his arm, getting the sleeve of her red silk dress soaked in the process. "Let's go into the back."

They stepped into the kitchen, where Betsy was arranging a tray of eclairs and chocolate-dipped strawberries. She looked up and gasped. "Robert! My goodness, what happened to you?"

"Later," he said. Taking Marie's arm, he pulled her

around the corner and into a walk-in storage closet
filled with stacked chairs. He flipped on the light and
closed the door.

"What on earth . . ." she began.

"Marie, I'm so sorry." His eyes held a depth of emotion she hadn't seen in a long, long time. They looked as
if they might even be holding back a tear or two, but he
was so wet, she couldn't be sure. "I'm sorry for everything. I've been a jackass. I meant to tell you about the
trouble at work, but I kept putting it off because I didn't
want you to think less of me."

"I wouldn't have! Larry told me you were framed. I
knew it wasn't your fault."

"No, but I was pushed out all the same, just as if I was
guilty, and . . . God, Marie, I can't tell you how that hurt."

Marie's heart turned over. "Of course it did. It must
have been awful."

"It was."

"The injustice of it all . . ." She shook her head, words
failing her. "And to know you couldn't fight it without
bringing the whole department under scrutiny."

He nodded. "It was killing me."

"So, why on earth didn't you tell me?"

He shoved a wet lock of hair out of his face and
looked at her. There was no pride or pretense in his
eyes, only regret, pain and sincerity. "I wanted to. I kept
trying to find the right time, but you were so busy and
excited with your new business, and, hell—I didn't
want to ruin that for you. And then the retirement party
happened, and after that . . . how could I explain why I
hadn't told you earlier? The longer I waited, the harder
it became. I finally convinced myself that you really
didn't need to know, that you'd be happier not knowing.
But it was a big, ugly secret and it was eating up my insides. And the fact that I was keeping it secret started to

eat at me, too, until keeping the secret hurt even worse than the secret itself."

"Oh, Robert," she whispered.

He put his hands on her arms. "It was stupid pride. I felt like the world's biggest loser just as you were becoming a success—as if I'd been put out to pasture just as you were sprouting wings. I felt old and inadequate, and then . . . hell, I became that way." He drew a ragged breath. "And I blamed you. I'm so sorry. It was unfair and selfish and stupid. I guess I just couldn't bear to put the blame where it belonged because I already felt like such a loser." He lowered his voice to barely a whisper. "And I was scared."

"Of what?"

"Of losing you. And yet there I was, pushing you away." He shook his head, then gave an embarrassed smile. "I guess I need to see a shrink, huh?"

"No. You just need to see me."

She laid both palms gently against his cheeks and looked directly into his eyes. "You need to see into my heart. Because if you look there, you'll know I'm here for you. You'll know I love you, and nothing will change that. But if you don't want my love . . . Well, I won't keep trying to force it on you."

His hands moved from her arms to her shoulders. He drew her closer. "I *do* want it. I love you more than life itself. I guess I just haven't been feeling like I deserve you." His gaze poured into hers, sincere and honest and true. "I want to make it up to you. I'm willing to do whatever it takes. If you want to go to a marriage counselor or a psychiatrist or a two-headed witch doctor—you name it, and I'll go."

"You know where I'd really like to go?"

"Where?"

"Home," she whispered.

He pulled her close and gave her a lingering kiss, slow and sweet and tender, full of emotion, warm with promise. "I feel like I'm already there."

Tears slipped down her cheeks, but this time they were tears of joy. He kissed her again, and this time the warmth flashed to flame. She pressed against him, feeling the heat of his skin through his wet shirt. He tightened his arms around her and pulled her flush against him, full against the hard proof of his arousal.

There was no need for Viagra—only a need to have no barriers between them, and they had already bared their hearts. Robert wedged a chair beneath the doorknob, then reached for the zipper on her dress.

Chapter Thirty-nine

Stevie awoke exhausted the next morning, exhausted and depressed. She found a note by the coffee machine:

> Big meeting today—Went in early. I'll be home late. Don't wait up.

Tears puddled in her eyes as she mixed Isabelle's cereal. It had been well past midnight before Holt came home last night. He'd crawled into bed and turned his face to the wall, and when she'd reached out to him, he'd muttered he was tired. It was the first night since Stevie had moved into his bedroom that they hadn't made love. Stevie had lain awake until the early morning hours, her stomach gnarled up like the roots of an old tree.

At the first disagreement, he'd pulled away. He hadn't stayed and talked things out; he'd simply walked out the door. She'd thought she'd nearly scaled that high wall around his heart, but at the first sign of trouble it was back, taller and more insurmountable than before.

It was discouraging, to say the least. So was the fact that Holt was hiring Charlotte to do the interior design of the house across the street. What bothered her most wasn't even the fact that he'd hired Charlotte; it was the fact he was getting the house into move-in condition. He was still planning to leave. The fact he'd hired an old girlfriend to feather his post-divorce nest just poured salt in the wound.

It wasn't that he didn't care about her, Stevie thought as she lifted Isabelle into her highchair. He simply refused to acknowledge it. He was convinced that he couldn't maintain a marriage, that divorce was inevitable and that Isabelle would suffer if the divorce came later rather than sooner.

Stevie was convinced that actions spoke louder than words, and Holt's actions had been loving. He kissed her when he came home, nuzzled her neck for no reason, and he cuddled with her on the sofa as they sat talking after dinner. He got up with Isabelle in the mornings so Stevie could get extra sleep. And he'd obviously been reading her pregnancy manual, because he'd brought Stevie crackers and soda in bed after reading that eating something before rising might ward off morning sickness.

And as for his lovemaking—Holt was the most exquisite, tender, passionate, considerate lover imaginable. He thrilled her beyond words. The attraction was reciprocal; there was no mistaking that.

She only hoped she wasn't mistaking fantasy for reality. She was banking on the hope that by the time the new baby arrived, Holt's fear of commitment would be a thing of the past.

Last night had been a setback. How much of one, she didn't yet know. At least time was on her side. She had the better part of a year to change his mind— which was a good thing, because the way things were going, it looked like she was going to need every single minute.

Isabelle seemed to have caught Stevie's unhappy mood. The baby fussed and squirmed as Stevie fed her, practicing her newly acquired razzing skills with nearly every mouthful. When the doorbell rang a little after ten, Isabelle was crying, Stevie had a backache and the baggy gray sweats she'd thrown on when she awakened were spattered with baby cereal and peaches.

Carrying the squalling child on her hip, Stevie walked through the toy-littered living room to the front door and looked through the peephole.

Great. Just great.

On the other side of the door stood the interior decorator, her hair shining, her makeup impeccable, wearing a sleek gray suit that clung to her skinny curves and showed off her long legs. Shifting the disgruntled baby to her other hip, Stevie opened the door.

The scent of expensive perfume wafted in. The woman ran her eyes over Stevie, taking in her disheveled state and no doubt comparing it to her own glorious appearance.

Her perfectly pointed lips curved in a phony smile. "I don't know if you remember me, but I'm Charlotte Ferguson."

"Yes, I remember. You're the woman who delivers dead flowers at night."

The plastic smile cracked a bit. "I'm Holt's interior designer. And he told me I could get the key to his new home from you."

His new home. The words rankled. Stevie's stomach

tightened. "Yes. It's in the kitchen." She pulled the door wider.

Charlotte stepped in and looked around. As they headed for the kitchen, Stevie imagined how the place must look through the woman's eyes—a baby blanket thrown across the living room floor, a baby swing in the corner, breakfast dishes on the counter, a high chair spattered with baby food, toys scattered everywhere.

"I'm sure you like what I've done with the place," she said in a droll tone.

The woman was not amused. "So . . . you're still watching Holt's baby?"

He hadn't told her they were married. Stevie's heart fell to the floor. She lifted her chin. "Actually, she's my baby, too. And Holt and I are having another."

Charlotte stared at her with wary disbelief, as if Stevie were psychotic.

"Didn't he tell you?" Stevie asked. "We're married."

The woman faked a small smile. She obviously thought Stevie was lying. "All I know is that he's hired me to do the interior of the house across the street because he's moving there."

Stevie lifted her head and mustered all the bravado she could gather. "Yes. We think a little distance will help keep the mystery and romance of our marriage alive."

A cereal-soaked strand of hair fell in Stevie's face, somewhat ruining the effect. As she brushed it away, Isabelle loudly filled her diaper.

Charlotte stared at the child, her expression aghast, as eau de dirty diaper scented the air.

"Would you like to hold her?" Stevie asked sweetly.

"Um—no, thanks. I'd better get to work."

"You do that." Stevie held out the key. Charlotte took it with her thumb and forefinger, as if it were unsanitary.

She hightailed it to the door, high heels clicking on the hardwood floor like the toenails of a poodle as Stevie followed with the malodorous baby.

Stevie paused in the doorway as Charlotte scurried onto the porch. "When you select furniture for Holt's bedroom, be sure and give him a four-poster bed," Stevie said with a wicked grin. "He really likes it when I handcuff him to the bedposts."

The shock on Charlotte's face gave her a burst of satisfaction. But her bravado crumbled when she finally closed the door, because there was no satisfaction in the realization that Holt was really going to leave.

When Stevie arrived at the parenting center to teach a noon class on coping with colic, Michelle hurried up to her.

"Stevie—have you seen the newspaper?"

Stevie settled Isabelle beside another baby on the play mat in the infant area, then rubbed her aching lower back. "No. Why?"

"Your father's a hero!"

"What?"

"He rescued a man whose car went off the causeway last night."

Michelle scurried across the room, plucked a newspaper off her desk and handed it over.

Stevie scanned it. Sure enough, there on the front page was a photo of her father, standing by a police car in a dripping wet shirt, his hair plastered to his head.

Above the photo, the headline blared RETIREE SAVES LIFE. Stevie scanned the article.

"Why was Dad on the causeway?"

"I don't know, but that guy's awfully lucky he was."

"Wow. I can't believe my mother hasn't called."

"Well, call her! I can't wait to hear the details."

"I think I will." Stevie pulled out her cell phone and punched in the speed dial number. She frowned as she hung up a moment later. "That's odd—the answering machine's on, and the message says they're out of town until next Monday."

"Maybe they don't want to deal with the publicity."

"Maybe. It's unusual, though." Stevie winced as her backache spread to her belly.

"What's the matter?" Michelle asked.

"I've got a stomachache. I must have eaten something that didn't agree with me."

Michelle's brows pulled into a frown. "Maybe you should go home. We can reschedule the class."

"No. I'll be fine."

But she wasn't. As Stevie discussed methods of soothing fussy newborns, the cramps continued, low and hard, too intense to be ignored. She fought off a sense of rising panic. *No.* She refused to even consider the possibility.

But as the afternoon wore on, it became unavoidable.

"Stevie—are you okay?" Michelle asked again as the class ended.

"No." Hot tears formed in her eyes. "I-I think . . ." She couldn't bring herself to say it. She squeezed her thighs together, as if sheer willpower could prevent the inevitable. "Michelle—can you drive me to my doctor's?"

But by the time the doctor examined her, it was all over.

"I'm sorry, Stevie," Dr. Arnold said gently. "About twenty percent of all pregnancies end this way in the first trimester."

Tears streamed down Stevie's cheeks as she sat at the end of the examining table, clutching her blue paper gown.

"It wasn't caused by anything you did, and there was

nothing you could have done to prevent it." The doctor handed her a tissue. "It might help to know that ninety percent of the women who miscarry go on to have other full-term pregnancies and healthy children."

"Not me," Stevie said bitterly.

"There's no reason to think that."

Yes, there was; her marriage was over. Now that the adoption had gone through and Isabelle had bonded with Holt, there was no reason for him to continue their sham of a marriage. Stevie had thought the pregnancy would buy her some time, and in that time, Holt would grow to love her. But time had just run out.

She'd not only lost a baby; she'd lost the man she loved.

Chapter Forty

Holt's administrative assistant stuck her head into the boardroom where Holt was meeting with the top executives of Allen Industries, her round face puckered in a frown. "I hate to interrupt, but a Michelle Blanche is on the line, and she says there's an emergency involving your wife."

Holt's heart slammed against his ribs. He abruptly rose from the conference table. "Please excuse me."

Something had happened to Stevie? A sickening anxiety crawled through his chest as he strode down the hall toward his office. He grabbed the phone at his assistant's desk, not wanting to waste the extra few seconds it would take to go into his own office.

"Hello?"

"Holt, I hate to call you like this," Michelle said. "Stevie said you were in an important meeting and didn't want to disturb you, but I thought you should know."

"Know what?"

"Stevie had a miscarriage."

Oh, jeez. His throat went tight. "Is . . . is she okay?"

"Physically, she's fine. She's seen her doctor, and he sent her home. But emotionally—well, she's devastated. And I thought you should know."

"Is she at home now?"

"Yes. I offered to stay with her, but she didn't want me to. She said she was fine and perfectly capable of taking care of Isabelle, but I don't really think she should be alone."

"I'm on my way. Thanks for calling."

Holt hung up the phone and looked at Lanie. "I've got an emergency at home. Tell the board I'm sorry, but we'll have to reschedule the meeting." Then he rushed out the door.

A clammy emptiness gripped him as he steered his car through the traffic on St. Charles Avenue. His harshness last night couldn't have been good for Stevie or the baby. He'd lain awake much of the night, and from the sound of her breathing, he knew that Stevie had, as well. Had he caused this to happen?

He arrived at home to find the shades drawn and the lights out. He didn't see Stevie at first, because she was laying on the sofa, staring into space.

"Stevie?"

She moved her head, but nothing else.

He crossed the room and knelt beside her. "Stevie, I'm so sorry."

"You don't have to lie to me." Her voice sounded flat and lifeless. "I know you didn't want this baby."

Hell—was it true? Maybe at first, but the idea had grown on him. "I hate that this happened."

"Well, it did. So you're off the hook." The words carved a hole in his heart. "Stevie—I feel terrible about this. Maybe if I hadn't been such a prick last night and gotten you all upset . . ."

Her eyes softened, and so did her voice. She slowly sat up and swung her feet to the floor. "No. It's not your fault. The doctor said it wasn't caused by anything we did or didn't do. It just happened."

Holt sat beside her on the sofa and lifted her hands. They felt cold and limp. "I'm so sorry," he repeated.

She stiffened and pulled away. His insides felt all torn up and overturned, like a freshly plowed field.

"Your interior designer friend came by this morning," Stevie said.

Oh, hell. Holt's stomach sank farther.

"I guess your place will be ready soon."

"Stevie, that's not something we need to address right now."

Her mouth firmed with resolve. "Yes, it is. Since I'm not having a baby, we might as well revert to our original plan. We'd agreed to file for divorce as soon as the adoption went through and Isabelle bonded with you. Well, both of those things have happened."

His blood turned to ice. "This isn't the time to be talking about that. You've had a rough day, and—"

She broke in before he could finish. "Holt, I can't do this anymore." Her eyes held the determination of a woman who'd made up her mind. "I love you. I was hoping that by the time the new baby came, you'd love me, too. I know that wasn't fair of me; it wasn't fair to expect you to change. But life is about change, and the baby was going to be a big change, and . . ." She looked away. "I guess I was hoping you'd have a change of heart, too."

His heart felt like a raw wound. "Stevie . . ."

She held up her hand. "Don't say anything. I know you

feel bad. I know you didn't intend to hurt me. I know you want to console me about losing the baby. But you're going to hurt me more if you say a lot of loving things right now, just as I'm finally accepting the truth."

Her eyes held so much pain that it hurt to look into them. She drew a ragged breath. "There's no baby, and you and I have no future. I can't keep pretending that this is a real marriage when it's not, and the longer it goes on, the harder it is on me. It would be cruel of you to stick around and be kind, and to make me love you more. I want to make a clean break."

"Stevie . . ."

"You can see Isabelle anytime you like. The more, the better. You can come feed her breakfast and stop by after work. But, Holt—I can't live with you anymore."

The last thing he wanted to do was hurt her more. He had no choice but to do as she asked. "When do you want me to leave?"

"Now."

"Do you want me to call someone to come over—Michelle, or your mother?"

"I don't need anyone to come." He voice held a resolute note of finality. "I just need you to go."

Chapter Forty-one

Stevie's heart felt as empty as her womb as she watched Holt load a suitcase in his BMW, then slowly back out of the driveway half an hour later.

It wasn't like she hadn't seen it coming, she thought as his car disappeared around the corner. She'd known better than to get involved with Holt. But she'd let her heart override her head, and she'd started believing the lie she was living. She'd even made herself believe that Holt loved her, too.

She wiped away a tear as she turned from the window. She hadn't wanted to send him away, but she was too vulnerable to let him stay. If she clung to him tonight, if she let him comfort her for the loss of her baby, tomorrow she might not have the strength to do what needed to be done.

And it needed to be done. Better to end it now than to drag it out. Better to sever all ties before she got in any deeper. If she loved him this much now, how much harder would it be in another month or two—or twelve?

It was better to make a clean break. She knew that. And she'd known in advance that it was going to hurt.

She just hadn't known how much.

It was late afternoon as Holt left. He drove aimlessly down St. Charles Avenue, feeling grief-stricken and numb. He didn't want to go back to the office; he didn't want to have to face anyone or answer any questions. But he didn't want to be alone, either, and the idea of going to a bar held no appeal.

He wanted to be with Stevie. She was the one he'd gotten accustomed to turning to, to talking things out with, to confiding in. She was the one who understood him and accepted him, no matter what. There was no one else in his life like that. There never had been, and there probably never would be again.

He flipped through his mental rolodex, trying to think whom he could call. He didn't have any close single male friends. The buddies he felt closest to were all happily married, and they'd be busy with their wives and kids.

But there was his father. Vince had recently moved

into a temporary apartment in the suburbs while he oversaw the renovations on the house he'd bought with Caroline. Holt and Stevie and Isabelle had taken him a pot of Stevie's homemade stew the day he'd moved in. Holt had even agreed to be the best man when he re-married Caroline in City Park next week.

On impulse, Holt drove to his father's apartment and knocked on the door.

Vince opened it, his reading glasses on his nose. His face lit up in a smile. "Holt! What a nice surprise. Come in—come on in."

Holt walked into the Spartan apartment.

"Can I get you a Coke?" Vince asked.

"Sure."

Vince opened the fridge, pulled out two cans and gestured to the couch. "So what's going on?"

Holt accepted the can and blew out a harsh breath. "It's a long story."

"I'm all ears."

Holt popped the top on his soda, and spilled out the whole tale—how he'd really met Stevie, how he'd per-suaded her to temporarily marry him, the nature of their arrangement, the miscarriage, the separation.

His father's eyes were sympathetic. "Sounds like you got exactly what you wanted out of the deal," he said when Holt finished talking.

"I guess," Holt said glumly. "But if that's the case, then why do I feel so lousy?"

"Maybe you started wanting something more."

Holt shook his head. "I don't want to stay married only to have it fall apart in a few years."

"Who says it has to fall apart?"

Holt lifted a sardonic eyebrow. "You, of all people, are suggesting it won't?"

Vince leaned forward, his elbows on his thighs. "Let

me ask you—where are you going to find a better wife than Stevie?"

"Nowhere. But I'm not looking for a wife."

"Why not?"

Maybe it was a mistake to come here. His father seemed to have entirely missed the point. But what had he expected? "Because I don't want to be married."

"And why is that—because you're so happy being single and you've been so miserable being married?"

"Well, no." Come to think of it, just the opposite was true. He'd loved coming home to Stevie. "I just I don't think marriage is a good risk for Isabelle or me."

"Why? Because your mother and I goofed up?" Vince shook his head sadly. "Don't base decisions about *your* life on *our* mistakes."

"I'm not. I'm basing them on my own experiences."

Vince set down his Coke on the coffee table. "When my business started going south, I thought I had all the answers. I'd built a lot of houses, so I figured all I needed to do was keep my head down and plow away and do what I'd always done. I didn't stop and look around to see how things had changed—how consumer tastes had changed, how the competition had grown, how the housing demand had slowed."

Holt took a swig of soda, wondering if his father had a point and if he was likely to get to it anytime soon.

"It seems to me you're doing the same thing here. You have it in your head that you can't fall in love and get married because you think love doesn't last, but you're not factoring in new information. In case you haven't figured it out, son, you're in love with Stevie."

It wasn't anything he hadn't thought himself, but it was startling all the same, hearing it said out loud. By his father. *You're in love with Stevie*. He turned it around in his mind, examining it on all sides, weighing it, trying it on for size.

"Even if I am," he said cautiously. "That's not enough. There's no guarantee we'd make for the long haul."

"You don't let the lack of guarantees stop you in other areas of your life. It all comes down to what you're willing to put your faith in."

"Faith," Holt scoffed. "Sorry, I'm fresh out."

"No, you're not. You don't let the risk of food poisoning stop you from enjoying a good hamburger, do you?"

"Well, no."

"So you're willing to put your faith in whether or not some two-bit fry cook has heated your hamburger to the right temperature, but you won't trust your heart to the woman you love. Now, I ask you—does that make any sense?" Vince looked at him hard. "Especially when you take into account that burger-flippers are usually not the sharpest tools in the shed, and love is the strongest force in the universe. Hell, son—God is love, and there's nothing stronger than the Big Guy upstairs right?"

"Marriage is a lot more complicated than cooking burgers."

"Only if you make it that way." Vince rose from his chair and strode to the window, his hands in the pockets of his khakis. "Any relationship is going to have some problems. No two people see eye-to-eye on everything. But if you can put personal pride aside and think in terms of 'us' instead of 'me,' well, it's not complicated at all."

"There's still no guarantee I can make it work."

"Life doesn't come with many guarantees, son, but I can tell you two of them: If you don't get down on your knees and beg that woman to take you back, your child will never know what it's like to be part of a real family, and you'll spend the rest of your life looking for something or someone to fill up that Stevie-shaped hole in your heart."

Holt stared down at the carpet. "I don't want Isabelle to ever go through what I did when you and Mom divorced."

"Make sure she won't." His father's voice was sure, his gaze confident. "Your mom and I didn't have a clue how our divorce was affecting you; we were ignorant, and I'll regret that until my dying day. But you're not ignorant. You'll make mistakes raising Isabelle, there's no doubt about that, but they won't be the same ones I made."

His father cocked his head and looked at him, his eyes sad. "Of course, when I think about it, it looks to me like you're following right in my footsteps."

Holt looked up, surprised. "What?"

"The worst mistake of my life was letting your mother go. You're about to make the same mistake with Stevie."

Looks to me like you're already following in my footsteps. His father's words replayed in his head like an annoying song as Holt backed his BMW out of the apartment parking lot half an hour later.

Damn it, he didn't want to be like his dad—especially not when it came to marriage. He didn't believe in any of that till-death-do-us-part business. His father was full of it. He wasn't following in the man's footsteps at all.

Against his will, more of his father's words floated through his mind: *It all comes down to what you're willing to put your faith in.*

Boy, that was another gem. A muscle twitched in Holt's jaw as he steered the car from the side street onto Veteran's Boulevard. Well, that's what he got for talking to his father. He should have known better than to seek wisdom from a guy who'd been KO'd three times and was about to climb back in the ring again.

The thought of his parents' impending remarriage set off a weird churning in his gut. Their reconciliation no longer made him angry; it simply left him confused. It flew in the face of all his beliefs about love and marriage and relationships. Did they really still love each other, after all they'd put each other through? Could love really be that forgiving, that enduring, that strong?

Holt was so lost in thought that he didn't see the red light until he was nearly in the intersection. He slammed on the brakes, but an eighteen-wheeler was barreling down Clearview, heading straight toward him.

He was about to be hit! There was a split-second sense of inevitability, a hair's-breadth of a moment when his life flashed before his eyes.

But it wasn't his life. It was Stevie's face.

He was going to die before he ever really lived. Stevie would never know how he really felt about her.

Everything seemed to happen in slow motion. His car fishtailed to the left. The truck veered right. The shriek of his tires and the loud bleat of the truck's horn ran together, forming a shrill, ear-splintering cacaphony.

He didn't realize he'd shut his eyes until he opened them to discover that his car had stopped sideways in the middle of the intersection. His heart was somewhere north of his tonsils. Around him, angry drivers blared their horns and swerved around him.

The light changed. Holt's leg shook as he pulled his foot off the brake and onto the accelerator. The easiest way to clear the intersection was to head in the opposite direction. He did just that. After driving two blocks, he pulled into the parking lot of a fast-food restaurant and stopped the engine.

He sat behind the wheel for a good long minute, his heart beating like a machine gun. *Good God.* He'd nearly gotten himself killed. And if he had, Stevie's face would have been the last image in his mind.

He got out, his legs as rubbery as banquet chicken, and went into the restaurant. He ordered a cup of coffee, then spilled some on the counter when he tried to pick it up because his hand was shaking so.

He carried it to a table and sat down. Man, that had been close! Slightly less luck and his car would have looked like an accordion. He glanced out the window, and his gaze caught on Isabelle's car seat in the back.

Dear Lord. She could have been with him.

He stared at the little safety seat. It was nothing but plastic and fabric—nothing that would really protect her in a bad accident. It was a sobering thing to contemplate.

A chill chased down his spine, and his father's words chased through his head: *It all comes down to what you're willing to put your faith in.* When he buckled himself or his child into a car, he was putting his faith in a bunch of metal and rubber and glass. He was trusting in his own ability to drive safely, and in the ability of every other driver on the road to do the same.

It was a terrifying thought.

"You don't let the lack of guarantees stop you in other areas of your life," his father had said.

It was true. He couldn't keep Isabelle locked up in a padded cell for fear she might get hurt, and he couldn't stop driving for fear of having an accident.

He didn't let the risk of failure stop him from going after new business accounts. He didn't let the risk of falling keep him from climbing a flight of stairs. So why should he let the risk of failure stop him from going after the sweetest thing life has to offer?

A loud sizzling sound drew his attention to the front

of the restaurant. He looked at the grill behind the counter as a pimply-faced teenaged boy with a bored expression flipped a hamburger.

Holt smiled. *Okay, Big Guy. I get the message.*

His heart floated free, like a boat cut loose from an anchor. Why had it taken him so long to figure it out? He was just like Isabelle. The thing he wanted most in the world was the very thing he'd been trying hardest to avoid.

He wanted love—the lasting kind, the kind that had deep roots and tall branches, the kind that sheltered and protected, that was steadfast and strong and ever growing.

And he wanted it with Stevie—with Stevie and Isabelle and any other children they might have. He wanted to share it with his parents and her parents and their entire extended family, then the neighborhood and the town and the whole big damned world. He might even want to include a dog and a cat or two; and hell, who knew—maybe even some fish.

He wondered if Stevie wanted the same. He wondered if she'd still trust him with her heart, or if she'd decided he wasn't worth the risk. Dear Lord, he hoped he hadn't blown it. He prayed she'd give him a second chance.

He needed to tell her how he felt. He needed to let her know he'd had the change of heart she'd hoped for. He needed to convince her that he believed in love, he believed in forever and he believed they belonged together.

Chapter Forty-two

"This is Stevie Stedquest with Parent Talk. You're on the air."

"Stevie, I have a three-year-old who keeps taking off his clothes in public. It's very embarrassing, and I don't know what do about it."

Stevie looked down at Isabelle, who was playing on a blanket on the studio floor. "This sort of behavior is usually a bid for attention. How have you been handling it?"

"Well, I scoop him up and leave the store or restaurant or wherever immediately."

"Which is probably exactly what he wants. Does he do this when he's bored?"

"Come to think of it, yes."

"Well, the first step is to limit the amount of time he's bored. The next is to tell him, before you go into a public setting, that big boys keep their clothes on, and that you expect him to do so. Let him know that if he takes his clothes off, you will no longer take him home. You're going to take him to the restroom to put his clothes back on, and then you are going to finish your shopping or meal or whatever. Then give him an incentive. Tell him that if he acts like a big boy, you'll give him a reward. This doesn't have to be a new toy or candy; it can be taking him to the park or spending some time playing a game with him."

"Okay. Good ideas. Thank you."

"He's likely to test you on this. If he does, remain calm and follow through on what you told him."

"Thank you so much."

Stevie glanced at her watch. This hour usually flew by, but today time was dragging.

Face it; *life* was dragging. It had been three days since Holt had moved out, and his absence had torn a big hole in the fabric of her life. He came by every morning to feed Isabelle breakfast, and he stopped by every evening after work, but Stevie went upstairs when he arrived and didn't come down until she heard him leave.

She knew she'd eventually have to face him, and she'd have to face other people as well. She dreaded telling her parents that she and Holt had separated. They'd called Saturday from Cancun, and they'd sounded so happy and carefree that she couldn't bring herself to give them the news. With uncharacterisitic impulsiveness, they'd flown there Friday and were apparently having the time of their lives.

She dreaded telling Holt's parents, as well. They were getting married next weekend in City Park, and Stevie was supposed to serve as Caroline's matron of honor. How ironic it all was: the marriage bringing Vince and Caroline back together was dissolving just as the older couple were reuniting.

Stevie stared at the row of blinking lights on her phone. "We have time for one more caller."

Through the window, Hank held up three fingers, indicating which line she should pick up.

"This is Parent Talk. You're on the air."

"Yes. Do you know anything about Attachment Disorder?"

Stevie's pulse quickened. The voice sounded a lot like Holt's, but it must be her imagination playing tricks on her. He knew as much as she did about Attachment Disorder. He would have no reason to call and ask about it.

"As a matter of fact, I do. For our listeners not acquainted with it, it's a syndrome where a child has difficulties forming attachments. The child pushes away people trying to love him or her, because the child never learned how to form a bond and fears being abandoned. What's your question?"

"Well, I think I have it."

Stevie looked at Hank. He smiled and made a circle in the air by his head, indicating that he thought the call was a whacko.

Stevie's heart thought differently. It pounded hard. "You think you have Attachment Disorder?"

"Yes."

"Well, I'm sorry, sir, but this is a parenting show."

"I know. But I'm a parent, so it's a relevant question."

It was Holt. She was sure of it. "What makes you think you have it?"

"Well, I have all the symptoms. I've become very attached to someone, but I've been holding back and not letting her know how I feel. I didn't even want to admit it to myself. And I think it's because I'm afraid that sooner or later, I'll mess things up and she'll leave me, and that would not only break my heart but the heart of our daughter."

Stevie felt light-headed, then realized she'd been holding her breath. "So what's your question?"

"How can I overcome it?"

Stevie struggled to tamp down the sparks of hope kindling within her. "Well, the cure for Attachment Disorder is love and trust."

"That seems to be the cure for lots of things."

"Y-yes." Her heart beat like a tom-tom. Through the window, Stevie saw Hank making a circle in the air with his finger, signaling that she should wrap it up. "I'm sorry, but we're out of time. Thank you for calling." She clicked the off button, her hand shaking. "That's it for to-day. Join us again next week for more Parent Talk. Good night, and good parenting."

Stevie turned off the mike, took off her headset, then gathered up Isabelle's things. She moved methodically and deliberately, forcing herself not to hurry. She would not let herself get worked up into an emotional state. If she was wrong, she couldn't bear the disappointment.

All the same, her heart was thrumming like a hummingbird's wings as she set Isabelle in the stroller, folded the blanket the baby had been playing on and put it in the diaper bag.

"That last caller was really weird," Hank said as she pushed the stroller out of the studio and into the control room.

"Yes."

"Must be another full moon."

"I guess so." If the caller was who she thought it was, it wouldn't surprise her if the moon was blue.

Pushing Isabelle and lugging the diaper bag on her shoulder, Stevie headed to the elevator. The ride down two floors seemed to take forever, and the short walk to the exit seemed like a marathon. She held her breath as she opened the door to the parking lot.

Sure enough, there stood Holt, his cell phone in his hand. Hope rose inside her. She tried to keep it grounded, but it had powerful wings.

The streetlamp gleamed on Holt's face as he grinned. "Any interesting calls tonight?"

"Just the last one," she said.

"So . . . how do you think that guy ought to handle things?"

"I think . . ." Stevie's heart crashed against her ribs. She drew herself up and looked into Holt's dark eyes. "I think he ought to be very, very sure of what he feels. Because if he's just trying to do what he thinks he's supposed to do and not what he really, truly wants—well, that's not good enough." She paused and drew a tremulous breath. "It's not enough for a man or a woman to marry for the sake of a child. The man needs to love the woman for herself, with his whole heart, like she's the only woman in the world. Because if he doesn't love her that way, he's not truly committed. And if he's not truly committed, then their relationship is built on sand."

"But if he *is* sure, what should he do?"

Stevie's skin tingled, tingled from her head to her toes. "Well, if he's absolutely, positively sure, then he needs to let her know."

"Okay. Here goes." He went to his knee on the middle of the asphalt parking lot. Isabelle laughed and waved at him from her stroller.

Holt looked up Stevie. "From the moment Isabelle and I first heard your voice, we knew you were our answer. The problem was, I didn't know the right question. I thought all I needed was someone to take care of the baby. I didn't know I needed someone to love."

Stevie's heart thundered like a summer storm.

"You once said that love could work miracles. Well, it has. Your love has not only healed a broken baby, but a broken man. I didn't think I was capable of love, and now I find myself head over heels."

Overhead, a cloud shifted to reveal a full moon. Stevie's heart soared up to it.

"The last time I waylaid you in this parking lot, I wanted to marry you for Isabelle's sake. This time, I want to marry you for mine."

Stevie's heart rocketed past the moon and into deep space.

"Stevie, I love you. It's taken me a while to realize, but

I do. I love you in all the ways a man can love a woman—as a friend, as a partner, as a lover, as a playmate, and probably in a bunch of other ways we haven't even discovered yet. I want to spend the rest of my life with you. I want to fall asleep with you in my arms, and wake up with you beside me every morning. I want you to be the mother of my children and the grandmother of my grandchildren. What I'm trying to say is—Stevie, I want to be married to you. I mean *really* married—heart and soul, forever after, till-death-do-us-part married."

"Oh, Holt!"

"The last time I proposed to you, I gave you my grandfather's compass. So this time, I want to give you this." Rising to his feet, he reached into his pocket and pulled out a horseshoe magnet. It was a baby's toy, padded and encased in red plastic. He pressed it into her hand. "Magnetic force is what pulls a compass needle in the right direction. And that's what you do to me, Stevie. You give me direction and purpose and a reason for living."

His eyes searched hers, and in their depths, she saw the mate of her soul, the very heart of her heart.

"So what do you say? Do you think you could marry me for real and forever?"

In her heart, she already had. She nodded, too choked up to speak. Then she handed the magnet to Isabelle and threw her arms around Holt's neck. As their lips met, no compass was needed, because they both knew they'd found true north.

Epilogue

The Reverend Alan Pitcher's wife looked up from her needlepoint as he walked through the door of the parsonage a little after nine o'clock the following Saturday evening.

"How was the wedding, dear?"

Reverend Pitcher dropped a kiss on her forehead and sat down beside her on the green floral couch. "Beautiful. Small, but very beautiful."

"This was the one in the rose garden at City Park, right?"

The minister nodded.

She put aside her needlework and looked at him expectantly. "Tell me all about it."

After thirty-two years of marriage, this was a familiar ritual. His wife always wanted a play-by-play description of the weddings he performed, so he'd schooled himself to notice the things that interested her.

He spread his arms along the back of the sofa. "Well,

it was lovely. The roses were all in bloom, and the air smelled like perfume. They had a harpist and lots of candles in those tall candle thingies."

"Candelabra."

"Right."

"How many people were there?"

"Just the bride and groom, their son, their daughter-in-law and grandbaby, and the daughter-in-law's parents."

"This was the divorced couple that was remarrying, right?"

"Right."

"What were they wearing?"

"Well, the men wore tuxedos. And the bride had on some kind of cream-colored suit with little pearls all over it."

"Was she beautiful?"

The minister nodded. "She reminded me of Jackie O."

His wife gave a blissful sigh. "What about the other women?"

"The daughter-in-law wore a pale blue dress with skinny things holding it up."

"Spaghetti straps."

"And her mother was in blue, too. Her dress had see-through sleeves."

"I bet it was chiffon. Did the bride and groom look very much in love?"

"Yes, indeed. But then, everyone did. It was the darnedest thing—while the bride and groom were saying their vows, I looked up, and the other two couples were looking at each other, whispering the vows, too."

"That's so sweet!"

"And when I told the groom he could kiss his bride, all three couples kissed."

"Oh, how touching!"

"It was. You know, I've performed hundreds of weddings, but that's the first time I've gotten a little misty-eyed myself." He put his arm around his wife's shoulders. "It made me think how love is like ripples in a pond—how it grows and spreads and touches the lives of others. And it made me think about you, and how much I love you."

"Oh, Allen!" She gazed up at him with tender eyes.

He drew her toward him and into a kiss, which unexpectedly took on a life of its own. She smiled as they drew apart. "That must have been some wedding."

"It was," the minister murmured. "It was."